THE
LAST SONG
OF
PENELOPE

CLAIRE NORTH

THE
LAST SONG
OF
PENELOPE

A SONGS OF
PENELOPE NOVEL

orbit

orbitbooks.net

ORBIT

First published in Great Britain in 2024 by Orbit

Copyright © by Claire North 2024

The moral right of the author has been asserted.

A CIP catalogue record for this book
is available from the British Library.

HB ISBN 978-0-356-51611-0
C format 978-0-356-51612-7

Typeset in Bembo by M Rules
Printed and bound in Great Britain by
Clays Ltd, Elcograf, S.p.A.

Papers used by Orbit are from well-managed forests
and other responsible sources.

Orbit
An imprint of
Little, Brown Book Group
Carmelite House
50 Victoria Embankment
London EC4Y 0DZ

An Hachette UK Company
www.hachette.co.uk

www.orbitbooks.net

DRAMATIS PERSONAE

>>

The Ithacans

Penelope – wife of Odysseus, queen of Ithaca
Odysseus – husband of Penelope, king of Ithaca
Telemachus – son of Odysseus and Penelope
Laertes – father of Odysseus
Anticlea – mother of Odysseus, deceased

Councillors of Odysseus

Medon – an old friendly councillor
Aegyptius – an old, less friendly councillor
Peisenor – a former warrior of Odysseus

Suitors of Penelope and Their Kin

Antinous – a suitor, son of Eupheithes
Eupheithes – master of the granaries, father of Antinous
Eurymachus – a suitor, son of Polybus
Polybus – master of the docks, father of Eurymachus
Amphinomous – a suitor, warrior of Greece
Kenamon – an Egyptian suitor
Gaios – a soldier for hire

Maids and Commoners

Eos – maid of Penelope, comber of hair
Autonoe – maid of Penelope, keeper of the kitchen

Melantho – maid of Penelope, chopper of wood
Melitta – maid of Penelope, scrubber of tunics
Phiobe – maid of Penelope, friendly to all
Euracleia – Odysseus's old nursemaid
Otonia – Laertes' maid
Eumaeus – Odysseus's old swineherd
Priene – a warrior from the east
Teodora – an orphan of Ithaca
Anaitis – priestess of Artemis
Ourania – spymaster of Penelope

Women of Ithaca and Beyond

Semele – an old widow, mother of Mirene
Mirene – Semele's daughter

Mycenaeans

Elektra – daughter of Agamemnon and Clytemnestra
Orestes – son of Agamemnon and Clytemnestra

The Gods and Assorted Divinities

Athena – goddess of wisdom and war
Ares – god of war
Aphrodite – goddess of love and desire
Hera – goddess of mothers and wives
Artemis – goddess of the hunt

Pets

Argos – Odysseus's old dog

CHAPTER 1

>>

Sing, O Muse, of that famous man who sacked the citadel of Troy, and after wandered many years across the sea. Great were the sights he saw and many woes he endured as he tumbled tempest-tossed, always seeking one destination: home.

Sing his song down the ages, sing of heartbreak and cunning devices, of prophecies and honour, of petty men and their foolish ways, of the pride of kings and their fall. Let his name be remembered for ever, let his story outlast the high temple upon the mountain peak, let all who hear it speak of Odysseus.

And when you tell his story, remember: though he was lost, he was not alone. I was always by his side.

Sing, poets, of Athena.

CHAPTER 2

>>

O f the many kingdoms that make up the sacred lands of
Greece, it is generally agreed that the western isles are
the worst. And of the western isles themselves, comprising
many parts of some diverse merit, everyone concurs that Ithaca
is the pits.

She rises like a crab from the sea, black-backed and glistening
with salt. Her inland forests are scraggy, wind-blasted things,
her one city little more than a spider's town of twisted paths
and leaning houses that seem to buckle and brace against some
perpetual storm. By the banks of the twisted brooks she calls
rivers there are shaggy goats who nip at scrubs of grass that
sprout like old men's beards between the tumbled boulders of
a bygone age. At the mouths of her many coves and hidden
bays the women push their rough boats onto the grey, foaming
sea to catch the morning harvest of darting silver fish that play
against her shores. To her west are the richer, greener slopes of
Kefalonia, to the north the bustling ports of Hyrie, south the
generous groves of Zacynthos. It is absurd, those who account
themselves civilised say, that these richer lands should send their
sons to pay homage in backwards little Ithaca, where the kings
of the western isles have built their crooked excuse for a palace.

But look again — can you see? No? Well then, as I am mistress of war and cunning I will deign to share something of my insight, and tell you that the wily kings of these lands could not have chosen a better place to set their throne than on the back of mollusc-like Ithaca.

She sits like a fortress in a place where many seas meet, and sailors must travel beneath her gaze if they wish to ply their wares in Calydon or Corinth, Aegium or Chalcis. Even Mycenae and Thebes send their merchant vessels through her harbours, rather than risk a voyage through the southern waters where discontented warriors of Sparta and Pylos might plunder their barks. Not that the kings of the western isles have been above a bit of piracy in their time — not at all. It is necessary that a monarch occasionally demonstrate the power they can wield, so that when they choose *not* to wage war, but rather invite in the emissaries of peace, peace is especially grateful and cooperative in light of this merciful restraint.

Other accusations levelled against Ithaca: that its people are uncultivated, uncivilised, uncouth, with the table manners of dogs and a repertoire of poetry whose highest form is little more than a bawdy ditty about farts.

To which I say: yes. Why indeed yes, these things are true, and yet you are still a fool. Both things may be true simultaneously.

For the kings of Ithaca have made something really rather useful of their ruggedness and uncultivated ways: behold, when the barbarians of the north come with cargoes of amber and tin, they are not shunned at the mouth of the harbour, nor berated as ignorant strangers, but courteously they are led into royal halls, offered an inferior cup of wine or two — most wine on Ithaca is appallingly sour — and invited to speak of the misty forests and pine-dark mountains that they make their home, as if to say well, well, are we not all just salt-scarred children of the sea and sky together?

The civilised dolts of this world gaze upon the merchants of the west where they stand upon the shore in dirty robes, chewing fish with open mouths. They call them yokel and crude, and do not realise how easy this opinion makes it to prise silver from the greedy fingers of men dressed in silk and gold.

The palace of her kings may not be fine, no marble columns nor halls steeped in silver, nor why should it be? It is a place for business, for negotiations between men who append the word "honest" to their names, just in case anyone might doubt. Its walls are the island itself, for any would-be invader would have to steer their ships beneath jagged cliffs and through hidden shallows of biting stone before they could land a single soldier on Ithaca's shores. Thus I say: the kings of the western isles made canny, shrewd decisions on where to lay their heads in this rough and ragged land, and those that condemn them are fools, for whom I have no time.

Indeed, Ithaca should have held for ever, defended by stone and sea against all intruders, save that the finest of its men sailed with Odysseus to Troy, and of all those who went to war, only one is now returned.

Walk with me upon the stone-glistening shores of Ithaca, to where a man lies sleeping.

Shall I call him beloved?

This word – this "beloved" – is murder.

Once, a long time before, I came close to saying it. I laughed in delight at the company of another, cried praise upon her, smiled at her jests and frowned at her sorrows – and now she is dead, and I her killer.

Never again.

I am shield, I am armour, I am golden helmet and ready spear. I am the finest warrior of these lands, save perhaps one, and I do not love.

Well then, here he is, this man who is everything – nothing – everything to me.

Huddled, knees tucked to his chest, head buried in the nook of his arms as if he would block out the bright morning light. When the poets sing of him, they shall say that his hair is golden, his back broad and strong, his scarred thighs like two mighty trees. But they shall also say that at my touch, he was disguised as a crooked old man, hobbled and limping, his great light diminished in a noble cause. The humility of the hero – that is important in making him memorable as a man. His greatness must not feel unobtainable, unimaginable. When the poets speak of his suffering, hearers must suffer with him. That is how we shall make a tale eternal.

The truth, of course, is that Odysseus, son of Laertes, king of Ithaca, hero of Troy, is a somewhat short man with a remarkably hairy back. His hair was once an autumnal brown, which twenty years of salt and sun faded to a dull and muddy hue, crackled with grey. We may say therefore it is of some colour that has been so much overgrown with disarray, shorn with stress and faded with travel that it is hardly a colour at all. He wears a gown that was given him by a Phaeacian king. The negotiations as to the quality of the gown were fantastically tedious, since Odysseus's hosts had to insist that please, no please, their guest must be dressed in the finest, and he as guest had to reply that no, oh no, he couldn't possibly, he was a mere beggar at their table, and they said yes, but yes you are a great king, and he said no, the greatness is yours oh great one, and thus it went for a while until eventually they settled upon this middling garb that is neither too fine nor too drab and thus everyone could come away feeling satisfied in their social roles. The slaves had fetched the gown long before the agreement was struck, of course, and laid it ready out of sight to be presented. They have too much to do in a day to waste time on these performances of civilised, song-worthy men.

Now he sleeps, which is an apt and suitable way for the wandering king to return to his island, indicative perhaps of the weight of the journey that he has experienced, the burden of it, the crushing passage of time, which now shall be redeemed by the peaceful breezes and sweet perfumes of dearest Ithaca and so on and so forth.

Vulnerability – that too must be a vital part of his story, if it is to live through the ages. He has performed so many vile and bitter deeds that any opportunity to embody some sense of the innocent, the man cruelly punished by the Fates and so on is absolutely essential. Throw in a few verses about meeting the hollowed form of his mother in the fields of the dead to really emphasise his qualities as a valorous man who keeps striving towards his goals despite the burdens of a creaking heart – yes, I think that will do.

That will do.

I do not expect you to understand these things. Even my kindred gods barely manage to think more than a century ahead, and save Apollo their prophecies are flawed, cripplingly naïve. I am no prophet, but rather a scholar of all things, and it is clear that all things wither and change, even the harvest of Demeter's field. Long before the Titans wake, I foresee a time when the names of the gods – even great Zeus himself – are diminished, turned from thunder-breakers, ocean-ragers into little more than jokes and children's rhymes. I see a world in which mortals make themselves gods in our places, elevate their own to our divine status – an astounding arrogance, a logical conclusion – though their gods will be vastly less skilled at the shaping of the weather.

I see us withering. I see us falling away, no matter how hard we rage. No blood will be spilled in our honour, no sacrifices made, and in time, no one will even remember our names. Thus do gods perish.

This is not prophecy. It is something far more potent: it is the inevitable path of history.

I will not have it, and so I put mechanisms in place. I raise up cities and scholars, temples and monuments, spread ideas that will last longer than any broken shield, but when all else fails I will have one more string to my bow – I will have a story.

A good story can outlast almost anything.

And for that I need Odysseus.

Now he stirs on the beach; naturally the poets will report that I was here to greet him, a good moment for Athena to appear at last, a revelation of my role, my support – let's not call it that, let us call it . . . divine guidance – my noble presence that has always been with him. If I had appeared too soon it would have made his journey easy, a man overly aided by the gods – that wouldn't have done at all – but here, on his home shore, it's just the right moment, a kind of catharsis even – "Odysseus at last meets the goddess protector who has all this time guided his trembling hand" – it is the perfect narrative beat to insert myself into . . .

Well.

If the poets have done their work, I hardly need to recount this business further. If they have sung their songs as I intend they shall, then their audiences should now be tearing up, hearts fluttering, as Odysseus finally stirs, wakes, sees this land that he has not set eyes upon for some twenty years, struggles to understand, cries out in rage against betrayal, against the perfidious sailors who spoke so gently only to abandon him once again in he knows not what cursed place. The poets too can then describe how he slowly calms, steadies himself, looks about, smells the air, wonders, hopes, sees at last my divine form, standing above him.

I shall say, "Do you not know this place, stranger?" in a

manner that is both irreverent – I am after all a goddess, and he a mere man – but also gently fond, and he at last shall cry out: Ithaca! Ithaca! Sweet Ithaca!

I will let him have his moment of passion, of purest delight – this is also an important emotional part of the overall structure of the thing – before guiding him to more practical matters and his still unfulfilled duties about the land.

This shall the poets sing, and when they do, I shall be at the heart of it. I shall appear when it matters the most, and in this way, debasing though it is, I shall survive.

I loathe Odysseus for that, sometimes. I, who have wielded the lightning, reduced to mere adjunct to the tale of a mortal man. But loathing does not serve, so instead, I swallow my bitterness, and work. When all my siblings are diminished, when the poets no longer sing their names, Athena will endure.

The poets will not sing the truth of Odysseus. Their verses are bought and sold, their stories subject to the whims of kings and cruel men who would use their words for power and power alone. Agamemnon commanded the poets to sing of his unstoppable strength, his bloody flashing sword. Priam bade the poets of Troy raise their voices in praise of loyalty, piety and the bonds of family above all else, and look where they are now. Wandering through the blackened fields of the dead, slain as much by the stories they sang of themselves as by the blades that took their lives.

The truth does not serve me, it is not wise that it be known.

Yet here my dual natures tug upon me, for I am the lady of war, as well as wisdom. And though war is rarely wise, it is at least honest.

Truth, then, to satisfy the warrior within my philosopher's breast.

Listen closely, for this is the only time I will tell it.

A whispered secret, a hidden tale – this is the story of what actually happened when Odysseus returned to Ithaca.

8

CHAPTER 3

>>>>>>>>>>>>>>>>>>>>>>>>>>>>>>>>>>>>>>>

At the edge of a sheer black cliff spotted with the nests of precarious birds, a stream tumbles, thin-fingered and glistening, to the sea below. Follow the water inland a while and one may find a pool where sometimes the maids of Ithaca bathe and sing the secret songs that the men will never hear, a woman's voice being considered of impure stuff best left to funeral dirges. Here mossy rocks glimmer amongst the cool flowing water, and silver-limbed trees bend as if ashamed to be seen bathing in summer light.

Climb a little over scrubby branches and broken thorns that catch at the hems of wanderers, and one will reach a promontory that bulges from the land to peek up like a naughty child between fingers of faded leaf and broken stone, commanding a view upon sea and town, the crooked roofs of the palace and curling groves of rough-boughed trees. This is not usually a place disturbed by human voices, being a solitary kind of locale fit for a prowling lynx or yellow-beaked hunting bird. Yet now as we draw near, we may hear something truly remarkable for Ithaca – not merely voices, but that most unusual combination of melodies – a man and a woman, speaking together.

The man says: "But they are gods."

The woman says: "While still living?"

"Yes, of course."

"Not children of gods? Children of gods are a fairly common feature of Greek nobility, you see."

"No – they are the actual god."

"But what if they are fools?"

"They are not."

"Of course they are – some of them, I mean."

"Well, in that case the Pharaoh who supplants them erases their monuments, steals the gold from their tomb and scours their name from the temple."

"So they are gods until it is decided otherwise."

"Exactly. If they were bad Pharaohs and the flood failed, then clearly they were not gods."

"How . . . flexible."

"And Egypt has stood for eternity, and shall stand an eternity more, no?"

Let us look a little closer at this pair, resting by the water's side. The man is called Kenamon, sometime a soldier of Memphis. The woman is Penelope, queen of Ithaca.

When she introduces herself, this is not what she says. She is Penelope, wife of Odysseus. The stone she sits upon, the water she drinks, the sunlight that touches her skin in the morning – all of these, she says, are his. She is but the steward of his land, for she herself is his too. It is very thoughtful of you to call her queen, but she is simply the humble wife of a king.

She too has tacked her fortune to the name of Odysseus, and by that name she lives or dies. We have much in common, in that regard.

Wives of kings, of course, do not sit alone with soldiers from far-off lands as the sun rises above the isle. Such a thing would be scandalous for even an ordinary woman of some meagre propriety. Penelope knows this, and therefore two concessions have been made to this encounter. Firstly, they are seated high above the town, far from the eyes of her people, and came here both by separate ways, and will by separate ways depart when their conversation is done, he to wander the island and think of home, she to inspect her flocks and her groves, maybe call in on her revered father-in-law or conduct such business as a good steward must.

The other concession is the two women sitting nearby, at far enough remove to not intrude on the conversation, but near enough that they can say under oath, why yes, I was there, I saw all that happened, and by the gods attest that not a fingertip brushed another, not a breath was shared in too much proximity, and when our lady laughed – if she did – it was in a sad sort of manner as though to say "Well, one must laugh at adversity, no?"

These two women are Ourania and Eos, and of them we shall have more to say anon.

"It does strike me," the man called Kenamon concedes, "that there are certain ... similarities in some of our divinities. The details may change, but there always seems to be a rebirth, an afterlife, a great battle, and a promise of something more to come."

"A promise of something more to come is extremely useful," Penelope agrees. "There is nothing quite like being told that the lash you endure is but a fleeting shadow on the way to some Elysian field to encourage meekness in your torment. Remarkable how much people will endure for unproven promises."

"You sound ... not entirely orthodox in your opinions on this, my lady."

"The songs of the priests are ... *useful*." She says this word as I sometimes do – *useful*. A useful plague upon an enemy camp, a useful murder in a shadowed hall, the son of a king smothered

11

in his swaddling garb, a daughter dragged by the hair to the marriage altar – barbaric, of course, unhallowed and cruel, but yes: *useful*. Useful cruelties to bring about a satisfactory end.

Wisdom is not always kind, truth not gentle, and neither am I.

Kenamon's skin is the colour of sunset, his eyes flecked with amber. Aphrodite calls him "dishy", mingling appetites for food and physicality in a way I find frankly distasteful; Artemis remarks that his hands are more suited to the spear than the bow, then loses interest. The men of the isles do their best to ignore him entirely, for they cannot help but suspect that he has actually done some of the deeds of which the petty boys of Ithaca merely boast. He came to these isles looking to woo a queen. The queen politely informed him that of course, he was welcome here. She was a woman alone, a widow in all but name, and Ithaca needed a strong king to guard its shores. This being so, naturally she would not turn away anyone who sought her hand, not least because if they were busy wooing, they would not be busy plundering, raiding or enslaving her peoples.

Equally, her husband's body had not been found, so naturally she couldn't marry any man who came to try his luck, but he shouldn't be disheartened by such a thing, insurmountable as it was. No one else had been, after all.

"Though Ithaca cannot afford the riches of many other lands of Greece," Penelope continues, "when I was a girl in Sparta I remember hearing that there were nearly five times more men and women living in bondage than roamed free through the streets. The warrior men punished and tormented extraordinarily any who dared show even the slightest whiff of disobedience, to cow the population with terror. But the priests . . . the priests offered a whisper of something else – they offered hope. I never forget the potency of those chains."

When Kenamon left his home, far to the south, he had a shaved head, jewels about his arms and neck, and a commandment from his brother not to return until he had made himself a king. This commandment was of course absurd. There was no world in which a foreigner would ever win the hand of the queen of Ithaca – but that was not the point. Kenamon's absence was desired, and in the moment in which he was sent away he had to choose between staying and fighting against his own family, raging in blood and quarrel until his brothers, his cousins, maybe even his sisters too were slain; or slinking across the ocean to a land where no one knew his name. He chose what he thought of as the path of peace. He had seen too much war, and for so little consequence.

His hair has grown now, dark and curled. He wanted to shave it, as is the proper way – but in this land there seems to be some significant weight given by the menfolk to the quality of their natural locks and the magnificence of their beards. At first Kenamon thought such vanities ugly, but as the time has rolled by he sees now that it is nothing more and nothing less than the usual business of jostling comparison that the men of his home country would perform, whether that be expressed through hair or teeth or strength of arms or width of leg or set of jaw and so on. The ways mortals have to set themselves up or push others down are so numerous even I am sometimes amazed.

"I took slaves, when I was a soldier," Kenamon blurts, and is surprised to hear himself say it. Kenamon is often surprised by the words he speaks when in the company of this woman – she has that effect on him, at once exhilarating and terrifying to his heart. Penelope waits, listening, curious perhaps, any judgements she may have hidden beneath her plaster smile. "I remember telling them that they were lucky to be taken by me. I was angry that they were not more grateful."

No poets sing the songs of slaves. It would be extraordinarily dangerous to give voices to the less-than-people of this world, lest it turn out they were people after all.

War is not merciful, wisdom is not just, yet people still pray to me for kindness.

They would not if I were a man.

I trail my fingers through the gentle sea breeze, let its coolness play upon my skin, feel the warmth of the sun upon my back. It is the most pleasure in physicality I permit myself, and even that is dangerous.

Penelope, queen of Ithaca, was given the slave-girl Eos as a wedding gift. How lucky, everyone said to Eos, how lucky you must feel, to be taken from your squalid little rat-hole of a home and your common little family, put upon a ship to a far-off land and given a nice gown in which to serve a queen.

Eos's name will not be sung; her story would add a complexity that will only confuse the hearer at a time when I need their attention fixed upon other matters.

By the edge of the water, there is silence a while. It is a silence that is strange to both people sitting upon this promontory. They are of course used to many other kinds of silence – the silence of loneliness, of loss, of distant yearning for impossible things and so on. But a silence shared? A silence held in contented company? It is alien to both of them, if not entirely unwelcome.

At last: "Amphinomous invited me to spar," says Kenamon.

"I trust you said no?"

"I am not sure. He will not be seen to eat or drink with me, as that might acknowledge that I am in any way his equal or that my friendship could offer any value to his cause about the court. But if we are two warriors engaging in matters that transcend courtship or politics – matters of war, I mean – then that is acceptable without being meaningful. I think he means well by the invitation."

"I think that if he cannot recruit you as an ally, he would be wise to maim or wound you in some accident upon the training field," she replies, her eyes half wandering to a flash of colour in a nearby bush, perhaps the wing of a butterfly, the back of a glistening beetle; a lovely thing of brilliant crimson is more of a novelty to the queen of Ithaca than casual talk of betrayal and death.

"I am not convinced that is his intention. He seems ... sincere. Ever since the affair with Menelaus and the children of Agamemnon, I think he has felt a certain obligation."

"Well, he did aid Antinous and Eurymachus in trying to raise a fleet to murder my son upon his return to these islands," muses the queen, her eyes still searching for that flicker of light, that dance of life moving in the air about them. "He has a lot of work to do if he wants to redeem himself from that particular undertaking."

"Has there been any word from Telemachus?" Kenamon does not ask this question as much as he would like. He would like to ask it all the time, to hop up and down outside Penelope's door demanding to know, how is Telemachus, where is Telemachus, is the boy I helped train in the sword safe? Is there news? He is surprised how much he worries for the lad; he tells himself it is merely some passing affection, a kind of lonely fantasy concocted from being far from home. He tells himself that whenever he talks with Penelope too, and worries that he might be going mad.

"Ourania has a cousin in Pylos who reports that my son recently returned from his wanderings to the court of Nestor and is looking to take ship again. To where, she is not sure. Telemachus himself ... does not send word."

Telemachus, son of Odysseus, set forth nearly a year ago to find his father.

He has not succeeded.

Sometimes he thinks he should send some message to his mother, let her know that he is well. Then he does not. This is a greater cruelty than if he had not thought of it at all.

15

"Be careful with Amphinomous," sighs Penelope, a little shake of her head as if all of it – the talk of her son, of violence, the sight of a butterfly's wing – can be brushed away in a thought. "Spar with him if you must, but if Antinous or Eurymachus make the same offer, they will absolutely be conspiring to murder you upon the training ground, where they can say it was an accident rather than a violation of the sacred laws of the land."

"I am aware," sighs Kenamon. "And I will politely decline should they ask. Say that I am no warrior fit to match with them. But I believe Amphinomous is in his own way not too dishonourable. And it will be pleasing to talk at the feast with someone who is ..." His words drift away. There is no good ending to this sentence, rich in possibilities though it be. Someone who is not a drunkard suitor, pawing at Penelope's hem? Someone who is not a wheedling boy, desperate to win the crown of absent Odysseus? Someone who is not a maid, rolling her eyes as the men call for more meat, more wine! Someone who is not a queen who must be conversed with only in secret, and to whom there are things that no man will ever be allowed to say?

Perhaps none of these. Perhaps all. Kenamon has not heard the tongue of his people for well over a year, save in odd snatches at the wharves. When the Egyptian traders come, he is at once there, babbling with them like a fool, nothing of any meaning to say but delighting, revelling in the ease of the language of his birth as it flows from his lips. Then they sail away again; then he is alone once more.

For a while he wandered through the hills of Ithaca by himself, and in his loneliness he could perhaps close his eyes and imagine he was not in this place at all, but back upon the waters of the great river that scythes his homeland. Then he wandered these hills with Telemachus, before that young man sailed; then

Telemachus left to forge his own story, to grow from a boy to a man in a journey across the sea – that at least is how the poets will tell it – and Kenamon was alone again. But now the queen of Ithaca – shall we say rather the wife of Odysseus – sits by his side. And Kenamon is perhaps a little less alone, and even more lost than he was before.

"I should go," Penelope declares with a shake of her head. Every time they meet, she is on her way somewhere else. The isles are full of groves and herds of goats, fishing boats and busy workshops that toil in her husband's name – busy, busy, busy, always so busy. And yet every time, her departure is a little slower, her business a little less urgent. Nothing should alarm a monarch more than the moment she realises that the people she has promoted will be absolutely fine labouring without her. Such thoughts should raise uncomfortable questions about the value of kings and queens. (Very few monarchs have these thoughts, and thus do their dynasties die.)

There was a time when I had no interest in Penelope, queen of Ithaca. Her role was merely to serve as motivation for her husband, her existence justifying his sometimes more questionable deeds. My eye was entirely on Odysseus. It was Hera, of all people, who pointed out that the women of Ithaca – mere shadows to his tale – might be something more. Hera who suggested that Ithaca's queen should merit some of my attention after all.

Here then, let us peek inside the mind of Penelope:

She tells herself that she sits with Kenamon because he has been of service to her. He defended her son, defended her, in a time when violent men came to her isle. He has kept secrets that she might otherwise have had him killed for knowing; he does not wheedle for her hand, when they converse, but speaks to her – how remarkable this is – almost as easily as if she were a man!

She tells herself that she has no interest in him as a husband.

17

Of course not. It is entirely unacceptable to even imagine such a thing, and so she does not. She does not imagine it when she sees him walking by the shore, or hears him singing in the little garden beneath her window, where only he and the women go. She does not imagine it when he says thank you to a maid, nor when she catches him sparring with shadows, a bronze blade gleaming in his hand.

Penelope has spent a long time learning how not to imagine all sorts of distracting and unhelpful things. It is another of the qualities she and I share.

Now she rises.

Now she will depart.

Any moment now . . .

. . . any moment . . .

I nudge her in the small of her back.

You are no use, I breathe, *if you permit yourself to dream.*

She staggers slightly at my touch, a movement that becomes a step, that becomes walking away. But as she does, a question forms on Kenamon's lips, a thing that will perhaps hold her here a moment more, blurted at the very moment she was to leave: "I heard a ship was wrecked on the eastern shore, a Phaeacian?"

She is grateful that his question stops her, irritated that it is in her way. "Worse: a ship came, it left, without so much as calling at the harbour or bartering for fresh supplies or trade. I haven't had any trouble from Alcinous and his people before, but if this is going to become a habit – if they think they can just bypass my ports altogether – then something will have to be done. His wife's not unreasonable, but since Agamemnon's death the fear that kept even the more ambitious kings subdued has been weakening."

"I thought Orestes would help. Bring back some of his father's security? Enforce order in the seas?"

"Perhaps," muses Penelope. "But Orestes is young, and still

18

asserting his power after fending off his uncle's claims. Nor is it entirely to Ithaca's advantage to be constantly leaning on Mycenae for support. It makes us seem even weaker than we are." She shakes her head, stretches her neck from one side to the other. "We'll think of something. It might be nothing. Like I said: the Phaeacians are more pliable than many of the petty kings nipping at Ithaca's shores."

Kenamon nods, but says nothing more.

He thinks Penelope is at her most beautiful when she speaks of politics, when her eyes narrow in the concoction of some slow-burning scheme. Sometimes, when she talks of barter and bargains, of plots and petty princes, he has to stop himself from blurting: come away with me. Come to Egypt. I cannot offer much, but all I can, I will.

He does not, of course. They are both wise enough to know that it would be madness, death.

Wisdom is not loud, is often unseen, unpraised, unremarked.

Perhaps, if I were not also the lady of war, I would be wise enough to be content.

A while therefore in silence they remain, even though both should be about their days; but this moment, pleasing enough as it is, cannot last for ever. Too much is afoot in the island, and even now the first sign of great change approaches in the form of a woman with autumn hair and forest eyes, striding up a winding path, gown hitched to reveal her knees and a skin of water upon her back. Her name is Autonoe, maid of Ithaca, and she has come with word of the first event that will tear the land asunder:

"Telemachus's ship is in the harbour."

Thus begins the end.

CHAPTER 4

>>

It is not apt that a queen should run. By the poets' reckoning, the only times when it is acceptable for a queen to run is to greet her long-lost husband, who still glistens with the blood of his slain foes and the sweat of war as he returns unto her heaving bosom, or when she throws herself in an uncontrolled passion upon said husband's bloodied corpse before proclaiming her intention to drive herself through with his blade as she cannot live without him. In this latter scenario, it is the duty of any nearby maids to grab said blade from their mistress's hand before she can do any harm upon herself, at which point the lady might fall into an elegant but profound swoon from which she later wakes distressed but less immediately suicidal.

A queen should also run when the soldiers of a foreign power have burst into her city and are about to set upon her in a most barbaric and savage way – ideally her run should be to a cliff edge from where she can throw herself, and if there is no convenient cliff then she should not run at all but rather trust to her sheer matronly dignity and force of character to dissuade at least some of the soldiers of a finer sort from raping her then and there, instead giving herself to their captain, who may at least be more exclusive in his cruelties.

These are, if you believe the poets, the only circumstances under which it is acceptable for a queen to run, and the majority tend towards supplication and death.

Such are the stories woven by my father, Zeus, and my brother-gods, and what power they hold. I would burn it all, if only I had the strength.

Penelope understands her duties as set down by the poets and the words of men, and does not run to the harbour where the ship of her son, Telemachus, is newly docked. Rather she moves at that brisk, breathless pace that one may see when a house is on fire and the leader of the bucket chain knows the difference between haste and panic. Her dearest maids, Eos and Autonoe, flank her as she descends through the town, with the third lady of this group, the somewhat older and more breathless Ourania, bumbling along behind with a muttered, "This is not dignified!"

Kenamon is nowhere to be seen. This is the wisest course of action for everyone concerned.

The ship of Telemachus is an adequate vessel, capable of carrying some thirty rowers and a fair stash of fresh water and dry meat below. It is poorly suited for battle and has little of note about its sea-scarred sides or oft-patched sails, but that was one of the qualities for which I, as I guided the son of Odysseus to his quest, chose it. Telemachus naturally wants to be a hero, as his father is, and what a weight of heroism his father's legacy is indeed. It would undermine the value placed upon Odysseus's story for his son to be a useless pipsqueak, implying perhaps that the father's glory is merely a fleeting, futile thing; thus, the bare minimum of valiant quest for Telemachus is essential. But the greatest heroes first need to survive to reach the object of their quest, and discretion is a valuable commodity for those who wish to live long enough to be praised. Odysseus understands this, appreciates the fine line between being seen to be heroic and being secure enough to get away with it. The son is more doubtful in his intellect.

Thus: a merely adequate boat.

It is with this dichotomy in mind that we should not be surprised that though the ship that carried Telemachus from Ithaca some many moons ago is now sitting like the proud male duck at the quay, Telemachus himself is nowhere to be found.

Breathless, Penelope slows, asks: where is my son? This is his ship – where is he? Has anyone seen him?

There is a question, too, on the tip of her tongue, on the edge of her lips, which she cannot breathe, cannot even begin to shape; it catches in her chest, it is a stone pressing down upon her heart. I will say it for her now, whisper it, choke it out: is he dead? Has my son's ship returned without him, is he lost?

Were a reputable sailor of assured honesty to walk up to Penelope now and say: good my lady, apologies my lady, I saw your *husband's* corpse pinned upon a white wall, it was him, I knew him perfectly and everyone who witnessed it agreed, Penelope would listen to his tale, nod once, thank him politely, and head immediately to the palace to commence her requisite seven days of mourning and enact some very thorough, well-thought-through plans.

Were this same man of the sea to now approach her and say: good my lady, apologies my lady, I saw your son drown, as sure of him I am as of the waxing of the moon, Penelope does not know what she would do. Would she fall weeping? Would she turn to stone? Would she thank him politely and walk away without another word? She has no idea, and though I am a goddess of great potency, neither do I. Very few thoughts there are which are inconceivable to the queen of Ithaca. Calamity, destruction and disaster – all these are regular contemplations. But for her son to die? She has not permitted herself to think on it. It is one of the very few blind spots in her otherwise remarkably clear vision.

So now she calls out: where is my son? Has anyone seen Telemachus? And people stare, because this is an unusual, disconcerting thing. They are used to seeing their queen by the harbour, face veiled and voice hushed. Her immutable form is a marble statue of monarchy that no storm can shake. Yet now, embarrassing almost, awkward and uneasy, it seems that a woman — a mother, even — stands upon the quay, shaking, crying out, my son, my son! Has anyone seen my son?!

It is not a huge performance of emotion, of course. Penelope has spent too much time being ice to truly know how to let any fire burn. But still, eyes are averted, toes shuffle to point away, voices mutter as she grasps the hand of her nearest maid and stutters: where is Telemachus?

Telemachus is on the way to the hut of the old swineherd, Eumaeus. He has not found his father, nor news of his father's death. He is therefore a failure, and cannot possibly face the censure of laughing, mocking men. Better to have drowned, he thinks, than be anything less than a hero — but it is also profoundly less than heroic to throw yourself into the foaming depths without having at the bare minimum slain your wife or mother or *something* noteworthy on the way — even an unusually large boar or particularly ill-tempered bull would do — and so, wretched and without any better idea, he has returned. There was simply nothing better for him to do.

He will have something of a shock when he gets to the hut and finds someone else waiting there, salt in his beard and sand between his toes — but that is a story for the poets. For now, I sing this other melody, of a mother looking for her son who has sailed far from home, and who she cannot find.

It is a sailor from Telemachus's ship who at last sees the queen in her frantic prowling by the seashore and descends to say, forgive me, ma'am, as I may, ma'am, I sailed with your son and can say he is safely returned. No doubt he has gone straight to the palace to see you – you must have just missed him – but he is safe and well and absolutely will be waiting to show you his duty no doubt.

Then Penelope gasps and says: of course! Of course he will be waiting for me! And together they scurry to the palace, much to the chagrin of snow-haired Ourania, who has only just made it to the shore and is far from enamoured at the idea of having to climb the hill she has just descended.

"For goodness' sake, it's Telemachus!" tuts the maid Autonoe, who for all that she doesn't particularly like the son of Odysseus finds to her surprise that she is at least somewhat concerned for the welfare of the boy, in as much as she cares for those things that Penelope cares for.

So in a flap of gown and veil, breathless shuffling and mutter-ing from old Ourania, the group scuttle up to the palace gates, Penelope not even bothering to step within the hearth before calling out: "Telemachus! Telemachus!"

The palace is ringed by walls that are precisely high enough to be a hindrance to an attacker and not a handspan more. The kings of Ithaca had neither resources nor inclination to build for glory or to make a point – function is the only issue at stake in the faded bounds of this place, in her cracked stones and creak-ing old doors. The courtyard that leads from the main gate to the entrance of the great hall is large enough to accommodate a small muster of armed men who might be gathered before a raid, but not so large that it is a pain to keep it ordered and clean. The great hall itself has but one large fire, still being cleaned and prepared by the morning maids, and the empty chair of Odysseus is raised upon a plinth at its northern end precisely so high that any king sitting upon it may observe all who sit at the long tables below, but not so high that it's difficult for an old monarch to climb or has any great risk of an embarrassing fall.

The most extensive parts of the palace are the kitchens,

24

the quarters for the maids, the pig pens, the grain stores, the carpenter's workshop, the timber shed and the long latrines. Though rooms aplenty have been stuck on the side of teetering walls and perched precariously on crooked stairs above sagging halls, each one is in its dimensions and attention far less significant than all of these. More likely you are to sniff the innards of a gutted fish or hear the snuffling of a snout than catch the aroma of sweet incense or the raised lyric of a soothing song. As a child, Telemachus would sometimes run through these corridors to hide in hidden nooks, and the maids who searched for him would hardly bother to seek him out from the palace's weaving shadows but merely wait for him to get bored and emerge of his own accord, as the latter was frequently more reliable than looking.

Penelope rarely went searching for her child. There was always far too much to do. She promised that she would get round to it, that she would be there for her son. But every time she found a free moment to play with him, to hold him close, to be merely present by his side, there was another messenger from Troy, another request for grain, gold, men, something else a queen had to do. "I'll be right back," she'd say, and eventually Telemachus gave up waiting for her to keep her word.

Yet now: "Telemachus!" she calls. "Telemachus?!"

There is no answer.

When Telemachus sailed from Ithaca to find his father, he did so without a word. He could not see what possible benefit there would be in speaking to his mother of his plans. She would say it was folly, rash, that he was abandoning her for his own foolish pride, his own selfish desire to be a hero – a *true* hero of ballad and song – rather than face up to the web of politics and indignity that reigned on Ithaca. He told himself it was better to spare her from her wretched tears, and save himself the tediousness of having to argue with a woman. When a storm broke over his

25

vessel on the second night at sea that threatened to pitch them all into the tempest waters, he stood upon the prow and did not blink at the sight of lightning. When, while travelling with Nestor's son to Sparta, they were set upon by bandits, he fought with the lion's fury, blind to blood or danger, a snarl of blade and tooth. He does not, therefore, consider himself a coward.

"Telemachus?! *Telemachus!*"

Penelope moves through the halls of her palace, and he is not there.

"Where is he? Where is my son?"

"Perhaps he has gone to see his grandfather . . ."

"Before his mother?"

"Perhaps he has . . . news?"

"If he has news he should have come with an army! If his father is alive he should bring back an army – if his father is dead he should bring an even bigger army! Telemachus!"

"My lady – he is not here."

Penelope catches Eos by the hand as the maid says it. She will not stagger, will not fall. Eos is a short woman, barrel-shouldered and bronze-jawed. Compared to many of the maids in the palace, her hands are not splintered with wood nor burned from cooking, yet still her skin is worn to dried leather, warm and unyielding where she grips Penelope's fingers tight within her own. Outside, a few of the lazy suitors, the bedraggled boys and wretched half-men who plague her court, have been drawn by the noise of her cries. She will not weep before them. She will not show the slightest sign of wretchedness. Instead, she draws her chin up, which straightens her neck, which straightens her back, and lets out a single breath, and nods just once, and remembers to be merely a queen again.

"Well," she says. And again: "Well."

She will not speculate on where her son has gone.

Perhaps he has some plan.

Perhaps he has some clever scheme.

Perhaps there is a reason why the boy who left without a word to his mother does not seek her out when he returns. Some good reason of ... of state. Of high and important matter. Of ... something like that.

He is, after all, Odysseus's son. And she Odysseus's wife. These are the only things that matter now.

"Eos," she breathes. "I believe we were to inspect the grain?"

"Of course, my lady," replies Eos, as she lets Penelope's fingers go. "I have prepared everything."

The suitors watch from the open windows of the hall, the shutters drawn back, as the wife of Odysseus and her maids drift away.

CHAPTER 5

>>

In the hut of the old swineherd Eumaeus, voices can be heard:
"Father, I . . . I . . . "

"My son!"

"There are suitors, all throughout the palace, they have been . . . "

"They shall be punished, my son, I swear it . . . "

Tears are shed.

Womanly tears are tears of self-pity, of feeble despair, of powerless grief, of attention-seeking hysteria and emotions that overpower good sense. At most, they are to be tolerated – women can't help themselves, after all – and at worst, derided as pathetic indulgence. So say the poets, and it takes so little time, so very little time indeed, for the lies of the poets to become the truth of the land.

These are not those tears.

These are manly tears welling up from two heroes who have overcome and endured torments with a strong-jawed silence and now are releasing the profound suppressed emotions that have been lurking for so many years beneath their rugged exteriors. Such tears are acceptable for warrior men and entirely different from the weaker feminine sort of weeping, and no one had best dare suggest anything other.

After, a plan is devised.

In the palace of Odysseus, the suitors are settling in for their evening feast.

There are approximately one hundred of these men, and they present something of a novelty on the island of Ithaca in that there are within their ranks not merely foreigners from far-off lands come to woo the mourning queen, but also men older than twenty-five but younger than sixty. When Odysseus sailed to Troy, twenty years ago, he took the flower of the western isles with him – any would-be warrior over the age of fifteen or a few years shy of being a grey-bearded old man set sail with the king, and in the ten years in which he laboured, many more boys were sent with helmets too large for their heads and sacks of grain beneath their feet to fuel the endless demands of blood and war. Of those who sailed, many died at Troy. Some were eaten, so the poets will say, by cannibals on their way home, or lost while plundering on their westwards voyage. One tripped and fell from the roof of the house of Circe in a manner that frankly even I struggle to find poetic valour in; some were plucked from their seats by many-headed Scylla as they rowed beneath her lair in the crashing cliffs. The rest drowned. Their names will be sung only to help contextualise the valour of brave Odysseus, the last man left alive. The poets will be at pains to point out how prideful men, greedy men, thoughtless men die. Only the wise man makes it home.

The youngest of the suitors who paw at Penelope's gown are Ithacan. They were children, whelps as Telemachus was, still cradled in their mothers' arms when Odysseus left. Too young to fight in Troy, raised on the stories of their absent fathers' heroic deeds, they laugh and jostle and snarl and snap, each one eager to prove that he too is a man, a soldier, a bringer of greatness, and each one entirely untested in their little courage, which only makes them bray the louder. It takes strength for a man to be confident in his silences. Kenamon is often silent, but that is largely because there are few who will speak to him, being a foreigner and maybe even a threat.

Of all these beardless boys who would be kings, the two considered most prominent are Antinous, son of Eupheithes, and Eurymachus, son of Polybus. This is how they speak:

"Eurymachus, you simpering mouse! Put down a proper wager and prove yourself a man!"

"I don't need to wager with you, Antinous, to prove anything, thank you very much."

"Is Daddy still angry with you? You can tell us, we won't judge."

"Go away, Antinous!"

"*Go away, Antinous!*"

The sycophantic fools who have each set their stars by the rise and fall of either suitor, clusters of boys hovering at their backs, respectively laugh or glower. This is the quality of dolt who has of late resided on Ithaca. Their mothers cannot understand how it happened – how did they raise their boys to be such men?

(Why, it was their love, misplaced. For they told every boy how big and brave and strong and mighty he would be, how he must never let anyone tell him that he is wrong, must never flinch or show weakness, never cry when hurt or wounded or broken or afraid – only girls do that. With love, they poisoned their children, and here we are. Here indeed we are, and I am not innocent in this creation.)

On tables a little away from the hearth, men from further afield. Would-be princelings from Athens and Pylos, Calchis and Mycenae, third sons of second sons, all sent a-wooing to the western isles to try and win themselves a kingdom, there

30

not being any really good wars brewing where they could win themselves anything else by more manly deeds. They have grown used to the diet of the isles (fish) and the paucity of the company (backwards, uncivilised), and even those amongst them who were once soldiers are becoming fat and lazy on the parade of water and wine that is poured into their cups by their ever-aloof hostess.

"Well then why don't you leave?" asks Amphinomous, some-time warrior with flecks of gold in his russet beard and a jaw like the prow of the ship on which he first sailed to this isle. "If you are so sick of waiting for a woman to make her mind up, the sea is wide and the world still full of wonders. Sail away!"

"But," whines his drinking companion, "what if she was going to choose me?"

"She is not going to choose you," opines another. "She is not going to choose anyone."

She — the lady of the palace — sits apart from them all at the furthest end of the hall. Her husband's throne, a modest chair of carved wood without jewel or gaudy adornment, is set behind and a little above her. She has never sat in it. Her cousin Clytemnestra sat in her husband Agamemnon's throne when he sailed to Troy, and ruled like a queen, and where is she now? Grey and empty, wandering the fields of the dead, her heart still bleeding where her son drove his blade. No, Penelope sits merely *near* her husband's throne, its perpetual guardian, the loyal wife holding still to the memory of her beloved, absent Odysseus. There was a time when she occupied herself at these feasts with weaving a funeral shroud for her father-in-law, Laertes. The fact that Laertes is still living was merely a minor impediment to this enterprise — always best to plan ahead, the women of Ithaca like to say. That at night she unpicked the work she had woven by day, having pledged to marry a man

31

of this hall when the weaving was done – that was a far more controversial and serious matter.

Tricksy, the suitors said of Penelope after her deception was exposed. She is a tricksy, tricksy queen.

She should really have married one of them when that little act was discovered. Put an end to this whole sorry affair. But which man to marry?

Penelope sits above the feast, and her eyes flicker about the hall. Antinous doesn't meet her gaze, has not met her eyes for many months. He has given up pretending not to despise her. He does not know enough of her as a woman – no one there truly knows her as a woman – to hate some piece of her humanity. Rather he loathes what he feels she has done to *him*. He should be a warrior-king, a man sung in the ballads who goes forth and takes what he wants, conquers all who challenge him. But she has made him less than a man – she has made him one who has to wait on the whims of a woman, she is to blame for all his deficits. He will never forgive her that, and should they ever wed he has sworn that he will make his feelings known upon the marriage bed.

Eurymachus smiles, crooked-toothed and trailing loose limbs, as her gaze passes him by. He has no illusions about being a warrior-king as Antinous has. In a way, he thinks it's a nice sign how loyal Penelope has been to the memory of her dead husband. She is a woman who knows her duty, which means if they are wed – when they are wed – she will show the same duty to him. Perhaps she will stroke his hair, as his nursemaid was wont to do when he was a boy, and listen patiently to the moans and petty gripes that brim within his bosom but which he dare not give voice to, being as they are too small to merit serious attention from grown-up sorts. He doesn't mind that she's getting old and is almost certainly barren – it could be nice, he thinks, to have an older woman look after you. Eurymachus's mother died giving birth to a baby boy who did not survive the night. His father, Polybus, did not enjoy the company of females after.

Penelope's eyes drift past Eurymachus's without acknowledgement. Amphinomous nods once, leading with his chin – a polite acknowledgement that seems to suggest a degree of equality, of mutual respect and understanding between these two that Penelope is confident has not been earned.

She does not look at Kenamon. His insignificance is his safety, and she finds with a strange ferocity that sticks in her throat that she would have him safe.

The evening light through the windows of the great hall is flecked with crimson and blazing fire. It drives the shadows up the painted walls, layering the distorted forms of these suitors over the painted daubs and frescoes of brave Odysseus doing heroic deeds that Penelope commissioned to adorn as many public surfaces of the palace as she could. Odysseus slaying a boar as a young man; Odysseus sailing to Troy. Odysseus locking blades with fearsome enemies, Odysseus striking them down. Odysseus with his bow. Odysseus devising the wooden horse. Odysseus fighting in the companies of the great kings who are his sworn allies. There is a recent addition to these frescoes – not of Odysseus at all. Rather the son of Agamemnon, Orestes, has been added holding his father's bloody sword, his dark eyes staring out of the wall with a decidedly determined expression while at his side soldiers and kings all do homage. Penelope thinks it a good idea to remind her guests just how potent her new allies are, in these changing times.

There are no images of Telemachus.

Penelope doesn't know what they would depict if there were.

By the hearth, the bard sings a ballad of Troy. He sings of the bravery of men lost, of their valour, of an age of heroes that will not come again. Penelope likes that part in particular, but alas, her status obliges her to seem weepy-eyed when it comes up, to cry out, "Oh woe is me, my heart is breaking for my poor brave husband!" on a regular basis, just in case anyone in the hall might forget why and why and why they are waiting. The chorus is coming now. Usually she would start preparing herself for a bit of a swoon and an early night, Eos catching her as she droops in her womanly distress. Tonight she does not blink, does not flinch, her thoughts in some other place.

The maids move about the room, serving plates of lentils and fish, meat and bread with which the men can scrape at the feast within their bowls. There are nearly forty women of the household of Odysseus, from young Phiobe with the laughing eyes and merry lips to old Euracleia, ancient nursemaid of Odysseus, seething in a shadowed corner. Phiobe doesn't mind the many men who linger in the palace — she enjoys the stories of far-off places and the attention of tongue-tied youths who have no hope whatsoever of seeing the throne of Ithaca, let alone surviving the inevitable war that will be unleashed should Penelope ever name a man — and for their part, they enjoy her easy company and merry wit. Euracleia despises the men, the maids and everything about the house. It is disgusting. It is a disgrace. It is the betrayal of everything her beloved Odysseus stands for. Yet she does not entirely blame the men for their actions — they are but men, ambitious and bold in seeking to be made kings. Rather it is the women, the *women*! The maids and yes, she hardly dares say it, but Penelope too, who look upon and smile at the men as if somehow giving *permission* with their eyes. As if there were some sort of . . . *accord* between them. Euracleia shudders to think on it, and therefore does not.

Penelope dislikes Euracleia. If her dead mother-in-law, Anticlea, had not made her swear to do right by the old nursemaid, she would have been dispatched to some harmless villa on Kephalonia many years ago, to live out her elder days berating ducks and geese, rather than maids and even queens in the house of Odysseus.

Telemachus is not at the feast.

Penelope has sent word to certain women of her acquaintance – to old Semele and her daughters, to Anaitis, priestess of Artemis, and to Teodora, who knows the secret paths of this land better than almost any other who treads upon it – to find her son. Word came back fairly quickly from Semele's daughter, Mirene, that she has seen Telemachus in the house of old Eumaeus, the swineherd. He seems unharmed and sober. He does not appear to be in a hurry to return to the palace to greet his mother.

"Oh," said Penelope, on hearing the news. "Then he has found nothing and failed in his efforts to be a man."

In a way, this is a relief.

It is politically the least unhelpful outcome she can think of – a maintenance of things as they are, her husband neither alive nor dead, no clear answers any which way.

It is also emotionally something – anything – that she can cling to. For if Telemachus has failed in his quest, then of course he is ashamed, he is shattered, his heart is rent in two, and that goes some way – if only some – to explain why he is not by his mother's side. This at least is what Penelope tells herself. It is the only thing she can.

In the great hall, the bard reaches the chorus. It's fairly standard fare – a lament for the many lives lost to the betrayal of Helen, for the great soldiers cut down in their valour, the kings slain, the heroes who shall not breathe again and so on and so forth. The really good bit is coming, about how Odysseus is returning still to Ithaca, guided by honour, guided by love. A few of the suitors who have been here the longest stir a little, glance towards Penelope. They are aware that this is another of those musical moments that she is prone to fluttering on, before

35

retiring to her room, overcome with a womanly weakness that curiously enough excuses her from the lingering tedium of the feast. Kenamon watches too from beneath long black lashes. He observes Eos shuffling her feet a little wider apart, rolling her shoulders, a veiled glance passing between mistress and maid as though to say, here we go ...

A shadow, a presence at the door.

It is enough of a presence to draw attention, and attention drawn, voices fall silent. The silence spreads through the hall like the last wave of the high turning tide, sweeping all before it, drawing every eye, until even the bard by the fire hesitates, quavers, coughs his way to a stuttered end-note. Penelope too looks towards the boy – he would insist on being called a man – who stands with his back to the light of the fading day. Catches her breath, and the catch is real.

Telemachus, sword at his hip, cloak upon his back, dark hair growing curly about his skull, a thin beard doing its very best to make itself known about his sunken chin, looks around the hall of his father. The son of Odysseus is not especially tall, and has some of his mother's pallor, a hint of the ocean in his skin. But a year of salt and travel has broadened his back, scraped a little softness from his cheeks, fattened his wrists and narrowed his eyes into a slight squint as if he is expecting even now to have to pick his way across a hostile land of danger by the thin light of the moon, or beat against a raging summer storm.

The last of the suitors are hushed at the sight of him. They are not armed. It is one of the sacred rules of this place that guest and host alike go without a blade, though plenty have hidden secret daggers about their gowns. Telemachus's hand opens and closes about the hilt on his hip, his eyes sweeping across the room, until at last they settle on his mother.

Penelope stands, slowly, gripping Eos's arm tight.

Telemachus walks to the fire.

Warms his hands, though the air is mild and there is no biting chill to it, his back to the room, his mother, the world.

Turns.

Surveys the suitors.

They watch him, and do not move. There are some amongst them – Antinous and Eurymachus included – who at one time conspired to catch Telemachus on his return voyage to Ithaca, slaughter him at sea, far from the sight of his home harbour. But their plans were thwarted – the poets will say by the gods, by sacred Athena, though perhaps a little more pragmatically by Telemachus's mother first commandeering their vessel of war and later having it burned to a scarred bone of blackened timber whose bones still now blot the harbour mouth. However, a mother saving her son would not a good heroic fable make, unless said mother perhaps dies after in an act of magnificent self-sacrifice to teach said son a valuable lesson, and so we shall ignore it. Telemachus certainly will, if he even bothers to make enquiries. (He will not.)

It is Antinous who at last dares to speak, since whoever goes first will be clearly the boldest of the suitors, even if what he has to say is inane. Volume is of more value than content. Thus: "Telemachus!" he cries. "You grace us with your presence!"

Telemachus once nearly punched Antinous in the face in this same hall, an act that would have precipitated a bloodbath that would have washed these isles crimson. Naturally I intervened before anything too dramatic could unfold, but this time, as the young man's eyes lock with Antinous's, I do not feel any need to act. Rather, a curl of lip, a pulling back of shoulder – it is not a sneer of contempt that is drawn upon Telemachus's face, as there might have been in the past. Rather a look dawns that seems to say "how strange that I ever despised you, since the energy it takes to hate one as low as yourself vastly exceeds the effort that you are worth".

I am familiar with this expression; it is one I have sometimes caught upon my own visage, when I see its reflection in the corner of my eye. Unlike foolish Telemachus, I have laboured to wipe my expression clean.

"Antinous," he replies. "I am glad to see that you are still being so graciously attended to as you eat at my father's table. What great comfort it is to me to return to my father's house and see all of you so well fatted by his hearth. Truly the hospitality of Ithaca is unbending."

This is not the reply Antinous was expecting. He understands hatred, fury, passion, rage, jealousy, indignity – in Antinous all these things blaze hot, the same roaring scarlet that burned in the hearts of Achilles and Ajax, Agamemnon and Menelaus. He does not yet understand how these things might creak as ice, a slow, cold glacier that rolls across the heart. Such things confuse him. He does not react well to being confused.

"And dare we ask where you might have been, Telemachus? Your presence was dreadfully missed at the feast – I'm sure your mother wept rivers for you!"

Telemachus's eyes flicker to Penelope, but he turns away immediately, to focus on more important matters. "Why, honoured guest," he drawls. "I am glad you asked. I travelled to Sparta to meet with my father's sworn brother, Menelaus, and to Mycenae to speak with Orestes, that great king. I travelled with the sons of Nestor and scoured the land in search of news of my father, and am now returned to you."

"And what news do you have? Did you see his corpse? Or was your quest a failure, a little ... family outing rather than anything of real import?"

The smile that flickers on Telemachus's lips is so fast that Penelope thinks she has imagined it, cannot believe it is there, knows it was. It passes in the beating of a butterfly's wing, and then Telemachus is dismissing the question with a wave of his hand. "I have a great deal to report, and have learned many things," he says. "But this is not the time for it. Please – you are feasting. You are enjoying the feast. Carry on. You are my mother's guests."

He walks now towards the creaking door that leads to the innards of the palace, as all around the suitors start muttering and spluttering, rising to their feet – Telemachus, Telemachus! What news, Telemachus! You can't just come in here and say there is news and not tell us, where have you been, what have you seen, what news of your father, *Telemachus*?!

He pauses by his mother for just a moment as his steps carry him past her chair. Bows a little – the bare minimum of courtesy and respect, so bare as to be entirely disrespectful – then turns his head from her and heads into his father's palace.

CHAPTER 6

>>

S hock.

Penelope is shocked.

This is an unusual sensation for her.

She has stood up to princelings and kings. She has defended her islands from pirates and veterans of the great wars of Troy, locked wits with the king of Sparta and won, been abused and threatened in her own home, and yet she could not say she was ever particularly astounded. The worst of all things has always seemed a likely possibility in the great game of kings. Saddened, she might say. Disappointed at the situation. But never especially surprised.

Penelope has always been blind where her son is concerned. It is one of her few failings as a queen, and her greatest regret as a mother.

Telemachus leaves the hall, and for a moment all is stunned, all is silenced. Penelope is frozen where she stands like a startled forest creature that hopes that if it does not move, it will not be perceived. The suitors do not speak, the bards do not sing. It is Kenamon at last who breaks the spell, coughing and exclaiming a little too loudly for his place: "Well, a drink to welcome back the son of Odysseus, yes?"

40

No one wants to drink to the son of Odysseus, but the words themselves are the noise that pushes back the wall of hush that has descended like a stone upon this place. Antinous blusters; Eurymachus mutters that Telemachus seems very strange, Amphinomous says well, well, he looks ... doesn't he look well ...?

The bard begins to sing again. Penelope's fingers are white where she holds Eos's arm, and the maid does not say how much the queen's grip hurts.

The women follow Telemachus into the palace.

He has not waited for them beyond the door.

Is not in his room or council chamber.

Melitta, wide-hipped maid with a slaughtered sheep slung upon her back, blurts that she saw him go this-a-way. Autonoe approaches them as they weave through the halls of the palace to whisper that she has seen Telemachus head to the armoury. Penelope and Eos quicken their steps, scuttle through the spider-halls to the darkened room where the meagre arms and weapons kept by the few soldiers of the palace are stored.

The door is indeed open, and in the last light of the evening sun through a high square window Telemachus stands inspecting a spear, feeling the weight of a shield. Why – this might be the same spear that he held in his hands when, many moons ago, he set out to fight pirates, and was nearly slain for his rash efforts. This might be the same shield that was dented by a raider's blade as the youthful boys of his short-lived militia fought and died against those brutal men who would have taken these isles. Kenamon saved his life that night – at the time he was grateful, but now he understands that gratitude does not serve a hero, let alone a king.

The boys are dead now, but so are the men who killed them. They fell in what the poets have been instructed to call "Artemis's arrows", if they talk about it at all. Generally they do not. There are very few in the palace who really understand what force it was that slew Ithaca's invaders, and they do not consider it politic to discuss the subject anywhere but in the midnight shadows. Penelope in this matter, as with so many, would far rather a fanciful story is told than a true one.

Now Telemachus examines these few weapons in the gloomy room, as his mother stops breathless in the door. Sensing her presence, he looks up, sees her standing there, nods as though to say "ah yes, this business too" and resumes his inspection. "Mother," he says, running his finger along the blunted edge of an axe.

Eos stands a little further back. She was present at Telemachus's birth, held him up by his armpits when he peed himself as a young child, knows every secret of both mother and son. But still, this is not her place. Not in his eyes, at least.

"Telemachus," stutters Penelope. When he does not reply, she draws herself up a little straighter. Her adoptive mother, Polycaste, and her mother-in-law, Anticlea, were both princesses and queens. Though they differed in many qualities, they both agreed on one point: that as a queen, when you are bending, when you think you might break, that is when you must straighten your back. "You are alive then," she barks, harder, bolder, not as a mother might.

"Yes. Alive." A dagger is drawn from a sheath, examined, returned.

"You left without a word."

"It was necessary. The suitors would have tried to prevent me."

"And that meant you could not tell your mother?"

A half-shrug, the snicker of bronze sliding back into the scabbard. "You would also have tried to prevent me."

"And my word would have been enough, would it? My tears, my warnings . . . that would have stopped you?"

A sigh, a huff. Euracleia huffs and sighs like that. Penelope

42

feels a twist of sickness in her stomach, a knot of shame. Her mothers only ever taught her how to be a queen, as they themselves had been taught by their mothers before them. Tenderness was not in the art of a monarch, their children given over to nurses and maids for such matters, and now Penelope has . . . many regrets. More than she herself can know.

Telemachus turns to her, and there is none of the simpering half-stumble of the boy she knew when he departed these shores. Something has changed in him, but she cannot know how recent that change has been. "Where is Father's bow?"

"What?"

"Father's bow. Where is it?"

"In the council chamber. On the wall. It is hanging as a reminder that—"

Telemachus tuts, shakes his head, cutting her off. "It shouldn't be in there. It is not good for the wood."

When Penelope last checked, Telemachus knew and cared as much for the maintenance of his father's bow as she did for the lives of squid. Her mouth shapes sounds that do not come, indignant cries that have no meaning, imprecations, implorings. She should be running towards him. She should be throwing her arms about his neck. She should be weeping into his shoulder, my son, my son, you are alive, my beautiful boy!

She wants to do all of these things. Were Hera or Aphrodite standing by her side, perhaps they would nudge her into this course of action, bid her fling herself upon him and cry, my son, my son, my heart is made whole again, my son!

But only I am here, goddess of war and wisdom, and in these regards I am . . . deficient.

There was perhaps a time, a long time ago, when Penelope could have been tender, and her son would have thanked her for it. That time has passed.

Telemachus returns a sword to its place, nods – he is satisfied with his inventory. He moves to leave, but Penelope is in the door. A little puff of irritation as he waits for her to move, and she does not.

"I have business to attend to," he barks, at her lumpen, frozen feet.

"What business could be more important than seeing your mother?"

"There is much in this isle that has been neglected," he replies, with a wave of his hand. "I was gone too long. For that . . . " For that he should apologise. It would be the gentlemanly thing to do. He waves the thought away. "You should tend to your guests. Be the hostess."

"Telemachus, I—"

"You are in my way, Mother."

If he had shoved her, both hands pressed into her chest, knocked her off her feet, the blow could not have landed more heavy upon her. Eos's gasp is audible from the shadow where she waits. Penelope feels something hot and strange upon her cheeks, pricking her eyes. It is impossible, unacceptable, and must not be seen. Queens do not bend. It is this instinct, this training, this truth that must rise above all other truths, that makes her stand aside – not as a mother, but as a queen. Telemachus marches by her, and down the hall.

CHAPTER 7

⪼⪼⪼⪼⪼⪼⪼⪼⪼⪼⪼⪼⪼⪼⪼⪼⪼⪼⪼⪼⪼⪼⪼⪼⪼⪼⪼⪼⪼⪼

Later, Penelope weeps.

Autonoe guards the door of her bedroom, so that no one might gain entry.

Eos sits on the bed that Odysseus carved for himself and his wife from the still-living boughs of the olive tree, and holds her mistress as Penelope sobs. As Penelope bawls and shakes and sniffs wet snot and shudders and shakes and weeps some more, Eos strokes her hair, squeezes her shoulders tight, says nothing, there being no words that can make this right.

Penelope tries to say: it's my fault, it's my fault, why didn't I say the right things when it mattered, why couldn't I be there like a mother should – it's my fault! But the words are hiccupped between gasps of breath and as with most things to do with her maternal duties, it is far, far too late.

She tries to say: I love him so much, when he was born he was the most beautiful, the most beautiful, but my husband left and I had to be a queen I had to keep the kingdom together I had to be – he was so beautiful my son!

Eos pats her gently on the back. She has quietly disliked Telemachus since the boy, aged thirteen, was introduced to the concept of "whore". He took to the notion with mortified

45

fascination, constantly peeping round doors to see if here – yes here – there was a whore doing that whoring she did, the most outrageous thing in the world, the most disgusting, the most repulsive – goodness he would find it out so he would and be very thorough indeed in his investigations.

Telemachus has never lain with a woman. Once, on his travels with Nestor's son, he came close, the sound of rutting from the room next door stirring even his loose nether parts. But he found at the moment of truth that he was repulsed by the willingness of the proffered lady, sickened by her enjoyment of the experience, and so he drew away. None of this must ever be sung of the son of Odysseus. The men of our songs are incapable of imagining themselves as anything other than thrusting and virile, and though most heroes' sexual organs fall within a harmless average, and every man will at some time experience a certain flaccidity, the astonishing violence that is unleashed upon she who so much dares as whisper this truth sometimes surprises even me, and I am difficult to amaze. No – the most I can do is ensure that when the poets sing of Odysseus's exploits, they shall be tinged with a hint of courtesy towards the ones he lies with, if that is what the listener chooses to hear.

There was a time when men cowered before the name of Hera, mother-goddess. When warriors bent the knee at the mere mention of Athena, when kings humbled themselves beneath lady sky, lady earth. Gone now. Now courtesy is about the most the ladies of above and below aspire for, and then say "thank you kind sir" and "oh you flatter me, kind sir", gnawing on those scraps of dignity that are tossed our way.

I tried to scour the woman from my soul, the female from my skin, but it is never enough. Never quite enough.

The moon is rising, the sun is set, when Penelope is done with her tears.

She straightens a little, does not meet Eos's eyes, lest she weep

46

again, nods once at the distorted reflection of her own face in the muddy mirror of bronze that sits near the door, says: "Well then. My son clearly intends to kill the suitors. What shall we do about this?"

Eos has been waiting for this question, this return to pragmatic business, since the first snotty tear. "I have sent word to Ourania, Anaitis and Priene. They are gathering tonight."

"Good." Another involuntary snuffle, which Penelope and Eos both choose to ignore, wiped away quickly on the back of Penelope's hand. A long, shuddering intake of breath. A letting go. There is no time left for sorrow. It was a moment of weakness – nothing more. Nothing more. We will not speak of it again. "Find out how many spears Telemachus has mustered. If we cannot stop him going through with this madness, we may as well give him the highest chance of not dying in the attempt."

"You should flee," murmurs Eos. "Even if your son succeeds, it will spark a war that he cannot win. Not without help from Mycenae, and I doubt he has appealed to Orestes. Anaitis can give you sanctuary in the temple of Artemis, then a temple on the mainland, or with Elektra . . ."

"Not at all. If my son is to fight and die, then it is all over anyway. I have had a good life, all things considered. We will have to make the most of things."

Now it is Eos who is shocked. This maid, who was given to Penelope as a wedding gift, a young companion to bring the queen comfort as she journeyed to her new dominion, has never heard Penelope speak so easily of death. Never seen her so casually dismiss a clever scheme, or lightly throw aside a plan. That said, she has hardly ever seen Penelope weep – no, not even when Odysseus sailed for Troy. There has always been work to be done, business to attend to, matters to keep the women of Ithaca busy. Tears would have to wait for some other time, for a day of rest when all struggles might cease.

Now Telemachus has returned, and Eos cannot help but wonder – if the suitors are to all die by his hand, what then will happen to the maids? Usually such questions would also have occurred to Penelope, but tonight . . . Eos does not know what to make of her queen tonight. She is not blind to Penelope's faults; a slave will always know when her mistress is fallible. But tonight – tonight is the worst of all possible times, Eos thinks, for her queen to start making mistakes.

A knock at the door. Autonoe's voice drifts through. "My lady?"

Autonoe rarely calls Penelope "my lady", let alone "my queen". It is a sign of how rattled she is by Penelope's unexpected outpouring of sentiment that she has moved into this particularly respectful vein.

Penelope wipes the last tear from her eyes, draws the veil about her face, removes her hand from Eos's own, turns away from her reflection in the twisted mirror. "Enter."

Autonoe does not enter, as if to come into a room still hot with salt might somehow contaminate her with sentiment. Instead she murmurs, head half through the door, "There's a beggar downstairs with Eumaeus, asking to be served."

"Then serve him."

"The suitors are not responding well to his presence."

Penelope sighs, rolls her eyes, but is immediately a little straighter, a little firmer in her voice. She knows in her heart that she has failed as a mother, and for that she thinks she is likely to die. But though this particular maternal identity has slipped her grasp, other manifestations of her nature still blossom, given her strength. She is still a queen, and more than that, she is still a consummate hostess.

"Can't Medon or Aegyptius do something? I am busy contemplating my son's imminent, sacrilegious murder and the violent end it means for all of us."

"Medon is asleep, and Aegyptius cannot be found."

Another sigh, but in a way Penelope is grateful for this news. Doing something practical is far, far easier than feeling this great wellspring of shame, grief and dismay that still clogs the passage of her throat. "Where is Telemachus?"

"Downstairs."

"Has he done anything foolish or barbaric yet?"

"No. He is remarkably calm. Polite, even. He told Melantho that he likes what she's done with her hair. Everyone is unsettled."

"I will be down directly."

CHAPTER 8

>>

Four gods there are who have much in the way of interest on the island of Ithaca.

Artemis, goddess of the hunt. She was drawn to Ithaca by the sound of arrows flying and the snapping of snares in the midnight wood. The prey that was being hunted were men, not rabbits, and the huntresses who notched their arrows to the bow moved in darkest secrecy as they dispatched their quarry, and the goddess approved.

Aphrodite, lady of love and lust. Her eye was drawn by her favourite plaything, her little mortal pet, her mirror made flesh, Helen of Sparta, Helen of Troy. Why then her gaze drifted from Helen to her cousin Penelope was, I am ashamed to say, something of a mystery to me. I, who am wise in all things, have never fully fathomed what moves the lady of love. Sometimes I reflect upon this, and it brings me pain to think how far from companionship my soul has fled – but I will not flinch. Athena never flinches.

Hera, queen of the gods. She came to this island when her beloved Clytemnestra did, holding the hand of that vengeful queen and wiping her brow as she fell beneath her son's bloody blade. She said she was on Ithaca to protect the mothers of the isles, and I dismissed her without a thought.

50

"Who gives a fuck about the mothers?" I exclaimed, for of course, no one does. No poets sing of them, or when they are named, they will be merely motivation, adjunct to some hero's tale.

In this matter, of course, I was mistaken.

Wisdom must be honest with itself, even if it is sometimes wise to lie to others.

For though they were not sung, it was the mothers, the daughters and the wives who kept the world turning, the fires lit, the lights burning.

"Stepdaughter," Hera tutted one moonless night as we stood upon the edge of Olympus, gazing down to the sleeping world below. "You have forgotten that you are a woman."

I have very little time for Hera, but in that moment I felt my body tense as if struck by a thunderclap.

"I understand your relentless chastity bit," she went on, swirling her cup of ambrosia thoughtlessly, as if impossible sediment might have formed in the bottom of the golden brew. "You're a tedious prude, but at least if you pretend you're like a man, it might make some men think twice about having a go at you. Never going to work, of course – to some men it's just a challenge, something to break. Someone to break. My husband likes breaking things. It's the only thing he's really got left that makes him feel like a man."

Distasteful though it was, I could not help but agree with Hera's assessment of my father's inclinations.

"And as for the rest of it – well, you may act like you're a man, but they'll never accept you. You can out-grunt them, out-fight them, out-kill them, anything you like really, but that doesn't mean you'll belong. There is no brotherhood waiting for you. There is no fellowship or companionship or trust – not at all. Not between them. And not for you. Goodness, did you learn nothing watching Agamemnon and

Achilles sulk and pout at each other over who has the biggest cock and where they get to stick it? And this business with Troy is only going to make it worse. All those dreadful idiot boys with dreadful idiot notions in their heads about what it means to be a *real* man, and who are they modelling their behaviour on? Shitty little murderers and shitty little rapists who understand power only by swinging their shitty little fists into their brother's piggy little faces just to prove a shitty little point. Pathetic."

"Not Odysseus," I said. "He is not like that."

"Isn't he? Are you really telling me he isn't vengeful, proud, deceitful, manipulative, determined that everyone knows he's the smartest man in the room? Maybe it's not quite as obvious as walking into the palace scrotum-first, but it's still a story sung to the same end. Power. Position. Above others. Above all other men. And of course, above all women too. I had hoped Circe might knock some sense into him, maybe even that slut Calypso, but no. He's still got to be greater than them all. He'll be greater than you too, if you don't watch it."

In silence a while we stood, she and I, upon the edge of the world.

It occurred to me that if I was Aphrodite, I would have burst into tears. I would have wrapped my arms around Hera's neck and blubbered: it's all so true, all so sad, so sad, my little heart is breaking! And perhaps Hera would have sighed and rolled her eyes and patted me on the back and for a while she and I would have held each other in mutual sorrow, before remembering again that we dislike each other intensely and parting ways.

And it occurred to me that if I was Zeus, I would have struck her, then and there, for daring to question my wisdom and my power. Whore, I would have said. Bitch. No one will ever love you. I'm the only one. Look at what I have to put up with, with you. Look at what you made me do.

This is what the poets would expect, and sometimes it is just easier, time-saving, energy-saving even, to just do what everyone thinks you should, until at last the story becomes the truth.

CHAPTER 9

>>>>>>>>>>>>>>>>>>>>>>>>>>>>>>>>>>>>>>>

In the great hall of the palace of Odysseus, a beggar arrives.
His hair is matted with dirt, his shoulders hunched and
swathed in rags. He does not look up at the maid Melitta when
she greets him at the door, eyes down and chin tucked in as if
he is fearful of blows, but asks for a few scraps, something to
ease his journey.

Melitta welcomes him in. It is the noble custom of the house
to ensure that none, no matter their status, are turned from the
door. It is also useful, Penelope feels, to have the suitors' feast
occasionally interrupted by the lowest of the low, a reminder
that in her eyes their place is not so different from that of a
starving vagabond clawing at another's feet.

The beggar goes from table to table. Amphinomous says,
"Oh, so sorry, I seem to have eaten . . ."

Eurymachus says, "It's filthy! What's it doing here?"

Kenamon says: "Of course, sir – I hope you do not mind the
taste of fish?"

Antinous strikes him across the brow for the impertinence
of being, of breathing in this place. The beggar falls, crawls a
little along the floor. Antinous likes this. Antinous crawls this
way, sometimes, when his father hits him. His father seems big

when he looks up from his cowering place to behold the old man's blazing face. Antinous must therefore be big too, when he beats another down. This is how things work.

Telemachus rushes to help the old man rise, and is shaken away. Telemachus's face is crimson with rage, indignation, a passion and a fury that is only not recognised by the suitors because they have no reference for ever seeing anything quite like it on his features before. If anyone listened closely they might hear a murmur of, "Let's kill them now!" but the sound of laughter and merriment from the suitors is too loud for the whisper to travel, covering the beggar's snarled "Not yet!"

The beggar rises.

When the poets sing of this, they shall add another beggar to this scene – someone who is not enfeebled, not grateful for the scraps thrown his way. For the great and the powerful – those who can buy the stories that are sung – would have the world know that if you are base, and humble, and beg meekly for scraps, you may be rewarded with some throwaway flesh, and grovel in thankfulness for this gift. But if you are loud, and indignant, and blaze with rage and injustice at the cruelty of your station, at the barbarity of a world in which the powerful may feast and the poor may die, skin and bones at the great man's door – well then, you deserve every foul thing that's coming to you, no?

It is wise for gods and kings to tell this story. Wisdom is not a universal truth – it serves. Oh but how it serves.

What else? As Telemachus backs away from the beggar man, blood in his skull and fire upon his tongue, I think I feel another presence move too. I freeze the air, slow time to a snail's crawl, cast about for it – no. Not for it. For *him*. He should not be here, he is not welcome, the poets will not speak his name, and yet I look, I listen, and I think I taste the iron scent of him on the

55

very edge of this scene. Another god of war, a foul taint at this feast. I whisper: *Ares?*

But he is gone.

My brother will be a problem to be solved before this song is song.

Then Penelope is in the doorway and mortal speed returns to this bustling tale. "What do you think you're doing?" she snarls, as Antinous prepares himself for another kick at the fallen old man. Antinous nearly trips over his own feet. He will not stop in his aggression for a mere woman, of course, but neither is he particularly comfortable being berated by one, let alone in public. He puffs, he swells, he shrivels, he shrinks. He wants to tell her that it's none of her business what he's doing – but of course, even if she were not a woman, she is the hostess, so all of this is her business. He slinks into his seat. Telemachus withdraws to a seething corner, to watch the veins pulse in the necks of the feasting men. Eos and Melitta help the beggar to a stool near the fire. He staggers a little between their supportive hands, though there is something off about his motion. Muscles in his arms, in his wrists, taut from rowing, not yet wasted by deprivation and impoverishment. He should crush the maids with his leaning bulk. Yet he moves lightly, carries himself in an uncanny place that is neither withered nor full, crippled nor strong. Eos's lips thin, but she says not a word as Melitta fetches the beggar food.

Then Penelope is by his side, the words already tumbling out before she's given the man another glance. "My humble apologies, sir, for your treatment," she is saying. "It is utterly unacceptable that you are received so poorly in my husband's house. Please, you must eat, you must rest, my maids will see to it that—"

Here now she turns to gaze fully upon him, having thus far directed her attention in glowers towards sulking Antinous and his leering boys. Here now her words stop. She looks upon the beggar. The beggar does not look upon her. He mumbles, saggy-lipped and heavy-tongued: "Thank you, my lady, but there is no need. No need at all. You have already been kind enough."

Penelope looks at the beggar.

Looks across the room to her son.

Looks back to the beggar.

It is now perhaps helpful that she has shed so many tears for Telemachus.

Perhaps of great advantage that she has already seen her son caress the edge of a bronze blade, observed him with a throat-cutting glimmer in the corner of his eye.

Of course, she thinks.

But of course.

Of course this is how he became so bold.

Of course this is how he found his courage at last.

She should speak. Her silence has lasted too long, will be remarked upon, noted. She opens her mouth, has no idea what she is going to say, and is saved for a moment by the return of Melitta with a bowl lined with soft bread and cooling fish, which she folds into the beggar's curled hands. Those hands, though – streaked with mud, dirt under the fingernails, the fingers bent as if they can never uncurl, clumsy in their usage, scarred and calloused by time and the sea. And yet, like the rest of him, there is an imbalance to this sight, an artifice perhaps to their apparent weakness, an act to their supposed deformity. Penelope is suddenly fascinated by his hands – easier to be fascinated by the beggar's hands than his face – and that curiosity gives her the space to breathe: "I wonder, traveller, where you came from?"

"I am a sailor of Crete," the beggar replies, through a scoop of fish that he chews through an open, churning mouth. "My ship was lost at sea, I was the only survivor, barely made it to your shore."

"That is ... terrible," opines Penelope, the word meaningless on her tongue, the emotion that should accompany such a sentiment entirely misplaced. "I had not heard of any wrecks nearby – are you sure that there are no other survivors?"

"Forgive my ageing eyes," replies the man, his gaze still firmly cast down at his grubby feet and tattered gown. "If any lived besides myself, I did not see it."

"You will be tended to," Penelope proclaims. "You will have a warm place to sleep and fresh clothes."

"I could not—"

"Nonsense. You are on Ithaca now – hospitality is our sacred trust. But I wonder, if it is not too great a burden, may I ask you some questions? You must have travelled far, heard many things."

"I have travelled a bit, my lady, though I was just a humble sailor."

"And did you, in your travels, hear anything of my husband, Odysseus? I know it is a foolish thing to ask, but forgive a wife. I ask everyone who comes to my door."

"Odysseus ..." murmurs the beggar. "I think I saw him once, many years ago, when he sailed to Troy. He had a purple cloak, held with a brooch. I remember the brooch – none who saw it could forget it. It had this device of a dog holding down a fawn, I recall. Very fine workmanship, a beautiful thing."

Penelope's voice catches in her throat, and it is not a feigned or false thing. "I gave him that brooch," she blurts. "It was a wedding gift."

"It was a fine thing, and he a fine man, who spoke of his queen with great affection," murmurs the beggar.

"Alas – it is surely lost, with my beloved husband."

The beggar stirs in his seat, shakes his head. "I do not think so, my lady. For I heard not four moons since that your husband had been seen alive, that he was even now coming here, returning to Ithaca with great wealth to reclaim his throne."

"It is kind of you to think so, but why would he not send word ahead if he was? Why let me suffer all these years, plagued by suitors and cruel men who would dishonour Odysseus's name in his own home? No. My husband would not do such a thing. It would be too unwise for his kingdom, and dare I say, too cruel to me, if indeed he ever loved me as I am sure he did."

The beggar says nothing to this. He is, for the briefest moment, annoyed. Not with himself, per se, but with, of all people, the queen. He is not a man used to reporting a thing as true and having it immediately rejected as false, impossible. He is not used to being challenged by woman or man, and few who do so have ever lived long to relish the experience. However, annoyance is not a helpful emotion right now for a humble man of bent spine and bowed neck, so he shakes his head a little and mumbles: "Well, my lady, I am as I said merely a humble sailor."

"Not at all," she replies, a little lighter, a little louder, straightening up to survey the room as if this address were now for all within, not just the beggar before her. "You are my honoured guest. I will have a bed prepared for you and fresh water to bathe your feet in, to wash away the sea—"

"Forgive me," he blurts, then at once turns his head away, for it is really quite unacceptable for a beggar to interrupt a queen. "Forgive me," he repeats, softer, trying again. "I am so used to sleeping upon rough decks, to having no blanket but the stars, I do not think I would feel comfortable on any softer thing. And as for washing, I would not have your women dishonour themselves with my wretchedness. Perhaps if there is an older lady in this palace, one who would not be so offended by my disfigurement . . . ?"

Penelope's lips thin.

Across the room, Kenamon is watching her. Not as the others do – not with side-eyed resentment or petty hunger, but with the attentiveness of one who has seen his lady tense, and hears the whispered word *danger*, but is unclear on the danger's source.

Usually, Penelope would look up, meet the Egyptian's gaze, nod without smiling – she never smiles upon a suitor in public – and turn away. This would be more conference than most men could ever imagine with the Ithacan queen. Not now. Perhaps never again.

Instead, for a moment Penelope considers slapping the beggar, hard, once, across the cheek. If she's going to do it, this is the only time. The only chance she may ever get. She has never hit a man. She wonders what it feels like. It would only be one slap – a really good wallop, just to get it out of the system; none of this flapping, pawing nonsense you sometimes find from a woman enraged enough to want to express it with her hands, too frightened to make it count. She imagines the sound, wonders if it would be enough to silence the hall. She thinks that Clytemnestra would hit the beggar full body, arm extended, a great big follow-through, and then maybe a backhand on the return. She is not sure what her cousin Helen would do, but imagines it would be done with a simper.

She does not hit the beggar. Does not smile. Does not frown. I love her then, and it terrifies me, and no one must ever know.

Instead, with the barest exhalation of breath, Penelope murmurs: "Of course. There is one in this household, a loyal woman by the name of Euracleia, who I am sure would be able to assist you. I shall send her to you, and see that a place is prepared for you near the fire. Please do not be troubled by the suitors. They will be too drunk soon enough to do more than swagger and scowl. No harm will come to you from them."

"You are too kind, my lady – too kind. I had heard of your generosity, but did not dare to hope."

Her smile is the edge of a knife. "You are welcome, sir, to my husband's palace."

The beggar reaches for her hand to clasp it in gratitude, to press it to his brow, to feel its touch, but she has already turned her back on him, and is heading for the door.

CHAPTER 10

>>>

In the great hall, a beggar watches the evening feast.

Antinous: "I heard a Phaeacian ship was seen near Phenera yesterday, well where are they now? Bloody Phaeacians . . . "

Eurymachus: "When I am king, the Phaeacians will know their place, you'll see, I'll . . . " A hiccup of strong wine from a near-empty cup. "Melitta! Wine! More wine!"

Amphinomous: "Telemachus looks . . . different. Changed."

"Well of course he's different! He's been on an adventure, hasn't he? Gone and talked to Nestor and Menelaus, done that flattery that his family's so good at. We should have nipped him before he got back to Ithaca, we should have taken him out at sea, but now . . . now we've all got a problem."

"Melitta – where's the wine?!"

Outside the palace of Odysseus, the swineherd Eumaeus digs a hole in an unmarked scratch of ground for the old king's dog, Argos. That ancient animal lived long enough to smell the hand of a friend, and then died. That is how the poets shall sing of it. It is important that their tales be spun with themes of loyalty, duty, the savagery of debased humans contrasted with the simple affection of quiet, noble creatures of the earth. This too has power, and I am grown so desperate for it that I will tolerate, of all things, a sentimental verse or two about a dog, if it serves my cause.

Kenamon exclaims: "Telemachus! Telemachus, my dear friend! How are you? Where have you been? Tell me everything, tell me—"

Telemachus cuts him off. "I was about royal business," he barks. "You could not understand." And then, because Kenamon's face is split with betrayal, with sorrow even to hear the young man who so recently he taught in matters of spear and blade, Telemachus hesitates. Lowers his voice. "I am surprised you are still here, Egyptian. I thought you would have sailed home before now."

Kenamon opens his mouth to blurt – he is not sure what he shall blurt, perhaps merely "Telemachus?", a sound to invite explanation, that seems to exclaim: my boy, my dearest friend, what has happened to you?

For a moment, perhaps Telemachus will speak. Words of: it is good to see you, I am glad you are well, there are things you should know, things I might say . . .

But I stand at his side, turn his chin a little so that he sees the beggar again by the fire and at that sight seals his lips. Shakes his head. Turns away without another word.

Wise, I tell the boy, as Kenamon's heart cracks a little further through the splintered hollows of his wandering soul. *You are making a wise decision.*

By the fire, the beggar watches the suitors, and the beggar watches the maids.

Melitta laughs as Eurymachus tries to pinch her bottom, swaying easily out of the way. She and he have long had a complicated relationship of give and take, one he has barely understood, for all that he has sometimes enjoyed a few of its consequences. Loose-lipped in the night, he has tumbled into her embrace and laughed and wept and complained about the unfairness of it all, and she has soothed his brow and said, "There, there, lovely man," before vanishing back into the duties of the palace again without any sign that tenderness has ever passed between them.

Phiobe sits in the lap of one Nisas, a boy-suitor who knows he will never be king, and pinches his cheek and says: "You're hilarious, has anyone told you that you're hilarious?" and laughs and leaves before he can wind his arms about her waist.

Autonoe stands in the door to the kitchen and proclaims with a wry twist in the corner of her mouth: "Always wanting more, aren't you, Antinous?"

Melantho jests about the length of a suitor's sword; Eurynome cannot hide the curl of her mouth at a merriment she should not find amusing.

The beggar watches the suitors.

The beggar watches the maids.

Then Euracleia comes and grumbles, grunts, resentment ringing in her voice: "I am sent to tend to you, sir."

Euracleia's neck sticks out nearly horizontal from her neck, and she struggles these days to raise it, her eyes perpetually scraping along the floor. Her hair is faded to a few puffs from a spotted skull, but her hands, when they ruffle the tresses of some young scamp, are astonishingly warm, soft and beautiful, remarkable in their contours and history of a life told. They are, alas, the last thing about her nature that is of pleasing note.

She finds it despicable that she – she! – the oldest and wisest and sometime most beloved of all the maids of this house – should be sent to care for some *beggar*. For some washed-up vagrant, some filthy, shit-soaked wanderer to their doors. It is further proof, as if Euracleia needed it, that she is loathed by the haughty maids of Penelope, mocked by proud Eos and cruel Autonoe. But she will show them. She will do her duty, as a maid must, because she knows what it is to serve. And so she leads the beggar away from the fire to a room where a bowl of water has been prepared, and says: "Please, sir, sit. I will wash your feet . . ."

The door closes behind her, and that way shall it stay, for the moment.

Another door opens.

It is a side door that leads from the women's quarters into a garden where, in fragrant daylight, bees buzz between purple flowers and the sweet smell of honey may be found on the morning breeze. By night, it is a subdued, hidden corner away from walls and windows, with depths of twined branch and twisted leaf that may cover hidden gatherings by shuttered lamplight, and where many a plan has been schemed, a plot hatched in these long, waning years.

Here footsteps hurry over worn stone, cloaks are drawn tight about bunched shoulders, voices whisper on the faint midnight breeze. I peer through the darkness, draw away the shadows from the hooded faces of the women who are gathered here, know them all.

Some we have met already. Autonoe, Eos, maids of Penelope. Ourania, hair like snow, lapis lazuli on her sagging wrists. She served the old queen of the house, Anticlea, mother of Odysseus, until Penelope bargained for her freedom. Ourania has proven more useful to Penelope as a woman of the world than a slave of the palace, her many "cousins" in many places constantly relaying news of the outside world back to the western isles.

Who else? Anaitis, a priestess of Artemis, at whose temple sometimes gather those secretive women whose notched arrows and fast feet first drew the huntress's attention to these isles. She smells of old leaves and woodsmoke, barely even notices how her knife moves when she skins a rabbit, does not understand the things that people ask of the goddess, yet sees the blessings of Artemis in every dawn and every sunset as surely as if the huntress were her sister laughing by her side.

Priene, her sandy hair cut short and sticking out wild about her little round ears, a cloak barely covering the array of swords and knives strapped to her hips, her thighs, her calves, her back, her belt. She should be mine, this warrior-woman, but alas, Priene has two qualities that keep her from being truly beloved of Athena: firstly, she is not from the islands of Greece, and still casts her prayers back to the ladies of the winding eastern river and open steppes of yellow grass. Secondly, her heart is full of passion, fury, love, fear, delight, hope and desire – and she is not wise. I sometimes envy her that.

Priene is the captain of the women who meet at Artemis's temple. These women were once forty, then fifty, then a hundred, gathered in secret in the night. Now there are more besides, secret conclaves of widows and daughters who will never be wives who meet all across the isles. Their work keeps Priene busy, but to her surprise, she does not feel it as labour.

This is Penelope's midnight council.

There is a council who meet at noon, of course – a council of aged and learned men appointed by Odysseus on his departure, who have these twenty years blustered and made some loud, loose proclamations upon the island. But they have only limited use to a queen, and so this other council, this hidden convocation of women, was formed, to meet where no eyes might see them.

Penelope is the last to reach this gathering, accompanied by Eos as they slip through the night of the sleeping garden. Loyal Ourania squints through the gloom to see her, asks as she draws near: "Did you find Telemachus?"

"Telemachus," replies Penelope, a little breathless from more than just the scuttle through the dark, "is the very least of our problems."

There is a slight stirring, a shifting of muddy shoe; nothing good can be portended by Telemachus being merely a moderate pain, instead of the persistent thorn he has always threatened to be.

Penelope takes in a long breath, lets it out slowly, and at the very end of the exhalation proclaims: "My husband is returned."

The silence lands like a rock in a pond.

It is Ourania who finally blurts: "He what?"

"My husband," repeats Penelope, more for her own benefit than that of any other, confirming to herself that these words she speaks are true, "is returned."

Again, it is Ourania, who is perhaps as near to a friend of the queen as any woman can be and thus feels a certain liberty to speak the things that others are merely screaming silently inside, who exclaims: "Odysseus. Your husband. Odysseus. Here. Are you sure?"

"I was a little concerned that I had lost my mind and was mad," muses Penelope, her audience not much more than a mirror to her own absolute bafflement at this scene. "But then he asked for Euracleia to attend to him with, may I say, the nuance of a fish. Of all the women in this palace, it stands to reason that he would trust his old nursemaid, so of course I sent her down to him. Autonoe stood listening at the door when she went in. Autonoe?"

"There was a lot of muttering about how undignified it was for her to attend to a beggar," Autonoe says. "Followed by a shriek, a clattering of copper and the spilling of water. Since then Euracleia has been engaged in trying to pretend not to be jubilant, and failing spectacularly."

The women of the council glance at each other, trying to read expressions in the settled shadows. At last Anaitis, priestess of Artemis, a woman who has more time for the simplicity of the forest than the bewildering noise of the town, raises her hand.

"Is that . . . proof?" she asks. "I mean, if Odysseus is back, what happened to parading through the streets with spears and drums and that? I thought that was what kings were meant to do."

"Well," sighs Penelope, "I imagine he *would* do the parading with spears and drums, and preferably a sizeable amount of golden treasure, if he had any. I can only conclude that the fact he has returned alone, and in rags, is because his entire army is dead and he without so much as a silver chalice to his name."

Another silence. Very few of these women knew the men who sailed with Odysseus to Troy. Eos and Autonoe were barely girls, pink-lipped and giggling in their youth, when Odysseus departed with the greatest of Ithaca's manhood. Priene perhaps did know some of the warriors of the western isles — but she knew them as enemies on the wrong end of her spear, faceless men to be cut down in the fury of the battle, the blind desperation of the sweat-stained melee where every second is an eternity, every eternity passed in the blink of an eye. Anaitis finds the company of men even more baffling than the general company of women, and so it falls to Ourania to half close her eyes and think a little on some of those warriors she saw sail with Odysseus to Troy. She does not weep for them, does not mourn them — she has had twenty years to grow accustomed to their absence. She cast libations for those few she cared for many moons ago; acknowledged all others as dead and drowned long before this moment. Indeed she would be more surprised had Odysseus returned with bands of warriors at his back, alive and trumpeting their great success, than she is to think upon their deaths. But still. Still. It seems to her important that someone offer up a prayer to the men of Ithaca, however they died, wherever their ghosts may be.

Anaitis is unashamed to ask questions, oblivious to how uncouth it is considered not to immediately understand all things, to not be proud in your deductions, even when wrong.

"So, if Odysseus doesn't have an army, and is disguised as a beggar ... what does this mean?"

"It means he's scheming," barks Priene, scarred arms folded across her chest. "That's what Odysseus does."

Priene, who once rode in the chariot with Penthesilia, warrior-queen who should have been one of mine but never offered any god her prayers, does not like Odysseus. She knew that she did not like Odysseus long before she entered the service of his wife, for Odysseus was a Greek, and therefore an enemy. The certainty she had that he was dead was one of the few mitigating factors in the bargain she struck with Penelope when she agreed to be a secret captain to the queen.

"Sometimes Greeks pay me to kill Greeks," she said that night they made their accord.

"Priene," Penelope replied, "I rather think I'm offering precisely that."

Since then some nuance has been added to their bargain, but even so the possibility that Odysseus lives, let alone that he is now upon these shores, is a source of some inner conflict for Priene, and she has always preferred her conflict clean, bloody and in the open.

Penelope sees this, knows it, looks Priene straight in the eye. "You are correct, of course," she says. "And my son is clearly part of the plan. They will begin by slaughtering the suitors."

Again Priene is not sure how to respond to this. She is naturally in favour of slaughtering the suitors – it is something she has long advocated for – but that was before a returned tyranny of bloody kings might claim the benefit of this action. Now she stands stiff, eyebrows drawn, saying not a word.

"When you say 'they'," murmurs Ourania, "do you just mean Odysseus and Telemachus? Two men?"

Penelope shakes her head. "Odysseus came to the palace in the company of Eumaeus, and Telemachus returned with a dozen men who I can only assume are loyal to him. Eumaeus might be able to round up four or five more spears, so perhaps . . . fifteen, twenty men?"

"That is still twenty men against one hundred," muses Ourania. "With all respect to your husband's manly strength, I do not see how that will end well."

"Agreed," barks Penelope. "It was madness when my son was going to do it; it is madness now that my husband is involved. However, I do not see that they have any other choice. If Odysseus has not returned with an army, he cannot simply march into the palace in pomp and demand that the suitors leave by the mere threat of his presence. He does not have the power to just persuade them to go. They would say that he was not Odysseus, call me a liar if I swore that he was, declare it was some conspiracy hatched between me and my son and disfigure his corpse before anyone of nobility or note might come to identify him. Then we would be precisely where we already are, but with my husband truly dead and my son with him. No. Odysseus must kill the suitors before they realise who he is. Even if there was not an immediate necessity to do it for his safety, it is an act of power. In the absence of an army, he must prove that he is still to be feared, still the great warrior of these isles. He must use his name, create a story about himself, mighty Odysseus, to keep his kingdom safe. It must be told that with bloody warrior strength Odysseus returned, slew a hundred men, reclaimed his wife and with spear and fury once again ruled over his kingdom. The story – the story is his safety."

"Stories are fine," grunts Priene, "but they don't kill one hundred men."

"Agreed. Clearly we must offer some assistance."

"I can muster the women, we can—"

"Without being seen. My husband's safety – my kingdom's safety – depends on any victory seeming entirely his own."

Priene's scowl deepens. Autonoe clears her throat. "There are those tinctures your cousin Helen kindly sent from Sparta," she muses. "A little of the something she put in the wine of the men when your son visited her court, as well as more . . . potent brews."

"We would have to ensure any such potions are administered at the same time Odysseus is ready to make his move," Eos adds. "If they are to be effective – and unknown."

Penelope nods, considering this. "I think we can find a way to make these things align. What else? No doubt the suitors will try to rush the armoury when they find they are attacked. My husband will think of that and try to defend it – unless the years have truly addled his wits – but perhaps we can further assist there as well."

"If we are doing all this, would it not just be easier to talk with Odysseus directly?" asks Anaitis, and is rewarded with a slight intake of breath from Eos.

Penelope smiles upon the priestess of Artemis, and her smile is the skull-toothed grin of the damned. "Not at all," she sighs. "Not at all."

"Um . . . why?"

"Because my husband also is testing me. This business with disguising himself as a beggar, this sailor of Crete nonsense . . . it is a test. He will doubtless have heard what happened with Clytemnestra, not to mention the ten years he spent stuck on a beach in the name of my cousin Helen. It's all very well getting the poets to talk about pious Penelope, loyal Penelope, cold-bedded, barren, heartbroken, lonely Penelope. But he is still a man, his honour resting upon the dominion he holds over his kingdoms, his warriors and his wife. He needs to determine for himself whether I am chaste. He needs to behold my inno-cence, a desperate woman who has these twenty years occupied herself with mourning for her dear husband without so much as a jot of pleasure to her days, valiantly performing her duty in his honour.

"Naturally I can be allowed a degree of cleverness, so long as it is in defence of his name and his son – but cunning? Strength of arms, force of will, the power to rule, the wits to succeed? Absolutely not. Far too dangerous. For if I am cunning in my queenship, what else might I have been cunning in? If I can deceive all of Greece, raise an army of women, manipulate and scheme my way to success, then who is to say that I have not also cunningly bedded some man, or do not have a trap lying in wait for my husband? The merest suspicion that I am in any way disloyal and he will cut my throat. Of course he will. Of course. And no one will question him. Penelope the whore. Penelope the wife who thought she could be a queen. If every other lady in Greece has done it, why not me? That would not in any way diminish his story. If anything it might benefit him. Poor wandering Odysseus who all these years travelled across the seas in his desperate journey to come home, overcoming no doubt a great many obstacles that would have stopped a lesser man, only to find his wife a traitor to his bed. Naturally he would have to kill me. Weakness not to. Another whore who should have been kept under guard, another woman who cannot be trusted, another betrayal by our weakling sex. And so you see, the game must be played, if I am to survive."

The women consider this. Priene and Anaitis speak nearly at the same time, their truths breaking through their discretions:

"We should kill him."

"This game is stupid."

Penelope's smile does not flicker before either of their sentiments.

These thoughts – they have crossed her mind.

They had not occurred to her until the very moment she saw

72

through the beggar's disguise, but in that second, the idea had sprung: *what if?*

What if she cried out: this beggar, this vile, debased man! He tried to touch me! He tried to kiss my lips, how dare he?!

The suitors are always hungry – hungry for meat, for power, for blood, for anything to prove themselves men of substance – and Telemachus would have been caught off-guard, unable to do anything but shriek and wail as his father was dragged out into the yard and beaten to death by the mob.

Then things could have gone back to normal.

An empty bed, a quiet kingdom, the promise of war deferred.

It would have been so simple. So very, very simple.

But then this word – *deferred.*

Blood will be shed. She knows this too. At some point the peace will crack and blood will be spilled, and whether Odysseus is alive or dead, this will come. But if he is dead – worse, if she has had any part in killing him – what will her son do then? He will be another Orestes, she thinks, driven mad by so much blood.

And so it cannot be.

And so her world, instead, must end.

"I have had a good twenty years," she breathes, to the night, to the quiet, to the soft sea breeze, to no one in particular. "I have been a queen, whether people acknowledge it or not. I could have been born a slave, or a woman of Troy. This has been better. Ladies: being a queen with you as my council has been better. But we knew this day would come, one way or another. Either Odysseus's corpse would be found, and I would have no choice but to marry again and see my isles plunged into war; or Odysseus would return, and I would relinquish my power – this power, this thing that we together have made – and be his wife once more. Odysseus is returned, and yes, it is a bit of a surprise for everyone here, and no, his return has not been particularly helpful, since he has not in fact come back with an army of loyal men to enforce his reign. But it has happened. It is happening. How we face it now is everything."

Priene's brow is descending towards her nose. She wants to kill Odysseus. She knows it in her heart. Of all the kings of Greece who sailed to Troy, he was one she had fewest feelings about, for it seemed to her even in the heat of war that he was just some petty king who had no choice but to obey when his more powerful bully neighbour demanded his aid. But now this petty king has returned to Ithaca, these isles where inexplicably, unexpectedly, Priene has found a sort of home, a sort of peace, when all that she had before had burned. He will burn it all again. She knows this. Her knuckles are white where she grips the hilt of her blade, and yet she does not draw it, does not scream, does not bare her teeth and give her battle cry. Perhaps she can become wise after all, my warrior-lady. Perhaps she will hear my whisper in her ear, before the end.

Then Ourania raises a wrinkled, spotted hand and says, "Forgive my bluntness, but even if by some miracle Odysseus survives fighting a hundred maybe intoxicated men, what happens then? These are the sons of princes and nobles of Greece. They are the sons of the great men of the western isles. Eupheithes controls the grain from Dulcium, Polybus controls the shipping from Hyrie, the merchant fleet in Leucus. What happens when Odysseus murders their sons in his own palace? Yes, I know it is his palace and technically he will have the right in the eyes of the gods to kill any man who looked sideways at his wife – that is all fine and good. But do we really believe the battle will end there? It will ignite the very war that you have spent ten years trying to prevent. Fathers who were enemies will become sworn brothers to avenge their slaughtered children, and then what? Perhaps Odysseus and twenty men can kill a hall of surprised drunkards. Odysseus and twenty men cannot hold the palace. What then?"

No one has an answer. Ourania huffs, throws her hands into the sky. "Well, though I am with you until the end, I hope you'll understand if I am with you from the prow of a fast boat. You are all of course welcome to join me. I have a cousin in Pylos with a lovely—"

"They must be made to understand," cuts in Penelope, her voice a little loud, a sliver of uncertainty pushing through. "These fathers sent their sons to beggar themselves at my feet. To take that which was not mine to give. It was already obscene. My husband is, as you say, by the laws of the gods within his right to slaughter them. We must . . . make them understand. If I killed the suitors I would break every vow as woman and hostess. My husband is not bound by my rules. But you are right. The grief of a father . . . there will be consequences."

"What should we do?" asks Eos, soft as the feathered wing.

Penelope half closes her eyes, nods at nothing much. "Send to Elektra in Mycenae. Discreetly, of course. Ourania, how soon can you get message to her?"

"With a fair wind? Three or four days if the gods are with us."

The wind will be fair; Poseidon will not notice my touch upon the breeze.

"Do it. We have given good service to Orestes and Elektra, much of it . . . beyond the normal duty of mere allies. They owe Ithaca. They owe *me*. We must pray that they respect the debt, and act appropriately and in time."

"That doesn't sound like it suits the story of Odysseus," grumbles Priene.

"Loyal allies come to celebrate his return? The children of Agamemnon joyfully sending ambassadors and emissaries to honour the great hero? That is the story that will be told," Penelope replies. "Heroism and valour – not civil war."

"And if Mycenae does not come?" murmurs Eos.

"Then we must hold. Priene . . . I know you fought for Ithaca, not me, and not my husband. I know that. But I think now you maybe fight for something more. If it comes to it, will the women – will you – stand?"

Priene has never looked away from the eyes of death or monarch alike, and does not look away from Penelope now. She takes a long time to answer, wants to make sure she is right when she speaks, certain of her path. As certain as she can be. Finally: "We fight for Ithaca," she declares. "I do not know your husband. I do not like your husband. But if we can with one battle prevent a war that would burn these lands to the bone . . . I will fight it. For now."

Penelope nods her head, a little bow, a little acknowledgement. "Thank you, Priene. Have the women prepare."

A nod in reply, a bare twitch of darkness in the shadow.

The women of this council do not take hands, do not press brow to brow nor shoulder to shoulder as they depart. There are some who would happily do so at a quieter time – why, Anaitis once convinced Priene to dance by the fire as it blazed before the forest temple, to sing and laugh and spin with the merry women of the isles; and Eos and Autonoe have over the years learned that one's ice and the other's fire when combined make for a most potent friendship. But tonight there is no time for affection, no place where they should say, sister, my dear sister, good fortune be with you, my heart sings for you, my soul bursts to think upon any harm that might befall your tender grace.

It is the same manner, the same weight of a crisis yet to unfold, Penelope thinks, that made her a terrible mother. The same grinding necessity of labour, the same not daring to breathe of things that might break a soul in two that silenced her when she should have held Telemachus. The thought makes

76

her turn back, makes her want to cry out to the women of her council: my dearest ones, my friends, my truest hearts!

But they are already heading away, about their labours, and the moment, as with so many, is gone.

CHAPTER 11

>>>

B y dawn's light, a ship slips from the island of Ithaca, heading west, for Mycenae. The messenger is a man who found
himself in a spot of bother with services owed to another who
lacked a sense of humour. Ourania stepped in and wiped the
bond, and now he has a new kind of debt to a new kind of
mistress, not that either of them would describe it that way. "I
feel we can be of use to each other," Ourania would say over
a cup of watery wine. "I feel that there are mutual benefits to
be had for all."

When Ourania was a slave in the palace, she could not make
such promises. When she was freed, it was as if her bound wings
were at last unstrung and like the snowy swan she was revealed.
It is an uncomfortable pattern that Penelope has occasionally
observed with more than a few of the women who have been
freed from service, but one best not dwelt upon by the kings
and queens of this or any land.

"Find Elektra," Ourania commands. "Don't waste time seeking audience with her brother – go directly to the princess of
Mycenae. Tell her that Penelope calls for aid."

The messenger nods, and does not question his duty.

*

A bed of straw has been laid near the kitchen fire, on which a beggar sleeps.

Telemachus does not sleep at all, and bounds out of his bed at the first glimmer of day to run along the cliffs, to prowl along the sea, to draw and sheathe and redraw his sword away from the sight of men, to laugh, to choke on a sound that might almost be weeping – but surely can't be, for he is a man now and his weeping is all done. To flit from place to place as reckless and unsteady as the fluttering of his heart. He will soon remember himself, collect himself, sneak back to Eumaeus's pig farm – his father's pig farm, he corrects himself, the pig farm that the swineherd has kept in trust for his father all this time – and there they will meet with a small handful of barely boys and ageing slaves who Telemachus feels can be trusted for what must be done. The poets will not sing of these bow-legged men, dressed in scavenged pieces of bronze and holding old, blunted blades. The fewer people who can assist Odysseus in his return, the more valiant it will be – and leave more room naturally for myself to take a certain prominent role, recasting the affair to my needs, bitter as they may be.

In the morning, Eos combs Penelope's hair. The light of dawn is reflected off the sea far below her bedroom window, playing with shadows on the ceiling as the day grows fat, caressing the barely slept-in bed that should be for two, and has these twenty years held only one. Eos is not very skilled with hair. She knows two or three things to do to it, all of which she learned from Ourania, who had them from Euracleia, who considered two or three things more than adequate for any woman of modesty. Eos has perfected these outdated and unfashionable drapings of locks but has very little interest in trying anything new or more, since the whole business is clearly absurd when the only thing that truly matters is keeping one's hair from one's eyes when stomping across the island checking on the goats or crossing the waters to Kephalonia to examine a winding olive grove.

But someone must be a brusher-of-hair for a queen, and it is a position of great honour, and greater intimacy, since the movement of hands over a skull and the caressing of fingers about a protruding ear or long, sun-stained neck may lead to conversations about secret, complex truths and simple, difficult things. It is this latter that Eos is gifted at – the quiet as her comb moves in which she hears Penelope thinking, her judicious silence as she considers a reply, her clean assessment of a dangerous thing, words of murder and betrayal delivered with the soft touch of fingers brushing aside a wayward strand. Eos has no interest in hair. But she loves those mornings when it is simply her and the queen of Ithaca, talking aloud of what they are going to do to solve a crisis, to feed greedy men, to eliminate a threat, murmured by the tug of a shell comb through hair.

No one has touched Eos's hair since she was a child, before she was sold as a slave. She sometimes steals Penelope's comb, and uses it to tease out her own tangled locks, but knows the feeling is not the same. She thought once of asking Autonoe to comb her hair, or even Melitta, but didn't quite have the courage to do it. Neither mistress nor maid is comfortable with vulnerability, save perhaps together, and what is more vulnerable than desiring the attentive touch of another, given tenderly, to satisfy a human whim? What is more dangerous than admitting you are not a creature of stone, copper-souled and wise in all things, but that you are in fact of flesh and blood and have a heart that can be broken, a soul that can love and be betrayed, a mind that yearns for companionship and a body that desires to be more than a stiff and unbending tool?

Nothing, Eos thinks, as she combs her mistress's hair.

Nothing, Penelope concurs, as she watches her twisted reflection in the cloudy mirror.

Nothing, I howl to the stars and the sun, to the endless night and cruel breaking day. There is nothing so dangerous as the need to be loved, as the desire to be seen, to be held, to be known in all your failings and loved despite them all. Nothing as heart-cracking, as soul-sheering as to love and be loved and be seen to laugh and seen to weep and known to be afraid and so away with it, let it be gone!

It is cruel to be wise, and yet still to yearn.

The suitors are still snoring in a haze of meat and wine when the council – the midday council, the council of men – meets. These are the elder men of Odysseus, ancient gentlemen too old to sail to Troy even twenty years ago, or of such inclinations that Odysseus decided it might be wiser to leave them behind, rather than have them sour the mood of his army as it set forth across the wine-dark sea.

Aegyptius, a twisted willow of a man with yellow spots upon his lumpy skull: "So where is Telemachus? Why isn't he here? Why hasn't he brought us news of his father? Doesn't he realise that everyone is speculating? They say that Odysseus must be dead otherwise surely Telemachus would have returned with him – doesn't he understand how dangerous the situation is?"

Aegyptius is not prone to getting overexcited about anything, but like most men of this assembly he has spent the last ten years growing increasingly aware that his power stems from the authority of a king who may be dead, and when dies Odysseus, so dies that thin semblance of relevance that Aegyptius may have crudely retained.

"He's been talking with some of the survivors of the militia," mutters Peisenor, one-handed veteran of a hundred ancient raids, back in the days before Agamemnon told the kings of

Greece that it was no longer acceptable for them to raid each other, and that they must set their eyes upon greater, further-off prizes. "Seems to me his father must be dead, if Telemachus is trying to muster men."

Aegyptius blanches, which is a remarkable sight given how much the old man has striven to avoid the sun. "Not battle? Not on our islands? Against the suitors?"

"Boy can't be so stupid, can he?" The last of the councillors, Medon, a warm-sunshine face above a great full-moon belly, wispy hair fading to a spindly winter fern on his skull, glances at the corner where the last, unspeaking part of this assembly sits. Penelope rarely says much in these council meetings – it is not her place – but attends to show willing, to make it clear that she is a loyal wife to her absent husband who cares deeply about the business he would conduct, were he here. It is not expected that she herself should have opinions, rather provide a certain comely adornment to affairs. Autonoe sits at her side, a lyre in her lap, which just this once, she does not play. Autonoe's brow is furrowed, her eyes set on some distant place. Penelope too – her thoughts are fled, gone elsewhere. Medon is the only one who notices this; the only one who cares.

"We should find Telemachus," grunts Peisenor, who also is feeling a certain mortality creep in at the edge of these shaded walls. "Demand to know what he knows. Maybe his grandfather—"

The old soldier's words are interrupted by a pounding of feet, a shuffling of robe, a woman's voice raised indignantly – you can't, wait, you mustn't – but too little, never quite enough. The door of the council chamber is pushed open. The intention was perhaps to slam it open, to burst into the small room with its round table inlaid with gleaming shell glittering brighter than any of the council assembled around it, to spring upon them with a dramatic cry of "Ah-ha, now we have you!" But the door to the room, like so many in the palace, is a heavy, crooked thing that has shifted in its frame as the palace itself has swayed and settled over the years, so the thrill of the moment is somewhat lost with a slow scraping like the cracking of a dead man's jaw.

Peisenor is already blustering before it is apparent who stands in the doorway, a cry of "How dare you, sirs, how dare you disturb—"

He is silenced before he can continue what was already quite a weak sentiment, by the two men flanked by slaves who have entered the room. They are both old, their eyes growing misty and backs beginning to bend with time. They were sometime friends, allies even, dear servants of Odysseus and his kin, husbands who valued their wives and fathers who wondered aloud what their grandchildren would be. But those days are past. Eupheithes, father of Antinous, is shorter now than his dark-haired son, but that merely makes him shout the louder, sneer the greater, hit the harder. He must never let his son realise that he is ashamed, not just of who his boy has become, but of his own part in creating him. He must never let his son know that the father wishes occasionally to throw himself at Antinous's feet and weep and say forgive me, forgive me, forgive me my darling boy, I did not know what to do when your brothers did not come back from Troy, I love you though I only ever spoke of them, forgive me. To do so would break Eupheithes' soul, and so he never will, never can, and will die unrepentant, without mourners to his grave.

Polybus, father of Eurymachus, is as oar-long and stick-thin as his son. His golden hair is turned to a white mane about his head, and he is missing several teeth, which he disguises by barely moving his lips when he speaks, and only rarely smiling. He loved his wife, more than he ever knew how to express, and when she died, a part of him died too that he cannot name, can

83

barely remember. He did not know how to be a father without a wife. When he looks in his heart, he is astonished to find that he still grieves, though he can hardly remember the face of the woman he loves, merely the pain of her absence.

It is not noble that the sons of noble men debase themselves in competition for a crown – or worse, in competition for a crown whose gift is in the hands of some mere woman. Yet Ithaca must have a king, and what kind of fathers would Eupheithes and Polybus be if they did not envision the diadem for their offspring? It is a strange kind of ambition, a cruel form of nobility, that to become the greatest amongst men first their sons must become mere woman-pleasers. No man can reconcile this. Having failed to reconcile it, the fathers of Antinous and Eurymachus cannot reconcile anything much at all in their hearts or their heads.

Alas, what these men lack in wits, they make up for in power – mastery of granaries, mastery of ships. They are not skilled in grain nor sail, but both possess a singular quality that has kept them in their state – the absolute conviction in their own worth, and a willingness to destroy any who stand in their way. Thus it often is with the great.

I grit my teeth at their presence, silence the crackling of my displeasure.

"So," says Polybus, "Odysseus is finally dead."

"We don't know that—" begins Peisenor.

"Of course he's dead," snaps the old father. "He hasn't come home with Telemachus and that means Telemachus didn't find him and that means he's dead. Even if the others haven't understood it now, they will soon enough. It's over."

Eupheithes, loath to agree with his paternal rival in any matter whatsoever, folds his arms and nods his chin, just once, a mere half-acknowledgement that despite his enmity, he finds Polybus's logic flawless. Their sons are not here for this encounter. They are in their beds, sleeping off the wine of the night. The wishes of these young would-be kings are irrelevant to matters of great state.

"There still isn't a body—" Aegyptius tries.

"And?" snaps Eupheithes. "There are no bodies of any of the men Odysseus dragged with him to Troy. None of our sons have been buried, but we understand that they are dead. We have mourned for many years. So what if there's no body of Odysseus? Telemachus went away to find his father and has returned without him, so that's settled now. We can stop with this women's nonsense and choose a king. Ithaca needs ruling, and without a strong leader now there will be war. You know this. *She* knows this." He jerks his chin towards Penelope, sitting in her corner, but does not grace her with a flicker of his eyes.

"This is happening fast—"

"Twenty years!" Eupheithes roars, and even Polybus flinches. Does Polybus hear passion in Eupheithes' voice, hear the grief for sons lost at sea, hear the rage, the despair, the broken heart of a soul who knows he will never live to see those grandchildren after all? Perhaps he does, but no – no. He cannot permit himself to hear the humanity in this rival father, sometime friend. That would oblige him to ask too many questions of himself. "Twenty years," repeats Eupheithes, a little lower, stocky body shuddering as if an earthquake rocks beneath his feet alone. "Ithaca needs a king."

Penelope clears her throat. It is a polite, little sound, and when she speaks she addresses the ceiling, as if the cracks alone are a court worth attending, a matter that needs her most urgent and intense consideration. "These good men are right."

Medon's jaw drops to his chest. Aegyptius's fingers curl around the edge of the table, Peisenor feels the ghost of where his shield hand used to be. These are not sentiments that any in the room expected to hear from the wife of Odysseus. They will break everything.

Break it, I whisper, my hand upon her back. *Break it all.*

"They are right," she repeats, rolling the words around her mouth as if curious, testing the weight of them, feeling their warmth. "My son has returned, and he has not brought his father with him. My husband is therefore either dead or out of the reach of mortal men, and my son has not proven himself capable of raising an army to conquer these islands in his father's absence, and thus is not strong enough to hold the throne. Thus I must settle matters as quickly as possible to prevent the – as you say – inevitable bloodbath, and marry."

"Penelope," begins Medon in a low, warning tone – but his voice is cut through by Aegyptius.

"This is an important matter – too important for, if you'll pardon me saying, a woman's whim."

"Antinous is the only one strong enough to hold the kingdom," barks Eupheithes.

"Antinous is the most hated man in the western isles," retorts Polybus. "If you are serious in wanting to avoid a war, Eurymachus is the only choice."

"The council will decide—" Aegyptius tries again, feebly.

"No." Penelope rises as she says the word, and it is the first knock of the battering ram against the city gates. The men recoil, for they cannot remember ever hearing such a sound spoken so directly, so firmly, from this woman's lips.

"Um, but—" A limp nothing sound from Aegyptius, and again:

"No," barks Penelope, louder, raising her chin as sometimes her mother-in-law would do, pulling back her shoulders. There it is – the hint of a Spartan princess, the cousin of Clytemnestra, the daughter of a naiad of the raging sea. "This matter will not be decided by you. I will determine the fairest way to choose my husband – a way that ensures the safety and rightfulness of my choice. Tonight at the feast I will declare my intentions. Between then and now I will make sacrifices for my dead husband and pray. You men will not be so brutal as to deny me that."

Feet shuffle slowly on the dusty floor. These men were perfectly prepared to be entirely brutal and prevent Penelope from so much as sneezing any notion that was not the name of a new man, the new king – but sacrifice and prayer is a tricksy move from this tricksy queen. By the rites and rituals of these lands Penelope should really have seven days at least of weeping and rending of garments, seven days to fall sobbing to the ground while crying out "Odysseus, Odysseus, Odysseus!"

In the broader scheme of things, her willingness to compress this process down to a mere afternoon is not entirely unreasonable. Practically cooperative, they think. After so many years of waiting, matters are suddenly unfolding fast, chaotic, dangerous. The breath that this land has held all this time is being expelled and even these old men, who thought themselves prepared, are swept up in the tempest of it.

The councillors have spent a long time deliberately not choosing a candidate, deliberately keeping themselves safe in their neutrality. They thought they had for ever, and have not prepared for when their time runs out.

The fathers do not have this concern. Time to them has been the enemy, as if this whole world, this glorious expanse, were merely a barrier to some imagined, petty glory.

So it is with mortals. So often it is with gods as well.

"Tonight," agrees Polybus.

"Agreed," grumbles Eupheithes. "It is time for Ithaca to have a strong king."

There are mutual nods, and no words. There is nothing words can add that will in any way ease this situation. Then the old fathers turn from the room, and march out into the spider-halls of the palace. No one marks the beggar, slouched near the door, too stupid and dull no doubt to have paid any attention to the half-heard words spoken within these halls.

CHAPTER 12

>>

Medon says: "It will be a massacre, it will be war, and Telemachus . . . "

He is struggling to keep up with Penelope as she strides through the palace. She is heading for the pigsties, hardly an apt place for a woman to pray and weep for her beloved husband at a time of intense and foreshortened mourning, but still, Medon is not going to question this now. "Tell me you have a plan," he blurts, breathless as he wobbles along behind the queen. "Tell me you have any kind of plan."

"I have a plan," she declares, stepping out into the light of the yard where the animals range.

"This is happening too fast," Medon whines, as Penelope prowls up and down, examining livestock for the feast, still not a whiff of pious prayer or desperate wailing about her presumably mournful self. "Where is Telemachus? Does Laertes know? Whoever you choose, Telemachus will challenge them, he will . . . Are you hoping for single combat? Do you think your son can win? Amphinomous is a good fighter, and I know he's fond of the boy, but if Telemachus comes up against him—"

"Medon!" There it is again — that strange quality of voice that rang out when Penelope said "no", something shocking, hard, unexpected. I lean in closer, put my hand on the queen's shoulder, feel her shudder a little at my touch.

I see you, I whisper in her ear. *I am here.*

"Medon," she repeats softer, quieter, taking his hands in hers. "You have been ... When I came to Ithaca all those years ago ... I was a girl. A child. My duty was to produce an heir, and I did. I was not my cousin Helen, I was not Clytemnestra marrying Agamemnon, I was not the daughter of a great king. My mother, my heritage was ... Even my husband would sometimes talk down to me. Call me a 'delightful thing'. A 'charming creature'. We are not ... I was not here to be a woman. Barely even a queen. But you treated me as both. You spoke to me about serious matters as if I was worth sincerity. You answered my questions without belittling me for asking, you were ... I have lived longer on Ithaca than I ever did in Sparta, and though I do not know if my father would have ... if with time and age maybe he would have looked upon his daughter with ... You have always spoken to me as if I was worth speaking to. For myself. For who I am. I am not ... It is not my place to say things that are ... but I think ... "

Here it is again, the place where queen meets woman, and only one can live. The mother who should cry out to her son – Telemachus, Telemachus, my Telemachus! My love, my dear boy, my beautiful child! The daughter who should take Medon by the hand and say, kind Medon, generous Medon, I have had many mothers and many fathers, but none of them were like you. If I were to have chosen the father I wanted to have, he would have been you. He would be you.

Eos will never ask another woman to comb her hair, and Penelope has failed. She has failed as a mother, as a daughter. All that is left to her is to be a queen. Maybe even a wife. These are the only things that matter now.

Her hand falls away from Medon's. Instead, a little limply, she pats him on the shoulder, and eyes fixed on some other place says: "Ourania has not seen you for a while, I think? Perhaps you should visit her. She has a house on Kefalonia, the blossom in the evening smells divine, it is really quite restful. A very restful place. For a few days, perhaps. Just a few days."

Here also is where Medon should say: Penelope. I did not have a daughter. I did not have a daughter, but if everything is to end, if the world is to be pulled apart, let me stand by your side. These are the words he should say, but today the woman standing before him is not the frightened princess of Sparta he once knew, not the newly wed child nor the freshly weeping mother. It is not Penelope who bids him go, but the queen. Medon did not think his heart could break. He is surprised, relieved almost, to realise that it can.

"My lady," he says, and finds he is not sure what else to add. Then: "My queen." His hand clasps hers, water brimming in the low paths of his eyes.

She squeezes his hand in reply, but doesn't know how to say any words that would be meaningful and true.

Let us quickly glance towards those other matters currently unfolding in the palace, and in particular to the one slave of whom the poets will have some positive things to say: Euracleia.

Euracleia is not in the kitchens.

Euracleia is not in the great hall.

She is not fetching olives from the stores, nor pounding grain, nor gutting fish, nor berating the younger maids who bring water from the well.

Her absence is not noticed by many. Rather it is felt as a slight uplifting in their day, a place where a scalding tongue and a blazing glower should be. Too rarely we stop to notice the beautiful dawn, the brightness of a glorious summer morning, the caress of a gentle evening wind, fixating instead upon the storm and the shuddering downpour. So it is with the absence of Euracleia.

Autonoe is the only one who, a little after the sun reaches its zenith, glances round the palace walls and wonders where the old nursemaid has gone. She whispers it to Eos, who nods without raising her eyes from her work, replies that they should say nothing, show no sign. These things must be as they must be. Do not trouble yourself over the old maid.

In a darker place, a hidden place where the air hangs perpetually cold, untouched by any angle of the sun's light, voices:

"And what of the maids?"

"Whores. Sluts. The lot of them."

"Impossible. She would never allow—"

"Allow? She cannot stop them! You've seen how they are with the suitors. Touching. Smiling. *Fondling.* And that's not the half of it."

Euracleia never imagined being anything other than a slave. The freedom to dream was not permitted to her. One slice at a time the optimism of her childhood was carved away – not to marry, not to be a wife, not to be the mother of a living, breathing babe born of her own blood, not to raise a child who was her own, not to laugh at the touch of a man, not to rejoice in the company of strangers, not to possess anything that was her own, not to run free upon the hills, not to grow old surrounded by doting family, not to love, not to wonder, not to hope. As each part of her was removed, cut down, the only things that remained of any value were the prohibitions of her life. She has grown proud of the things she is not – not a dreamer, not full of hope, not merry, not compassionate – these absences have become her sacred whole. Sacred unto her, and therefore sacred unto the world that she perceives. Thus will mortals and gods both try to make something of the life they live, even when the simplest kindness due to the mewling babe has been stripped away.

The poets will love Euracleia when this tale is sung. The kings who buy the poets' songs will make sure of that.

I struggle to look upon her, even when she is not whispering poison in the dark, for it seems to me that sometimes her eyes flash up from their submissive place, and gaze straight into the most secret parts of my soul.

"*Whores*," she breathes, eyes shining in the dark. "Whores and traitors, all of them."

In the evening: a feast.

The last great feast on Ithaca.

Word has gone round, whispered from Polybus and Eupheithes to their sons, from their sons to their men, from their men to those boys who know they will never be king, and thus have pledged themselves to anyone and everyone they can, that they may have the greatest chance to survive the coming change.

The suitors arrive in the hall, dressed in finery. They have not adorned themselves in such a way since Menelaus, king of Sparta, last visited this palace, and gracious if that wasn't an unpleasant experience for all. Arms of gold, oiled hair and belts of glittering silver adorn the long, low tables of the palace of Odysseus. Antinous and Eurymachus sit nearest the front, at opposite tables, surrounded by their retinues of men who cannot be king. Amphinomous too, with his gaggle of foreign princelings and hangers-on, a golden cup between his great clasped hands as though to say: what, this? Oh, I found it under the bed. Funny old thing.

The king and princes of Troy adorned themselves in finery too, the night their city burned. They imagined, perhaps, that they had won. They imagined that their suffering had meaning, that the blood, the loss, the pain – it had been worth something. Worth anything at all. But when the sun set over the scarlet sea, they still could not say what it had been for. They could not see a reason, nor find any truth that made their suffering any more or any less than a brutal tearing in their souls, a screaming of rage, a crying-out of despair and broken promises.

So they put on gold.

Perhaps, they thought, the envy of others at the glint of yellow metal might fill the endless, crumbling dark of their hearts.

(It did not.)

Tonight, the only suitor who seems to have missed the message regarding the end of all things is Kenamon. The Egyptian is notably less adorned than his peers, though when he came to Ithaca it was with a great many gifts to be bestowed and markers of his family's greatness. He has over time, much as have the rest of them, grown more casual in Penelope's hall, easier in his disposition, since to remain stiff and upright amongst the tumult of men would to always be alone – and even the noblest of hearts cannot long endure loneliness. Now he stands out again, not merely for his darker skin and wide, deep eyes, but for the absence of glittering presentation upon his body. Baffled he looks from man to man, and uneasy his sword hand rests at his side, at the place where a blade should be.

The beggar is there too, of course. Telemachus has insisted on keeping him in the hall, stinking and wretched though he is. "He is my honoured guest," he barks. "A man as good as all of you – better."

Telemachus also does not fully understand why the suitors are adorned tonight. He did not attend the council meeting, and has not been in the palace all day. Even if he were, who would have told him what was transpiring? Most certainly not his rivals – and he did not think to ask the maids.

So it is that when Penelope emerges from upstairs before even any wine has been served, any meat presented, with no veil upon her head and ashes drawn across her brow, it is Telemachus's gasp that is loudest of all. Penelope this warm evening is flanked not just by loyal Eos, but by Autonoe and Phiobe, Melantho and Melitta. All the women of the house – save Euracleia – have smeared ash across their skin, rubbed their hands in it, clawed it into their gowns. Now they array themselves at Penelope's back, heads bowed and hands clasped, a silent wall of mournful womanhood.

The men have not seen the women like this before. They had not perhaps realised how many they were, nor indeed stopped to consider them as a collective entity. Not just "that woman" serving them at their seat, dodging their clasping fingers, whispering promises with a smiling mouth. But "these women", a collective body sharing goals, hopes, needs. Buttocks shift uneasily on long wooden benches. A few tongues lick lips that feel suddenly dry, eyes are turned downwards and away from this solemn presentation.

Penelope lets the moment last, lets it linger. She has rarely had so much silent attention from almost anyone in these halls, let alone so many suitors at once. Her eye roams across all of them like the light of the wandering moon, until it flickers over Kenamon.

What is this?

The tiniest nothing in the corner of her mouth?

The smallest suspiration of breath?

The unheard skipping of a heart?

No mortal may see it, save perhaps one.

Then Kenamon looks away, and Penelope's eyes have moved swiftly on.

"Suitors," she declares, voice a whip snapping across the silent hall. "The time has come. For ten years I have waited for word of my husband. Ten years I have wept for him, watched the eastern horizon, prayed, lamented, made sacrifice, cried out to the gods. I know it was ... selfish of me. When he left, he entrusted me with these lands, with the safeguarding of his kingdom. Ithaca needs a king, but I, being weak, being sentimental, was not waiting for a king to return. I was waiting for my husband. I let my own desire, my own heartbreak, be more important than what Odysseus's beloved people need. That must now end. I must accept that I am a queen as well as a foolish, doting wife, and do what is right for my kingdom. I must choose a new husband, and he must be king."

There should be cries at this, triumphant stomping of feet, roaring, a rush of manly breath and body towards her, a stampede of exultation. This thing on which they have been waiting, on which their lives depended – is this it? It has been imagined so many times that now it is here, it is somehow lesser than their fantasies, a disappointing note at the end of a swaggering ballad. They believed their own stories of what it would be when this moment came; in that as with so many things, they were fools.

Besides, the few wise amongst them know: this is just the beginning. This is just the first beating of the fatal drum.

Telemachus's knuckles are white, his breath short and sharp. He wants to shout, to scream, to let his palm beat across his mother's cheek. How dare you, roars his heart, how dare you? How dare you do this, now, *ever*, how dare you?

But the beggar's hand grasps his wrist as he starts to move, a grip like marble, and holds him in place.

"She betrays—" Telemachus hisses.

"Watch," the beggar replies, dark eyes glinting behind a mane of dirty hair and grubby beard. "Watch."

Antinous is the first to rise, in the silence that echoes from Penelope's speech. "My lady," he declares. "We are glad that you have finally come to your senses! May I be the first to say—"

She silences him with a raised hand. He is outraged,

indignant – but not entirely surprised. Antinous is growing used to having his words cut down in this hall. "When my husband left," Penelope declares, "he ordered me to guard his kingdom until our son should be a man. Telemachus is, as you can see, now fully grown, and I am proud . . . " She trips over the word, stumbles – is this deep feeling, a wellspring of emotion that cracks in her voice? Or is it the lie? As always, it is likely to be both. " . . . I am proud of who he has become. He has sailed forth and proven himself a warrior, a great prince, honoured in Sparta and Mycenae alike. But blood alone is not enough to rule. A man must show that he is truly great, worthy of sitting on my husband's throne."

She steps aside. From behind her, Eos and Autonoe come forward, a cloth-wrapped object borne between them, which Penelope unfolds with slow twitches of fabric as if each corner were coated in poison that she barely dare touch.

From within, a bow.

It is not of a Grecian design, but rather was had by Laertes, father of Odysseus, from a warrior of the eastern steppes, who could fire it from the back of a moving chariot at a speed that even cocky Apollo might have respected. The arrows it sends forth are, if you are careful in choosing your heads, capable of penetrating even the finest armour of bronze, which makes it something of a novelty in the field of war as fought between Grecian kings. For this reason, as well as matters of poetic honour, Laertes and Odysseus both tended to keep the bow away from the battlefield, lest it cause the following conversation with their regal peers:

"Good grief, Odysseus, you are saying that bow can kill a man in full armour?"

"Why yes, Achilles, so it can."

"And how long does it take a man to learn to aim and fire it?"

"I would say that a few good months of training might be

97

required, but that were you to fit out a troop of say, one hundred slaves with the weapon, they could provide a proficient source of death within a few weeks, if they were to shoot and run away."

"An army of slaves, you say? You mean warfare could be waged by the oppressed and the humble, the downtrodden and the merely quite indignant, all without years of preparation and vast investment of wealth and energy? Just by arming them with simple tools and some big ideas? That the tales of war could be transformed from ones of great kings and heroes proving their strength, honour and valour, becoming immortal in the hearts of men, to lines of nobodies standing a hundred steps apart showering each other with impersonal, inescapable death for causes *other* than the personal glory of a single, brutal man?"

"I suppose one could see it that way . . . "

And so on. My brothers and sisters on Olympus, when I try to explain this notion to them, laugh without understanding, without conceiving of the end of a world that such things might bring. Only Hephaestus, who understands that a good tool in the right hands may change more than just a cracked wheel in boggy mud, frowns and nods and shows the slightest consideration of the thing. The rest will understand only when their heroes – and then their gods – are swept away before the horseback bow and nameless ranks of marching men.

For now, then: the bow.

"This is my husband's bow," says Penelope, hand resting on the bare wood as if she might feel some touch of its absent master through the grain. "Tomorrow you will try your hand with his weapon in a test of your martial skill. He who wins, I will wed. For now, I invite you one last time to feast, and drink, and honour my dear husband's name even as I mourn my loss and prepare my broken heart to do what needs to be done."

She is angling for a quiver in her voice at these last words, a little gasp, a turning away of her head, maybe an apt tear or two. But in the moment she is so busy thinking on her plans, on needful labours and important contingencies that must be prepared, that she quite fails to focus on the production of a single salty tear. In the instant in which her last words are spoken, she remembers, and jolts almost with surprise and horror to discover herself so unprepared to produce an appropriate dewy performance. It is Autonoe, always a little faster and a little rasher than Eos, who sees this, and in the gap where Penelope's sigh should be gives instead a great big sniffly sob. She swallows it down as soon as it is produced, as though embarrassed to have been caught showing such frail womanly weakness at this time and before her mistress, but it is enough to buy Penelope space to press a hand to her brow as though she is growing faint, which allows Melitta to step forward to place her own hand beneath Penelope's elbow to support her should she swoon clean away.

This at once permits a bustle of female activity, as like a black cloud the ash-stained maids sweep in upon their mistress to shroud her with their bodies, encircling her with soft murmurs of "Oh Odysseus" and "Our dear master!" and so on and so forth.

The performance from many is crude, shallow. Phiobe's sob is a crinkle away from a giggle as she squeaks, "Oh no, dear Odysseus!" – a man she never even met, being born too late to know the missing king. Melantho nearly rolls her eyes as she moves through the display. The suitors see some hint of this, of course, but none of them will be the first to interrupt a pious performance of womanly grief – especially not at this time. Not when their eyes are now entirely fixed upon the bow that Eos is wrapping once again and hurrying away, or upon the faces of their enemies, rivals and sometime could-have-been friends.

The beggar sees all, of course. Or at least, he thinks he sees enough.

CHAPTER 13

>>>

Penelope does not return to the hall that night for the feast. Indeed, a great many of the men who had assembled leave as soon as it is polite, to try and find a bow of their own and a place to practise, or to scheme with their fellows who know that this is a skill they cannot master in so short a time.

Antinous is one of the first to go, and his departure immediately provokes Eurymachus into leaving, for if Antinous is scheming something then Eurymachus must absolutely scheme something else, even if he is not sure what that might be.

Amphinomous stays as late and as long as he can.

He is good with the bow.

He knows he is.

Artemis would snort at his skills; Apollo wouldn't even deign to consider the quality of his meagre shot.

But compared to the other suitors, as far as he knows?

Amphinomous is better than them.

His heart rushes in his chest, blood pounds in his head. Does this mean she has chosen him? Has she determined a challenge that will specifically play to his strengths, give him the greatest chance at being king? Is this a cunning device that all but names him the new ruler of Ithaca, without saying his name out loud?

Clearly she cannot show him outward favour, must seem to be aloof, but a challenge with a bow, *with a weapon of war,* of which he is a master, surely this must mean something?

He wonders if she loves him.

He had hoped, when he first came to Ithaca, that she might.

That hope faded, but has never entirely gone away. Amphinomous wants to be a good king, wants to be a good man, a good husband. He does not know if he can be all three, but he has promised himself: he will try. Whatever happens, he will try. Has Penelope seen that at last? His mind reels, but he is still wise enough to know that there are others here who will have had this thought as well. He will not be safe stepping outside these walls tonight.

"I was wondering, perhaps I might sleep within the palace?" he murmurs as Autonoe passes him by.

Autonoe doesn't mind Amphinomous. As suitors go, he is not a particularly offensive member of their tribe. He has shown remarkably little interest in the maids, save once when he sat by moonlight with Eos by the sea and told her of how much his heart yearned to return to his home, to see the land where he grew up and share in honest talk with his beloved friends and still-living family. He has not been so indiscreet since, but that has hardly been a problem given how many of his companions in the palace have been willing to spill their hearts and minds for a sweet word and sly caress of a maid.

She knows it would be simplest to throw him out, let him be murdered by some jealous man in the dark of the city streets, his body thrown into the sea – "Oh no, is dear Amphinomous not here to try his luck with the bow?" they will say. "Whatever could have happened to him? A coward after all, perhaps."

"I will have a place prepared for you," she says instead, and is surprised to find her heart flutter a little as she turns from him, a taste in her mouth that might almost be . . . regret?

How strange, she thinks, and resolves to not think on it any more.

Melitta weeps.

"Stop it!" snaps Eos. "Stop it right now! Someone might see you!"

"Eurymachus isn't a bad man," whimpers the maid. "He's not a *bad* man. It's just his father, he doesn't give him the chance to be who he wants to be, to find himself—"

"Stop it!" repeats Eos, eyes flickering through the blackened night to the open windows of the palace. "Stop it at once!"

When Melitta does not cease her sobbing, Eos grabs both her hands between her own, presses her face close to the weeping maid, hisses: "If Eurymachus was king, there would be a war and he would die. You would die. We would all die. And no one would care. No one cares if we die. Do you understand? No one cares."

Melitta sniffs, sniffs up snot from the end of her nose, nods. They all understand. They have always understood.

They return inside the cool palace walls, as a beggar watches from the shadows.

Kenamon of Memphis finds Telemachus upon the walls, watching the horizon as if he would by will alone command the sun to rise, the sun to set.

He had not set out to find the boy – his heart still hurt too much from their first greeting. And yet how rarely the mind is honest, even unto itself, for having resolved not to go looking, Kenamon absolutely went directly to the place where the prince was most likely to be upon this hour, his familiar haunt gazing out to sea. There is a thing unresolved, a burning, blazing anguish, a desire to scream: do you not know me, boy?! A desire to implore: are we not friends? And beneath it all, a growing fear, a gnawing terror: what will you do now?

Will you hurt me?

Will you draw your blade, call me enemy, now that all things are changing?

And if wounded, will I wound you?

Is this truly how we die?

Kenamon has not thought these precise thoughts – not out loud, not with the mind-that-is-formed-of-words. But if interrogated, he would blurt these questions and at once clasp his hands over his mouth as if horrified at the notions that emerged from within.

I sigh as he passes me on his way to the battlements, but do not stand in his way.

"Telemachus?"

The boy jumps, reaches for a blade at his side – he is not carrying one, this is his palace after all, it would be ridiculous, obscene – hesitates when he beholds the Egyptian.

On the one hand, Kenamon taught Telemachus to fight. With his father gone, it was this stranger from a distant land who sparred with him in the hills, who commanded, move, *move*! If you go backwards I will follow! Why are you attacking my sword when you should be attacking my head, *move*!

Kenamon did not fight like Telemachus thought heroes should. It was grubby and breathless, as much about the mind as the body.

You've got two hands, haven't you? So grab the damn spear!

Telemachus feels . . . *gratitude* towards this man.

Gratitude is an incredibly uncomfortable experience for Telemachus. His whole life has been geared towards resentment, to a story of bitter betrayal and harsh cruelties. This narrative, woven from petty slights and outright lies, is the only way he can explain why he is so much lesser than the man he thinks he should have become.

"Kenamon," he blurts, a little slow, a little too late to be courteous. "What do you want?"

"Telemachus, I . . ." Too many emotions may stop a mouth as soon as open it. "How are you?" This is all he can bring himself to say, but there is genuine curiosity, affection almost in the Egyptian's voice. For a moment of pure terror Telemachus thinks that Kenamon might be about to hug him – the idea is torture, and his eyes flicker about immediately to see if a certain beggar is watching. "Your voyage – your adventures. You look . . . well. Are you well?"

What happened?

What have you become?

It is not wise to ask these questions.

It is also entirely essential that they be asked.

Wisdom is rarely easy, too often an unwelcome guest.

Telemachus shuffles back an instinctive little step before Kenamon can draw too close. It is small enough to be nothing, grand enough that the Egyptian sees it, hesitates, almost seems to flinch. "This . . . this business with the bow," Kenamon tries, slower now, his accent showing a little more plainly in his speech, his fingers suddenly lumpen and clumsy at his sides. "You know. Whatever outcome. Whatever happens. I will always defend your mother. I . . . if there is some way . . . if there is . . . I hold her in the highest regard, but I would never seek to disinherit. I would . . . I know I cannot be king, but if there is some service I can . . . I can render to you. To your family. It would be my honour."

For an instant, Telemachus wants to blurt out everything, to run to the embrace that seemed just a moment ago offered, to cry out, "My friend, my friend, my dearest friend, my soul is the tempest and I do not know which way to turn!"

Then he sees the beggar.

Always the beggar.

Watching from the door.

So instead, he turns away. "Thank you. Your words are noted. We will see what tomorrow brings."

Kenamon stands a moment more, waiting, hoping, holding back his hands from reaching out to touch the boy on the shoulder. Telemachus does not look at him, does not acknowledge his existence, and so at last, the Egyptian bows his head, walks away.

In her bedroom, Penelope is examining tinctures, powders and sweet-smelling perfumes in clay pots and bottles.

They came from Sparta, sent by her cousin Helen. This one will whiten your skin – dreadful how much you've let the sun beat upon you. This for drawing on a great dark brow that runs almost ear to ear, very fashionable, very chic. This for rubbing into your cheeks, this for brightening your eyes, and this . . . ?

Penelope picks up a bottle whose purpose the messenger who delivered it did not know.

Cousin Helen is skilled with many plants and powders to alter a state of being. How one is seen. How one might see. Women's tricks. How strange it is, Helen might muse, that our husbands demand that we are beautiful, but scorn us for putting effort into our beauty.

Penelope puts a bottle into Eos's hand.

"It will be enough," she murmurs. "Not too much, just enough."

Eos slips the bottle into her gown. "They will bring knives tomorrow. The suitors."

"Some. Not all. And it may not be to their advantage if they do."

"Amphinomous has asked to sleep downstairs tonight. Autonoe permitted him."

"I didn't think she had such a soft spot for the man. And where is Euracleia?"

"Tending to the beggar. She insists on bringing him the finest sweets of the palace, honey and tender fruit. She thinks we do not notice, and he sends them away untouched, snaps at her behind closed doors, tells her she will ruin everything."

"He is in bed, then?"

"Yes, but he sneaks out as soon as he thinks it is safe to do so. He knows the palace, knows how to move through its shadows."

"Of course he does," sighs Penelope. "Thank you, Eos. For . . . Thank you. Good night."

Eos wants to caress Penelope's hair. She wants to twine it round her fingers, point out another sprouting grey, brush it back from Penelope's ear. She does not.

"Good night, my queen," she says.

CHAPTER 14

Penelope lies in the middle of a bed made for two, and does not sleep.

When she first came to Ithaca, her husband showed her this bed, carved from an olive tree that grew through the house itself. A living monument, he called it.

The practicalities of the thing have of course proven absurd. The tree, while still living, caused endless cracks and tears in the structure of the room, culminating in one night when a wall fell entirely, nearly suffocating Penelope and her infant son in a shower of mud and dust. The women of the palace most skilled in construction tutted and looked at the wreckage and said: "We see what your problem is, my lady. Your problem is the tree growing into your bedroom. That'll be it, right there."

But this bed is a living monument, young Penelope objected, and the women said well be that as it may, lovely gesture and everything – but still a hazard.

In the end, Penelope had the olive tree severed at the trunk, and a new tree planted right next to the remains that could be allowed to grow in a way that looked as if it absolutely could be entwined with the walls itself, without the actual architectural inconvenience of having a tree trying to sprout twigs through the sheets. She felt that the essence of the thing was still being honoured, emotionally and, perhaps more important, visibly, should anyone in the know ever ask, even if a certain practical mindset had needed to be applied to the problem.

When Odysseus had shared this bed with Penelope, he somehow managed to dominate most of it. He had started out trying to sleep only on one side, but he tossed and turned and she, even as her belly swelled with Telemachus, didn't think it appropriate for a wife to complain as her husband moved steadily more diagonally into her space. He was also a dreadful snorer, a roaring snuffle as loud as the snorting boar he liked to hunt. Penelope would lie awake imagining that his grumbling, throaty exhalations were like the gentle washing of the sea, but alas, they came in such fits and starts that no sooner had she lulled herself to sleep than a thunder of phlegm would at once rouse her back to full, startled wakefulness.

When he went to Troy, she stayed sleeping on just her own side, tight and compact near Telemachus's crib as she had been wont to do. She had wanted to cry herself to sleep, felt that was the very least a mourning queen could do, but in truth on the first night of Odysseus's absence the failure of the room to shudder with snoring had been such a novel relief that she had gone straight to sleep with a little half-smile on her face. She felt dreadfully embarrassed about it the next morning and did indeed manage a few tears at her own terrible hypocrisy. The fact that she had slept well did not make it easier for her to muster the depths of emotional torment required for said weeping, but she was determined to put the effort in.

As the years went by, Penelope herself began to drift across the bed. First a leg stretched a little to the side, then another. The day after she ordered the living tree from which her bed was grown to be severed from its source of life, she finally sprawled across the whole thing, arms outstretched and legs splayed, just to see what the experience was like. Both disconcerting and delicious, she concluded. A very unqueenly kind of luxury.

When news came that Troy had fallen, she shuffled back to her side of the bed and tried sleeping in a tight little ball, just to get used to the notion again. When after a year her husband had not returned, she tried sleeping on the floor for a night, imagining what it might be like for Odysseus in his rough travels, without comfort for her head or blanket for her spindly limbs. That experiment lasted less than the hunting of the midnight owl, before she got back into her bed with bumpy skin, sore back and shivering. After a meagre few weeks of this, her orientation drifted again to the middle, and there she lies tonight, staring up at the moonlight spilled across the ceiling, one woman in a bed made for two.

After a while, she moves to the side.

Then she is not sure if the side she is on is hers, or her husband's.

It has been so long; these things that once seemed as natural as breath, as simple as blinking, are now somewhat more obscure.

She moves to the other side.

Neither feels correct.

She rolls back into the middle.

Stretches out her arms, her toes.

Thinks she should feel guilty at how much she enjoys it, appreciates the space that she has to herself. She is not getting any younger; limbs that as a youthful princess were perfectly content to be snuggled into a ball now appreciate a certain room to roam, and her body is becoming ever more particular about the angles in which it lies.

She tries to muster a pang of remorse, of self-reproach at her selfishness.

Does not.

She thinks of touching herself. She came upon self-pleasuring through listening to the half-intuited whispers of the maids. No one was going to tell her about it, or if they were then doubtless they would have said it was foul, grotesque, wrong. The first time she experienced sensual delight from her own ministrations, she felt abhorrent, worried that she was destroying her ability to have more children, that people would smell the profanity upon her. Then one night she caught sight of a maid and a man in the throes of copulation and it was all a bit much really and so she touched herself again and thought diligently of Odysseus throughout, which while it didn't have a particularly detrimental effect on the experience neither was a significant stimulant. His face was already growing dim in her recollection at that time, memory layered over by year after year of living.

Aphrodite, were she to report on this matter, would shrill with fantasies and ecstatic delights for the Ithacan queen to indulge in, and doubtless become highly anatomical in her assessment of what Penelope should do next.

I consider pronouncing on such things to be crude and unnecessary, save where the thoughts of a woman portend to the fate of a king. Naturally, my siblings can never know that I consider sexual matters in even the most brisk of tones, for what if I want pleasure? What if I need comfort, desire intimacy, yearn for companionship?

Farewell then my power.

Farewell wisdom, and force of arms.

Farewell the mind that will make the choices – the cruel choices, the hard choices, the choices that must burn and blaze and rend the world in two, irrefutable in their calculation, unbiased by such petty concerns as hope, trust, loyalty, desire, fear, yearning, longing or love.

Farewell my strength, the shield and the spear.

Love is of course, the most unacceptable.

There was once one I contemplated sharing my heart with, but she died by my hand and for the pleasure of my kin, who love nothing so much as to make themselves large by making others small, and I swore: never again.

Never again.

Thus, in simplest terms: Penelope contemplates pleasuring herself, largely out of curiosity to see if she can still be pleasured. She imagines that sexual acts will be performed upon her by some man or another in the coming few days. She thinks that if her husband dies tomorrow, the suitors will not feel any inhibitions about raping her and her maids. The failure of Odysseus to initiate a successful massacre will almost certainly provoke a violent reaction from those who survive upon the nearest creatures they see – that is the way of things. The idea destroys even the slightest chance of pleasure she may have experienced, sticks in her throat, makes her stomach twist, her lungs ache. She has already determined that she will fight until she dies, with what strength she has. She does not dare to think of what will happen to the women who serve in her house. It is yet another topic on which the queen of Ithaca averts her thoughts – and thus we see how sentiment once again clouds the mind. I will have none of it.

She is not sure what her husband will do with her, if he survives. He was a perfectly polite and tender lover when they were wed – but it was also clear that lovers they would be. "Are you ready?" he asked, as they lay together beneath the olive tree, his hand upon her breast, his hairy leg already half drawn across her own.

"Are you ready?" is not asking "Are you willing?" or "Should I stop?" Certain assumptions have been made that move beyond both those enquiries. From such a place, it is hard to go back. Odysseus had looked into her eyes as he did his business. She was not sure what he saw there, but appreciated in an unclear kind of manner that he didn't turn away. She wondered after what he discerned in her face. Neither Anticlea nor Polycaste had instructed her in what she should do other than lie still and obey, but Clytemnestra had said that you were meant to moan – as if in pleasure – when a man did his business, and that if maybe you did, he might get it over with faster. It all really rather depended on the man. "Helpfully, men tend to assume any noises you make are sounds of pleasure," she had explained. "So if you just want to whimper he'll probably think he's doing well, and that's enough."

That had been before Clytemnestra was dragged by the hair from the body of her first husband, who Penelope had always considered a fairly harmless if slightly dim sort, into the arms of Agamemnon.

Thoughts of Clytemnestra are not soothing for the queen of Ithaca.

Penelope rises from her bed.

Lies back down.

Rises again.

Goes to the window.

Looks down to the sea.

Pulls a cloak about her shoulders.

Eases open the door to her room.

Eos sleeps outside on a pallet of straw. There has been a maid sleeping outside Penelope's room for as long as her husband has been away. When Odysseus's mother, Anticlea, was still alive, that maid was usually Euraclea. When Anticlea died, Penelope chose her own maids, each taking turns, night after night, to guard her door.

Eos is also a snorer, but far lighter and more consistent than Odysseus. One might indeed imagine the gentle washing of foaming waves upon a shingle shore, to hear the soft sighs of the maid. Penelope steps gently round her, moves without lamplight or guide through the palace. She knows every step, could travel blindfold, navigating by toe-touch and the familiar smells of every corridor. A whiff of the animal pens, of slumbering pig and hairy goat. A sniff of woodsmoke from the kitchen stoves where the great fire gutters in the hearth. The thick aroma of oil from a still-flickering lantern, the soft, dry scent of mud and clay from a wall freshly repaired after a storm, of damp straw on a patched leaning roof, of freshly washed tunics laid out to dry.

She moves by touch and memory down through the narrow, twisted corridors to a door to her midnight garden that smells of little white flowers that shed yellow pollen on their snowy leaves, of purple blooms that seem to swallow the busy bees whole, of fat green leaves that catch the morning dew on their sharp tips and black damp earth whose belly glistens with busy, happy worms. An owl shrieks overhead, watching the dark with sharp yellow eyes – it is not mine, but I salute it nonetheless. The gulls are slumbering in their cliff-edge perches, and the crows have finished their bickering to settle in for the night.

Penelope drifts through the scent of her garden, hears the bubble of the little stream that runs behind it, tumbling away towards the steep cliff beyond the palace walls and down, down to the sea. This place was Anticlea's once, a haven of fragrance and shelter where the old queen would sit, eyes closed, leaning back into the sun. No one disturbed her when she came to these bowers, and as she grew older and more frail, Penelope and her maids would carry her into its embrace, hang sheets between the walls to give her shade when she drifted to sleep upon a wooden bench, hands folded beneath her cheeks and knees tucked to her chest like a child.

When Anticlea died, Penelope's first thought was to turn the whole thing into an extension of the long vegetable garden that runs from the rear of the palace past the great well and to the edges of the walls. There were always mouths to feed, even

113

with so many men gone from the island. But in some very short passage of time, she learned to value this place as her mother-in-law had before, to appreciate just one corner of her life that wasn't entirely defined by harvests and dung, the abundance or lack or water upon a field or the skinniness of a goat. A small corner of honest luxury, that was entirely her own. It felt a little naughty – she was, after all, a queen, above and beyond petty desires and personal sentiments.

"For goodness' sake," Ourania had tutted, when Penelope explained this. "Who do you think you're fooling, girl?"

No one else would have dared to say these words in quite this way to Penelope, and for a moment she did consider chiding the old maid. But then she had stopped – she had considered – and she had concluded that perhaps, in this particular matter, Ourania had a point.

Now she moves through this garden that is entirely her own, astonished tonight to discover a wellspring of gratitude she had never known she had before for this quiet, this dark, this peace of being alone.

Although, as it turns out, not quite alone. For as she moves through the dark, a voice says:

"Um . . ."

Penelope stops dead, her eyes slowly adjusting to the fading moonlight as she blinks into the shadows of the garden. A figure moves, spreads its arms in a kind of apology, tries again. "I, uh . . . thought everyone would be asleep."

Kenamon of Memphis, soldier far from home. All that may be said of the sanctuary this garden gives to the queen of Ithaca by day may be said of the pleasure it gives to this warrior by night. He did not find it by himself, of course. Even with his many wanderings and explorations, there are doors in the palace he knows not to open. But one night, not so many moons ago, Penelope said to him: come, there's a place I'd like to show you.

114

She led him, Eos at her side, to this oasis of fragrance and quiet, away from all the eyes of the palace, and gestured to a wooden bench and said: this is a place I like to go. When I am thinking. You are welcome here, sometimes.

'Sometimes' is a word of many meanings, and none at all. Yet she had meant the offer sincerely. There was a debt she felt needed to be repaid, and since it could never be repaid with such things as honest affection, open friendship or sacred marriage, she offered one of the few precious things she had to give.

Come, she had said. Sit a little. Tell me about Egypt. Tell me about yourself.

Now in the dark the two blink at each other, and Eos sleeps upstairs, and together they are entirely alone.

"I'm sorry . . . " she begins, and all at once:

"What has happened?" he blurts.

He reaches for her, his hands upon her arms – his hands upon her arms! I glance heavenwards to see if any others are looking, any gods or creatures of the divine, and see none. If my brother Ares is in these isles, he has hidden well – and he does not like to hide.

Medon wanted to put his hands upon her arms like this, Eos wants to hold her tight – even Autonoe sometimes thinks that what they really need is to tangle their fingers in sisterhood and secrecy, an innocent intimacy, a connection that is more real than mere words can say. None of them do it. He does, without even thinking – it is merely the human thing to do, the right thing that needs to be done, almost childlike in its simplicity.

She flinches, but does not pull away.

"What has happened?" he repeats, voice a bare whisper, for he too has learned that Ithaca is a secret place.

"Nothing. It is time. That is all. It is time."

"Is this because of Telemachus? He has said something? Seen something? If he is going to fight, I will join him. I will fight for him. I know I can never be . . . I know he would never allow you to marry – cannot allow you to marry – but still, if I can serve, I will serve him. Does he know that? Will you tell him?"

"I . . . I don't . . . "

Now she pulls back, shakes her head, rubs the place on her arms where his hands had been, feels his lingering warmth, feels how cold she is where his fingers did not touch her skin. He does not seem to see, to understand, steps after her, close, voice rising a little, though still not enough to break the quiet of night. "If this . . . business with the bow is real . . . then I have a hope. But you said yourself I can never be king, so what are you planning? I will keep the secret, you know I will, anything you ask for, anything you need, I will serve. I will serve you, Penelope. You must know it by now."

"I . . . I do. I do. I know, but . . . "

Penelope is rarely lost for words. I feel my lips curl. Here it is again – sentiment, fondness, maybe even something more – they muddy her mouth, turn her words to dirt. She should be speaking with clarity, strong and clear and calm, the things that are needful, the necessary things, but no – no. All tangled. All useless. And for what? For the things I have denied myself, so that I should never be so witless in my speech.

As much as I loved her when she was ice, I hate her in this moment of fire. It is a hate born of jealousy, and I am immediately ashamed.

"I will not take up the bow if you tell me not to," he breathes. "Whatever it is you need, whatever is happening – I am yours to command."

"I know."

She knows, and the knowledge destroys her from the inside out.

There was a night, many moons ago, when I took Kenamon of Memphis by the hand and led him into the fray, made him a

116

vessel of my might, of my divine glory. There was a night when Spartans chased the queen of Ithaca through her own lands, and he took the life of those who would have made her a slave, and asked nothing in return, and sang songs of his homeland in the secret places where the women were, and for a moment forgot to mourn for his distant home. He is not a great man. He does not come from fine blood, is not a son of the land of Greece. There is no place for him in this story, and yet . . .

. . . and yet, what use are the gods if we do not occasionally repay even our mortal debts?

I clasp his shoulder, as a warrior will. Press my forehead against his own. He does not know what divinity he feels, cannot name it, will never understand. Yet he draws in a shuddering breath, and in that moment at last comprehends the impossible thing.

"Is he . . . is he back?"

The whisper hangs upon the air, and Penelope shakes her head, cannot meet his eye, cannot answer. I let go my warrior, my loyal servant, this strange and distant man. Turn to Penelope. Brush her chin with my fingers, raise it, let her look one more time upon him, then turn her head a little to the door so that she might see.

With mortal eyes she could not, but my touch gives her a tiny flicker of my radiance and so she glimpses – just a shadow, just a turning of black in black – the beggar man as he pulls his face away into the darkness.

She snatches in a little breath and her eyes dart back to Kenamon's own, searching his features, not for anything in him, but for a solution, an answer for herself.

Be brave, my warrior, I whisper into her soul. *Do not flinch from battle. Be wise.*

Kenamon's breath comes fast and thin, his hands want to hold her but he does not. "Penelope?" he whispers, and there are those words again, on the edge of his breath, the question he does not dare utter. *Is it him?*

His body is between her and the door. A little step, the tiniest movement, and his face hides hers from any within who might try to see it; his chest hides her hands, the movement of her fingers. The smallest motion, a little shuffle – there. There it is.

The beggar in the dark looks, but for a moment cannot see past Kenamon to behold the queen of Ithaca.

And at last – at long, long last – she smiles.

She has not smiled upon a man in this way for . . . she does not know how long.

Tears hot in her eyes, warm on her cheeks.

She presses her hands against his chest, feels the beating of his heart.

He catches her fingers in his own, holding them tight. He is not sure if the racing pulse he feels through them is hers, or his. He thinks perhaps this is it – perhaps there is hope – maybe not here, maybe not on Ithaca, but perhaps the two of them, a place where the waters of the Nile run clear . . .

She raises her gaze, looks into his eyes.

What shall we say he sees in those eyes?

Each creature, mortal and divine alike, spins their own stories, creates tales in their own image, weaves their own reality.

Thus, my stepmother Hera might say: *He sees a queen who has burned away all other parts of herself, all pieces of a woman and a woman's desires, to be only the monarch she has to be.*

Or Aphrodite: *He sees all the things she cannot say, bursting at once from within her soul.*

Or maybe even Artemis: *He sees a woman looking at him and finds this confusing, that way men do.*

This is of course one of the problems with divinity – we tend to be somewhat extreme in how our aspects shape our perceptions of events.

But I, who am wiser than all the others combined, see the truth of it, and the truth is that all of them are correct. Mortals are more capable than gods of being many things at once, of holding many great truths within their bosoms. It is why they blaze so brightly, yet fade so fast.

So let us simply say that Penelope, queen of Ithaca, wife of Odysseus, widow of some twenty years, daughter of a naiad and a king, mother of a prince who cannot hold his own kingdom, smiles up into the eyes of a soldier from the south, lays her forehead upon his chest as if she would fall into him. Feels his warmth. Breathes his breath. Shares in the beating of his heart. Lingers a moment, then pulls away.

Is this love?

I do not know.

I am the wisest of all living things, and to my shame, I do not know.

Have mercy on me, for I do not know if this is love.

Enough, I whisper, half closing my eyes so I do not have to look upon this thing. *It is enough.*

She gazes upon him, remembers his unanswered question hanging in the air, nods, just once. Whispers: "He is here."

Enough. It is too much. It is enough.

Kenamon understands.

For a moment, he thinks of reaching for his sword, but he does not have one by his side. A rock from the garden, then, or some tool – there must be something nearby. He contemplates turning to the darkness in which he now feels the beggar lurking, grabbing whatever shadow waits there and strangling him with his bare hands. Kenamon has felt this fury before, back in Egypt, back when he rode through the southern lands in pursuit of the bandits who'd burned his home, and again when his brother laughed and said: *What can I say? Papa always loved me more.*

He has heard rumours of Odysseus. Does not deceive himself into thinking this will be an easy fight. Wants to fight it anyway.

And what then? I whisper in his ear. *What will you do when the battle is done?*

And Kenamon, for all that he is a warrior, is also wise.

I would love you too, I breathe, *if love were not a foolish thing.*

He closes his eyes, lets out a little breath, and at last sees a future – the future, the future that must be, that all things have been leading towards for a very long time. It is very short, very bloody, and there is no way out. Not for him, and not for her. That is the truth of the thing.

She sees it too. The knowing of it in his face, in his shortened breath, in the fluttering of his heart.

She regrets that there has not been more time.

Time to say sorry, perhaps. Or thank you.

To say: I valued you, I laughed with you, I enjoyed the sound of your voice, the words you spoke, the stories you told. It pleased me to gaze upon you, and for you to gaze upon me. In your eyes, I was a woman, whole and beautiful. I felt that. I even sometimes believed it. It felt good. With you, I was whole.

Or to say perhaps a thousand other impossible, forsaken things.

Instead: she steps away, finger untangling from finger one digit at a time.

Draws in a final breath, inhales the smell of him, the warmth of him.

Lets it go.

Lets go of hope, of sentiment, of trust, of joy, of companionship, of dreams of something more.

Makes herself instead what she has to be: a warrior, wise.

And at last, with a shove and a snarl: "How dare you approach me?" she barks, voice ringing in the dark. "How dare you come into this place? What kind of ignorant barbarian are you?"

He should stutter, protest, be amazed.

120

There are tears in his eyes and he is not so good at pretending, so he does not.

"Get out of here!" She raises her voice a little more, shriller now, pushing it as hard as she dares. A difficult balance – loud enough to be heard by any hidden hearers, but not too loud to rouse the house. "Get out of here, this was his mother's garden, how dare you think you can just . . . be here?! You disgust me. Of all the foul, stinking men to come to my hall I thought I had seen the worst, but you . . . a foreigner. A stranger to these lands. What are you? Not even a prince. A merchant's son. The younger brother of a younger brother sent to whore at a widow's door, having no prospects in your own home. I pray that the sea takes you – not fast, not easy, but as my husband was, washed for ever from the ones you love, alone and out of sight of land."

She spits.

It is not a very impressive gesture – she can only muster a little saliva, and not much range. But that little is enough. The foaming moisture hangs upon his cheek, drips slowly down.

He steps away.

Wipes it from his skin.

Nods.

I do not need Aphrodite's sight to see what that look is upon his face. I hear Penelope catch her breath, feel her regret like a spear through the heart. Not at what needs to be done – that is a wound that burrows far deeper and far more bloody than mere regret ever can. Rather it is at the sight of his understanding, his knowing of what this is, and worst of all: his forgiveness.

I'm sorry trembles upon the edge of her lips.

I'm sorry.

I'm so sorry.

She wants to scream it, to throw the words upon him.

She cannot, and even that, he seems to see.

Kenamon nods once more, smiles, touches his fingers to his

chest. His back is to the door, hiding the salute. Raises his fingers from his heart, presses them to his lips. Kisses them, turns his warm fingertips towards her, a promise of a thing that shall never be, a farewell that can never be pronounced. There are tears in his eyes, but she thanks the gods they have not fallen yet, may pass without being seen. The tears running down her face are, she thinks, more useful. She focuses on that. Useful tears – always find the useful. These can be tears of rage, of indignation – of grief even, but not for him. Never for him.

She catches his fingers, her movement shielded from sight by his body, squeezes them, immediately regrets that she did so, that she felt his warmth again, presses them back against his chest, lets go.

He smiles at her, and thinks he will never smile again.

Then Kenamon straightens, raises his voice loud and steady, proclaims: "You have always made it quite clear that you despise me, queen of Ithaca. Always made it quite clear where your heart lies. If I can do one good thing with my life, it will be to leave you now. Goodbye, majesty."

It would be easier, she thinks, if he screamed. If he pouted and sulked and raged. He did try to find those sentiments, push them into his speech – but he could not. Even now, at the end, he could not do it.

The moonlight cannot hide her tears, which now tumble glistening down her face. I bid the clouds skim a little thicker across that glistening orb, command the breeze to turn to catch and pull her half-suffocated sob away from the palace walls.

I take Kenamon by the hand.

Come away, I say, to his rushing heart.

Come away.

His feet will not turn, save with my divinity. I nudge his ankle, press his knee into bending. He nearly falls at the first step, and I catch him.

Come, warrior, I whisper. *It is time to go home.*

I lead him towards the door, and for a moment he too half glimpses the beggar in the dark, before that shadowed man darts away.

CHAPTER 15

>>>

Penelope in her garden – weeping.

Kenamon shuffling like a drunk blind man towards the harbour, towards the sea.

There is a wind in his face that dries any tears before they can form. I send dreams to rouse a servant of Ourania's, that will have her scuttling to the docks before the first light of dawn. She will find him there, wretched at the harbour's edge. She will lift him up, carry him like an old man to Ourania's home, and there the maid will say: "I have a cousin who sails the amber routes to Egypt, you know."

Kenamon was raised to worship the falcon-headed god, the bringers of the flood and the passage of the sun. When he came to this land, he prayed still, for a little while, but without the pomp of the temple and the beating of the drum, his prayers seemed empty and cold. He has not prayed for a long while, and I do not know what god will hear him should he call again.

"I do not remember what home is," he says at last.

Ourania is kind, in her way. She lays her hand upon his shoulder, but cannot find suitable words.

"I should go back," he says. "I should protect her."

"Darlingest," Ourania replies. "All you can do now is get

yourself – and her – killed. If not today, then tomorrow – that was always going to be the way."

He knows the truth of it, hears it in her words, and swears at that moment that he shall never love again, and I am sorry for it.

I will leave him here. The poets will wipe him from existence. Even in the southlands, where they inscribe their tales in ashen ink and carved stone, there will be no monument raised to him, no honours given to his name. He will vanish into history, a merely ordinary man.

I salute him, nevertheless, as I go.

Brother, I proclaim, *warrior-wise. Go home, and lay down your blade. I release you from my dominion. Diminish, and be a fool, and love again.*

Kenamon does not hear me, his head bowed to the stones.

In her garden, Penelope weeps.

She puts her head in her hand and sobs until her breath chokes in her chest.

She cannot stop the water upon her eyes. Her body is in rebellion, twenty years of stillness, of silence, of folded hands and thin pursed lips finally cracking from the inside out. Not now, she thinks. In the name of all that is sacred, not now!

Her body does not appear to wish to listen. How strange, she thinks, that she can rule a kingdom, but not have any mastery over this.

I sit on the bench at her side and take her hand. Let her weep a little longer – but not too long. It would be prudent to enquire: *What manner of tears are these?*

For a while, she does not hear me, so I whisper to her again. *Are these tears useful? How may they be seen?*

Her sobbing slows a little. She draws down long, shuddering breaths.

She knows that she cannot, of course, be weeping for Kenamon.

That would make her a whore, a slut, a harlot, a weak woman of desire and foolery, no better than her cousin Helen, for whom the world burned. Such an outcome would be entirely unacceptable – dangerous, indeed.

Yet the reality is that she is weeping, and there is still a beggar hidden in the shadows of the door, so really . . .

I resist the urge to drum my fingers, hear the wind rustle at my impatience, and instead try with what little compassion I can muster to nudge Penelope with the edge of my foot.

What use is weakness now? I ask. *Come now. Come. Do not be a fool when it matters the most to be wise.*

She takes another slow, shuddering breath.

Does not look towards the door.

Clasps her hands in prayer.

"Oh blessed Athena," she begins, pausing to gurgle down a little more air between the gasps of mourning. "Lady of war and wisdom."

Kenamon, wails her heart. *Kenamon! Kenamon, forgive me, forgive me!*

I do not mind. The words she says out loud are the needful component of her prayer, not the spirit within. They are what the poets will recall.

"Blessed Athena," she continues, "who has long watched over our house. If my husband is truly dead, if I must cast ashes upon his name, then I beg you . . ."

Forgive me, beats her heart. *Forgive me!*

" . . . take my life!"

I squeeze her shoulder as another bout of weeping sweeps across her face, trickles down her nose and into her mouth. She hauls down a ragged lungful of air, keeps going, just to make sure. "If my husband is dead, then let me join him! I beg you, goddess, do not leave me in this torment any more!"

I spin the wind again – such changeable weather we're having tonight – to ensure her words are carried to the shadow in the door. The beggar has pressed his back to the wall, is gasping quick little breaths. In the poem, this will be the moment that strengthens his resolve. It is a necessary beat, a vital part of the song that will be sung. I cannot make Odysseus a hero if he merely murders unarmed men at a feast; such things violate all the sacred laws of Greece, cast him as a monster, or worse – just another man led by vengeance, honour and pride. No. He must be motivated by a higher power, must be given reasons, take his time to reach thoughtful conclusions, and when he strikes, the poets will say his blood was roused by the prayers of his tearful wife. Thus the monster may be redeemed. Thus Odysseus's name may yet be saved, and with it, my own.

Penelope, having done her duty, puts her head in her hands again, uses the huddle against her own skin to slow her breath, lets the cold seep through her burning eyes, her burning heart, her blazing soul. Begins to compose herself.

Away, I whisper to the beggar in the door, and he, blood thundering in his ears and fingers shaken into claws, scurries into the dark.

A while longer then, I sit with Penelope, my hand upon her shoulder.

Slowly she straightens.

Slowly she draws in calmer, steadier breath.

Slowly she raises her eyes to heaven. Then out loud, without looking upon me, she spits these words: "Gods. Kings. Heroes of Greece." There is something she wants to address to these ideas, something complex, rich, bitter. She looks for the words, and can only find these: "Fuck you all."

Then she rises, and I let her go.

CHAPTER 16

>>

These are the great goddesses of Olympus:

Hera, who was once mother-earth, mother-fire. Her brother Zeus raped her, after he had grown bored of all her sisters, and made her his wife. Even then, even in those early days, the gods had begun to shape the world to say that woman who is violated may not seek punishment against her attacker, but should herself seek to be redeemed for the thing that was done to her. Thus did Hera's power wane, and instead of fresh blood on obsidian blade, endure, endure, endure became the mantra of the mother-god. We cannot punish our men, so we must take our punishments where we can. We punish the whores they fucked, the children they made, the daughters they raped. Cling to what few shreds of power you have, to the bitter throwaway offerings cast from your husband's table, and endure. What else is there to do?

Thus fell the first of us, the mother of the flame.

Aphrodite, who the gods feared for they knew that they themselves desired her, and if they desired her then that meant she had power over them. To diminish her strength, they belittled her, mocked her greatness, called her whore, slut, tits-and-no-brain. For if love, delight and intimacy were so powerful – well then, these must be things to be *owned* by the powerful, a marker of their status as sure as golden cups and blades of gleaming bronze. The slave may not rejoice in pleasure, the woman may not exult in her body; only for kings and heroes may be the ecstasies of delight, and even then love – love was always too dangerous to be endured.

Demeter did her duties without complaint, as a woman must, until her daughter went down to the underworld. Then she broke the world as mortals starved, children died, ice consumed the world. Her daughter's relationship to this was not of interest to the gods – motherhood, as possession, as ownership, as the right to break the world in your own personal grief, was far more important than Persephone's wishes.

Well of course she's a bit, you know, muttered Zeus. *She's a mother! Mothers do the most unreasonable things.*

Artemis shut herself away from her fellow Olympians, with her nymphs and naiads in the woods. For her there would be no sexual concourse – at least, not with any man – and she would live detached, untouched, uninterested. In time the gods largely forgot about her, save when some fool shed blood upon her holy lands – and even then, they indulged her, as one might tolerate a sexless child, hardly a woman at all.

My father raped my mother, his sister Metis, and, upon finding a prophecy warning that the child of this union would be wiser than he, swallowed my mother whole. This did not prevent me bursting, fully formed, from his skull.

After, he said he was fond of me. Fondness was a tool by which he could seek to control me, while also asserting his dominion over me, as thus: I'm fond of the little darling, isn't she adorable? I wonder what's going on in that funny little head of hers?

Naturally, I yearned for his respect, his love, his admiration. What child would not? But I learned in time that these were merely his hidden weapons, as potent as the spear, injuring until your soul was scarred with wounds of his choosing. I was his darling little one, his sweet owl, his baby girl – anything except the lady of war, lady of wisdom, the only other divinity to wield the thunder and the lightning. For a while I found deference and demure wit useful tactics to bend him to my will, diminishing my dignity to pander to his. These things were necessary, for both my safety and my goals.

Inevitably he began to look upon me as a sexual creature. If he could take my body by force, then could he not also take my mind, my soul, reduce all of me to a mere adjunct to his will? To get ahead of this, I swore myself a virgin. I pulled my helmet over my face, strapped my shield to my arm, renounced all signs of desire, longing or passion. I shuttered my body and my soul, and more – much more – I punished women for the things men did to them, saying that they too should have shrouded themselves as I did, and what really did they expect to happen to them if they dared to laugh out loud or be seen to exult in joy? It was hardly the man's fault if he could not control himself; it was just how things were. I laughed at the deaths of nameless thousands, shrugged to hear of some broken ship torn apart on the rocks by my uncle Poseidon, showed interest only in tests of power, strength and might of arms.

In short, I made myself like a man of Olympus.

I thought, if I did so, that I would finally be able to show my power, to blaze – not as some silly woman, but as wisdom and war incarnate, bright amongst the gods.

In some small ways, it worked. I was not mocked, as Aphrodite is; not dismissed so readily as Hera or Demeter when they speak. It was never quite enough, but it was something – and something was all I could grasp.

I did not then appreciate what else would come from making myself a man. For these are the things a man may *not*

130

be: frightened, ashamed, guilty, doubting, hurt, ignorant, ful
of need. The need to be seen. The need to be touched, the
yearning to be held. The need to belong when broken as well
as whole, in this ever-changing world.

Then came Odysseus.

CHAPTER 17

>>>

Four suitors die in the night.

They are all of them reputed to be good archers.

Only one of their bodies will be found in the morning – the other three are judiciously disposed of – and word of their deaths will not reach Penelope until much, much later.

Another thirteen suitors flee.

They cannot draw or fire a bow if their lives depended on it, and today their lives do. So, in a rare flourish of minimal wisdom, they run. They would be judged as cowards and fools, their honour lost – but they shall not stir in the minds of the busy, important people who might employ a poet, and thus are accounted merely amongst the nameless dead. Moreover, they shall live. How rash it is that we sing more of the honourable dead than the silent living. I thought once to remedy this deficit in our stories – and have not found a way yet.

Two spend all night practising with bow and arrow, and accidentally sleep through their summons to the palace.

This leaves eighty suitors, once one also observes the absence of an Egyptian.

Of these eighty, nineteen are convinced that they are going to die, but their honour does not permit them to flee, and so, weak-bellied and knock-kneed, they come to the palace of Odysseus. Seven of these nineteen have angered Amphinomous, and are sure that he will win and have them put to death. The remaining suitors have angered either Eurymachus or Antinous, and though neither of those two men are considered much good with a bow, their fathers command the largest number of friends and slaves upon the islands and are unlikely to take their defeat gracefully, and so, again, a likely slaughter will ensue.

Eleven have brought their own bows, having somewhat mis-understood the nature of the day's festivities. Autonoe greets them at the gate, and politely asks them to leave their weapons outside. Peisenor, the old soldier, is also in attendance, along with a few of the palace guards. They watch the bows as they are assembled in a little pile near the palace walls, along with the odd sword and miscellaneous dagger that a suitor has neglected to hide, and say not a word.

Telemachus is waiting in the hall, unarmed. He has brought with him six companions from his voyage, boys becoming men from that generation of youths who were babes when their fathers sailed to Ithaca, never to return. They stand, legs splayed, chins out. The mannerisms of men are things they have observed on their travels, studied and studiously copied, and like most imitations of a thing lack all nuance and natural grace. Another six wait outside the palace gates, lolling about, their blades hidden beneath their cloaks. They are as inconspicuous as dropsy, but today at least most of those heading to the palace are too preoccupied to care.

Eumaeus stands near the door that leads to the armoury, five loyal slaves and an oath-sworn guard at his side. He should not be here – none of these strangers should be here – but Penelope's maids do not question them, seem to move past them as if they were invisible, or mere paintings on the wall. Besides, they do not have weapons; so where's the harm?

Speaking of weapons, Odysseus's bow, unstrung, is laid upon a yellow cloth at the centre of the hall. In front of it, running in a line straight to his empty throne, are the axes. Their shafts have been hammered into the tables from which they stand – they will not be detached easily or soon – creating a straight line of bronze that rise as stiff as any guard for a royal king. This assemblage has disrupted the normal layout of tables about the hall, forcing the gathering suitors to mill in awkward groups, backs pressed to the walls, as the maids drift between them pouring the sweetest wine into the finest cups.

The beggar curls himself into the deepest dark of the place, shoulders hunched, chin down. Euracleia kept on trying to bathe him, and he kept on rubbing dust and ashes into his skin in retaliation. No one has stopped to question why, after some days in the palace, this man still looks like a huddled bag of rags – Penelope would never let any guest, no matter their situation, go so untended. But his quality is of such a low sort that people do not choose to look, or if they do, their eyes skim straight over him like breeze over stone.

As the suitors move into the hall, blocking out the light of the morning with their backs to the open windows, their alliances grow more pronounced. Now is the end of all deceptions, and there are little gasps as look – look – this man who has for so long been close to Eurymachus now stands by Antinous, and that fellow who everyone swore was Antinous's man is now throwing his lot in with Amphinomous, standing shoulder-proud by the would-be king's side. A few men mutter curses at each other; one spits on the floor. The maids move through the hall, pouring wine.

Amphinomous sips from the offered cup, as is the required courtesy from a guest – no more. Eurymachus takes a cup without thinking. Antinous drains his down, defiant, the apple of his throat rising and falling with each huge glug, glaring round the room. Holds out the cup at once for another slosh, licks stained lips like the hungry wolf, grins.

Many suitors have brought gifts, a final desperate plea. They are politely received by Melantho, their offerings carefully arranged along a table against the wall of the hall nearest the kitchen, so that perhaps Penelope, when she arrives, might drift past them and say: gracious, what a lovely thing; or perhaps: why Nisas, I didn't know you had such an eye for pearls, and so on.

Two of Odysseus's council are present – Aegyptius and Peisenor. They mutter between themselves, ask, have you seen Medon? He should be here. Melitta stands by their side. She has orders not to leave until they are safe and this business is done.

The poets have not been invited. Everyone understands why. Afterwards they will be informed of the outcome of events and how gloriously and nobly the winner behaved. The last thing anyone needs is a clever man with a gift for words reporting on the reality of whatever is about to unfold.

The maids are making their second pass with jugs of wine when Penelope descends. She has wiped away her mourning ashes and put on her finest gown. Her veil flutters softly about her brow, Eos holds her hand as if she were a delicate waif incapable of walking without support, guides her to the foot of her husband's chair like one approaching a sacred throne. Lets go. Stands back. The suitors turn to stare upon her. The beggar stares most of all. All is hushed. Penelope takes a moment to savour it. It is rare – most rare – for the men of this hall to hang upon her every word, to listen with anything resembling even feigned attentiveness.

"Gentlemen," she declares, voice washed grey stone. "Honoured guests." These words are ice in her mouth; they burn, they numb her lips, she is not sure what they mean any more, thinks they have perhaps grown profane, though she has not committed any sacrilege. "Thank you all for your presence, and the many fine gifts you have brought to my husband's house. But I am not looking to be flattered, nor can my affection be purchased with trinkets." A loose flick of her wrist. She has practised this motion, tried mimicking the way her cousin Helen might twitch a finger as though to say "Ah, bring me a plume of feathers for I am delicate yet must be obeyed" – Penelope has never quite got it right.

Autonoe lifts Odysseus's bow, shows it to all assembled.

"My husband was a great warrior, and a mighty king. The test therefore is simple. That man who can string my husband's bow and fire an arrow between the heads of these axes – he will I marry."

There is a mutter of discontent, a murmur of dissatisfaction. This is all nonsense – all of it absolute nonsense. Eyes turn to Amphinomous, already rolling his neck side to side. Antinous licks his lips, steps forward. His father has started mustering men for the inevitable fight, but they are not yet enough to take the palace – not yet. It is a source of some surprise to many of these suitors after so many years how quickly things have unfolded, how ungraciously they must scramble to muster arms. Antinous opens his mouth to speak, to throw some scorn upon the hesitant mass of men – when another interrupts.

"I will do it."

Telemachus steps into the middle of the room.

He has not spoken to any man of his intention, and indeed the beggar curled into a corner has to swallow his own tut, his own hiss of disapproval as the young prince comes forward. The suitors shake their heads, grumble – this was not the plan at all, not at all. But Telemachus's raised voice cuts through. "This is my father's house, my father's bow. I will string it and shoot it and then there shall be no further question as to whether I am his worthy successor, equal in might to any man here. That done, by all means one of you marry my mother." His lips curl into a sneer around the sound, his eyes flash scorn towards the stiff veiled figure of Penelope by her husband's throne. "Marry her and be done with it. She is not my father's legacy."

Eurymachus makes to say, "Um, well, actually, that's not . . . "

But Antinous raises his hands, barks: "By all means, Telemachus! If you think you can string and fire your father's bow, by all means do it!"

Antinous does not care who fires what shot – whatever the outcome, his father will come with sword and spear, even if they do not make their move until the wedding feast itself.

I sigh as Telemachus's glower deepens, and he strides towards the waiting weapon. He takes the string, grips the bow, pulls and bends, pulls and bends, pulls and bends – and fails. Laughter begins around the room, little murmuring waves of it, titters and chuckles that grow to a cheek-flaming snort of contempt. It is not that Odysseus is remarkably strong, nor his father before him. There is a trick to this kind of weapon – but of course, and with all things, there is always a trick.

Telemachus only stops trying when he hears something click in his neck, when he feels his arms about to break, and when he looks up to see through the now peals of merriment the beggar in the corner gently shaking his head.

He sees something else too, as he lays the weapon down, fighting back tears, forcing himself to believe the burning in his eyes is anger, fury, not shame and regret. He sees Melantho, where she guards stone-faced Peisenor and Aegyptius, who despite herself sniggers, just once, as he steps away from the bow.

"Don't worry yourself, Telemachus!" coos Antinous. "When I'm your daddy I'll teach you how to string a bow!"

The failure of Odysseus's son to master the weapon should serve as a warning to the suitors, a portent of what's to come. It does not. Rather it seems to fire up their blood, stir their arrogance – for here now steps forth Antinous to try his luck, still cackling at the falling-off of his opposition. Antinous is not a particularly strong man, and certainly has spent less time pulling an oar than Telemachus. When he fails, he makes a joke out of it, points at Penelope and barks, "She has given us a length of solid wood to bend, not a bow at all! Another woman's trick!"

In other circumstances, maybe some of the suitors might have agreed with Antinous. But now they are trapped in the gambler's error, seeing each man's failure as proof certain that when they try – when *they* try – they will surely succeed. This is the madness by which many a mortal has damned themselves, and from which many gods grow fat upon fervent, futile prayer.

The suitors strain, and the bow does not bend.

Unlikely alliances suddenly begin to form and break, as one suitor tries to help another curve the wood. Here, says one, if I hold it with my knees . . . Are we sure this is the right string, perhaps a longer . . . ? Wait, I think I have the trick of it, oh no, it's not quite . . .

Penelope watches, a frozen statue at the head of the hall.

"We need tallow and wax!" barks one. "We need to soften the bow by the fire!"

This rather implausible notion is at once taken to heart by every dolt who has failed so far in their labours with the weapon, and away is sent Phiobe to fetch tallow. As she darts through the nearest door, Eumaeus and his waiting men slip out after her. The path to the armoury is unguarded, all attention put upon the hall. Pushing back the heavy door, they look for the many weapons that Telemachus has promised them and find . . .

Precisely twenty spears, precisely twenty swords. Twenty plumed helmets, twenty bronze breastplates, left each in a set as if waiting for these exact same men with their exact requirements to enter this room. Eumaeus is not the smartest of

Odysseus's servants. He will not mention this coincidence, nor wonder at it in the future. It is merely the goodwill of the gods, he will think, that the number of weapons available exactly matches the number of Odysseus's men strewn about the palace. Only later, when the blood is being washed from the walls, will someone discover the rest of the armour carefully stowed under cloth and straw at the back of the furthest washhouse.

Eumaeus and his boys begin to arm, shushing each other whenever metal clatters, eyes flickering anxiously down the empty corridor beyond the door.

In the hall, the bow does not bend.

As a philosopher, I should feel compassion for the sweating, beleaguered men.

As a warrior, I must declare that these suitors with their wax and their mutterings about string are abject fools, who would not have lasted a day on the fields of Troy.

Then the beggar says: "Let me try, lords."

No one listens to him.

A little louder: "Good lords, let me try."

"Does someone hear a buzzing?" barks Antinous, not looking up from his by now profoundly suspicious study of the recalcitrant weapon.

"My travels have made me strong. Perhaps if I can bend the bow . . ."

"Who let this filthy creature into the hall?"

"Let him try!" barks Telemachus.

"What, you'd be fathered by a stinking beggar? Are you so desperate, Telemachus?"

"If I can do it, I won't ask anything," grumbles the beggar. "Just for my own sake, to know whether these old hands still have it in them. I think I saw a bow of this kind once, there is a trick to it . . ."

"Let him try." Penelope's voice lashes across the hall. Eos is already moving, uncovering a wooden box from a shadowed corner, revealing within it a sharp bronze blade and dagger on which is carved the image of a hairy tusked boar. "If he succeeds, he can have these fine weapons," a loose gesture towards the blades as they are brought nearer the waiting beggar, "as well as a cloak and javelin to see him on his way. And you suitors will be able to match your strength in taking aim and firing with my husband's bow. I see no harm in that."

"Nor I," intrudes Telemachus again, a little too loud, a little too eager. I struggle not to roll my eyes. "So it will be done. Now, Mother – go to your room."

"I beg your pardon?"

"Your presence is not required for this. You will be informed of the outcome."

"This is my—"

"This is *my* house." His voice rises, and the suitors shuffle awkwardly at the sound. They did not think they could feel embarrassed for Telemachus, not really, but this whole thing, after his failure with the bow, his failure to find his father and his pouting displays, even the lowest of the suitors think actually it's a bit much.

Telemachus should be wise enough to sense something of this, but alas, he is addled almost as one who is drunk. In one form or another his whole life has been leading to this moment, and now the fantasies he has played through his mind drown out all realities, all common sense. I lay my hand upon his shoulder just as he opens his mouth to blurt another banality, another declaration of a pomp he has not yet won.

Enough, I whisper. *This is not the way.*

He barely hears me; I am a little startled to find him so far gone from the touch of my power, think I smell something else upon him. "Mother," he repeats, a little softer, a little less absurd. "Go to your room. This is man's business now."

Only the faint fluttering of her veil about her breath shows any sign of life in Penelope, as for a moment longer she stands, frozen to stone. Then another breath, a shrouded blinking, and she turns on her heel and marches for the door.

CHAPTER 18

>>

In the great hall:

"There is a trick to it, you see," says the beggar, as his hands encase the bow.

In the armoury:

"Funny how there seems to be exactly enough . . . "

In the kitchens:

"That is the last of Helen's tincture. It will work upon them soon."

"Good. Tell the maids to withdraw – discreetly. Bar the doors when the last is out, and retreat to the wall that looks over the cliff. There are ropes there if we should have to flee."

By the side of Peisenor and Aegyptius:

"Good sirs," breathes Melantho, "Medon asks for you in the council chamber."

"What, now?" barks Peisenor. "At this moment?"

"He should be here," adds Aegyptius, gaze fixed upon the beggar man with the bow. Aegyptius's eyes are growing old and weak, but there is something in that beggar, in the way he turns his head, the way he moves. A thing settles upon the old councillor's heart, a certainty that cannot be true.

"If you will attend him—" Melantho tries again.

"Absolutely not!" retorts Peisenor, and then feels Aegyptius's hand upon his arm.

"Peisenor," murmurs the old man, a most unusual thing to use the warrior's name, a strange kind of urgency in his voice. "We should attend Medon."

"But I—"

"We should attend. Now."

Peisenor makes to splutter, to exclaim, what rot, what absolute ... and then follows Aegyptius's eyes to the beggar as he begins to string the bow. Sees perhaps, just perhaps, a hint of the same thing that his colleague sees. A memory of a younger time, his missing hand itching with it, a recollection of impossible things.

"Gentlemen," breathes Melantho. "If you will follow me."

They follow, and no one marks them, these old men of Odysseus's court.

"There is a trick to it," the beggar breathes, as the bow begins to bend. "See – see if you just understand the wood – see ... "

And in the place where the queen has slept alone for all these twenty years?

Penelope closes the door to her bedroom softly, as Eos scuttles away through the halls, gathering up the last of the maids to run to their place of safety. Considering this, the queen of Ithaca hesitates, then drags her small table, still laden with pots of Helen's powders and ointments, in front of the door. For good measure she adds a stool, barring the way, then steps back to consider her work. It is feeble. She knows it's feeble. But it still makes her feel a little better.

"I brought rope," says a voice behind her.

She spins at once, reaching for the little blade she always keeps concealed in her gown. Priene, sword at her side, knives attached to every spare extremity, lies propped up on her elbows on Penelope's marital bed, a coil of rope at her side. "For

143

escaping through the window," she adds. "To make it easier for you to get down, if they beat at your door."

Penelope lets out a little huff of breath. Technically Priene's presence so casually draped across the bed is a kind of sacrilege, but she long ago relented of trying to get the warrior to conform to such civilised ways as the use of stairs or doorways, let alone private spaces. So she sits down on the opposite side of the pallet, removes her veil, shakes out a little of the tightness in the binding of her hair, sighs again.

"I didn't expect to see you here," she says. "I thought you'd be massing with the women at the temple of Artemis."

"Teodora has it under control," Priene replies. "And it seemed to me that you could use a little protection too, should the worst come to pass."

This is the most sentimental thing Priene has ever said. Penelope's voice catches in her throat; for a moment she is dumb. Priene appears oblivious to this, utterly at ease in her body and her poise.

"It's in my husband's hands, and my son's now," Penelope blurts at last. "We've done what we can."

"You should have let me bring the women. We could have killed the suitors easily."

"And what then?" Penelope shakes her head, swings her legs up onto the bed to match the loose sprawl of Priene's posture. "My husband discovers that the power he holds in this island is not his own, but mine – yours and mine, I mean – the power of women. He will see it as a coup, utterly unacceptable, a great shame, a dishonouring of his valour and his name."

"We could have killed him too, you know," Priene breathes. "No one need ever have known."

"And after?" sighs Penelope. "If we have learned one thing from Clytemnestra, it is that the kings of Greece do not take

144

kindly to a woman killing a man. How many armies could we have held off? For how long? And at what cost?"

Priene's lips curl in displeasure, but she cannot fault the logic.

You could be mine, I breathe. *Forsake your gods, forsake your heart, you will need me in days to come . . .*

"No," continues Penelope, with a little huff of breath. "We need Odysseus's name. The protection his story brings. Without it every petty king in Greece would see us as a target. And Odysseus and Telemachus both – they need to feel like they're doing something for themselves. At least for now."

Priene tuts, shakes her head. "And I thought he was supposed to be clever."

From below, a sudden roaring of men's voices. It is a strange sound, a medley that is hard to unpick. Priene angles her head to hear it a little better – a mixture of adulation and despair, a cry of emotion upon emotion that is too layered to pick apart and say of it cleanly, here is this one thing, this simple truth unfolding through breath and air.

The beggar man has strung the bow.

"If my husband and son do die, as still seems very likely," muses Penelope as the roaring fades, "will you help me to Ourania's boat?"

"Of course."

"I appreciate that. Very much. It is . . . I am grateful."

Priene shrugs. "Anaitis says that it shouldn't matter too much to the women who wins – the men will still fight it out amongst themselves, boy against boy, in the resulting civil war."

"Yes, that seems most likely."

"If they bring in mercenaries, though – if they touch the women . . . Even if you do not make it out of this palace alive, I want you to know that I will fight to defend them. I will fight for that."

"I know. Thank you. And thank you also for being here, for me."

"You are ... useful. To the women, I mean. You are not without use."

This is a lie. Priene knows the warrior's truth: that affection, sentiment, trust, kindness – they die first, when battle is drawn. She had thought she had rid herself of them, purged them from her bosom, burned them on the funeral pyre of her dead queen, Penthesilia. Not enough, of course. Sometimes she looks within herself, and finds that her heart betrays her. It makes her, she knows, a worse captain, a dreadful general, and yet here she is.

Here she is.

I am here, I whisper. *I am waiting for you, when the time is right.*

Another roar from below, this one deeper, richer, resounding in dismay.

The beggar has shot an arrow from the bow. Through the line of axes it has passed like the lightning bolt, slamming square into the wall beyond. The suitors could not have imagined anything like this would come to pass. Some sway towards the beggar, to snatch the bow from his hands – but their feet move oddly, strangely, a tangle of sodden limb. One drops a wine cup. Another tries to stand, and almost immediately falls. No one notices. All eyes are fixed on the old man with the bow.

Priene's head is turned to one side, listening, but her voice is light and sure. "If your husband survives – if we all survive the coming days – I will leave this island. I came here to fight for the women. Not for him."

"I understand," Penelope replies. "My husband's reputation, especially if he does succeed in massacring all the suitors, will act as a shield enough for now. The women can lay down their bows and knives. No one need ever know what we built here. No one need ever ... It is for the best. I know that. It is for the best."

146

Another roar: the beggar has done it again! It wasn't a coincidence, it wasn't a lucky shot, he really is good with a bow! Also, there's something about the way he's standing now, isn't there? A little straighter, a little taller, shoulders back, eyes bright. Limber – that's the word that is coming to mind. *Limber.*

"It has been . . . I have found myself . . . appreciating . . . a little something of this place," Priene muses, as the rolls of sound reverberate up from the hall below. "I did not think when I came here that there would be . . . After my queen died and I left the ashes of the east, it seemed . . . I do not know who to be, if I am not fighting. Not killing Greeks. But Teodora says . . ." Her voice trails off. Teodora says things that are as strange to Priene's heart as they are to mine.

"You know, there's very good hunting on Kephalonia," murmurs Penelope. "And even if we do get a king, whoever he may be, there will still be wolves to contend with and not enough men to do it. I notice that my husband has returned without the flower of Ithaca's manhood, and so . . ."

A final roar from below interrupts Penelope's sentence. This roar will not end until the lungs that gave it voice are silenced, for this is the roar that comes when the beggar man shoots his third arrow, clean into Antinous's throat.

Priene listens, seems to hear the blood pop from the suitor's neck, his last gurgle, his gasping final breaths, nods at nothing much.

". . . What I am saying is should you and maybe Teodora want to take up an unofficial role on that island, there will always be women who would be honoured by your strength," concludes Penelope, as below the screaming begins.

"Thank you," Priene says. Penelope thinks this is the first time she has ever heard these words from the woman's mouth. "My people are travellers, always moving across the plains." Her people are dead, or scattered to the winds. This too is her

147

truth. And so ... "I would be ... curious to see what it is like to have a home."

From below – howls of death, screams of pain. Some suitors are trying to rush to the doors, to escape the armed man who now rains barbed death upon them, only to find that the doors are mysteriously closed. Others as they rise find themselves swaying, bewildered – one laughs hysterically and does not know why, another cries for his father. Not a maid is in sight, nor the old men of Odysseus's council, and as they hammer upon the heavy wood they find more men are drawing blades, Eumaeus and his gang bursting forth from the passage to the armoury in full plate that barely fits their stick-skinny bones, spears in hand and swords at their hips. Telemachus rushes to them to grab a blade, turns and drives a spear straight through Amphinomous's back even as the suitor staggers and tries to grab a chair for a weapon.

Amphinomous turns to see Telemachus's bloody, grinning face standing over him. There is something in the wine, he tries to say, but the spear has plucked the words from his heart.

There is something in the wine.

Amphinomous's eyes are pricked with tears. He does not weep for his death. Rather it is the betrayal, the sheer betrayal. The cruelty of it.

He cannot understand.

And then he dies.

Around the edge of the palace, the maids wait. Some are weeping openly, only to be hushed by Eos and Autonoe. Others stand holding kitchen knives and hidden daggers, grimly waiting to see what might unfold. They have slung rope ladders off the sides of the wall, ready to run and escape should anyone emerge from that hall with bloody looks in their eyes. They will flee to the temple of Artemis, where the other women are waiting, bows in hand, axes at their side. They will flee until they are forgotten – this is all that they can do.

In Penelope's room, Priene listens to the sound of slaughter, of desperate, begging, drunken and drugged men. To the howls of pain and the cries of despair, the tears of the dying and the hollow defiance of the damned. She thought she would savour it more, this massacre of grotesque men, of monstrous Grecian princelings. She thought it would sound sweet in her ears. She is surprised to find that it does not. It leaves her hollow, sickly even, cold.

A cool hand enfolds hers. Penelope stares at the door of her bedroom and says not a word, face ashen as the cacophony rings up from the halls below.

Priene does not pull her hand away, does not squeeze the queen's fingers. Instead she tightens her grip around the hilt of a sheathed blade, and they wait.

When the poets are given gold to sing of these events, they will speak of a roaring battle that turned upon the edge of the deadly blade. They will speak of charges and counter-charges, of treachery and the rallying of warrior men. They will make it sound like a worthy slaughter by Odysseus and his son.

I will be there, of course. Intervening only enough to make it clear that I am blessing this event and desire a very particular outcome – not so much as to detract from Odysseus's righteous and manly efforts. Important, as Penelope says, that this battle is all his own. It must be sung of across the isles, played to drum and lyre in every palace of every petty king throughout Greece. Odysseus, the warrior-king, returns home and in great and bloody fight slays a hundred armed and entirely capable men. Don't you think about challenging Ithaca now, don't you dare raid her shores; her king is a man of infinite fire and vengeance, merciless with the bow and blade – you stay far away, you hear? You leave her shores alone. You leave her people to me.

This is the song that will be sung, and it is wise that it is so. Moreover it will be pleasingly less cannibalistic than previous odes of, for example, Atreus and his kin. The vengeance that Odysseus takes will be against overwhelming odds and to protect his beloved son and wife, rather than a simple expression of his regal power and tyrannical right. This is what I will have said about Odysseus. Perhaps if it is sung enough, one day even I will believe it.

What the poets will not say – and what Odysseus and Telemachus themselves will be too soaked in blood at the time to perceive – is how the suitors struggle to stand. Struggle to rise. Antinous, his lips stained with wine, saw Odysseus draw back the arrow that would fly through his throat, and thought it all a big joke, until it slew him. Eurymachus was preoccupied with the urge to be sick in a corner when the massacre began.

The wine, cries the broken lips of slain Amphinomous.

There is something in the wine.

Even those few suitors who manage to break down a door and rush to the armoury are staggering like men possessed, only to find that the weapons they expected are gone. The poets will reframe this in order to add a certain frisson of extra tension to the experience, rather than say how Telemachus stabbed each man in the back as he worked his way down the hall.

On the walls of the palace, the maids weep and huddle at the sounds of death, and Eos has stopped telling them to hide their tears.

In her bedroom, Penelope clasps Priene's hand, and waits.

Her breath is fast and shallow, but that is her only movement.

She barely blinks.

Does not say a word.

Does not rise, nor pace, nor weep, nor snarl, nor rend her hair.

Merely waits and breathes.

Breathe.

Breathe.

Breathe.

Until slowly – so slowly – the sounds of murder from below grow less.

Here: one tortured cry, cut short.

Here: a gurgle of distress, turned into a slice of blade across throat.

Here: a hammering against a barred door, which ceases.

Here: a body falls, and does not rise. Thump, it goes.

Thump.

And falls no more.

When the slaughter began, the few loyal guards Telemachus could find sealed the gates of the palace. They have stayed sealed since, hiding the sight of blood, the sounds of slaughter.

Outside, the slaves of the fathers wait.

The fathers themselves, Polybus and Eupheithes, and a dozen more aged men of the isles who have sent their sons to beg for an Ithacan crown, are absent. They are better set to the more urgent task of gathering spears and men to defend their sons upon their inevitable and predestined coronations. Thus, when word reaches these old men, it will come in pieces and rumours, half-truths and strange contradictions.

Antinous is slain – no, rather, Eurymachus is! Amphinomous shot an arrow that threaded the axes but killed a man – actually it is Amphinomous who is dead, slaughtered by the men of his own tribe.

The word that trickles from the palace will come out slowly, in half-whispers sobbed over the bloody walls. It is necessary that some whispers are released, rather than absolute silence. Silence speaks of a ringing, deadly certainty – half-truths will buy those inside the palace time. But still, truth will out. It will out.

Aegyptius and Peisenor wait in the empty council chamber. Peisenor sometimes marches to the door, says: "I must fight!"

Aegyptius stops him, shakes his head, holds him back, says nothing more.

Peisenor whispers, and the words nearly break him: "Was it him? Did you see?"

"It has been twenty years . . . "

"But was it him?!"

Aegyptius does not know. Thinks it cannot have been. Odysseus is dead. Odysseus is dead. That is the truth of it. And yet his eyes saw, and he thinks . . .

. . . He does not know what he thinks. The only thing he knows is that while young men scream and die, these two old men are safest behind a heavy barred door.

And then, at last, silence falls over the palace of Odysseus.

CHAPTER 19

>>

Telemachus, coated in blood.

He is proud of his crimson.

Proud that his skin crawls and itches with it.

Proud that there is no part of him that is not bloody.

Wants to lick his lips, taste the life of slaughtered men upon his tongue.

Knows it would be grotesque to do so.

Accidentally does so anyway, for his lips are broken and dry.

Tastes – perhaps Amphinomous, perhaps another man, the scarlet of their hearts upon his tongue.

Is repulsed.

Is enthralled.

Thinks he should be serious, sombre, head bowed, a steadfast warrior bathed in the afternoon sun. Wants to shriek with laughter. Shakes with it. Does not understand this reaction. Does not know where it comes from. Knows it is impossible. Knows it is hysterical, a strange, womanly thing. Blames his mother for having not raised him right, not taught him how to stand over the corpses of his enemies like a man. Does not recognise Eurymachus's face, now he is dead, when he nearly steps on the body of the fallen suitor. Has to stop and look again, really squint and try to see the man's features. Without life to animate it, the face seems like badly moulded clay, all bulging eye and lolling jaw. Telemachus has not appreciated how much life there is in even the most doltish of men, until he sees them without it.

Someone calls his name.

He does not answer. Pokes Eurymachus with a bloody foot, to see if the corpse is real. Is almost surprised to find that it is. That things upon this earth have weight. That Telemachus himself has mass to move, legs, arms, breath.

Someone calls his name again, and this time he looks up.

The voice is unfamiliar, strange, worn with time. It takes a moment to remember it, to place it, to give it a special kind of category: *Father.*

There it is. *Father.*

His father, giving orders.

For a moment, Telemachus almost baulks at that. Someone else — some other man — is giving orders in *his* house. Who does he think he is, this stranger crawled from the sea, that he can just saunter in here and then act like he owns the place? Telemachus has half a mind to snap at him, to tell him to mind his place, but then . . .

. . . then he remembers.

Father.

He had thought the sight of his father in this house would be something else. He had pictured men clad in bronze marching up from the harbour to horn and drum. He had seen his father, resplendent in gold, clasping him by the arms, embracing him, saying "My boy, I am returned, and I am so proud to see you a man." Then they would have sat together and talked long into the night and long into the day that followed, and his father would have held royal council and all the people of the island would have come to lay their homage at his feet and Telemachus would have been right there by his side . . .

154

. . . by his side.

There's the thing.

There's the thing that Telemachus is struggling with, now he tries to drag his senses back from the mires of blood into which they have descended. In his every fantasy, he has been standing by his father's side, but it has never quite been enough. Because in his *most* secret of fantasies, his most treasured, buried of dreams, it is Telemachus who is marching from the harbour to the palace, flanked by men of bronze, his father's body shrouded and borne behind him on a bier of gold. It is Telemachus who has sailed across the seas, slain monsters, driven back great evils and endured terrible storms, all to bring back the body of his father. Telemachus who lights the burial pyre. Telemachus whose brow is wreathed in metal as the ashes of the old world burn away. It is not that he ever wanted his father dead – not at all! Merely that he has always struggled to see how the son is the greatest hero in the land while the father lives.

Now he looks down, and sees his own tunic impossibly gored, his hands lost in drying, blackening blood. And this is of course correct. This is how it had to be. This is the battle he has fought by his father's side, the needful thing, the necessary thing, this is . . . He is not sure what this is . . . he is not sure of anything any more. He is not sure what the word "father" even means, or how it is to be a son.

"Telemachus!"

His father's voice – no. That's not right. Odysseus's voice. Telemachus has never known his father, but he knows the voice of Odysseus, he knows the sound of a hero, the sound of a king, has known it all his life, from the first stories whispered over his crib to the songs of the poets ringing through these halls.

Odysseus speaks. "Telemachus, where are the maids?"

"I, uh . . . I don't know."

"They fled to the walls." Euracleia in the door, Eumaeus

by her side. Her eyes glow bright and bloody in the reflected carnage, her hands shake where she clasps them by her bosom. It should be womanly distress, Telemachus thinks – it should be weakened horror. It is not. A primal thrill that would have stirred the Furies themselves ripples through the old nursemaid as she beholds the slaughter. He sees her nostrils flare as she drinks in the stench of slaughtered suitors.

"Fetch them here," Odysseus barks – there it is again. Odysseus. Telemachus looks at the old beggar man and sees not Father, not anything he can relate to this word, but something more. *Odysseus*. He does not move.

Eumaeus says: "We will fetch them immediately, my king."

The king of Ithaca nods once, brisk, as Eumaeus and Euracleia slip away into the hot afternoon light. He stands in the centre of the room, as bloody as Telemachus, the bow at his feet. He shot every arrow he could, and when there was no more space to move, he drew the bronze sword and dagger that Penelope had so fortuitously, so accidentally, placed at his side. Telemachus's brow furrows at that thought. There are a number of things about this whole affair that strike him as oddly fortuitous, but he cannot quite . . .

"Odysseus?"

The voice that says this word doesn't give it the weight it should carry. It should be said like this: *Odysseus, oh great hero, warrior, king!* Instead it is said like this: *Odysseus? Is that really you?*

Telemachus shuffles numbly on the spot, nearly slipping in a pool of blood, staggering to regain his footing. Amphinomous's body has fallen strangely, half propped up by the spear Telemachus drove through his back. The effect makes him seem more like crab than man, limbs in strange lines, head at a curious angle, enquiring, as though to say: *Did you do this to me?*

In the door, the man who spoke – Aegyptius, old Peisenor at his side.

Odysseus turns, looks his councillors up and down once, says simply: "Aegyptius. Peisenor. And is Medon . . . ?"

"Alive," says Aegyptius. "As far as we know."

A single nod. This is all the information Odysseus requires, after twenty years away from home. Meaningful greetings, cries of "But what . . . but how . . . but tell me all!" will have to wait for the bodies – so, so many bodies – to be burned.

A gasp from another door.

Euracleia and Eumaeus have returned, and with them, the maids.

They cluster in the doorway, holding their faces, their noses away. They do not recognise this place, this great hall of the palace. They have cleaned every stone and scrubbed every wall, swept ashes from the hearth and laid the table here for so many years, and now – now what a crimson hall of horrors has been made of their work. Phiobe shrieks and presses her face into a woman's shoulder, turning from the gore. Melantho vomits, tears and bile mixing about her lips. Eos holds Autonoe's hand, Autonoe grasps Eos. Melitta stands silently weeping, shaking but stiff. The women of the house of Odysseus – so many women – behold the slain bodies of the men who would have been their tyrants, their conquerors, their oppressors, their loved ones, their playthings, their sharers of secrets and maybe even – just maybe for a few of these slaughtered men – their friends. And if their hearts do not move to see such a kind of man as these dead, still they weep, still they sob to witness the bloody breaking of the world that was, the bloody birth of the world that is to come.

Then Odysseus, still wreathed in gore, says: "I am Odysseus, king of Ithaca. Take these bodies from the hall and pile them up by the wall."

It is Eos who tries to say: their fathers, their fathers will need the bodies for—

"You will obey your king!" roars Odysseus, and something

157

in his voice is enough to snap Telemachus too from his stupor, for he steps now towards Eos, bloody sword in hand, and looks for a moment as if he might run her through at her defiance.

This boy – this Telemachus. Eos has known him since he was a babe. She held his mother's hand as he was born, helped Ourania swaddle him and press him to Penelope's chest. She wiped his grazed knees when he fell, showed him how the women wove their garlands when he was still young enough not to understand the difference between men and women's things. And now here he is, blade in hand, blood in his eyes, looming over her and hissing like the wordless snake.

"Ladies." Autonoe's voice is shaking but strong. "Let us obey the king."

CHAPTER 20

>>>

By the time the sun is dipping below the horizon, the blood can be smelled from Penelope's room.

She stands in the window, Priene by her side. She can see the sea, hear the sounds of women weeping, of movement, of bustle and motion. But no one has yet come to her door.

Priene says: "I'll check . . ."

But Penelope grabs her arm, shakes her head, holds her back. "No. If my husband is dead then I would expect my door to already be battered upon by someone seeking to carry me away. And if he lives . . . then I must not be seen to be disobeying a word a man has said, even my son. My survival depends on it."

Priene clicks her tongue disapprovingly inside her mouth, but does not leave Penelope's side.

And yet another question, beating silently beneath their racing hearts: where are the maids?

A group of men is gathering at the gates by the time the first stars are pricking the horizon, demanding to know: what has happened? What is happening? Who is our king? They are not yet aggressive, not yet banging on the walls. But their impatience will only grow, as the night draws in.

The maids pile the bodies of the suitors by the wall.

It is a grotesque sight. Even I, who am steeped in blood and battle, am repulsed by it. It is the kind of disregard that would make Ares cock one bushy brow. The bodies of men, even men such as these, should not be laid one upon another within the reach of crows, like wet bloody bricks. The stench of them will soon reach beyond the palace walls, the roll of death drifting to the sea. It is a crude declaration of Odysseus's return to his kingdom.

Odysseus, I breathe, *this is not wise.*

In the hall, Eumaeus has given the maids shovels to clear the blood and gore. It is too thick, too gummed and sticky for mere scrubbing to remove. Instead, like mud, it must be slapped away and tipped into buckets. Not a stomach remains that has not emptied itself in a bitter pool at the work, nor are there tears left to weep in a single eye. Odysseus sits bloody upon his throne and watches the women work, sword still across his lap, while Telemachus snarls and paces across the hall.

Soon there are no bodies left within the place, merely scraped paths of gory crimson, and Euracleia lights a fire and throws sulphur upon it to drive away the fumes of death. Peisenor and Aegyptius sit as frozen statues beneath Odysseus's chair, eyes running at the stench, bones popping against thin, cracking skin.

My Odysseus, I whisper in the king's ear, *you have done what you needed to. The poems will be sung. Men will fear you. Your kingdom will be safe.*

He does not heed me.

I am briefly shocked, outraged even, to find his mind so shuttered to my imprecations. I touch him lightly on the shoulder, tempted even to shake him – just a little, that being all a mortal can handle of a goddess's touch – to remind him of my presence and his duty. He does not stir. His breath comes in thick, flaring sucks through his nose, mouth pinched tight. His lungs billow and deflate with each draw of it, each gasp. It is how he was when he clung onto that single trailing olive branch above the great mouth of the whirlpool, while Scylla hissed and snarled in her cave overhead. Hanging on. Just hanging on. When the past is meaningless and the future beyond your control, it is all Odysseus ever does. He hangs on.

Odysseus, I whisper, a pang of something lancing through me – what may we call this? Some notion of attachment, maybe even of regret, rippling through my chest. The knowing it is there hurts almost more than the feeling itself. *Odysseus, you are safe now. You are home now. Odysseus . . .*

He turns his face from me. I stop myself from gasping in outrage, from summoning my blazing spear. "Euracleia," he barks across the hall, to the watching old woman. "Come here."

She picks her way through the trails of blood and shovel-scraped floor, to avoid too much staining her hem, and leans in close by his side. "Tell me," he says. "Which of these woman have been disloyal to my house?"

Euracleia's eyes flicker round the hall. She draws in her lower lip, takes in a thoughtful, prolonged breath.

Odysseus, I breathe. *This is not necessary. This is not needful. You have done your work. Your name will secure your kingdom, no man will dare—*

"Her," whispers Euracleia, pointing across the hall. "And her. Her. She's a whore."

Odysseus nods thoughtfully, following each finger to the maid it picks upon.

Odysseus. My voice rises in a little urgency. *This is not necessary, it is not required, it is not—*

"Telemachus! Join us, please."

Telemachus crosses the hall to his father's side, nods as if he were wise while Euracleia points without naming, *her, her, her . . .*

I reach again for Odysseus, for his mind, his heart, *hanging on*, he is always clinging to that olive branch and hanging on . . .

I think I should see chaos. I should see a soul being rent in two. I should see something of Heracles' madness, an insanity bursting upon him.

I do not.

Instead I see fixed within him an absolute certainty, a calm as calm as any there has ever been. I see him sitting by the fire on Circe's island as the witch bade him journey to the grey lands and the realms beyond. I see him crying out in ecstasy beneath the nymph Calypso's body, weeping upon his white-stained stone as he beheld the endless sea that bound her island, kissing her fingers as she whispered: *I could make you a god.* I see him naked before a princess of the Phaeacians, humbly grovelling for her help. I see him, a beggar in his own palace, as the suitors hurl insults upon him. His face turned away from that of his wife.

And there it is. The beating truth that blazes back against even my divinity. The fire that burns through all of it, through Circe's caresses and Calypso's kisses, through the soft touch of that Phaeacian princess and the blazing ruins of Troy. There is it: four words.

Master of my house.

Then I look up, and there he is.

My brother Ares, leaning against the door.

He is picking dirt the colour of old scabs from beneath his nails with the tip of a blade, giving neither me nor the mortals about their business any attention. Yet clearly he has also been busy walking these halls, for his feet and ankles are smeared with clotted blood, and he draws in deep the breath of slaughter. I rouse myself to hurl scorn upon his name, to holler *how dare you be in this place?* – but stop myself.

His power does not work upon Odysseus's mind.

His divinity does not blazon through Telemachus's chest.

162

He is here, most assuredly, most maliciously setting foot on an island that all the gods had agreed would be *my* dominion. But he does not work upon it. Merely watches, and enjoys all that he sees.

He does not need to speak. Odysseus is mine, of course, but the others of Olympus – they are always watching, always waiting for a show of weakness. For the faintest sign of vulnerability in wise Athena, the slightest flicker of sentiment. They must never know.

War does not flinch.

Wisdom is not kind.

Ares looks up, sees me, smiles.

It is the smile of the wolf that smells the weakness of a faltering prey.

Then he is gone, as quickly as he came, and I gasp to shake the weight of him from my presence, even as Odysseus rises.

"Bring the maids into the yard," he says.

Telemachus nods, bids Eumaeus fetch some rope.

Aegyptius tries to splutter, Peisenor looks like he might be sick.

"Do not be gentle with any who resist," adds Odysseus. "All must watch."

Euracleia straightens, sways. Is elated. Is bewildered. She has yearned for power for so long, yearned to be seen, to be honoured, to be once again the greatest of the slaves – that was her only ever ambition. Now she has what she desires. Now there are consequences. Euracleia never considered consequences.

Master of my house, roars the heart of Odysseus, as the maids are gathered in the moonlit courtyard outside.

Master of my house.

Telemachus throws a rope across a beam that juts out from a supporting column.

Tests its strength.

Ties a knot.

Master of my house, thunders the heart of Odysseus, as Circe sings and Calypso laughs and the suitors bleed and die screaming at his feet. *Master of my house.*

And I? I, goddess of war and wisdom? The only creature living who, besides Zeus, dares wield the thunderbolt? What do I do?

I do nothing.

I do nothing as Telemachus makes a noose.

I do nothing as the men of Eumaeus and Odysseus's son form a circle around the maids, blades in hand.

I do nothing as Autonoe, then Melitta, Melantho, Eos and all the rest fall weeping, begging, praying – we are innocent, we are innocent!

I, the great goddess, wielder of the thunderbolt and the golden shield, do not draw my sword nor raise my spear, for my siblings are watching, and this too – why even this – is part of the story of Odysseus. It will be sung by the poets as purification. As the final cleansing of the house. It will join the ballads of the women of Greece – Helen the whore, Clytemnestra the murderer, Penelope who waited chaste and alone. It will be the final, necessary chorus that heralds the return of the master of the house.

And Athena does not weep for innocents, nor raise her hands for slaves.

Sometimes war is won by cowards.

Sometimes wisdom is turning your face away.

In that moment, I despise myself. That is also the truth of these things.

The maids begin to scream, as Telemachus grabs the first by the arm.

CHAPTER 21

>>

The screams are what make Priene draw her blade.

"Women," she whispers. "Afraid."

Penelope holds her arm, shakes her head, doesn't know what to do. How long have they stood in this window, waiting? She doesn't know. The stars tonight are beautiful. The sound of women's screaming suddenly seems to give their light a razored, bitter edge.

More wails, howls, imprecations – mercy, mercy!

Priene moves towards the window.

"It might not be . . . " Penelope whispers, her lips stuttering over the words. "Perhaps it is not . . . "

Priene's own lips curl in distaste. Cowardly lies, half-truths – she expects more from the queen of Ithaca.

Then: a hammering at the door. A thin, desperate voice calling out. It is Phiobe, one of the youngest of the maids. She slipped away when Euracleia gathered the women, darted through the halls. Her body is coated in the blood she has been shovelling; her voice is stained with horror and tears.

"Penelope!" she shrieks. "He's killing us!"

*

165

My kindred are not looking at Penelope; their eyes are all on Odysseus.

I help Penelope and Priene drag back the furniture that blocks her bedroom door. I carry them on silver wings through the palace, catch them when they nearly slip on the blood in the hall, turn their faces away, their eyes forward – no time to dwell on this now, only onwards, onwards!

I fill their lungs with breath as I propel them into the court-yard, give their eyes the sharpness of the gods, their voices the strength of the heavens. It is too late, of course. For the maids, for the poets, for the master of the house, for the stories that must be sung – it is too late.

Three bodies are already hanging, tongues rolling and blue, eyes bulging in their faces. Autonoe stands below, Telemachus by her side. There is a noose about her neck, she is screaming, clawing, fighting her fate. She has a hidden blade that she has drawn, nearly had Telemachus's eye out – but Odysseus caught it before she could stab and now she is one pull of the rope away from death, cursing without language, just a primal howl of fury and despair.

At this sight Priene draws her blade, and at once Odysseus turns, raising his own.

Penelope falls to her knees.

I catch her, hold back her hair from her face, my hand on her back as she gasps, gasps, raises her eyes, cannot look, gasps.

Odysseus lowers his blade at the sight of his wife.

Priene does not lower hers.

Penelope curls over her spine, and I hold her still, one hand on her back, breathing with her, slowing her breath down, slow now, slow now. Do not fall. Do not weep.

She presses her hands into the bloody earth for stability, rest-ing on all fours.

166

I raise her head, catch her before she can scream, breathe again my strength into her lungs.

Melantho, Melitta, Eos.

They dangle suspended above the ground, their arms loose by their sides. I help Penelope rise a little, catch her as she staggers, ease her once again to her knees at Eos's feet. The maid's hair has come loose and tangled. Penelope wants to reach up, touch it, run it through her fingers, but to rise now seems impossible, even with my godly strength. The soles of Eos's feet are bloody from her labours, walking through gore and hauling bodies to their end. Penelope kisses her toes, the tops of her feet, her bare, cold shins. Wraps her arms around Eos's legs, holds her tight, holds her close, and without sound, cries until the tears drip off Eos's pointed feet to salt the cruel earth below.

Priene stands by her side, something hot in her eyes, sword still raised, levelled towards bloody Odysseus's chest.

The others watch.

They watch the bodies swaying in the low night breeze.

Watch Penelope sob at the feet of her maid.

Watch Odysseus.

Watch Telemachus.

Hear only the gasping of broken breath.

Enough, I say to Odysseus.

"Odysseus," calls Peisenor from the edge of the yard, and finding nothing else to add, says again: "Odysseus."

Master of my house.

I brush the hair from Penelope's face one last time, then rise. I kiss Eos's brow, soothe down her rippling gown, turn and face the Ithacan king.

The relentless drumbeat falters within Odysseus's chest.

He turns and seems to see at last: his son, a noose about the throat of an unarmed maid. Bodies piled like clay against the wall. His councillors, shaking and pale by the door. The women, hanging. The women, covered in blood. His wife, weeping. Himself, painted in gore.

It is the sight of Penelope that he gazes upon the most. He is used to the cries of women, of course. He learned to ignore them, to shut them out – they were nothing more than the lilting accompaniment to the hollow drums of war. Yet now he looks upon the tears of one who has . . . *meaning* to him, and it is as if the shadows of the maids live again, the shadows of the women of Troy, as if all the work he had put into rendering their lives meaningless is now blasted apart and they are living creatures again, alive, vibrant, calling out in horror his name.

All this at last Odysseus sees.

At last Odysseus understands.

It is not perhaps mercy for the women that sways him. Merely an understanding that when the poets sing this part of his story, it will not quite be the song he imagined.

He sheathes his blade.

Shakes his head.

Turns to his son.

"Enough," he says. "It is enough."

Telemachus is reluctant to let Autonoe go. He sometimes wondered what it would be like, to feel her flesh so close to his, feel her heart, her breath. As a boy first coming into manhood, he would look upon her and feel . . . stirrings . . . and know that it was base and grotesque but feel them anyway. He would never debase himself with one of his mother's maids, of course, but still – but still. There is something in this moment, in her panting chest, in her face pressed so close to his . . .

"Telemachus," barks Odysseus, a little louder. "Enough."

Telemachus lets Autonoe go.

Euracleia opens her mouth to object, but a look from the king silences her.

He stares down at his wife, her face still pressed to Eos's feet. Seems as if he would say some words. Does not.

Turns, and finally, with slow, shuffling step, returns unto his palace.

CHAPTER 22

>>

The women wash the bodies of the maids in fresh water from the little stream that flows through the palace to the cliffs.

They sing the songs that only the women know.

Penelope places a silver necklace around Eos's neck, that no one might see the ugly tears of the hanging rope.

They burn the finest incense, lay the sweetest flowers.

Shroud the bodies as tenderly as though they are new-born babes.

There is nowhere convenient to bury them within the palace, and the gates are still barred. That growing crowd of men outside is growing more, drawn by the smell of death, the songs of mourning that drift through the palace walls.

The women stay up all night, to sing their sisters away.

Melantho, they cry, *who always made us laugh.*

Melitta, they sing, *quick and clever.*

Eos, they proclaim, *who only said things that were true.*

They comb the women's hair, wash the dirt from beneath their feet. The ministrations they receive in death are more tender than those they had when living.

And when the first touch of dawn comes, Priene lifts up the

mourners from the ground, one at a time, whispers, *come away*, and together they go to the palace gates.

The guards of Odysseus have been told to keep these gates sealed, but Penelope stands at the women's head and is still, technically, a queen. Moreover there is that in Priene's eye that brooks no disagreement and so, reluctantly, they unbar the gates – just a little.

The women walk out, charcoal upon their brows, ashes and blood upon their gowns, Priene in their midst. They carry their murdered sisters upon their shoulders, walking them to a place of sacred rest. The assembled people part for them, some crying out – what has happened? What has happened in the palace? Whose blood is this? Who is our king?

The women do not answer, and just this once, there is that in their funereal manner that brooks no sacrilege.

Penelope stays behind, watching them go.

Autonoe is the last to leave, glances back just once over her shoulder at her queen, before the gates close behind them and the palace is sealed once more.

Alone, Penelope returns to her room.

It is empty, the door unguarded and standing open.

There is no fresh water in a bowl, no sweet wine to drink.

She sits by the distorted mirror and sees a face that has not slept, smeared in ashes.

No maids pad through the palace halls.

No voices are raised in merry morning mirth.

She touches the comb with which Eos should caress her hair.

Knows she should stand. Take action. Be a queen.

She does not move.

Then he is in her doorway.

He has washed the blood from his skin, put on a new tunic

and cloak. He and Telemachus struggled to find these things without a maid to bring them, the organisation of the palace something of a mystery to both father and son. Only with Euracleia's help was the bare minimum of royal, unblooded attire achieved.

He carries no weapon. Eumaeus and Telemachus's men stand ready with spears along the walls about the palace downstairs. No one will be permitted to enter this place with swords again.

He says: "Penelope."

She closes her eyes, lets out a breath, does not look at him.

"Penelope. Look at me."

She straightens her back. The sight is magnificent and abhorrent; I confess to being fascinated by it. The queen of Ithaca wipes away her tears, wipes away her womanhood, wipes away her sorrows, wipes away her despair, wipes away the woman called Penelope. All that is left is a queen, hollowed.

"I do not know you, sir," she says. "It is not suitable that you are in this place."

"You know me," he replies. "You know who I am."

She rises from her chair. "You said you were a sailor from Crete. Lost at sea. And now you want me to believe you are . . . who? My husband? I have had plenty of men come to this palace over the years pretending to be him, or to have some knowledge of him, in the hope of winning favour. It has all been most crude and despicable."

He takes one step into the room, and she does not flinch, and she does not blink, and she does not welcome him in. "Look at me," he says. "You know me."

"Do I? Perhaps you look a little like my husband, but I have not seen him for twenty years. We were young, I even more than he, and who knows how he might have changed, or how my memory of him might have grown flawed. You could be any man, come into my palace. Not Odysseus."

172

"I am Odysseus. I am your husband."

A snort of contempt – she had this sound from Clytemnestra, and now she uses it well, finally knows how it feels, relishes the poison of it within her breast. Didn't think she understood her cousin until this moment. "If you are he, prove it. Prove that you are not just another liar, come to break my widow's heart. Prove you are Odysseus."

His eyes dart round the room, take her in, things that are familiar, things that are changed. It occurs to Odysseus that he has not yet looked upon Penelope as a woman. She is a queen, a wife to be reclaimed – but she has also aged. She was barely more than a girl when he saw her last, and he had somehow always pictured her as much the same when he returned home, hardly imagining that time might have acted upon this figure from his memories. In a way he is relieved – he was concerned that the grey in his hair might make her scorn him, but no, there is grey in hers too. Her skin has been worn by sun, her belly is a little softer than once it was, her hands more weathered, her face grown into something that looks with more – so much more – than the naïve curiosity of a child upon this world. She is, he realises, plainer than he had remembered her, and this is a huge relief that nearly staggers him off his feet. The two of them can be plain together, he thinks. Expectations can be lowered accordingly.

She stands, one hand resting upon the tabletop by her fingertips, the barest shimmer of support, waiting.

He looks away, about the room. "I told you of my brooch, the one you gave me . . . " he begins, and at once she dismisses it.

"A Cretan sailor could have seen it, as you claimed to have done. That means nothing."

"Our wedding day, the vows we made . . . "

"Many people were present there, and many more could have overheard our more private conversations. In matters of marriage between prince and princess, discretion is a disadvantage."

Again his eyes run round the room. "The bed," he says. "I carved that bed. From an olive tree. It grows through the house, it was my gift to you, a living monument. I did it without help from any other man, and you swore you would keep it a secret, just for you and me, so we would always know each other. Always be true. I am Odysseus. I am your husband."

He addresses these words to the bed itself, as if not quite believing it is still there. Then on finishing, raises his gaze, looks at Penelope, and sees.

Sees that she knows him.

Sees that she understands.

Her face is pinched pottery, but even if she were not his wife, he would know. She knows.

He moves towards her, raising his arms, but at once she steps back, draws a blade from within her gown, holds it defiantly towards him. He is astonished, baffled, dismayed.

"If you were my husband," she snarls, "*you would not have murdered my maids!*"

The shriek of it rolls through the house, echoes, fades.

Odysseus sways as if punched by the raging sea.

Then straightens.

Looks his wife in the eye.

"I did what I had to do," he declares, "to purify my house."

The knife drifts back and forth in Penelope's hand. She will not strike, but neither does she let go. He sees this also, sees the futility of it, straightens a little more, eyebrows rising. Perhaps his wife needs purification too; the thought has gnawed at his imagination these long, empty years. It was with him every time he told Menelaus: "my Penelope is loyal" and the Spartan laughed. On the tip of his tongue whenever Circe or Calypso mentioned Penelope, before they learned he did not want them to. And now here she is, weeping for whores and slaves. Here she is.

"They were *good*," hisses Penelope. "They were good, they served me, they were mine! Every day, every day you were gone, every day – how could you? How could you? She was ..." Her words choke, break, the knife sways again, she catches herself on the table before she can fall. I drift behind her, watching Penelope, watching Odysseus.

Downstairs, Telemachus sits in a chair beneath his father's throne.

It is the same chair he always sat in when his father was away.

Somehow he imagined that it would be different when Odysseus came home.

By dawn's light, the procession of women weave their way to the temple of Artemis. All along the road, other women have come to join them. They are armed with dagger and hunting bow, woodcutter's axe and pitchfork for bringing the harvest home. They sing the songs of loss, the songs of betrayal, as they carry the bodies of Eos, Melitta and Melantho to their rest beneath the cypress tree.

In the bedroom of the king and queen of Ithaca, Odysseus does not move.

He could take away Penelope's knife in a moment, of course.

Smack the blade to the ground, throw his wife upon the bed.

Make his feelings known.

He does not.

A part of him wants to. A raging, swelling, ugly part that threatens to burst through his chest. Any other man – any other king – would do it, and that is the primary thought that stops him, because if he believes one thing about himself, one thing above all others, it is that he is not like any other man.

Penelope sees this, supposes it is something she should feel grateful for. Her husband has in this one particular surpassed her expectations, such as they were.

Slowly, she lowers her knife.

Lays it on the table beside her.

Looks her husband in the eye.

Says: "By sunset, the fathers of the men you have slain will have heard what you have done. Eupheithes and Polybus can each raise fifty spears, and have the gold to muster at least fifty more in mercenaries, who they started recruiting the moment Telemachus returned home, knowing perfectly well that my son would be set on murdering theirs. My maids – Melantho, Melitta and . . . "

The name, the name, she can barely say it, swallows it home, chokes it back out again. " . . . Eos . . . plied their sons and their sons' retainers with wine, sweet talk and kind words to learn of this. You have twenty men at the most able to fight, along with some half-dozen or so guards of the palace who you can perhaps rely on. This may be enough to kill the unarmed suitors in the hall. It will not be enough to hold off a hundred armed, organised warriors."

Odysseus listens, and Odysseus does not move. In Agamemnon's tent in Troy, he became supremely gifted in this art, of staying so still he seemed to vanish into the fabric. He had not thought it would be of such service in his own bedroom.

Penelope takes in another shuddering breath, draws it all the way down. Removes her hand from the table. Steadies herself. Continues. "Twenty men can hold the palace gate, but are not enough to cover the walls. The length of the fortification is its weakness, and this place will shortly become indefensible. I am going to retreat to my father-in-law's farm in the hills. Its size negates any advantage of numbers and it has solid defences. You may come with me, or you can stay here, and die. I really don't care."

She grabs her cloak, makes to march for the door.

He catches her arm as she moves by him, holds tight.

Their breath mingles, eye to eye, skin to skin, fast, thin.

In all his imaginings – his bloody fantasies, his sentimental musings, his naïve dreams and bitter, vengeful thoughts of blood – he had not imagined this. Circe talked to him once in this haughty manner, and he held her by the throat as her magics failed, and smiled. Calypso never needed to speak to him so – her power was so thoughtlessly profound she barely even seemed to notice it for what it was. He wonders if he should grasp Penelope by the throat too, but as quickly as the thought arises, there are other, more urgent thoughts beating against his salt-stained skull.

Thoughts like: *we cannot hold the palace walls.*

For a moment, the two stand locked together, eye to eye, but his mind is already moving to another place.

Your wife can wait, I whisper in his ear. *She has waited this long, she can wait a little longer. The throne, however . . .*

Odysseus lets go of Penelope's arm. Says: "I will not abandon my palace," and knows even as he does that these are the kind of pig-headed nonsense words that have killed half the kings of Greece. Ordinary words, in short. The words of an ordinary kind of man.

"Then you will die in it," she replies briskly. "My husband was wise enough to know not to try and defend the indefensible. Eupheithes and Polybus will be here with their men before the moon rises. Do what you want."

Again she moves to the door, and this time he does not stop her, until his voice rings out behind her as she is nearly in the hall.

"I am Odysseus," he says.

He says it as much for himself as for her, a steadying thing. Odysseus: a man far too clever to make a mistake, no?

She looks back, considers him for just a moment, turns away. "You should have given the suitors proper burial," she replies. "That would have been smart, as well as just. You still have time to lay out the bodies in the yard and shroud them in whatever you can – that will incense their fathers less, when they break down the gates. Of course, now you have killed my maids and the rest are fled from your butchery, you'll have to do that for yourself."

So saying, she walks away, and he does not try to stop her.

CHAPTER 23

>>>>>>>>>>>>>>>>>>>>>>>>>>>>>>>>>>>>>>

Evening over Ithaca.

Penelope slips down the rope ladder suspended on the side of the palace wall. There are too many fathers of too many dead men arrayed around the gates to make that route appealing.

Below – a stick-narrow path above a sheer drop of cliff.

Beyond – the open scraggy island.

Old farmer Semele and Teodora, lieutenant of Priene, are waiting for her as she shuffles her way, unseen and unchallenged, away from the walls. Only Odysseus watches her go, from a high window of the palace, and he does not try to send men after her retreat. Not least because she is also correct in this particular – he does not have the men to send.

At the palace gate, the crowd has grown loud, angry, restless.

They hammer on the wood, speak of bashing it down, making their indignation known.

Word has reached the fathers of the suitors, whispered out through palace walls, of their sons' deaths.

Polybus falls to the floor, clutching his chest.

Eupheithes takes the news like a stone bouncing upon the wall of a cliff, and says simply: "Bring me my spear."

Both these men have been dreadful fathers. Their sons were not men at all, not creatures of flesh and bone to be nurtured and raised into the light. Rather they were extensions of each old man's identity, limbs to express the wealth of Polybus, the cunning of Eupheithes. Never was it said that these men were *Eupheithes, father of Antinous*, or *Polybus, father of Eurymachus*. Fatherhood was not a notion that served. Rather – Antinous, *son* of Eupheithes; Eurymachus, *son* of Polybus. Adjuncts to the glory of he who made them.

Did these fathers love their sons?

Or did they rather love some mirror of their own imagined glories?

I am no goddess of affection, but I know that even the simplest of creatures most often loves both.

The flies swarm above the bloated corpses of the suitors, flesh bubbling and skin sloughing away. Odysseus says: "We must shroud them."

"Father . . . " begins Telemachus, indignant, outraged.

"We do not have time to bury them," he snaps, "but neither can we leave them in this sorry state. They have been slaughtered to a man. That is enough. It is . . . it is enough."

This word, "enough", it is beginning to slip into him. To sneak through the sea-sunken and salt-storm tempest of his raging heart. He thought about it once before, when Calypso wound him in her sheets. Thought that maybe being contented on an island, not a king, merely a lover, might be enough. Then he rebelled against it. He had, by then, already begun to believe the story of himself that he would later tell others, and it could only end in glory.

Master of my house, he thinks, as Eumaeus and his men, choking on bile, cloths across their mouths, struggle to rearrange the piled bodies of slaughtered men into something resembling the minimum of dignity. Odysseus watches them work as the sun creeps towards the horizon, as fists bang against the gates.

"Father . . . " Telemachus tries again, and there is something in his son's voice that is really quite irritating for Odysseus. The boy manages to be both needy and officious, like a hungry dog that whines when it wants to bite.

"Your mother is correct," he snaps, and at once Telemachus flinches. He tries to soften his voice, to remember that this is a boy raised without a father, whose house was invaded and who has just fought savagely against men who – the more Odysseus thinks about it – did not seem entirely capable of fighting back. "The fathers of these men will not accept what has happened here. They will muster spears and march on the palace – and we are not enough to hold it."

"But you are here. You are—"

"I fight with my head, boy. These walls are too long to be defended. Against actual warriors, well armed and well pre-pared, we will be overrun."

"You can't – you are Odysseus – this is—"

"Penelope mentioned your grandfather's farm. Said it has walls. Is that correct?"

"What? I mean . . . when I left, they were rebuilding it, yes, there was talk of walls and—"

"What manner of walls? High enough to be hard to climb? Is there a gate?"

"I don't know. Grandfather wanted a gate, but I sailed before the work had begun."

A sharp nod. Odysseus remembers this feeling of authority, faintly, from years ago. Commanding men. It is an old habit, a recollection returning to the tip of his tongue. "We will go there. My father may be of some use in dividing our enemies. He was friends with some of the suitors' fathers, one time, may be able to talk some of them round. As soon as the bodies are prepared, we will leave secretly by the clifftop path your mother took."

"Mother is . . . "

"Gone."

"She left you?"

Telemachus doesn't want to say it, can't quite bring himself to utter the words, but surely – surely – this means his mother is the lying whore he's always feared? He saw what Orestes did to Clytemnestra, how brave Orestes was as he held the blade, and of course Telemachus is a good man, he doesn't want to have to kill his mother, but if she has dishonoured his father then . . . well then . . . the sons of Odysseus cannot be weaker than the sons of Agamemnon, no?

Odysseus sees his son, the anguish in his face, and does not yet fully understand what lies beneath it. The last time he held Telemachus in his arms, the boy was a babe, laid before a plough in an attempt to deceive the herald of Agamemnon. Odysseus has only his fantasies of a childhood, the loose sense of what he would like his son to be – no truth at all on which to fashion his opinions. He sees the son he wants his son to be, and for a while longer will shape the evidence of his eyes to concur with the desires of his heart. He knows that he has the right to call himself father, to demand piety, to act with command, to embrace his child and say "now, listen to me". He also knows, in a more honest part of his heart, that he has not earned these things that he now claims.

He puts his hand on Telemachus's shoulder.

The effect should be moving, a wellspring of connection re-forged between father and son. It is instead remarkably awkward, and I am once again pleased that the poets who will sing of this are absent. "Penelope . . . Your mother understood that this place cannot be defended. For me . . . for us . . . She and I need time." Odysseus is old now, he realises. He is old.

182

He does not dare let his son see it. "Perhaps . . . the way things have fallen . . . "

A shake of his head. He turns his face away from the lines of dead men, from his son's expression of hurt, confusion, betrayal. "Inform me when this is done. We withdraw as soon as it is dark."

And so, as the last light of day fades . . .

A hammering at the gate, a thundering, they have brought up ladders, they have brought up a battering ram – boom!

The gates of the palace of Odysseus burst open and men tumble in. Many are armed, the slaves and servants of suitors' fathers, and men whose blades can be bought. They recoil at once, not from the resistance of other men, but from the stench of death that fills the courtyard. The bodies of the suitors are laid out in neat rows, arms crossed and eyes closed. By the light of oil lamps every face is inspected, but even their own fathers struggle to recognise the waxen boys of their slaughtered kin.

Some fall weeping when they find their murdered child.

Some beg forgiveness. Forgive me, my boy, my boy, forgive me! I made you come here, I made you do this, it was me, my pride, my pride, my ambition, forgive me!

It is Eupheithes who picks these wailing fathers up, not bothering to even search the yard for his slaughtered Antinous.

"It was not us," he declares, eyes fixed on some other place. "It was Odysseus."

The men start searching the palace at a run, bursting through doors and crying out in battle fury.

They find no one. Not a trace of life, save the streaks of blood that the maids could not scrub from the stones.

Soon their run slows to a walk, as curious they pick their way through these unfamiliar halls by oil light, examining the frescoes and peering round open doors. Some talk of setting a fire, burning the whole thing to the ground, but no one does. The smell of death from the yard outside is a warning, a declaration, a threat.

He may be gone for now, but Odysseus will return.

"He is just a man," barks Eupheithes, face turned away from the moon as if even that light might blind him. "He is just a murderer on the run."

His soldiers and slaves look at the slaughtered corpses of their comrades, friends, brothers, cousins, laid out across the sodden scarlet earth, and are not sure they believe.

Believe, I whisper in their ears. *Let my stories spear your hearts.*

"He'll have gone to his father," mutters Polybus. "Or the temple of Athena."

Eupheithes nods, just once. "We bury our sons tonight," he proclaims, though he will never look upon his son's face again, nor say the name Antinous so long as he has power over himself. "And tomorrow we kill Odysseus."

CHAPTER 24

At the temple of Artemis, the women assemble.

Penelope has come here first, before going to Laertes. She addresses the women by torchlight. Says: you must stay here. It is not safe to leave this shrine.

Her maids – those who are left alive – look at each other.

Phiobe didn't stop crying until Anaitis gave her a little something in her drink.

Eurynome keeps on forgetting that thing she was about to say.

Some have tried to wash the blood from their clothes; a few have been given fresh, rough tunics by the women who have gathered at this place. Cold water is best for washing out a crimson stain, but even so, if you leave it too long, the colour goes deep.

Some of the maids hold knives, bows. They are not sure how to use them, but the other women – the secret women of the forest, the unsung widows and mothers – have lent them their weapons anyway. It makes the women of the palace feel safer, stronger. Just the thought of a knife in hand seems to steady some of them, make it easier to think. It is easier to think, Priene often says, when you are mulling how to avoid a fight that may lead to death, rather than thinking on how to avoid death itself, with no other options available.

Autonoe steps forward from the huddled women. "I will come with you to Laertes' farm," she says.

"No," Penelope replies. "It is not necessary."

"I will come with you," Autonoe repeats. "And if Odysseus looks at you, or speaks to you, or touches you or any woman in that place, I will cut his throat while he lies sleeping. This I swear."

Autonoe has always wanted power – what little power may be given to a woman and a slave. As the queen of the kitchens, as the confidante of the lady of the house, as the holder of secrets, as the manipulator of men and maker of secret plans, she had it. It was petty and slight, but to one who has never gorged on meat, it was a feast.

That power is gone now. Odysseus and Telemachus took it. And as she holds her blade, she pictures driving the point through the sleeping neck of Ithaca's king. She does not know if she can do it. She hopes that she can.

Penelope sees this, of course, and it occurs to her that this is not necessarily the kind of mentality that she should really be bringing with her into a potentially confined, potentially besieged space. She also finds herself weak at the knees with gratitude, aching to throw her arms about Autonoe and bury her face in her hair and whisper, *thank you, thank you, thank you.*

Anaitis says: "The women who remain will have the sanctuary of the temple," and because the sanctuary of the temple isn't always a guarantee against profanity, Priene adds: "We will keep them safe."

There are many gods who would be offended at the idea that mortal arrows need to guard their sacred sites.

Artemis is not such a one. I look about for her divinity, for a whiff of her presence, but do not see it. However, unlike my brother Ares, this does not mean that the huntress is not here.

As Penelope and Autonoe gather themselves for the short

walk up the valley to the farm of Laertes, Priene slips to the weary queen's side.

"The women are ready to fight," she says, "But I do not yet know who our enemy is. Are we fighting Eupheithes and Polybus – or Odysseus?"

"I am sure that will become apparent," Penelope sighs. "In some brief time."

"We can protect the walls, defend the farm, better than the temple . . ."

"Not yet. Not yet. I had Ourania send word to Mycenae, to Elektra . . . It is possible. If the message has reached her, then perhaps . . . but we will see."

"I will walk with you to the farm," Priene declares, and there is that in her voice that brooks no argument.

CHAPTER 25

>>

The farm of Laertes, father of Odysseus, was once a perfectly modest little holding deep in the hills of the isle, where the old man kept a few pigs, a couple of foul-mannered goats and grew a meagre harvest of somewhat unpleasant olives. Laertes considered this all entirely adequate – he put enough labour in to feel like he had something to do with his old age, but could also absolutely take naps as often as he wanted and get someone else to do any dirty work. This suited the old adventurer down to the ground.

When pirates attacked his farm, in an effort to capture and ransom the aged sometime-king, Laertes and the few slaves of his household hid in a ditch and watched the orange reflection of their home burning in the skimming clouds of the midnight sky.

When his daughter-in-law, Penelope, offered to rebuild his holding upon the same ash-strewn land where before his pigs had ranged, they both agreed that certain upgrades might be useful.

"Walls this big," he proclaimed. "Thick enough to be hard work, but not so long as we can just be overwhelmed. Always a mistake, walls too long to defend, too showy, too stupid. And spikes. And a ditch. Very important, your defensive ditch."

"Of course, Father," Penelope had replied, eyes down and hands clasped in humility before her. "Whatever you desire."

Laertes is napping when there is a pounding on his gate.

He snores as badly as his son, and does not stir.

Pounding again, louder.

I nudge him gently in the ribs, and also his servant-woman, Otonia, and with a start and a grumble of phlegm, the old king opens his eyes.

"Bloody late for a bloody guest . . ." he mutters to himself as he girds his loins in a tunic stained with streaks of faded yellow and blackened dirt.

"Who's there?" he calls into the fading dark, as he shuffles towards the heavy gates that guard his compound.

"Penelope," replies a voice from the darkness. "And Anaitis, priestess of Artemis, and my maid Autonoe and friend Priene." A moment of hesitation. "Also, word of warning – your son is back."

As the sun rises, Penelope sleeps.

Even Autonoe was surprised at how profound, how deeply the queen fell upon the offered bed, still in her travelling clothes, feet dirty and hair unkempt. No one shows any sign of wanting to disturb her.

Elsewhere, Laertes sits by an unlit fire in his favourite chair, a thing nearly as crooked and low-slung as he, and watches the waking women who sit opposite him.

Priene, sword at her hip. Autonoe, her eyes grey and baggy. Anaitis, priestess of Artemis, who prays with her lips moving in silence to the great huntress who protects these isles and who seems to mark nothing else in her devotions.

"So." Laertes addresses Priene, as she seems the most awake of them all. "He killed all the suitors, huh?"

189

"Yes."

"Well. Had to happen."

Priene's lips thin, but otherwise show no sign of sentiment.

"Imagine he'll be on his way here soon, yes? Show his respects?"

"He'll be fleeing the angry fathers of the sons he has slaughtered," Priene replies, stiff as the axe.

Laertes shrugs. This was also inevitable. He does not believe in getting worked up about things until they're actually happening, at which point he might permit himself a bit of a grump so long as it doesn't interfere with business. He jerks his head towards the room where Penelope sleeps. "She all right?"

"He killed three of her maids."

Laertes sucks in air through his cracked yellow teeth, tuts. Autonoe does not raise her eyes from the cup she grasps with both hands, shoulders hunched, knees locked together.

"Will you fight?" Laertes asks at last.

Priene raises her eyebrows. She would like to be able to raise one at a time, as she has seen Penelope do, but doesn't have the fine muscle control.

He spits into the fire. "I'm old, not dead, girl. I know who killed the raiders last year, and who got Menelaus from this island. But my son coming back ... that changes things. No one would blame you if you just ... disappeared into the hills. No one would know that you ever existed to blame."

Priene considers a while, then says: "The queen said I could kill Greeks. When I entered her service. I thought she was exaggerating, but she has kept her word. Greek pirates, Greek soldiers, maybe even Greek princes and kings. That's all I wanted. All that was left. It did not matter if I died, so long as I died killing Greeks. This seemed the best way to go about achieving that."

"And now?"

"Now ... now it is my duty to fight for something, instead of just against it. That is ... I promised myself I would not let myself get to that state again."

"But here we are," muses Laertes, a sound somewhere between a chuckle and a sigh. Easier, the old king concludes, to be amused by matters beyond all control than enraged by them.

Priene nods, just once, a grudging acknowledgement of a thing shared. Stares at her hands, her knees, the floor, as she answers, calm and clear. "I will fight for the women. I will fight for the maids. I will fight ... in some way ... to keep them safe. Even if that means," a scowl of displeasure about her lips, "fighting to defend some ... *Greek king*. If it needs a man on the throne to keep them safe, even a man like Odysseus, then ... they are what matter. They are ... everything."

Laertes clicks his tongue in the roof of his mouth – a sound meaning very little, an acknowledgement of listening to her words, nothing more, nothing less. He gave up on the tedious habit of caring about particulars a long time ago.

Priene indicates the room where Penelope lies sleeping. "I'll fight for her," she says. "I'll do that."

Laertes nods at nothing much, says nothing more.

They wait.

The sun crawls, muddy and pale, into the sky.

In the city beneath the palace, fathers prepare their sons for burial.

They do not know how to prepare the bodies.

How to say goodbye.

What songs to sing.

What tears to shed.

There is no song that has prepared them for this moment.

They think it is obscene, profane, unhallowed that these things should be so crudely done, or that so many bodies should

191

be arrayed together so no one father can tell which is his son from the line of shrouded dead.

There is also something about it that is tender, beautiful even. An intimacy to proceedings that would have been lacking were all rites and rituals properly obeyed, and if someone else's hand had twined the bodies of their boys in neat, impersonal robes.

They know they must carry on.

Carry on.

That is what men must do.

They must always carry on.

Odysseus reaches his father's farm just after dawn, his ragged army of boys and old men at his back. The gate is open, the old man standing in it with arms folded, robes hanging crooked about his knobbled knees. He has put on one of his better gowns, but not bothered to comb his wild, scraggy hair or scrape the dirt from his nails or his gnarled and curling feet. Odysseus should perhaps be shocked at his father's degeneracy – he is not. If anything, this is one of the few reassuring stabilities on the island.

"Father," he begins, stepping forward to bow his head, make a good, solid speech. "I am returned from my—"

"What have you done, boy?" snaps Laertes. "What the bloody hell have you done?"

CHAPTER 26

>>

It has sometimes been remarked upon how peculiar it is that there are two gods of war roaming the celestial palaces of Olympus. Besides some minor bickering over who is the truest lady of the hearth, or whether Apollo or Artemis is better with a bow, no other aspect of creation is so well catered for in the pantheon of divinities as bloody combat.

My brother Ares is, it is generally agreed, a god of savage bloodshed, of the brutal melee and the howling field. Whereas I am likely to be seen in the general's tent, strategising and concocting plans, or walking the ground of some marshy field before a battle to assess the terrain over which burdened warriors must travel.

There is some truth to this dichotomy, of course, but it also misses some important details. Ares too is often standing by the generals, proclaiming: "Send them all! What are they here for if not to die?" and often – far too often – his voice drowns out my own. Likewise, I am often in the field of battle, catching the arm of a fearful warrior and whispering: *Stand firm. Stand with your brothers. Keep their shields by your side.*

For I possess an aspect that my brother does not: I am the lady of wisdom, as well as war, and it is my opinion that war is almost never wise. It can be fought well; it can be waged with cunning and strategy, and I relish very little more than the sight of a small army cleverly led holding off a great and monstrous troop. But fundamentally there are very few battles drawn, very few horns sounded that were not blasted for reasons of foolish pride, greed, vengeance or fear.

Thus, by my very nature, I undo myself, and my brother laughs while kings and princelings wage war for petty pride and stupid, foolish honour, wisdom long since fled from their hearts.

Ares' simplicity is his power, his violence absolute. And gods and mortals alike find it easier to deal in simple, absolute things.

Once I rebelled against my father, tried to break the heavens – but I lost. I was betrayed by another woman, one who was favoured of Zeus, who found it safer to live under his arm than dare to be free. She was more afraid of the story of Zeus – of his unstoppable power, his mighty fury – than she was inspired by the stories I whispered, of freedom, change, something unknown and new. And when I was defeated, I knelt before my father and simpered and said "yes Papa" and "of course Papa" and whatever else was needful to survive.

Wisdom is not vengeful, but war often is.

"Does Papa still love you?" Ares asked, when our rebellion failed and Zeus blazed his fury across the heavens. "Did you sit upon his knee and tell him you were *swory Daddy?*"

I did, of course, do those things. Ares and Zeus both love to see a foe humiliated, dragged down in chains; it is sweeter to them than any divine nectar.

Since that time I have dimmed my light, kept my features empty and serene. I am sometimes even thankful for the lessons of my failure, for they showed me the cruel limits of my power, the opposition to my ambition. I learned that I could not with force alone strike down the gods, rend the skies in two and cry out across the shaking world: *Let us break these lies, crack these chains in two!*

My ambitions, diminished, would need to be quieter, smaller and cruel.

And so I set my sights on Ithaca.

The men of Odysseus guard the walls of Laertes' farm.

The walls are high without being extravagant, with a platform around the inner edge along which defenders may array themselves, albeit only one man deep. There were plans to raise up a barrier behind this same walkway, but the workers have not had time to finish their labours and a great many tools and fat logs are stacked in a lean-to beneath the eastern wall, ready for deployment. There is a squat gate in the northern wall through whose square jaws visitors must enter, and the walls about it and the platform overhead, though not great, are at least sturdy, and any enemy who wished to pass through could be herded by their dimensions into a narrow killing ground.

Surrounding the walls there is a ditch. The dirt from the ditch became the base of the wall itself, adding greater height to the otherwise unimpressive barrier. Laertes is proudest of this – he believes a good defensive ditch to be the best tool any soldier or king could require, and he is broadly correct. It is deep enough that a man dropping into it without care runs some risk of twisting an ankle or breaking a leg, and being in it, that same man will struggle to get back out the other side, his head all the time prominent enough to be a good killing height.

"Love a ditch!" Laertes proclaimed, as the women sent by Penelope to rebuild his farm laboured in the pounding sun to dig it. "Give me a ditch and then another ditch and maybe a bit of a palisade and I guarantee the other bastard will have given up before I've even finished running away!"

Laertes will not play a leading role in the poem that I shall spin of his son's life. This is not because he is not in his own strange way beloved unto me.

The land about the farm has been cleared on all sides to be sown with grain and worked by Otonia and the two former slaves who sometimes smelt tin in their crooked workshop on the edge of Laertes' little dominion. Beyond are the scrubby, grubby woods of Ithaca, thinnest to the east where they curl in ankle-catching scrub and thorn before reluctantly rising through tumbled stone and bitter earth into some sort of sulking greenery, and thickest to the west where black mats of trunk and bark obscure the curve of the hill as it rolls down towards the hidden valley where one might find the temple of Artemis. The farm itself sits at the highest part of all this, and on fair days you can see hints of the sea to both east and west from atop the defensive walls. Laertes is not particularly interested in the view. He likes it, however, when people who come to visit him arrive a little breathless from their climb; he enjoys watching people work for the privilege of his company.

Within the walls, the house. It is excessive for one man and his maid, and humble for a man who was once king. There are four fine bedrooms – "One for me, one for you, one for the grandson, one for Odysseus!" was Laertes' explanation to his daughter-in-law, who at least was mildly grateful at his assumption that she would not be sharing a room with her profoundly absent husband. In reality, the smallest room is inhabited by Otonia, but though meagre it is at least on the southern side of the house, away from the pig pens. The kitchen is the most impressive feature of the farm, after Otonia hinted that she would enjoy a little more room to work and the pleasure of morning light, and Laertes, who would never admit his fondness for anyone, let alone a loyal maid, turned to Penelope and barked: "And great big kitchens, with big windows and good shutters, stocked with herbs and good – *good* – wine!"

The well is right outside the kitchen door; Otonia is after all getting too old to carry heavy things more than a few paces, what with her back. No one has dared ask Laertes if he needs the aid of a younger woman – such a question would be a kind of profanity.

It is, in short, a stubby but moderately effective fortification. A hundred men with javelins and stones would thickly populate the walls and hold their place against most reasonable expectations of an assault. Though they would have to raise cloth throughout the courtyard below to find room to sleep, and the whole thing would be cramped, the tight dimensions largely mitigate any advantage in numbers that an enemy might bring, so that I say indeed a hundred, maybe even eighty men could successfully drive off all but the most wily of attackers, until their supplies of food ran out.

Odysseus, of course, has perhaps twenty.

Eumaeus has managed to find a further three men, all as old as he, willing to get invested in the return of Odysseus. These greybeards held swords some forty years since; now they will have to serve as body-draggers and shovellers of earth. Eumaeus had thought he could find more, imagined the whole island would at once rally to the return of their famous king, was indignant to discover how many doors were closed with a polite variation of: "Well, I hear the fathers of the men he's killed are arming, and anyway it's been twenty years, hasn't it? But if he survives the week then of course, but of course, we'll be ecstatic. Absolutely rooting for him. Let us know how it goes."

Eumaeus splutters that these cowards should be hanged as the maids were, that when Odysseus has destroyed his enemies he should rage through the streets of the city in vengeance and blood, plucking out every disloyal fellow by the hair.

Odysseus replies, eyeing up the old men the swineherd has found, that this will do for now. That this is enough. Knows

197

that in a way, the men of the city are right: he was gone from their island far longer than he ever ruled it.

Six palace guards arrive of their own accord to serve the king, weighed down with spears, javelins and armour. Odysseus thanks them for their loyalty, hears in their voices accents of other places – Aulis and Pylos, Calchis and Athens – asks how long they have served on Ithaca and how they came into the palace guard.

They eye each other up cautiously, then the bravest one says: "My king, we were passing through Ithaca after the war, looking for gold and glory. A cousin of a woman called Ourania approached us, asked us about our histories, gave us wine, riches. Then Ourania commissioned us to protect some merchant vessels in her care as they travelled through dangerous waters to the barbarian north or those seas where the hungry wolves who were not fed at Troy try to plunder their fellow Greeks. On hearing report of our good service, we were invited into the palace by Queen Penelope. She spoke to each of us in turn, offered us terms for our service, gave us our duties."

"Not Peisenor?" enquires Odysseus, keeping his voice light and curious. "Not Medon or Aegyptius or some man of my council?"

"No," they reply. "It was Penelope."

Odysseus nods and grasps each one on the shoulder and welcomes them in, and does not look towards the house where Penelope waits.

By the late afternoon, Odysseus has twenty-six men of fighting disposition at his command, as well as the old fellows who now annoy Otonia about the kitchen. This feels good. He was at his best, he feels, when he had the opportunity to know each man by name, and learn his weaknesses and strengths. Commanding large masses of faceless infantry required putting your trust in subordinates who were themselves trusted by their companies, and Odysseus will be the first to admit that the years have not given him much faith in subordinates. Twenty-six men, however, even if half of them are boys or of questionable merit – that is a solid number.

He sends as many as he dares out to forage for supplies.

They look a little bewildered. For the guards of the palace, for the friends of Telemachus, this is something they expect the women to do. Some of Eumaeus's old hands tut and step up to the front of their lines. "Younglings today," they mutter, as they shuffle into the sun.

"Father – do you have javelins, bows, arrows?" Odysseus asks Laertes.

The old man sucks in air through his gappy teeth, contemplates longer than he needs to, then snaps, "Of course not, boy! Who'd use them?"

Odysseus manages not to sigh. His father, even before Odysseus left, was a source of a not insignificant exasperation. Giving him a farm in the hills where he could only be exasperating some of the time was one of the family's wiser decisions. Laertes' eyes gleam; he watches his son try to resist the urge to huff, to puff, remembers how much he enjoyed making his offspring squirm, making the boy work. "Tell you what, though," he muses. "Got a lot of big rocks and rubble left over from rebuilding. Kept them specially, just in case I fancied myself a bathhouse or a nice little extension."

Odysseus's eyes brighten. He has never dropped rocks on heads, though he absolutely knows what it feels like to be in a press of men below the barrage. It strikes him as yet another cruel jest of the gods that he who spent so long besieging a place now must learn how it feels to be besieged.

*

Telemachus guards the gate of his grandfather's farm while the foragers go about their work.

It is the kind of suitable, down-to-earth business he feels he can get behind, and besides, the quiet of the watch, the stillness of the warm evening air – it seems somehow cleansing. There is no stench of death here. Even the manure of Laertes' animals is a bit of a relief. Telemachus needs space to think. Telemachus has never really before appreciated what space to think feels like.

In the kitchen, Otonia and Autonoe struggle to knock together a meal for nearly thirty. The maid of Penelope works without a word, gives no instruction, makes no requests. She carries a knife upon her belt, and makes no effort to hide the blade.

In the shadows outside the farm, Priene moves through the darkness. It is not considered entirely suitable that Odysseus meet the captain of Penelope's guard yet – not quite yet. Her lieutenant, Teodora, has come from the temple to join her, and other women too. Old mother Semele stands with her daughter by her side, an axe in hand. When people ask, "What do you want with an axe, good mother?" Semele replies that it is for the chopping of wood. This is not a lie. An axe is a tool for diverse purposes.

The women do not leave the cover of trees but silently watch the roads, the secret paths, the winding ways to the old king's farm.

Teodora says: "What's he like? Odysseus?"

Priene replies: "He murdered Eos, Melitta, Melantho. If he lives, he will be king of these islands."

Teodora thinks about this a while. Then murmurs: "And Penelope?"

Priene does not reply.

Women armed with bows and hunting knives, their faces daubed in mud, their hair twined with leaves, watch the farm in silence. And at their back, another. The lady of the hunt, vines twining between her toes, quiver on her hip, bow in hand – she watches too. I feel her presence because she wishes me to, but do her the courtesy of not trying to look for any further tracery of her passage.

Later, by the evening fire: Odysseus, Laertes, Penelope.

Autonoe roused Penelope from her room, whispered: "Your son and husband are here."

Penelope took Autonoe by the hand, regarded the knife on the maid's hip, thought of saying something, decided not to. Replied simply: "Well. Well. So they are."

The house itself is of course busy, each room rolling already with the sweat of men. But this place, this little room in the northern corner where Laertes likes to sometimes take his afternoon nap – it is just for family now. Telemachus still guards the gate. He does not think it appropriate to be seen doing much of anything else, and is grateful that people seem to accept this excuse.

Thus, the three elders watch each other in silence, picking over the food the kitchen has provided.

Penelope has slept, washed. Combed her own hair. She thought of asking Autonoe for help, decided it would be obscene. The result is more farmer's daughter than the wife of a king. She has none of the divine power of Circe, the beauty of Calypso, nymph of the sea. Her eyes are heavy and dark, her shoulders hunched. Odysseus finds himself staring at her, and then looking away as if he was regarding nothing much, nothing at all, whenever she catches his eye.

Laertes says: "So where's Medon, Peisenor, that lot?"

"I have sent Peisenor and Aegyptius to Kephalonia to try

and muster men," replies Odysseus, fingers stained with grease, chewing a little with his mouth open. "I think Medon is fled."

"I sent Medon to Ourania's house." Penelope's voice is calm and light, not a whisper of a scream, not a hint of the blaze that races through her soul. "For his safety."

"Ourania," muses Odysseus. "Who is she?"

"She was my maid, and my husband's mother's before that. I freed her, many years after Odysseus left, and she has continued to serve as my eyes and ears. She has informants in every court and knows every merchant from the Nile to the frozen north. That is Ourania."

Odysseus finds himself staring again at his wife. She does not meet his gaze, but concentrates on her food. Her hands are worn – he wonders how they got that way. She has been shearing sheep, holding goats by their bucking horns, inspecting the groves in the blazing sun, cutting the throats of pigs, counting bushels of grain, laughing in secret with her maids beneath the harvest sun. He tries to imagine all these things, finds he can, does not know if he can trust his imagination or not. Everyone told him his wife was sitting in her room weeping for him these past twenty years, it was her sole occupation – and though it seemed absurd, in time he'd almost started to believe the tale.

There is a kind of intimacy here, he realises. The story Penelope wove of herself, reaching out across the oceans, whispering its way even to the walls of Troy. In the absence of each other, stories were perhaps the only thing they could share.

He wonders with a start what stories she has heard of him, and if she believes them.

Laertes talks with a great slough of food still churning round his mouth, flecks of it on his chin. "So how many spears do you think Eupheithes and Polybus are going to muster?"

"At least a hundred," replies Penelope, as if she were pronouncing on buckets of fish.

Laertes considers this number with another round of jaw and lip. "And some real fighters amongst them too. Bloody mess that'll be."

Odysseus picks at his food, is astonished how good it tastes despite its simplicity, how much he missed this familiar warmth upon his tongue – does not think it would be appropriate to say so. He is not used to being lost for words. He feels inadequate, small even, sitting in his father's house. Realisation of this makes him angry. Anger is not helpful, and yet there it is, sticking in his throat, choking his wits.

I pat him gently on the shoulder.

Feel it, I breathe. *You cannot wish your anger away. Let it burn. Let it blaze. It is fire, undeniable, giving you strength. And understand too that when it matters the most, it will betray you, leave you cold and broken in the dark. Fire always does.*

Laertes, oblivious it seems to both mortals and divines in his presence, sighs, tuts. "Might be able to talk Polybus down. He was always more reasonable than he seemed. Eupheithes, though . . . he's tricky. Murdering his son." Another intake of breath. "Going to be difficult to reconcile that."

Penelope does not move.

Odysseus stares at his plate.

"Well!" The clap of Laertes' hands together rings brightly through the room, making both the younger people jump in their chairs. "Sure you can sort it, yes, let me know when it's done!"

With surprising energy for such an aged fellow, he leaps to his feet, bounds across the room and is gone in a miasma of sweat and eagerness to avoid further conversation. Odysseus is baffled. He had prepared so many things he was going to say – stories of his bravery and heroic sacrifice, of daring adventure and cruel betrayal. He practised it in the court of King Alcinous and his wife, and it received a really good response there. The least his father can do is wait to hear it . . .

But no. Laertes is gone. Laertes, it seems, doesn't particularly care.

A look flashes across Penelope's face, just for a moment – almost betrayal, perhaps, a shimmer of fear at Laertes' departure – but it is gone as soon as it came.

Penelope and Odysseus remain.

"My husband's mother is dead," says Penelope at last. "Anticlea. She died of grief for her missing son."

"I know," Odysseus replies. "I met her in the underworld."

Penelope snorts.

It is an ugly, cruel sound.

Odysseus flinches, but finds that his instinctive response – to strike, to lash out, to snarl with cutting wit that wounds almost more than the blade – feels petty and meaningless.

He stares at his food.

Penelope ignores hers. Somehow eating in front of him seems despicable, vulnerable, inhumane.

"Telemachus is . . . " Odysseus tries, and again words fail him.

Penelope waits. She has many words for what Telemachus is, but damned if she is offering them up as a gift to him now.

"I realise I have not heard much report of you, these many years," says Odysseus at last. "Save that you were here, waiting."

"That about covers it, doesn't it?"

"Does it? The islands seem . . . safe. Good trade about the harbour, as busy as I ever saw. I cannot imagine that it was . . . " A gesture. A loose encapsulation of things too big to be named. Of things that hang in the air, wet with shame.

"It was . . . ?" Penelope suggests. "Easy? Simple? My husband left me a council of three old men to run the isles in his absence. Three old men too old to fight in Troy, in charge of a kingdom. Surely you can have no doubt that when pirates ravaged our shores, when raiders stole our people, when Menelaus himself near as much invaded, they were more than up to the challenge of protecting me and my child."

This is the moment, I think.

This is the moment where the heart of Odysseus hangs upon an edge.

The heart of Penelope too.

There was such a moment, once, when Agamemnon saw Clytemnestra. A moment in which he could have struck, or could have repented. In which she could have pitied, or could have despaired. The blade tipped, the die was cast. They are both wandering through fields of blackened wheat now, calling out forgotten words to heedless mist.

Odysseus thinks about putting his hands around Penelope's throat.

He thinks of roaring, *Don't you talk to me like this, don't you talk to me like this! You bitch, you bitch, I wept for you! I sailed the world for you, ten years at war, ten years at sea, you have no idea the things I've done, the things I've seen, you cannot imagine! YOU CANNOT IMAGINE!*

He thinks of taking her right now, of throwing her to the floor and clawing away her gown, of howling, *Circe, Calypso, Circe, Calypso,* of throwing his humiliation, his fury, his loneliness and despair onto her. Into her. Maybe then he will be home. Maybe then the dead eyes of the sailors who disobeyed him, the drowned tongues of the men who ignored his advice — no, worse than that, the dead men he *could not persuade* — maybe they'll stop screaming at him from the raging whirlpool. Maybe then at last they'll call him king. Master of his house.

He could do it, of course, and no one would complain.

The first time he lay with Circe, he told himself that it was to seal a bargain, to make an oath with their bodies.

This was foolish nonsense, he knew. He just wanted her, and she wanted him, and both of them had notions about who they were and what they valued that made it pleasing to create some sort of excuse.

The first time he lay with Calypso, she had been on top of him, revelling, exulting in sex, in her ecstasy, in what he gave to her. He had never experienced anything like that. His father had always made it very clear that while it was useful for a woman to not experience too much distress upon copulation, and thus remain friendly and good-natured about the home, at the end of the day she understood that she was largely just there to serve a man's natural essences and ensure, by her body, that he too remained good-natured about the house. That was what sex was: a general strategy to maintain suitable accords through the pleasing and regular release of a man's natural essence.

Calypso, though – Calypso had laughed when he tried to show her what sex should be. She had laughed when he held her by the neck and drove himself into her, proving himself, being the man. Perhaps, he told himself, it had been her strange and unnatural nature. Her divinity, her nymph-like unknow-ableness. She hadn't shown any less interest in sex afterwards. Indeed, the next day she had mounted him with every sign of her normal enthusiasm, drawing his fingers to her nipples, between her legs, using him. Using *him* for *her* pleasure.

And Odysseus had wondered: will the poets say he is some-how to blame?

Will they say that he, who gave pleasure to women, is less than a man?

(They will not. At least – not yet. Not until the world is changed.)

Now he looks upon his wife, and knows that if he were Menelaus, if he were Agamemnon, he would hold her by the neck to the floor and crush the arrogance from her. She would survive it. If Helen could survive it, then he knows Penelope must.

Master of my house.

He looks at his wife. His strange, unfamiliar, old wife.

And realises with a start: this is what she is expecting too.

She sees all the thoughts that have run through his mind, and now she waits. More than that: she wants him to know that when he does it, if he does it, he does it without her consent. She wants him to know precisely what he has become.

Master of my house.

I lay a hand on his shoulder, and whisper: *Telemachus.*

And finally he understands: it is what his son expects too. This is why Telemachus is not in this room, why he has absented himself from this reunion. The thought is unexpected nausea, is shame, is sickness, is fury, is dread. His food is dry in his mouth, his stomach turns in protest. But not at the thought of what is expected of him, at what he might do to her – not that at all.

It is rather the notion settling upon him that this is what an *ordinary* man would do.

He looks away. I squeeze a little tighter.

And you are not ordinary, are you?

Odysseus raises his head.

Looks upon Penelope.

Enough, I breathe. *It is enough.*

"Enough," he whispers. The word is inaudible, Penelope barely twitching at the sound. He tries again. "Enough."

Troy burns, the seas rage, his men are drowning again and again and again, the eyeball of the Cyclops spurts black blood and ink, Scylla eats his neighbour whole, the sirens sing from their ruined island, he is hanging on, hanging on, hanging on and . . .

Odysseus closes his eyes.

Pushes aside his plate.

Stands.

Says: "I will sleep outside tonight. I will not disturb you further, my lady."

Penelope does not move, does not flinch, does not breathe, as Odysseus walks away.

For a moment, I love him, almost as much as when I first touched the cunning of his busy, turning mind. But love is a dangerous, reckless thing, and I will have none of it.

And so away.

CHAPTER 27

>>>

The time has come to speak to the lady of the hunt; she too has an interest in these isles.

I find Artemis skinning a deer on the steps of her temple. The maids are huddled within, out of sight, a certain merciful slumber cast upon them by the lady of the forest. The deer has been killed by mortal hands, left for the priestesses to skin and carve – but Artemis is bad at staying still unless she is about the hunt, where she may remain motionless for days, and so she has taken up the knife and bloody bowl and now shreds the animal in easy, thoughtless slices of perfection.

The moon is hidden by the time I approach, but neither she nor I need mortal light to see each other by. Our divinities alone are radiances blazing through the dark, calling to each other across the starlit hour.

I approach with respect for her holy ground, no weapons in hand or helmet upon my head. She barely glances up from her work as I draw near, her autumn hair wild about her head, her bare toes curled into soft earth.

"So," she says. "He's back, then."

"Yes. He's back."

"And hasn't raped his wife yet. I suppose that makes him what

209

you might call a hero." The sound of skin parting from flesh is dry and soft as she carves around a hanging hoof. "I imagine you're going to be taking more of an interest in these parts now Odysseus is returned," she adds. "Keeping an eye out for your favourite mortal and that."

"There is work to be done," I reply. "Stories to be told."

Artemis snorts, a damp, ugly snuffle of contempt. "Stories," she grunts. "Stories of your Odysseus to keep the island safe, when it was perfectly safe already when there were women to defend it. We were safe when we ran through the woods and cut down the men who threatened us. Now you want us to be safe because of your . . . your poet's words."

"Fewer lives are lost to a poet's song."

"If that's true, why was there all that fuss about Troy?"

I incline my head a little – though unexpected, the huntress has a point. "Very well, the poet's power cuts both ways. Either way, a well-sung story lasts longer than the string of a bow. Do you care?"

Another rip of flesh, a slip of blade against skin as she wipes a little clean blood against her thigh. "No. You and the others can play at shaping the world if you want. Heroes today, heroes tomorrow, new men, old men, glorious men, dead men. Whatever. When the winter comes and the dark curls in, you'll all be the same in the end. Whatever the stories are that mortals choose to die for, the forest will still take their bones. That's the truth of it. That's the only thing that matters."

"Perhaps you are right," I concede. "Even the gods cannot outlast the turning of the times. But if all we have is this life, this world, then I believe we should choose to live it well. Live it wisely. What else can creatures do?"

She doesn't turn away from her work, doesn't pause in her ministrations as she blurts: "Do you feel better, telling yourself that? Does it make you feel powerful, sister? Or are you just here because the only story you can make yourself part of is the story of some man?"

I shudder, but she does not see, or if she does, she does not say.

"I smelled him," she adds, face darkening. "Our brother. Ares. I tasted him on the air."

"Yes. There will be battle soon. And I think another after that. Usually he would not bother with such small affairs, but with Odysseus . . . I have spent so long making a story for him that perhaps the gods themselves have begun to believe it. Will you join me, sister? I cannot offer anything. There will be no poet's praise, no thanks or recompense. Will you join the fight?"

Artemis shrugs, but does not say no.

That night, the people of Ithaca lie dreaming.

Priene: of the touch of another's hand as they stand at the fire, of a thing that might be home, of the flames spreading and consuming the forest, the dark, the city. I brush the memory of it away before she can wake, put in its place the laugh of Teodora, the weight of the drawn bow.

Laertes: of the *Argo*. He has not dreamed of that ship for a long, long time, the crash of the sea and the strength of his youth. He sees his wife, Anticlea, waiting for him when he comes home. He sees her vanish and dissolve into a jug of wine, her face ripple into crimson tears before he can reach her, the shore always growing longer, harder, steeper, as he struggles to climb it to her side.

Telemachus: of how it felt to drive the spear through Amphinomous's back. In his dream, the suitor's head is trying to turn, trying to turn. If he turns all the way, he will look at Telemachus with dying eyes and Telemachus knows he will scream, he will shriek, he will wet the bed. So Telemachus keeps on moving, staying always behind the suitor as he thrusts the shaft deeper through his spine. If he cannot see Amphinomous's eyes, all he is doing is impaling meat. Just meat.

The wine, howls the ghost of the dead suitor, far below. *There is something in the wine!*

I look for the touch of Ares about Telemachus's mind, and think I catch a whiff of it – but it is gone before I can grasp it or drive it away.

Odysseus sleeps without dreaming.

He learned to sleep in all sorts of places, from a nap caught inside the belly of a wooden horse while the Trojans sang and danced around its feet, to a short series of tiny slumbers while clinging to a bobbing log on the edge of the storm. He should, he is aware, dream of his wife, his travels, the great deeds he has performed and will perform again. But frankly, the straw upon which he sleeps tonight is a more adequate bed than many he has experienced for quite a while, and the sound of his snoring can be heard through the shuttered windows of the house.

Penelope dreams of Melitta and Melantho, of her laughing maids.

Penelope dreams of Eos.

Of combing her hair.

Of her feet, dangling.

Of how, in death, Eos did not look like the woman she'd known. How, with the life gone from her, she was just a hanging mask, all weight without form.

And when she wakes, sweating and shaking and gasping in grief and dread, she opens her mouth to call for someone, for a protector, for a friend, and bites her tongue to hold back a name that is not the name of her husband.

Kenamon.

I cast my eyes quickly over the turning seas, looking for the Egyptian.

Ourania has already set him to sea – he is already gone. He

has not heard of what has happened to the suitors, does not know what fate he has evaded. He sits, his back turned to Ithaca, his face turned towards the sea. He is sailing past Zacynthos, heading south on a vessel carrying amber and wood, captained by a friend of one of Ourania's cousins.

He knows he is going home, and does not think he has a home to go to, and does not sleep or dream at all.

CHAPTER 28

⋙⋙⋙⋙⋙⋙⋙⋙⋙⋙⋙⋙⋙⋙⋙⋙⋙⋙⋙

In the morning, a scout is seen in the distance.

He is a slave of Polybus's house, sent to find missing Odysseus.

He stops where tree gives way to open grass around the farm of Laertes, and sees people upon the walls, water and grain being dragged through the open gates.

Telemachus is on watch, and calls out a warning, wants to run after the scout, chase him down, drive a spear through his throat.

"No, son, no," sighs Odysseus. "He is too far, and it is inevitable that we are discovered."

Telemachus fumes at this, but obeys. He knows his father is right. He is surprised how much he yearns to kill, astonished that when he is awake and closes his eyes he does not see the dead faces of the suitors, does not hear their voices call damnation upon him, but rather there is just crimson, pure in its beauty, washing across his vision. Only in his sleep do the dead rise up to condemn him.

I sigh and wipe a little sweat from his brow as the sun rises higher. *Foolish boy,* I whisper, *you will learn.*

*

Eupheithes and Polybus arrive in the afternoon, with a dozen more ancient men whose sons have been slaughtered, and who are astonished to discover that in the absence of their boys their hearts scream with a passion they never heard, never understood, when their children were still living.

Between them, these potentates have mustered one hundred and eleven spears.

It is fewer than they hoped. The name of Odysseus frightened some off; others were too lost in their grief to think on vengeance. What point is shedding blood, they weep, if it will not bring back their child?

Polybus wears torn robes beneath hastily borrowed, ill-fitting armour. He has rubbed his hands in ash, carries a sword at his hip that he barely knows how to hold. In life, he was a master of shipping, a man who could negotiate with sea captains and scarred sailors – not a soldier. He finds it strange that he thinks of himself already as the dead, as the time before the death of his son as the era in which he too was alive.

By his side, stocky Eupheithes has painted his face in the dried blood of his son, Antinous, rubbed char into his cheeks, his fingers. He wears only a helmet of bronze for protection, and bares his chest beneath his torn and bloody robe. He carries a spear, and his gown billows behind him as he walks as if the winds of Hades were already clutching at it. This sight, more than any other, sways the last of the men who doubted whether to follow him. There is something of the just about this grieving old man, something of the Fury. It is by my hand that these ideas – justice, fury – have become entwined, but I had not thought to see them blaze so brightly in Eupheithes.

Of the men who follow, a little over half are fully armed and armoured. The rest are slaves and servants, cousins and grieving family friends who have scraped together what instruments of war they can. They will mostly fetch and carry, do the vital unsung toil of war, while others array themselves in metal plate before the slim walls of Laertes' farm. They have a captain – Eupheithes was wise enough to know he needed such a man – whose name is Gaios. Gaios does not care if some fathers have lost their sons. That is just the way of things; simply how things happen. He cares that he receives reward for his labours, and that the fight, as it has been described to him, is winnable. And though he will not say it out loud, he is a little bit curious. It sounds to Gaios like he is being invited to kill Odysseus. The poets would make men believe this thing cannot be done. Gaios wonders what the poets will sing of him if he proves them wrong.

These men – we shall call them rebels for clarity's sake, if not accuracy – are seen approaching, and the gate of the farm closes as they draw near.

Telemachus places himself on top of the wall, spear in hand, as the few men of the army of the king of Ithaca arm themselves. His father does not join him, which Telemachus thinks strange indeed. Surely this is the moment in which they confront their enemies, proud and defiant, from above the gate?

It takes Telemachus a while to realise his mistake, for his enemies are in no hurry to present themselves for a suitably heroic conference of shouted insult and dire warning. Instead they circle the terrain at a safe distance, choose a place to pitch tents on the northern edge of a field, facing towards the gate, put guards on any paths that might approach, fetch water, commence the digging of ditches for soldiers to piss in, set a few cooking fires going, send back to their houses in town for blankets, any missing implements, and generally settle in. All watched by the now extraordinarily sweating Telemachus as he bakes in bronze upon the wall.

It is Laertes who comes out of the house to stand by him, in the end.

"Doing all right, lad?" he asks.

"Yes, Grandfather," the swaying Telemachus replies.

Laertes nods, spits, considers the encampment slowly swelling just beyond arrow-range of his wall. "They might not send a messenger," he says at last. "Might just decide to kill us all. Fathers can be like that, you know."

"Surely they cannot be so incensed as to want to kill *you*."

Laertes shrugs. "I'm protecting you lot, aren't I? My house, my walls. 'Sides, my son kills their sons, they kill my son in revenge, I imagine they'd expect me to kill them over killing my son and so on and so forth. Never-ending cycle of blood and all that. If you're going to slaughter family you've got to be thorough, everyone knows that."

Everyone does, save it seems Telemachus.

He did not see the Grecian kings throw babes from the walls of Troy. Stamp on the heads of infants, run knives across the throats of unmarried girls. He only heard the songs that the poets were commanded to perform by victorious, bloody men.

"Want to take a break?" Laertes asks, eyes fixed on the men at the edge of the trees.

"I am fine, thank you, Grandfather."

"If you're sure."

The old man will not offer again.

Odysseus finds Penelope dragging rocks onto the walls, Autonoe by her side.

"What are you doing?" he asks, careful to keep his voice low, level, polite.

"Fetching rocks to throw on the attackers' heads," she answers, not raising her eyes from her work. "When Eupheithes and Polybus attack, they will either try and ram the gate or put as many ladders as they can as far around the walls as possible to spread your men too thinly. Therefore we need to ensure that wherever your men go, there are rocks to throw, no?"

Odysseus cannot fault this logic, but still . . . "Your maid can do that. You are a queen."

"Who do you think fished these waters when Odysseus sailed away?" Still she continues with her work; still neither she nor Autonoe raise their heads to look on him. "Fetched the fire-wood, repaired the roofs, made the bricks, raised the animals, tended the fields, kept the roads . . . "

He raises his hands. "Though I cannot imagine it is spoken of, your question leaves only one possible answer."

This is one of the less foolish things Odysseus has said thus far to his wife, and so for a moment her labours slow. She straightens up, brushes dust from her hands, nods at Autonoe to stand a little further off. Autonoe is reluctant to move from her mistress, fingers brushing the handle of her knife, but eventually obeys.

Penelope now turns to look Odysseus up and down, as if taking him in again, wondering – was he always so old, so hairy, so worn down by salt and sun? She wants to ask him, who are you, stranger? Speak to me as if we never met, for frankly after so much time, it is as if we haven't. Only a fool would imagine that people do not change over all these years – and only fools do not change. So go on, stranger. Impress me.

Instead, she shakes her head. "I do not know if you are as good at defending against sieges as Hector was, but we will not survive ten years in this place."

"I know. And the longer they keep me here, instead of in my palace and showing myself to my people, the easier it will be to spread whatever story they want. They control the harbours, the granaries – they will be able to draw more grain and more men unless we can end it soon."

Penelope's lips thin, a moment of consideration, a place to say something more. Then she sees Autonoe again in the corner of her eye, the light gone from her eyes, the laughter from her lips. Just a woman, staying alive – and Penelope says nothing more.

"Your maid. Your . . . friend. Ourania." Odysseus is not sure how to refer to a woman who is neither slave nor wife nor widow. The categorisation of it is uncomfortable. "You say she shelters Medon. Can she . . . does she have . . . " A loose gesture around the walls of the farm. They are already feeling smaller, tighter, closing in now the gate is barred.

"You want to know if Ourania can help us?" muses Penelope. "Are you already growing desperate?"

No one calls Odysseus "desperate", unless it is himself. Unless he is invoking some state of pity – his own wretchedness, his own humble needs and so on – in the name of getting what he wants.

The old words flash to his lips, to his tongue. You have no idea, you do not understand, the things I've seen, the things I've done . . .

But the walls are closing on Odysseus too, and his wife is now staring straight at him, defiant – she was never defiant before, when she was just a girl. She said yes my lord, and thank you my lord, and laughed politely at his dreadful jokes, and then he left. He does not know what to make of a wife who looks upon him with hands upon her hips and a fire in her eye that is neither submission nor desire.

How extraordinary, I murmur in his ear, *it would be to live. How remarkable it will be for the poets to say you returned home after twenty years, and wooed your wife again, and survived.*

Of course, if he is to do these extraordinary things, if he is to reach the end of his remarkable tale in one piece, he may have to make some extraordinary decisions, embrace ideas that no other man would. Ideas that any king or warrior of honour and pride would dismiss out of hand. Notions such as humility, supplication, maybe even admitting to that most unkingly of attributes: having made a mistake.

I will love you then, I whisper. *No one will ever know it, no one must ever know, but I will love you.*

Odysseus has no qualms about feigning meekness, humility, so long as his audience understands afterwards how clever his performance was. To do these things for real, in front of his wife . . .

"You were . . . are . . . queen of these isles," he muses, eyes not quite meeting hers. "My son mentioned there had been . . . raiders. Attacks. And when you spoke of my council, there was that which implied you were not . . . entirely secure . . . in their watchfulness. I thought perhaps, my queen . . . my wife . . . would have taken some measures to defend herself."

She does not answer immediately, and that is enough to bring his eyes flashing back to her face, and at once they know the truth of each other, and he knows that when she next speaks, she is lying, and she does not care that he can see it. "What, I?" she asks. "A mere widow surrounded by *whores* in a palace I cannot control? Beset by suitors I dare not turn away, my son sailed to find his absent father? How would I even think to protect myself and my poor defenceless maids?"

For a moment they sway there together, eyes locked, shoulders square, daring the other to break.

Then Odysseus sees Autonoe in the corner of his eye. Euracleia had pointed her out, when they dragged the maids into the yard, said she was one of the worst, the greatest slut of the palace. Now she stands covered in dust, shoulder turned to Odysseus, eyes half closed against the beating sun, and he thinks . . .

. . . he thinks he can vaguely remember Ourania, or some half-glimpsed face of a maid his mother perhaps once called Ourania. He is not sure what she was like, or if she ever said anything useful, and yet now, how strange it is that *he* is asking if *she* can help. Not just the help of a woman – the help of a maid.

It is a baffling, impossible thing, but Odysseus has seen many baffling, impossible things.

He casts his eyes away from the glower of his wife, nods without knowing it, murmurs: "I will leave you to your work. For which . . . I am grateful."

I do not touch his arm nor kiss his cheek nor run my fingers across his brow as he leaves the women to their labours, for I am Athena, and my love is marble within my chest.

CHAPTER 29

>>

T he first attack comes at sunset.

They hear its preparation before it happens – the smack of axes into one of the few thick-boughed trees of the island, the rending of fibres as it falls, the snap of twigs and fluttering of dry leaves. The battering ram takes a little longer to make than the besiegers would like, for torches are being lit and fire shared from one man to another by the time the soldiers of Eupheithes and Polybus have stripped their trunk of its most thorny protrusions and lashed thick ropes to create handles by which it may be hoisted.

Telemachus asks if they should sally out, try and disrupt the creation of this weapon before it is ready, but Odysseus merely shakes his head, politely asks his father if there are any more household goods he would be willing to pile up behind the gate.

"Why not take it all!" grumbles Laertes. "It's not like it's not all new after my last home was destroyed by pirates! Easy come, easy go ..."

Odysseus chooses to hear nothing but affirmation in his father's voice. Most people find it easier to treat Laertes that way.

*

The sun is a bare slip of golden red vanishing into the west, the sky stained in strips of beetle purple and muddy orange as it dips below the horizon, when the attackers are ready.

They line up in unfamiliar rows, bullied into some semblance of cooperation by their captain. Gaios's proudest feature is his beard, which is indeed mighty, made the more so by the scar across his chin, which disrupts the curling patterns of hair and which, when asked, he can honestly say he got from a sword swung by a Trojan warrior, who died shortly thereafter.

At Troy, Gaios knew Odysseus by reputation more than sight, was never quite sure what to make of the man, chose not to think about it too much. Commanders were much the same, when all was said and done, and all the nameless soldier could do was focus on staying alive. In the ten years since he departed that war, empty-handed and battle-scarred, he has forgotten much of the mundanity of his experience. The poets have sung their songs and spun their stories and even he, even a man who was there, who saw these things, who should have known the truth of it, is not invulnerable against their power.

Odysseus, king of Ithaca, he muses, as his men assemble. *I wonder if you really can't die.*

A soldier should know: there is no man living who cannot be slaughtered by the blade. It is only the power of the poets that make Gaios doubt this truth, and he does not even know how much his heart has already been swayed.

You could be one of mine, I whisper in his ear. *You could serve Athena.*

He does not mark me, and I think I smell the hot iron of Ares' touch upon the breeze.

Odysseus does not know Gaios, but he recognises something in the order the man is imposing on the rebel men, the way he moves, holds his head up, how he barks commands. He thinks he sees a little of Agapenor, king of the Arcadians, in him, maybe even a hint of Thrasymedes, a princeling with half his father's intelligence but a carrying voice and somewhat unearned confidence that seemed nevertheless to inspire the more impressionable sort. Odysseus is not saddened, or even surprised, to find that he is about to be set upon by a fellow veteran of Troy. War is war, blood is blood, and as the world seems set to constantly remind him, Troy fell ten years ago.

As Gaios arrays his men, Odysseus arrays his, lined upon the wall above the gate, piles of rocks at their feet.

"Throwing rocks?" queries his son. "Is that ... Should we not ...?"

Telemachus wants to know: does his father not have some wonderful scheme involving liquid fire or secret traps or some ... some cunning trickery like ... well, Telemachus is not sure what, but he is sure his father will have it.

"Very effective, a rock on the head," muses Odysseus. "Hector's biggest mistake was forgetting it."

Odysseus has his bow by his side, a quiver of eighteen arrows. These are not the bronze-tipped arrows Penelope left in the hall the day he slew the suitors. Rather they were taken from a hidden place in the palace, their ends tipped with that most unusual and difficult of metals – iron. If it would have been unsettling to his fellow Grecian kings for Odysseus to go into battle with a bow instead of a spear, how disconcerted they would have been to see the power of this cold grey metal, both hard and brittle, deadly and rare.

Eighteen arrows. If every shot strikes home, he can do some impressive damage to his enemies. Not enough, however, to stop them. Not enough at all.

Penelope and Autonoe are fetching buckets of water from the well. They are filling every amphora and bowl, setting down their burdens near the straw roof of the pig's shelter and the dry timber of the gate. No one asked them to do it, and yet it is being done even as Laertes shoos his precious animals into the safety of the house with more tenderness and care than he has perhaps expressed to his own son or grandson.

Odysseus watches his wife prepare water, throw a bucketful onto the timbers of the gate itself in expectation of flame, watches her refuse to look upon him.

Turns his face away.

The rebel men do not start marching to the sound of a horn or a beating drum – none can be found on short notice. Instead they form up to a command from Gaios, and at an "Onwards!" begin to walk.

Polybus and Eupheithes stand behind, flanked by boy slaves and the few scurrying maids of their household they have brought to serve in their makeshift camp. Odysseus tries to put the distant face of a father half seen in firelight to the face of his child – was it Antinous who was Polybus's son, or Eurymachus? And did Odysseus kill Eurymachus, or was he dispatched by a blow from Telemachus? He knows he has killed many nameless men over many long years, but finds himself briefly troubled that here, on his island, he is not entirely sure which of his subjects he has slain. This is, he realises with a somewhat uneasy shudder, a poor start to his resumptive kingship.

No time to dwell on that now, I murmur in his ear. *No time at all.*

The line of rebels approaches. They do not run – that would be a pointless waste of energy, and it is hard to keep a formation over any great distance. Running is for the last moment, a final push of energy and enthusiasm to try and coax frightened men, sick with dread, into a charge that no one particularly wants to make. As they approach the gate, they are forced to bunch into a thinner column than perhaps they'd like to avoid the ditch that runs all around the walls of the farm, the makeshift battering ram at their centre. Odysseus fits an arrow to his bow, draws the string to his ear, picks out Gaios, lines up a shot. The veteran is in a plumed helmet, a Trojan thing no less, plundered perhaps from a bloody corpse in the ashes of the city. It occurs to Odysseus, as it has occurred several times prior, that the kings of Greece should have been wiser in their distribution of goods. They should have seen to it that more of their men received more of the treasure of the city, and thus avoided a generation of hungry raiders and angry soldiers with nothing but famine and regret in their hearts, set loose upon the tossing sea.

Another mistake; too late to fix now.

There is a narrow slit in the face of Gaios's helmet. Odysseus might make the shot, might just about be able to put an arrow clean through the nose of the rebel captain, break the spirits of his men right there. That would be ideal. But then again, the light is faded, torchlight flickers, and unlike a line of axes, Gaios is a moving target, and has absolutely spotted the archer on the wall, is watching him with something that is almost curiosity, fascinated to see what the great Odysseus might do next.

I look for Artemis, but she is not here. I am briefly disappointed, but not particularly surprised.

Odysseus lowers his bow. Eighteen arrows; one must use such things wisely.

The rebels near the gate. Odysseus picks up a heavy stone, roughly hacked from the mountainside, waits. The old men and boys about him do the same, looking to their commander. Telemachus wants to hurl his towards the advancing soldiers, though he would merely waste the rock, but reluctantly holds until his father gives a command. He suspects that his father has more respect for the nameless obedience of a group than he does for individual initiative.

Instead, a stone flies past Telemachus's head, and he stifles a yelp, almost drops the rock he is holding. Another smacks into the thin wall at his feet. Then another into the man who stands next to him, who howls and nearly tumbles from the wall. Telemachus ducks down as the stones fly, sees blood gushing freely from the shoulder of the fellow by his side, pain welling in his eyes. His armour bounced the projectile away from his collarbone, but in its journey it has still ripped through flesh, and now the blood twines freely down the soldier's left arm.

Below, at the back of the approaching line of men and their battering ram, the little gaggle of slingers fit more pebbles to their weapons. Telemachus has never trained in the use of the sling – it is not considered a suitable weapon for a royal man. Odysseus scowls as the stones fly, keeping his head low and knees tucked as he waits. The Trojans favoured archers on their walls, but when the Greeks went to scour the countryside for food – their predominant occupation for most of the war – out of the brush would emerge impetuous barrages of stones thrown by barefoot boys and half-naked men, claiming a constant trickle of broken bones that would take soldiers from the field as surely as any blade through the chest.

Odysseus is momentarily piqued to find that even here, even on Ithaca, there are other men wise enough to have recognised his own truth – that rocks are cheap.

A movement by his side. An unexpected presence distracts him from his thoughts.

Penelope.

She has climbed up onto the wall, head down, moving almost on hands and knees towards the bloodied soldier. Odysseus opens his mouth to object, to bark at her: get down! Get away!

Does not.

Briskly, as stones fly above her head, she crawls next to the wounded man, pulls back the bloody cloth from his arm and chest, feels about for breakages, pours wine into his mouth, murmurs nameless comforts, presses clean cloth into the wound. Getting him off the thin walkway is an awkward shuffle,

227

crawling round each other's cowering shapes, knee bumping knee, breath to breath. Pressing his back into the wall as his wife crawls past him, guiding the bleeding man down, is the closest Odysseus has come to touching Penelope since he returned home, and she doesn't even look at him.

Then the ram is at the gate.

Odysseus gives a wordless cry. He's delivered inspirational speeches as a leader, he really has, but the words were very hard to hear at the back, and by the time the gist had been whispered through the lines, his words had lost all meaning. Better, he'd concluded, to just go for a really good warrior roar, which he had practised in secret away from the lines when the wind was high and the sea crashed loud against the shore. It got the message across, expressed a primal sort of manliness. The poets could translate it into something suitably poignant later.

He pulls himself up, grabs a rock, drops it over the other side of the wall onto the mass of men below, not bothering to hurl it with any strength or aim particularly well – a rock on the head is a rock on the head. The others rise with him, Telemachus nearly tipping himself over in his enthusiasm to throw stones. A cry below, a crunch, a howl – a rock smacks into someone's arm, bounces off another's helmet, breaks someone's hand. The ram goes *thump, thump, thump* against the gate, which shudders and shakes in its frame.

Gaios commands torches thrown. Most don't have the angle, bounce harmlessly off the walls. A couple fly over and land in mud; one smacks against the gate itself on the outside, licks at its base, which begins to smoulder.

To some of the boys on either side for whom war is a strange unfamiliarity, this whole procedure is absurd, even laughable – clearly not how battle is done. Attackers just waiting while rocks are dropped on their heads, standing in lines hoping not to be slain. Defenders trying to find another stone to hurl, stepping

228

on each other's feet, working in busy grunts and half-muttered commands. Battle should be the clash of bronze on bronze, valiant duels and eye meeting eye.

Gaios and Odysseus know better. The vast majority of the fighting they did was in little knots and skirmishes about some half-burned farm, or over a cart of timber being dragged towards a palisade. It was groups of men who stumbled upon each other unexpectedly on a glorious summer's day, or an awkward stand-off across a narrow bridge that neither side wanted to be the first to cross, but from which neither could run away. This is a familiar warfare to these men; it is the kind of fighting where no cause is served save the ultimate one – stay alive. Stay alive.

Below, the slingers fit pebbles to string; someone on the wall gasps as a stone dents his armour, loses his feet and falls backwards, kept from tumbling only when he is grabbed by a flailing arm. The slingers are too far away from the wall for the rocks the defenders drop to reach them. Again Odysseus feels for his bow; again he hesitates. There are perhaps fifteen slingers – maybe he can kill them all, maybe he will miss one or two – and then his arrows will be done.

Thump, thump, thump goes the gate, and another man falls below without a sound as a rock hurled from the wall bounces onto his helmet, which caves onto his skull, blood in his mouth as he bites through his own tongue at the impact.

This battle is one of mere attrition. There is no cunning to it, no brilliant stratagem. The defenders on the wall will be eroded by flying stones until there are not enough left of them to hurl rocks upon the attacker's heads, or they run out of rocks to drop. Or the attackers will suffer enough injuries at the gate that they lose the will to step over their bleeding comrades to keep on hammering the ram against the wood and will break and flee. Very few men need to die for either situation to develop – they just need to lose the determination to stand. Bravery may hold a line against great odds, but one day the brave man will stand against a foe that is simply greater than he, and he will die, and damn all who stood with him. Courage is only of value in war when it has the wisdom to know when it is not.

And there he is.

There he is.

Ares, lounging by the stool upon which Polybus sits.

His sword is not drawn. He makes no move to enter the fray. Instead he chews bloody meat from bare fingertips, and sips wine from a golden cup, and seeing me upon the wall, raises his chalice to salute me, and stays where he is to enjoy the scene.

I scowl beneath my helmet, then immediately feel a pang of shame to have shown even that mild sentiment. Neither he nor I will unleash our divinities upon each other – not yet. These islands would not survive the clash of two gods of war.

Upon the wall, Telemachus rears like an angry bear, a rock raised in both hands overhead; flings it down upon the soldiers below. A slinger sees his target, hurls his stone. It comes out of the darkness like a mosquito, catches Telemachus in the middle of his chest, spins him, drops him down. Telemachus has been injured in battle before, thought that surviving such a wound made him impervious to pain, invincible. Cannot believe how much a simple stone striking bronze hurts, or the sharp-toothed dent it has scoured in the plate across his chest.

Odysseus sees this, smells smoke against the gate, and at last picks up his bow.

He targets a nameless man who holds the back of the battering ram by its rope handle. He is so focused on his efforts – on pull, swing, pull, swing! – that he doesn't see the archer pick him out. There is not fifteen paces between Odysseus and his prey. Armour or no, it is an easy shot, and the fellow falls with an arrow through his throat. He is caught at once by another, dragged back through the scrum of men – *move, move, out the way!* – but too late. There is no saving him. Someone else tries to grab the handle that has been released. He is the next to die. The swinging of the ram slows, wobbles. No one rushes forward to take the place of he who has fallen, as Odysseus lines up his next shot. The soldier who stood shoulder to shoulder with those who have just been slain is smart enough to recognise what is happening, and drops his handle to grab a shield from his neighbour, nearly wrenching his colleague off his feet as he ducks behind its surface.

Odysseus puffs out air, catches himself a second before releasing the shot, ducks down behind the wall again as the slingers, seeing their target, the most important target, hurl their stones towards him, kicking up dirt from the wall as they strike below, singing through the air as they soar high. I breathe one stone away that would have caught him in his side, knock it gently to the ground, huddle down with the king as he catches his breath, shakes his shoulders out, crawls a little further along the wall so he might re-emerge away from where the slingers are looking. These are not tactics befitting a heroic poem, or at the very best are the kind of base, scuttling things that whimpering Paris might have used – and yet Paris shot an arrow through Achilles' heel, and thus the greatest warrior of the age fell. Important to remember these details.

The pounding of the ram has slowed as the attackers scramble to get a grip once again on the trunk. Smoke is rising from the torches thrown against the gate, but it is still too wet to catch, spluttering and guttering in grubby black stains. Behind, Autonoe staunches the bleeding of a groaning man, while Laertes and Penelope hurl water onto the creaking timbers.

Odysseus has found a stretch of wall that is far enough away from where he last emerged. As Telemachus recovers his breath and fumbles once again for a rock to throw, Odysseus rises. I steady his arm as he draws back the shot, narrow his eyes, pick out the strongest man in the middle of the six remaining who hold the battering ram, place my hand in the small of Odysseus's back to steady him as he holds his breath, fires.

I am no goddess of the hunt, but this is still battle. The arrow flies true, snapping vein and tendon. The soldier drops, the beating of the ram slows again. Telemachus roars: "For Ithaca!" as he throws his rock. He is still absolutely convinced that inspirational speeches are the way to go, that one must bellow profound imprecations to honour, valour, bravery when one stands upon the field. He will learn – but for now at least the numbers of men upon the wall are few enough and bunched tight enough that most can hear what he said, and the rest get the gist, and so with a barrage of rocks they fling death upon the cluster of men about the gate, breaking bone and rending flesh – and with a howl and a shuffle of slipping steps, the attackers waver. They shudder, they falter. Gaios tries to rally them – "Keep going, we are nearly through!" – but an arrow drops another on the ram, and it falls. Men slip and slide from the narrow causeway towards the gate, losing their feet as they tumble into the ditches either side, unharmed but shaken, crawling hand over hand to try and scramble their way back up.

"Keep going, keep going!" thunders Gaios, and this time Odysseus takes the shot.

Even with my strength in his arm, it is not quite enough. Gaios whips his head away, ducks behind his shield. The arrow punches through the bronze as if it were cloth, missing Gaios's wrist by the thickness of a thumb. Odysseus's lips curl in frustration before he ducks back down behind the wall to avoid a shower of stone. But the shaft through Gaios's shield has briefly broken his cry, silenced his roars for obedience, dedication, and so now, in a muddy scramble of bronze and wood, the attackers turn, break, flee.

Telemachus howls, spittle and fury upon his face, snarls and roars and shrieks after them. His bladder suddenly feels incredibly full, his stomach incredibly empty, there is a thundering in his ears and he wonders if he is going to vomit, and still he howls and howls after the retreating figures in the dark, screams wordless profanities, wants to dance, to cry, to stomp on the crushed faces of the dead – until a hand on his arm slows him.

Breathless, swaying, gasping, he turns to see his father.

Odysseus grasps his son, and there is a look upon his brow – a frown that is perhaps calm reassurance, perhaps an expression that this too is all right, that it is going to be all right, a look of sobriety shared between warriors.

Perhaps it is something else.

Perhaps it is the same look upon Penelope's face, as she gazes up from the courtyard below. As she studies Telemachus, son of Odysseus, and wonders what kind of man he has become.

CHAPTER 30

>>>

H ere is the reckoning of the injured and the dead, as the
night settles over Laertes' farm.

On the rebels' side, there are six broken limbs, four minor
lacerations and five dead. This is not a great deal, in an army
of more than a hundred men – but in the narrow approach to
the gate, the bodies of those five are a barrier in themselves, a
pillowed wall of bloody flesh and shattered bone over which
their comrades must crawl towards the walls of the king of
Ithaca. The battering ram also is fallen, dropped with the rope
that supported it still entangled in the hands of at least one man
who died with an arrow through the throat.

On the defenders' side, there are two broken bones and two
minor wounds, all inflicted by flying stones. The broken bones
are a problem that is, to Odysseus, as near to death itself – for a
useless spear arm makes a useless man, and the diminishing of
Odysseus's numbers tells far more heavily on his plans than it
will upon the rebels.

The fire on the gate did not catch, but rather guttered in a
blackened stain on the soaking wood. By moonlight, Penelope
and some of Telemachus's men ease the gate open and scurry
outside, half blind on hands and knees, to recover thrown stones

sticky with blood, and to peel away any armour and weapons from the bodies of the dead.

Telemachus sits on the floor near the fire, there being no furniture left to sit upon, and shivers. Penelope tries to lay a shawl upon him, and he bats it away, nearly snarls at her, nearly spits like an animal, shakes his head. Laertes says: "Soldiers sleep so soldiers can fight, boy. Don't be an idiot."

It takes him a while to hear his grandfather's words, as if they were echoing from some far-off mountainside. Eventually he nods, bows his head, lies down. Penelope cannot tell, when her son closes his eyes, if he is sleeping or pretending.

Odysseus stands in the courtyard, looking at the walls that enclose him. Is this, he wonders, how it was for the princes of Troy, within their city? Did it take mere hours for them too to begin to yearn for the open plain and the blazing sun? He lets the thought linger, closes his eyes in imagination. When he fought at Troy, he never imagined what his enemies might feel, or long for, or believe. To do so would not have aided his cause. But now that he stands here, arms aching and walls hemming him in, it is almost a privilege, a great blessed relief, to picture the ghost of Hector by his side, to imagine conversing with him in another time, a more civilised time, as princes should.

Unconsciously, instinctively, his fingers brush the quiver at his side. He has thirteen arrows left.

Then Penelope is there, looking up past the walls at the same starlight that shines upon him, with a look of contemplation on her brow that seems almost familiar to the Ithacan king. "Well," she says. "I would call that a draw."

If Odysseus had dared say so in Agamemnon's tent, he would have been berated, roared at, condemned. The word "draw" was poison in the mouths of the Greeks, growing only more toxic as the years of endless nothing on the beaches of Troy dragged by. Only stories – stories of heroic victory or tragic despair, of things that were black and white, extraordinary or obscene – could possibly sustain a man through so much time.

And yet . . .

"I'd say so," Odysseus agrees, careful not to move too close to Penelope lest she flinch from his presence, lash out at the merest possibility of his touch. Autonoe stands a few paces off, hand tight around the handle of the knife on her belt. "Though it can be tricky to judge."

"Of course," muses Penelope, "Polybus and Eupheithes can send for reinforcements. I don't suppose you informed anyone of any significance that you were returning to the island?" she enquires. "Someone with sentimental attachment to your name and an army of loyal men who might come looking for you if they heard nothing good?"

This might have been, Odysseus is forced to concede, a rather canny notion. "On my return I considered it appropriate to be discreet, rather than bold."

"Ah. Well. So much for that, then."

Odysseus shifts his weight a little, is astonished to feel how heavy his legs are, how tired his eyes. "If we can get word to Menelaus, I am sure he will come."

"Menelaus attempted to invade and conquer these islands several moons ago," his wife replies, cold and bright as silver moonlight. "He did so in the guise of a guest, wearing the mask of friendship. He humiliated the suitors, pursued me into the countryside, attempted to poison the king of Mycenae, threatened your father and was finally convinced to abandon his quest by the recovery of Orestes and the imposition of Mycenaean authority, and by he himself falling victim to some of the same poisonous malady with which he had sought to impose his rule." Odysseus's mouth hangs agape, and he is too tired to know it. Penelope smiles, nods at nothing much. "So perhaps not Menelaus."

This is the place for an ordinary man to doubt his wife's every word, to call her a fool, a liar, to defend his sworn brother-in-blood. Odysseus does not. He is beginning to learn.

That is why you are mine, I whisper. *That is what makes you something new, something different. That is what makes you beautiful.*

"You must tell me more about that, when we have the time," Odysseus mumbles. "Perhaps Nestor? Pylos is only a few days away."

"Ah, Nestor. I heard one of his sons whipped my husband at Troy in a moment of mistaken passion, no?"

"The sons are not quite as wise as the father," Odysseus concedes.

"But Telemachus had a lovely time riding about with them, while trying to find his father's corpse."

"I hope my son was trying to find my living flesh," he replies carefully.

She shrugs. "One. Either. If Telemachus found Odysseus living, then he would be within his rights to demand why his father wasn't at home, defending his wife, his son, his kingdom. Unless Odysseus was cruelly imprisoned, in which case it would be an entirely different kind of reunion. The son rescues the father, establishes his valour as a great hero in the process – Telemachus would have loved that – but then that would been dreadfully detrimental to the security of the island if word had got out. Odysseus, the great king, imprisoned all these years, needing rescuing by a woman-raised whelp? Perhaps he is not the strong warrior everyone says. Perhaps he is just an old man, incapable of defending his kingdom. Such a story would have had long-term political consequences that someone would have had to deal with. Better for everyone that he found my husband's corpse. Odysseus's heroic name could still have been sustained, Telemachus would have had an adventure, returned puffed up on his exploits, raised an army in his own right as warrior and prince, fought a proper war with more than a handful of old men and boys at his back, and so on.

"As it is, this situation right now, it must be dreadfully uncomfortable for him." She shakes her head, though her thin, mirthless smile does not fade. "A man claiming to be his father is returned, and is acting the hero. Telemachus once again is just the son of Odysseus, a prince only by the strength of his father's arms, a warrior in the shadow of an ageing man. My son spent so many years longing to meet his father – no, let me say that differently. Longing to *be* his father. To be the man he believes his father to be. He never quite thought through the consequences of that desire. After all, there can only be one Odysseus."

Odysseus has not yet had the chance to know his son, but he did meet Neoptolemus, son of Achilles. He was little more than a boy when he came to Troy, a whelp in oversized bronze. His passion for slaughter had been nothing to do with war, nothing to do with victory; merely that he was the son of a hero, and there could never be enough throats cut to prove him more.

The thought is disquieting; Odysseus half closes his eyes, shudders it away.

"Nevertheless," he murmurs. "If we can get a message to Pylos, call for aid . . ."

"And how do you suggest we do that?"

"Perhaps your maid, she could—"

"You do not speak of her, you do not look at her!" Penelope's voice is the roused hiss of the cobra as it flares itself up to strike. She quivers for a moment, teeth bared, fingers turned to claws, and Odysseus shrinks. He has long known how to make himself small before the wrath of greater things – but he is astonished how naturally it comes now before the blazing of his wife. The thought should make him sicken, but it does not.

Perhaps, he thinks, as Penelope slowly unwinds from her coiled fury, it is because in this particular case, his wife is right.

"Autonoe stays by my side," Penelope continues, each word a controlled shudder on the air. "If she leaves, it is because her departure will keep her safe. She will be safe. Do you understand?"

"I understand." An afterthought, a strange notion. "Where did you send the rest of the women? The maids of the house?"

"To the temple of Artemis. They will have protection there."

Odysseus thinks there is meaning here, a thing that he should ask, a question that forms on the edge of his tongue – but he is not sure what it is. Something his wife is not saying, a truth just out of reach. He tries to grasp it, and it is gone.

Odysseus thinks that she is waiting for him to apologise.

Odysseus has never apologised to anyone in his life.

He never heard his father say sorry, nor his mother. The nearest either ever came to an expression of culpability would be if Anticlea murmured, "It is regrettable that you feel that way," and that was it. Even when Odysseus's men were drowning all around him, their lungs filling with foam, the words he wanted to say were: *Told you, didn't I? Told you and you didn't listen . . .*

Odysseus says: "The suitors. I thought . . . It was suggested . . ."

"You wanted to know if I had slept with the suitors. I have ruled Ithaca for twenty years – in these lands my name has legitimacy, my knowledge has power. And so whether you thought I was chaste or not, just killing me would have been foolishness of the highest degree. But you wanted to kill. You wanted to feel like the great man. The powerful man. It is wretched, is it not, that the only way you could find to do that was to kill unarmed maids."

Penelope now is silent.

Penelope now is watching the endless sky.

Odysseus thinks of striking her.

Thinks of falling at her feet.

Thinks perhaps that if he stands here long enough, in silence, she will forgive him.

She does not.

Penelope waits.

She is very good at waiting.

So it is Odysseus who turns, walks away.

CHAPTER 31

>>

The dawn is greeted with a herald from the camp of Eupheithes and Polybus, come to request permission to fetch back their dead.

Telemachus hisses: "We should let the crows take them!"

Odysseus replies: "The stench of their bodies will poison us if they remain."

The bodies are fetched away by unarmed men, carried back to their camp on the edge of the field. Odysseus watches, and thinks as he does that he sees something else move on the edge of the trees, away from the lines of Eupheithes and Polybus. A darting figure, a movement of a creature with a bow. He shields his hand from his sun and . . .

. . . it is gone, if it was ever there.

"Father," says Odysseus to Laertes, as the old man sits cross-legged on the ground sucking on dry strips of meat. "Have you ever seen . . . Are there others . . . do you have other allies on the island? Other men who might come to your aid?"

"Why'd you ask, boy?" demands the aged king.

"We are besieged," points out Odysseus in the calm, soft

tones of one used to unending frustration. "And I thought I saw movement in the trees."

"You took all the fighting men to Troy," Laertes answers with a shrug. "And only you came back. Doesn't leave many men to do much of anything, does it?"

There it is again.

A suspicion, glistening on the edge of Odysseus's thoughts.

A look in the corner of his father's eye.

The old man, just like his wife. Hiding something.

It is impossible, of course. His father would never hide anything from his son, or if he did, Odysseus would know. He would know.

And yet, the way Laertes inclines his head, the way he is so focused now on his eating, the way he does not entirely meet his son's eye, a certain curling of his lip.

Laertes has a secret – no, something more than that. Laertes is keeping the secret of another.

Odysseus looks for his wife, and sees her standing upon the walls, Autonoe by her side. The two women are holding hands, giving each other strength. They gaze towards the eastern forest as if they have never seen green before.

Throughout the morning, the sound of more chopping, hammering.

Telemachus squints towards the camp of Polybus and Eupheithes, trying to puzzle it out.

"They are making ladders," Odysseus explains.

"Is that . . . Can that work?"

"Ladders are a desperate tool," his father muses. "Easy to dislodge from a wall. But if they make many ladders, and as we are fewer men, then it does not matter how many we dislodge. They will encircle and overrun us."

"There must be something we can do."

"For now? All we can do is slow them down. Your mother . . . does she have . . . or your grandfather. Is there something they aren't telling me?"

"If they are, we will drag it from them."

"You don't know." Even Odysseus cannot keep the slight sigh, the whispering disappointment from his voice. Telemachus buries his flinch in a stiff spine, in a digging of teeth into lip. His father does him the courtesy of pretending not to see. Instead, he licks his finger, raises it to the wind, closes his eyes to feel the breeze.

"Father?"

"If I recall, the wind in Ithaca is . . . changeable," muses the old soldier. "And it has been a while, has it not, since it rained? We just need a little more time."

It is Laertes who walks out of the gates, in the end.

There was much arguing about who should do it, the merits and disadvantages of any particular choice, until at last Laertes snarled: "In the name of all the gods, either they'll kill me or they won't, but at least if they kill me, I'm just a grumpy old man!"

Telemachus spouted pieties at this, but Odysseus didn't rush to disagree with his father's assessment, and that was that.

Now Laertes marches, unarmed, elbows swinging and knobbly knees popping in his legs, out of his farm and across the bloody field towards the tents of Polybus and Eupheithes. He stops a little before halfway between the walls and the camp, and waits.

The rebels watch him, mutter amongst themselves, scurry back and forth, hold a brief conference, before at last, Eupheithes and Polybus walk out, also unarmed, Gaios a polite distance at their backs.

Eupheithes, swathed in crow-robes, patches upon his skull

where he has pulled his hair out, stops some few paces before Laertes like the rolling of a glacier coming to rest. Polybus sways by his side, as if the faintest breeze might knock him down. For a while these three old men regard each other, and just this once Laertes does not spit, does not churn phlegm about his mouth, does not sneer or leer or glower, but stands almost as if he were once a king of these lands; once a friend to these men.

Finally: "Your sons. They buried proper?" he asks.

Polybus catches his breath. Eupheithes does not blink. "All the honours befitting our children have been performed," he intones. "We cannot promise the same for your kin."

Laertes nods, digesting this thought like a comforting, familiar meal that he has not eaten for a while. "He's certainly made a mess of it, hasn't he? But thinking about it, not sure how else it could have ended really. Even if Odysseus came back home all trumpets and drums, your boys have been camped out in his palace too long, lapping at his wife's skirts and all that. No man of honour could have just said 'well thanks for trying, bye bye', not really. Knives at his back. Wolves at his door. Terrible message to send. But you know that, don't you? You always knew that. If it wasn't my Odysseus killed your boys, your boys would have killed each other. Eurymachus killing Antinous. Antinous killing Eurymachus. Something had to give."

The two fathers do not move, do not answer. Polybus wants to raise his hands to the heavens, to cry out, Eurymachus, Eurymachus, my boy, forgive me, forgive me! But like Odysseus, he does not know what it is to say sorry, and so the only words left in his vocabulary are these: my boy, vengeance, vengeance and blood, vengeance and honour, honour and blood, my Eurymachus!

Eupheithes is the cliff against which beats the endless sea, seeing straight through Laertes to some distant grey horizon.

"We were friends once," Laertes muses. "Now Odysseus is

hoping you'll remember that. Remember you were loyal, all that stuff. But I don't think so. He doesn't really get it, does he? Doesn't understand. He's got a son, sure he has, but he never knew him. Had twenty years to forget him, still thinks of him as this stupid little babe covered in snot, not that much has changed there. At least your boys got to spend time with their fathers, all things considered. Nice that. Good. A bit of time. The time you had. So anyway, my son, he's hoping I'll convince you to stand down. Take a load off. Maybe just one of you. Maybe you, Polybus. You're a merchant, not a man of war. Go grieve for your boy. Go home and weep. What even are you doing?"

Polybus would weep, would choke on tears, suffocate on his own breath. He cannot. That hour has passed, and there is no moisture left in him now.

Laertes sighs. "Well. No. Didn't think it would happen. Didn't think so. Not that I blame you. No hard feelings and that. You do what you have to."

The fathers do not move.

They stand, three wretched old men who led their children to war, to slaughter.

Laertes half closes his eyes, tilts his chin to the sky as if he might be able to hear again the crying of young Odysseus, the wailing of the infant Telemachus. As if he could perhaps roll back the years to hold the babes as they were weeping, to press them close to his chest and whisper, *My beautiful ones, you are safe, you are safe. Let me teach you how to be strong when you are weak, how to be brave when you are afraid.*

Instead, he handed the child over to nursemaids. Euracleia, doting, *Coo-cooey, who's brilliant yes you're brilliant, a little hero you are!* Slaves were not permitted to discipline princes, of course. Nor was it a father's place, each of these old men thought, to show anything other than those qualities of manhood that were needful to the raising of their children. Qualities such as dignity, composure, strength, honour. The endurance of pain without complaint. Swift violence when slighted. Anger when otherwise tears might flow. These were the qualities passed down father to son, father to son, and now here they stand.

Here they stand, as the soft breeze blows.

Let this world burn, I whisper on the wind. *Let it be remade.*

The gentle breeze flickers at my touch, twists, gutters, flares. Turns.

Laertes feels it, straightens at once. Looks Eupheithes in the eye, then Polybus too. Presses his fingertips together in front of his chest – it is almost a prayer, almost a token of respect, of understanding, a communication not between king and subjects, but father and father.

"My friends," he says, and then blurts, a strange, unexpected truth from his lips: "I will pray for our sons."

He turns, and walks away.

Strides with an energy he has always had, has enjoyed hiding, back across the plain towards the gates of his farm. Eupheithes and Polybus watch him, then return to their own ranks.

Odysseus is waiting for Laertes in the open gate. "I need a piss," barks Laertes, as he marches past his family, shoulders hunched and eyes down. "And a cup of wine."

Odysseus gestures at Otonia to attend to the king, then takes the burning torch that Telemachus already holds in his hand, and walks out into the field. He does not run – running might arouse suspicion – but strides calmly away from the farm, a guard of half a dozen men at his back. Stops in the knee-high scrubby grass, kneels down, runs his fingers through the stems in a way the poets will absolutely relate as a wandering king reconnecting with his homeland, straightens, and calmly sets his fire to the earth.

CHAPTER 32

>>

The fire burns all through the morning and into the afternoon. The wind drags it from the farm straight towards the camp of Eupeithes. It does not leap or billow like the storm, but rather spirals cloying, suffocating smoke into the men building their ladders, staining face and hand and fingers black, poisoning the sky with its reflected blaze, choking the air with its heat.

The men of Ithaca know when they can and cannot fight a fire. They pick up their camp and move away from the direction of the scalding wind, circling round to the east of Laertes' farm. There they will spend the rest of the afternoon and into the evening resetting their camp, digging new latrines, setting up new places to cook, while before the gates of Laertes the fire still blazes.

By sunset it is nipping at the forest itself, the leaves beginning to char and curl, shimmer with orange worms on the edges of the trees. I feel no great compunction to stop the burn. No tactical advantage is gained or lost by the burning of the trees. But I feel another move behind me, and Artemis is there, hands on her hips, a glower upon her face more vivid than the flames itself.

She tuts – annoyed rather than angry at this turn of events. She understands the use of fire in nature, in the hunt itself, knows the touch of heat upon the back of creatures flushed from the burning wood. But today there are more than rabbits hiding in these trees, and so with a huff of her cheeks and a flick of her hair, she twists the wind again, spins the flame back on itself, back towards the blackened ground where it began, but where nothing more now sits for it to consume.

"I thought you might not come," I muse, as we stand side by side watching the sputtering torrent.

"I won't come for him," she replies, a jerk of her chin towards the wall where Odysseus stands. "Even if he uses a bow."

The forest creaks a little with her displeasure, boughs bending beneath a twist of greying leaves, and she is vanished in a breath.

By nightfall, the fire is burning itself out. A tongue detached itself and crawled towards Laertes' farm, but couldn't cross the ditch before the night breeze brought a squall of rain that pushed it back into a smoking scar in the blackened earth.

As the clouds skim across the sky, Odysseus orders all lamps within the farm doused.

Telemachus is sleeping – he will wake with a start, hope no one saw him slumber, saw any sign of exhaustion or weakness. His father has not yet convinced him of how valuable a quick nap before a valiant deed is.

Laertes snores next to his favourite pigs. Autonoe has found a corner tucked in beside the bed of straw on which her mistress sometimes slumbers, and half snoozes with a knife clutched in one hand.

Odysseus stands upon the walls, looking towards the now relocated camp of Eupheithes and Polybus, where still figures move.

Penelope joins him at last, a rough blanket across her shoulders, her feet bare.

They watch the darkness as the owl cries and the last billows of sodden smoke spin and sting across the land.

"We have slowed them," Odysseus says at last. "But they will attack before dawn. They can rest, then choose their moment. We cannot sleep. We must watch. Will be exhausted when they come. That is a problem of being a defender – we cannot control the when, the where of the battle. We must wait, while our enemies sleep."

Penelope says nothing. Her face is stained with the smoke that drifted over the farm walls, her hair tangled and skin bumpy in the cold. Odysseus sees this, looks away. Addresses the night, the enemy without, in the low voice that is most suitable only for husband and wife. "I would offer to hold you, my lady," he says, "so you might not feel the cold so much. But I think you would object."

"My husband was very warm," Penelope muses. "I hope you won't think it too indiscreet of me to say it, but when we shared a bed I would often find the heat his body put out to be of a stultifying nature in the hottest months of summer. Not to mention the snoring."

"Perhaps he was just . . . a vital young man."

"He was not the tallest," she continues, as if he has not spoken, "yet somehow he managed to dominate almost the entirety of our bed."

"The bed I carved from a tree as a wedding gift for my beloved bride," Odysseus adds, "as a sign of our love."

"Yes, that was the one. Lovely sentiment, of course. Caused dreadful damage to the walls."

"It . . . what?"

"Hum, yes. A living tree growing through a supportive wall of the palace? Absolute disaster."

"I had . . . I had a plan to maintain it, there was—"

"My husband no doubt did have some sort of plan as to what

he was going to do as his romantic gesture began to sprout twigs in uncomfortable places," Penelope sighs. "But alas, he sailed away and never returned. So I had to take matters into my own, weak hands."

Odysseus lets out a slow breath, forces himself to linger in it, to be only a body, breathing. He did this a lot whenever Agamemnon was having another tantrum, or Achilles a sulk. "On the matter of your weak hands, my lady," he muses. "It seems to me that there is some . . . some business . . . that you are not telling me about."

"There is a great deal I am not telling you about, sir. Things I will only tell my husband."

"Penelope. Enough. It is . . . I know you know me. I know it. This . . . game. Tonight we will be attacked, again. We could die. The odds are that we will die, and you are still . . . obstinate . . . infuriatingly . . ." He tries to find the words, somewhere between pragmatic and tender, generous and indignant.

Penelope nods thoughtfully. "You are right, of course. We could well die tonight. But our deaths became probabilities the moment you and my son barged into my husband's palace and killed the sons of the most powerful families in the isles. If you had come with an army, with the support of some great king, maybe we would have survived. But you and my son had to be heroes. Had to do the heroic thing. So of course now we are very likely to die. Such a pity."

"You know I couldn't let them live. I couldn't—"

"My husband had to kill the suitors," she cuts in, sharp and cold. "My husband did not have to do so foolishly, rashly, without thought for the delicate political balance that I have spent twenty years – *twenty years* – fighting to maintain. He did not have to do so in a manner that may have glorified his name, his *story*, while plunging these islands into war. *He did not have to kill my maids.*"

"Penelope, I . . ."

Here it is again.

The stop in his voice where this word should be.

Are you sorry, Father? asks the ghost of Antinous above the ash-coated form of Eupheithes.

Are you sorry, Father? whispers the ghost of Eurymachus to shaking, trembling Polybus.

What is this feeling? wonders Laertes as he watches his grandson twitch in bloody dreams, hears the faint whispers of his son speaking to Penelope upon the walls. *What is this word?*

"I . . . I am . . ." Odysseus tries. "I thought . . . I was led to believe . . ."

"Interesting," murmurs Penelope, into the dead place where Odysseus's words are failing. "My husband, of course, was very good at making his own mind up. Slowly, carefully, he would assess the situation, gather information, and make an informed judgement. He wouldn't have listened to a bitter old nursemaid and a boy barely old enough to grow a beard, and on that testimony alone slaughtered innocent women. He might have asked other witnesses as to their conduct. He might have sought out Medon or Aegyptius and Peisenor, who would have been only too happy to inform him on matters necessary to the reclaiming of his kingdom. He might have spoken to his wife. Unless, of course, he was so embittered by war, so ground down by the churning sea, that all thoughts of what it is to be a husband had been beaten from him. So soaked in blood, so drowned in sorrows and dismay that he could not conceive of those qualities of husbandliness that are most needful to a man. Qualities such as trust, honesty, faithfulness, respect. That is possible. Perhaps my Odysseus died in Troy, and now you are come instead, a bloody, wretched ghost to take his place. Is a ghost my husband? What claim, I wonder, do the dead have on the living? Then again, it hardly matters if we are indeed to all die tonight, does it?"

251

Here it is, again. Here it is.

Odysseus screams, he rages, he foams at the mouth, he beats his wife about the face, he throws himself upon her, he howls, *you have no idea, you have no idea, you have NO FUCKING IDEA!!*

Odysseus weeps. He sobs, he falls at her feet, he clings to her legs, to her gown, he wails, he laments, *please, please, you have no idea, you have no idea, you have no idea.*

Both are options, unfolding before us now like the petals of the lotus flower.

Both will break him, of course. Both will leave him less than human. In one, he can still be a hero, of course – a hero who has reclaimed his wife and made his feelings known – but he will never be loved, never be welcomed home.

In the other he will be a human, a husband, a man who weeps the truth. But he will never be a hero ever again.

For a moment Odysseus teeters between the two.

I take his hand, and he closes his eyes at my touch, imagines for a moment that it is Penelope, it is his wife whose fingers brush against his own.

There is another way, I murmur. *There is always another way.*

He opens his eyes.

Turns to where his wife should be standing, opens his mouth to say . . .

. . . but it has been too long.

He was too slow.

Penelope is already drifting away, back down the wall, lost to the dark.

Autonoe says: "Will you call for Priene?"

Laertes has found a comb – something belonging to his dead wife. He said it was just lying around, a useless old thing. It is made of glistening shell, delicate and warm. Laertes never quite managed to tell his wife how much he loved her, and as the years rolled by, his failure to express this vital sentiment led her to believe he didn't possess it, and so apart they grew. He kept her comb, when she died. Ridiculous thing, he says. Can't imagine what it's doing here.

Autonoe combs Penelope's hair.

Then Penelope says: "Let me," and, awkwardly, combs Autonoe's.

A single oil lamp burns in the corner of the room. The shutters are drawn tight, the women loom over the light, their shadows huge and black behind them.

"Will you send for her?" repeats Autonoe, sitting cross-legged before the little glow, all furniture turned into barricade, as the queen works at a particularly tricky knot. "I know she's watching, on the edge of the forest."

"I'm not sure," Penelope replies. "I think sometimes it might be simpler if we just disappear. Vanish into the islands. Let Odysseus die."

Autonoe turns, catches Penelope by the wrist. "Do it," she barks. "I know you want to protect this kingdom ... maybe even protect Laertes. Your son. I know that's why you came here, that this is ... But they can't be saved. They are animals. Men are animals."

She should spit the words. There should be tears in her eyes, fire upon her tongue. There is not. She speaks as Eos might speak, calm, cold, the delivery of mere information, of a thing that is absolutely true – nothing more.

Penelope grips the comb like a sacred shield, a blessed artefact, as she sits on the cold floor before her maid, feeling the warmth of her worn fingers against her skin. Autonoe's face seems strange, unfamiliar, without laughter upon her lips, mockery in her eyes. There is now something of the Fury in her, which burns through even the cruellest merriment. "It's not too late," the queen replies, soft, so soft, lest she break the thin light that bathes this moment. "You can go. Anaitis and the women are waiting at the temple, you know where there is buried gold."

"And Odysseus?" Autonoe barks. "What about him?"

"Do you want him to die?"

"Yes." Not a moment of hesitation, not a second of doubt. Penelope flinches, but if Autonoe sees, she does not care. "Him. Euracleia. Telemachus. All of them. Ithaca was fine without a king. It was *good* without a king. If these are the kind of men who would govern it, then I would rather it burned. You don't have to die with them. What would be the point?"

Autonoe is baffled by tales of heroic sacrifice, of valiant death upon some bloody field. How much more could a hero do, she wonders, if he'd lived long and well, instead of died young and glorious? The poets have not yet mastered the art of praising that old man who lays down his blade to focus on developing new and interesting agrarian techniques, or digging wells where clean water is scarce. This would change, if I could reshape the world. I cannot.

Now she studies Penelope's face, tries to fathom out something – anything – that she can recognise in it. "Is it Telemachus?" she asks. "Is that why you're here?"

"I don't know," Penelope replies. "I thought . . . coming here . . . it was the correct thing for a queen to do. Laertes' farm is a defensible position, it affords the best chance for victory. I thought I was doing the right thing for Ithaca. Perhaps I am deluding myself. Perhaps you are right. All these plans I had. These schemes, these stratagems. I thought I was even prepared for what I'd do if Odysseus returned, but I had not thought it would be like this."

Autonoe grabs Penelope's hands, holds them tight between hers. "You owe him nothing," she snaps. "You were barely married before he left. This is your land. *Our* land."

There is some kindness here, in Autonoe's words – if you

can bend your ear to hear it. "Why did you come?" the queen asks. "You could have stayed with Anaitis. Why did you come?" Autonoe's face flickers into a scowl, her hand brushes the knife at her side. "Will you kill them?" Penelope asks, without judgement or malice – a curious thing, a thing to be factored into her considerations, nothing more. "Is that your plan?"

"I want to. I want your husband and your son dead. I pray for it." It is why Autonoe came here, and that is the truth. But the maid is also not deaf to the whispering of the gods, not blind to power and how power works, and so here is another truth, the cruellest truth of all. "But though I ... I hate ... I know. I do know. Some new king will come. Menelaus, perhaps, or Nicostratus. There's always another king." If bitterness could poison the land, then all the plants around Laertes' farm would now wither. "You failed them," she adds, eyes away from her queen, focused on some other place – the same place they always look now, whenever she does not look at the world around her. "Melantho, Melitta, Eos. You failed them. You failed us."

"I know. I'm sorry."

Three pairs of feet, hanging in the air. Penelope tries to picture the faces of the women who died, women she had known for years, for decades even – and cannot. All she can see are feet, suspended, a murderous barrier to any memories of the living.

"If you die, we'll be exactly what Telemachus says we are. Slaves and whores. I will never forgive you. Never. Eos would say I should, but she is dead, and I won't. But for the rest of us ... we need you to stay alive. Do you understand?"

Penelope thinks she does, but doesn't know what to say, and so in silence combs her maid's hair.

CHAPTER 33

>^{>>>>>>>>>>>>>>>>>>>>>>>>>>>>>>>>>>>>>}

The attack comes a little before dawn.

It is exactly as Odysseus said it would be, exactly what he would have done.

There is no cunning stratagem, no clever trick. When you have the sheer force of numbers on your side, some decisions become simple.

The soldiers of Eupheithes and Polybus sneak through the dark, towards the walls of the farm of Laertes. They have no torches, but crawl across the earth, dragging ladders with them in a stop-start of muddy movement beneath the scudding clouds.

They have constructed seven ladders, each carried by six men. Now they scurry forward. Now they think they see a movement upon the wall. Now they stop. Cower, faces to dirt, wait. Now the movement has passed, and they rise again. Odysseus has ordered all lights extinguished, that his men might better peer into the dark, unseen. This first contest is not one of blade and bow – merely who has the sharper eyesight, the better ears.

In the night, every sound is a threat. The slip of a foot into an unseen hole; the crack of a broken stem of some hardy plant that somehow survived the afternoon's blaze. The flutter of birds on the edge of the forest, the soft bend of the smoky breeze through the trees.

I bid the owl cry, and she does, but though the men on the wall stir, they do not see the figures moving through the dark. I bid the starlight shimmer a little brighter between the passing clouds, the hungry fox shriek, the sleepy crows scatter for the sky. It is not enough, and I dare not do more – not with Ares on these isles; I cannot predict what he might do in retaliation. That uncertainty frightens me more than knowledge does.

I look for the women of the forest, and there are four keeping watch from within the trees. They have not yet seen the ladders, though the youngest, a woman of long limbs and raven hair whose father died in the great storms Poseidon sent upon the men of Odysseus, thinks she sees something in the dark. Stirs. Nudges her sister. Points. Is not sure she saw anything at all.

Artemis should be sharpening her eyes, giving her the vision of the hawk. The hunter's vision is not my domain, but I can at least give her a certain something that so many others lack, a gift that is one of the most precious I can bestow.

Believe in yourself, I whisper in her ear. *Trust your senses and believe.*

"I saw something," she murmurs, reaching for the bow at her side. "I saw something."

The women lie flat upon the edge of the forest, and watch.

There is the thinnest line of grey upon the eastern horizon. It is a good killing light, not yet bright enough to see the danger, but promising no place to hide for those who are left alive.

"There," whispers the girl in the forest, just as the first ladder reaches the ditch.

And: "Did you hear anything?" asks a man with an arm in a sling as he stands upon the wall. He and his companion peer down into the darkness below, see nothing, but he could have sworn . . .

257

The ditch makes it hard for the rebels to position themselves, but they are not yet seen, not yet anything more than more muddy shadows in the dark. They try and raise the ladder, but this man is pulling down while this one is pushing up, and this fellow thought when you said left you meant the *other* left and they cannot shout or snap at each other as they might do in daylight hours and so for a moment there is confusion as they try to manipulate this thing between them. A few paces down, another little group is slipping into the ditch, while a third further along the wall thinks they have found a spot and . . .

"There!" the girl in the wood nearly calls out, nearly shouts the word, points, and by the dwindling dark of night, there they are. There is the ladder bobbing in the darkness as the men try to steady it, and no one on the wall has yet seen, there are too few guards and they are too sleepy, waiting for the relief of day.

"What do we do?" asks a woman, but the girl who knows to believe in herself, who knows to trust her senses, stands, cups her hands about her mouth and without hesitation roars across the night.

"Attack! Attack! Attack!"

Her voice does not travel particularly clearly or well, but it is enough. When men are primed for danger, they jump, they stir, and this at last is a human sound, inescapable and real. On the walls, men draw their swords, peer into the dark, look down, along – and one at last sees the threat.

There could have still been some uncertainty, save that one crew of rebels, on hearing a woman's call, assume that the element of surprise is lost, cast off the swaddling from their blades and give a cry of war.

"Alarm!" hollers a guard on the wall, and: "Alarm!" adds another, who hasn't actually seen anything but decides the least he can do is join in and make a good show of things.

The doors to the farmhouse open. Slumbering men stir. I

hurry them along, snapping a cold tendril of breeze into their dull eyes, shoo them towards the wall. Odysseus emerges at a full run without armour and barefoot, bow in hand, looks to the walls, cannot clearly see the threat, calls out: "Where is the enemy?"

The guards on the wall do not immediately know how to answer – but the attackers will answer for them, for the first ladder is now notched against the fortification and the first plume of a helmet rises above it. On the walls Telemachus sees this and cries out, and now all the men of the farm are rushing, half dressed and barely armed, to grapple with the oncoming threat.

A ladder attack is always risky. Usually to succeed it requires some complacency or even treachery from the defenders inside the walls. Warriors may only proceed up a ladder one at a time, and have to fight their way over a ledge while being battered from all sides without losing their footing on a precarious collection of sticks and wood – a hazardous task. Ares, of course, loves nothing more than a reckless charge into near-certain doom, the valour of the bloody man who must hold, hold, hold. He loves to cradle a warrior in his arms as he dies, one who did the impossible – and as soon as the life has faded from the dead man's eyes he stands, shrugs and moves on without a care. War has no time, he says, to remember the names of the dead – that is a problem for peace. Nothing will get done if we stop to linger. This moment – just this – is the only thing that matters.

And this is why I will always be the greater warrior, sister, he adds, when the others are not listening. *This is why you are weak.*

He is, of course, mistaken, for though I do not linger over bodies, the stories of the dead may be spun into something that will live on, and in doing so, serve me.

Well then – a ladder attack. Of the seven ladders that have set forth to scale the walls of Laertes' farm, three are already lodged in place, their feet stuck in the mud at the bottom of the ditch, the tops leaning against the high parapet. Of these three, one is steep, the top protruding high above the wall's edge; one is a little too shallow, an angle that leads to falling, and one has been fairly optimally placed and already has the first man upon it, another nipping at his heels.

Of the other four, one is in a ditch struggling to be raised – this one handled by the crew who cannot keep their enthusiastic roaring to themselves – and the other three are still circling. These latter now abandon any pretence of finding a discreet stretch of wall and merely charge straight towards the nearest bit of farm to attempt their scaling. This is foolish, but blood is now up and dawn is creeping upon the land. So be it – rash decisions are made under such circumstances.

On the walls, Telemachus makes it to the first ladder just as a warrior's head pops up above its rim. For a moment the two men are startled by the sight of each other. Telemachus has not been taught what to do when a man is scaling your walls; nor is the attacking fellow quite sure how he's meant to both climb and fight at the same time. So much for the training of the noble warriors of Greece. For a moment they blink dumbly at each other, before one of the loyal guards who has a little more experience with these things barrels to Telemachus's side, sees the ladder and at once gives the fellow upon it a great big shove in the chest.

The climbing man sways, but does not fall – grabs for the nearest thing he can find for support, which turns out to be Telemachus's arm, and for a moment these three sway and rock together as each tries to push the other off, clings to the other for support. This situation could continue an embarrassingly intimate while, but Odysseus, having finally made it to the wall, sees the tumult, grabs Telemachus's sword from his belt and with a great big swing of the blade severs the attacker's arm nearly to the bone.

The man does not scream.

His blood is too high, his heart too loud, his skin too hot. Nor does the release of the ladder really register with him as a mighty fall, as he and it are shoved from the lip of the wall. He feels he is in control until the moment he hits the ground below, when the shock of impact knocks some semblance of sense into him and he finally feels how there is something wrong – something wrong – something so terribly wrong with his arm.

Seeing lets him understand.

Understanding breeds feelings that he has never felt before.

He thought he knew the taste of death, the touch of pain, had faced his fears and reconciled them. He was wrong.

"Ladders!" roars Odysseus. "To the walls!"

The second ladder is found just before a soldier can reach its top, and a tugging ensues as the men above try to poke at the climbers below with spears and waggling blades. This fight distracts men who should have spread out to cover the entire circumference of the farm, and a little huddle instead coalesces in this place as one man finally grabs an axe and manages to split the top rung of the ladder, then the rung below, before a javelin bounces off the wall besides him, nearly taking his hand, and yelping he darts back into cover.

"The whole wall, the whole wall!" Odysseus cries, but it is too late – the third ladder is up in an undefended patch of darkness, two men already at its top. Two men are enough to claim this little space long enough for more to follow, and they have only just now been seen by Eumaeus from the courtyard below. The old swineherd can't muster much in the way of speed, but does his best, calling out, pointing and gasping between thin breaths, "They're here! Here!"

In the rush of blood and battle, he does not think he's been heard. Then another old man is besides him. Laertes, his night-gown tied up about his knees and a chipped blade in hand, looks up at the warriors on the wall, nods once and, rather than charge, hollers with a remarkably good bellow for one so crabbed: "GET YOUR ARSES OVER HERE NOW YOU BLOODY IDIOTS!"

Such is the kingly habit of Laertes' disposition, that for a moment the rebel warriors upon the wall itself hesitate, unsure if perhaps it is they who are being commanded to get said arses to Laertes' location. Odysseus has not heard his father roar in such a way for over twenty years, but he heard it enough as a child that even now the familiarity of it cuts through the sound of blood in his ears, and he turns to see.

"Telemachus," he barks. "Hold this side – there will be more ladders – do not let them up! You, take the south, you with me!"

Telemachus is not a coward. He simply finds, to his surprise, that more than anything, he wants to live. So he stays where he is commanded, and throws rocks upon the men below, and keeps throwing them until the battered rebels turn and run away, armour dented, bones cracked, bleeding from a dozen wounds. That then is the battle for the western wall.

Odysseus reaches the eastern wall as a third warrior mounts the ladder and lands lightly on his feet, ready to fight. Those already upon the wall wisely make the decision that they are not much interested in hand-to-hand combat on so narrow a ledge, and trot towards the stairs to the yard below. There wait the two old men, Laertes and Eumaeus, who draw a little closer together, Laertes now taking a two-handed grip upon his old blade, neither yielding ground nor rushing into the fray. Eumaeus has no idea how he will fight – he has a pitchfork with which he is most competent at the shovelling of manure, and some experience with the handling of difficult pigs. It was not considered prudent by the kings of Ithaca to teach their slaves more than that.

Laertes knows precisely how he will fight. The speed and

manoeuvrability of his youth is gone, and he will not survive more than a few seconds of intense combat before fatigue drains the strength from his arms. But as a young man he always observed how surprised even the most veteran of warriors were when you focused on simply trying to cut their fingers off; an efficient device for an old king.

The rebels move towards the pair. Eumaeus shakes and tries to give a ferocious cry, but his throat is tight, mouth dry. Laertes scowls. Eumaeus jabs limply at an approaching rebel, who bats the fork aside without caring, too small a threat to merit consideration. Laertes eyes up the bare skin of a hand as it moves, finds that he doesn't mind especially that this is how he dies, raises his sword.

Then Odysseus is there, charging between the two old men like a bull, grabbing the haft of a threatening spear and yanking it out of the surprised hands of he who held it. I lend him a little strength as he turns the weapon, slams the butt up to catch the rebel beneath the chin, knocking him backwards in a crack of shattering teeth. The other rebel takes a swing for Odysseus's head, and the Ithacan is forced to duck below it, a desperate dodge. He nearly slips as he comes back up, steadies himself with the stolen spear he still grasps; and then Laertes is there too, stepping neatly round the side of the soldier whose full attention is now focused on his son, to cleanly and calmly drive his blade into the warrior's throat. Just because Laertes prioritises cutting off fingers does not mean he will miss a killing opportunity when it arises. The rebel falls, amazed. Not at his death – he is one who turned his heart from all thoughts of living, all dreams of hope or family or future, many years ago, and became the living dead, a warrior on the twilight line between life and shadow. He does not fear death. He is merely surprised that it came from the blade of an old, gap-toothed man. I catch him as he falls, ease him down, guide the light from his eyes. He was not one the poets would name, yet even for men such as he must the gods sometimes take responsibility.

His comrade dies a moment later, still reeling from the blow beneath his chin. Odysseus has time to line up the killing strike, slipping into a gap between front and back plates of the man's battered armour to pierce through his lung with the end of the stolen spear. Though two men now are dead at Laertes' feet, time has been taken, and four more are upon the wall, weapons drawn. For a moment, rebel faces king, each unsure what the other might do. Then Odysseus throws down his spear, re-hefts his bow, notches an arrow to the string. The rebel warriors do not wait to see where the arrow might fly, but charge as one.

CHAPTER 34

>>>

As dawn rises over the farm of Laertes, let us consider the situation.

In the yard: four rebels descend upon Odysseus, Laertes, Eumaeus and a better-late-than-never warrior of the palace guard. How evenly matched this combat will be depends on the willingness of the rebels to work together, and how well they move their feet. A wise warrior will constantly turn and turn again to ensure that he can only be attacked by one blade at a time, positioning himself so that say, for Laertes to attack, he must shove past Odysseus. Or for Eumaeus to land a blow, he must first shuffle round Laertes. A foolish warrior will merely try to pick a single fight and fight it, oblivious to the threat of Laertes' finger-chopping sword, or even Eumaeus's pitchfork. I will return to them in a moment.

On the western wall: Telemachus has seen another ladder being raised, and now runs with his little gaggle of loyal boys to hurl rocks upon the heads of the men who are trying to climb it. He is struggling with how effective stones are proving. Does a hero lay down his sword in favour of a rock? he wonders. Achilles never did, and neither did Hector, but they were both in positions of some authority. Rather, Achilles would stand, blade in hand and shield glinting, while about him men dug another ditch around the camp; and Hector, plumes billowing upon his head and sword gleaming in the sunlight, would prowl upon the walls of Troy declaring: "That's the spirit! More rocks here!"

In short: a great warrior such as the poets sing of need only lay down his sword and pick up a big rock when enough of his men are dead that he has no other option. One day Telemachus will understand this too.

This leaves three ladders unaccounted for. One is bogged in the ditch below the walls, its hasty construction showing as rungs start to pop from their bindings. One was detected by Odysseus's men as it pressed against the southern wall, a little too late – men were already upon it, already reaching the top by the time the defenders arrived, and now blades rend flesh and voices cry and blood is spilled in the chaos of battle. There is little space upon the wall, so each encounter is fought in a kind of queue, warrior replacing warrior as men fall or are hauled bleeding aside. One stumbles and tumbles into the dark in a crack of bone. Another is dragged, clutching a pouring wound in his thigh, behind the metal chests of his companions. An old man lies gurgling his bloody last; a boy is weeping in the dark. I hold them in my arms, whisper: *You die well. You die well. You are dying for something more.*

Just one ladder remains unseen. The men who crew it are perhaps the wisest of the attackers, for they have made no sound, given no battle cry, but rather maintained their crawl through the dark, avoiding the temptation to run straight to the walls even when battle is joined. Instead they have found a space near the smoke-charred forest, and here they secure themselves, and begin to climb.

They are not spotted as they ascend.

Not regarded as the first clears the top of the wall.

The crimson fog of battle lies too tight over the eyes of the fighting men. I look to the east and see the first fire of golden dawn, see it glint off bloody bronze. Only when the last man is upon the ladder, does an arrow fly.

It does not come from the farm. Instead it looses from the trees behind them, buries in a reaching arm, nearly pinning it to the ladder the rebel has halfway climbed. He stares at it amazed, as if he cannot comprehend this thing that is now protruding from his body. The next arrow doesn't manage to penetrate his breastplate, but its impact jars him back into reality, slams the breath from him. He falls. It is not a long way down, but it is enough to knock some part of his mind back into function-ality – and on hands and knees he scrambles from the ladder, arrow still protruding, near weeping with the shock, the shame even, of how much he wants to live.

I look to the forest, and think I see Artemis steady the arm of the woman who holds the bow. Then they both are gone, leaving the bewildered soldiers still standing upon the wall.

In the yard, a rebel swipes for Odysseus and has his sword turned away – but he is skilled enough that he does not stay locked in his enemy's motion, but rather snatches his arm back, looking for another strike. Odysseus too is hunting for the kill. Like his father he loves to attack fingers, little slices against bare pinkies, keeping at a distance, preventing his enemy's defence from turn-ing into attack. Everyone is tiring. More time passes between each slash; breath comes in heaving, panting gulps.

It is this, perhaps, that encourages to action one rebel who up to now has been too far back to make a difference in the fight. With a leap he throws himself from the stairs, dropping nearly the whole height of a man to land in a messy crouch near Eumaeus, and with a roar sends his blade towards the swine-herd's head. Eumaeus lurches clumsily out of the way, loses his footing, falls. The warrior stands upon his chest, raises his blade for the killing blow.

Odysseus does not move to defend him.

It is not that he does not feel affection for the old man. He does. Eumaeus in particular did good work looking after Odysseus's old dog, for whom the Ithacan felt a great deal of fondness. It is merely that, in the tactical assessment of the moment, of all the people he can afford to let die, Eumaeus is high on the list. He does not want him dead. Nor is he willing to risk losing his own arm to save him. In the balance of the thing, Odysseus needs to keep fighting. Eumaeus does not.

The palace guard by Odysseus's side does not know this. He thinks his king is a good man, has heard stories of the valour of noble Odysseus. He thinks he will be rewarded for doing the right thing. That is why he throws himself towards the swineherd, deflects the blow that was otherwise marked for Eumaeus, and with his attention so focused on the fallen man does not see the fist that is thrown by the warrior who opposes him, which lands squarely in the middle of his face and breaks his nose.

The shock of blood and ringing of skull and cracking of inner parts of his face is enough to blind him for a moment. A moment is enough for the rebel who punched him to turn his sword away from the scuttling swineherd, and drive it up under the man's breastplate and into his chest.

The weight of the guard as he falls drags the sword down with him. Buried between bronze and bone, his killer struggles for a moment to get it out. That struggle is long enough for Laertes to perform his favourite trick of cutting the man's hand off, and as he falls screaming, Laertes calmly drives his blade into the rebel's throat.

Thus two men die, for what neither will never really know,

and they will be nameless, forgotten, and so the battle rages on.

Unseen, five men move along the walls.

They have three choices: to join their comrades in battle, to take the gates, or to take the house.

They could open the gate, but there is still a barricade against it, and moving that will take time and draw attention. Even if they succeed, there is no guarantee that Gaios and the remaining men of Polybus and Eupheithes will be able to cross the ground between their camp and the farm fast enough to storm the open maw before Odysseus retakes control and bars the path.

They could join their comrades. This would be the most companionable thing to do, sneaking up to perhaps run Laertes through from behind, or cut Telemachus's throat when his back is turned. However, they are not enough in number for even that surprise to necessarily turn the tide of battle – too few of their comrades have scaled the wall, their numbers are somewhat evenly matched, and though they fight mostly boys and old men, they also fight Odysseus. *Odysseus*, I breathe. *Odysseus! Fear the name of Odysseus, fear the cunning of Odysseus, fear him, my storied king, fear . . .*

Two of their number prowl along the wall and do indeed join the fight against Telemachus, cutting down a boy of Telemachus's crew before they are seen, oblivious to his youth, just another obstacle to their objective in this fight.

The remaining three slip into Laertes' house.

It is unguarded.

But not unoccupied.

At the foot of the stairs, Odysseus finally manages to kill the man before him. He sets a trap – exaggerates how much he gasps for breath, feigns a stumble, steps back. Into this apparent opportunity lunges the man, arm raised for a killing blow. The snap of Odysseus's sword across his neck is short and sharp. The Ithacan king barely needs to raise his blade to take the kill – the momentum of his enemy does most of the work for him. Laertes manages to cut the tendons on the back of the legs of one who still stands upon the stair. His fall knocks into the man in front of him, who stumbles, loses his footing. Odysseus does not hesitate to drive his sword through the soldier's chest as he tumbles, and rather than waste time on trying to remove the blade from the weight of the corpse that now crushes it, grabs his father's blade from his hand and drives it under the armour of the last man standing.

On the opposite side of the yard, Telemachus has nowhere left to go. The arrival of two new enemies has taken away all space, all opportunity. He is beset from both sides, his friends dying around him. He tightens up, shoulders bunched, feet square, focuses on the small, sharp power of his blade, on turning at his hips, on trying to get a counter in where he can, on shuffling steps and lunges side to side to claim what little space he can. There is a singing in his ears, heat blurring his vision, his heart thundering so hard he thinks it will burst. He tries to conserve energy, move only enough to stay alive, knows this will not be enough. He realises with a sudden lunge of terror that he has nothing left. He is surprised to find that he thinks in this moment not of his father, who will soon see him die, but of someone else entirely. Kenamon.

After all, it was Kenamon who taught Telemachus the blade, not Odysseus.

"Move!" shouts Kenamon in Telemachus's ear.

Move, I whisper.

"Every defence is an attack! If you can't be strong, be unexpected!"

Stay alive, boy, I add. *Stay alive.*

Telemachus wishes Kenamon was here now. He is astonished

at the thought. He is ashamed of it. Kenamon was a suitor, a stranger, a cursed man. And yet he also saved Telemachus's life, when pirates came. Asked the boy if he missed his father. As if he knew what it was like to have a father he could miss.

Stay alive, I murmur. *You are still of use to me.*

The tip of a blade ripples through the skin of Telemachus's arm. The thrust of a spear nearly punctures his neck, and the one who wields it drops his weight and uses the haft of the weapon to slam into Telemachus's chest, knocking him backwards. As Telemachus stumbles, he sees the body of a boy who sailed with him to Pylos, one of the few young men of the island he would consider friend, lying on the dirt below. He wishes the sight inspired him, sent him into furies of manly rage, gave him a second wind, filled his chest with cries of *Vengeance!!* Did not Achilles go mad on the death of Patroclus? Is this not how things should be?

Instead he feels for a moment: sad, empty, ashamed.

Telemachus has felt ashamed so many times in his life, but never known until now that this was what it was.

Then he looks up.

Sees an axe descending towards his skull.

Knows he will not raise his sword in time to block it.

Misread the angle of attack.

Misread the way it would come.

Will die for this mistake.

Closes his eyes.

He hears the arrow strike the man who would have killed him, and knows it must have been fired from his father's bow, because it punches through the warrior's armour like light through air. He opens his eyes, sees the man sway, shocked and confused by the shaft sticking out of his side, shoves him back with all his mass and keeps going, charging along the wall.

Another arrow smacks into the man behind Telemachus,

271

and then Odysseus is there, by his son's side, and the men who fought off the final ladder have also rallied, are turning now to fall upon the last soldiers of Polybus and Eupheithes within these walls. There will be no mercy. Telemachus drives his blade into the heart of one and keeps driving, pushes it all the way through his broken chest, howls, howls, howls, until his father pulls him away.

"Enough," whispers Odysseus, as Telemachus shakes and snarls and snarls and shakes. "*Enough.*"

Laertes stands below, looks up at his son, his grandson. Seems to now remember that he is old.

Eumaeus has not risen from where he fell. He is not dead, not even injured. He just cannot imagine moving ever again. The sky above him seems more beautiful than he has ever seen. He wants to weep with the beauty of the rising dawn. He has never wondered what it might be to be anything other than a slave. He will not conceive of it now, and yet – and yet – in this one moment of his life he wonders if there was something . . . something else . . . something unknowable and unnamed . . . that he has missed in his long and monotonous existence.

Telemachus always wondered what it would be like to be held by his father. He never thought it would feel like this.

Then a voice in the yard calls out: "Odysseus!"

The men on the walls are bloody, sweaty, sore, tired.

The light of dawn is high enough to pick out a world fringed in silver, prickled with pink.

"Odysseus!" calls the voice again, for he who calls does not know which one of these crimson-washed men still living is Odysseus.

And there they are.

The three who went into the house of Laertes are now emerging. One holds Autonoe by the arm. Another has a sword across Penelope's throat, his other hand tangled in her hair.

The queen of Ithaca stands stiff and straight and grey, a soldier's breastplate pressing into her back.

"King of Ithaca!" calls the man who leads them, standing a little to the side of the queen and her captor, blade in hand.

Odysseus lets go his son.

Rises.

Looks along the walls. Looks down into the yard. Murmurs: "Check that there are no other ladders."

Telemachus tries to speak, but the words won't come. His father takes his silence for obedience. Slowly begins to descend, a bloody sword in hand. He isn't sure whose sword it is, or where it came from. He picked it up from someone – friend, foe – in battle. It is a slightly odd weight, strangely balanced. He dislikes fighting with weapons he doesn't fully know.

Laertes is standing ten paces away from the men who now hold a blade to Penelope's throat. He is unregarded, just an old man, so no one objects when he picks up the sword of a dead man at his feet. Odysseus stops more than a spear's distance from the men who hold his wife by the throat. Looks them up and down. Says: "And what precisely is your plan?"

The leader of the group waves the tip of his weapon towards the king of Ithaca, but doesn't take a step. "Drop your weapon."

"And then what?" sighs Odysseus. "What happens then?"

The man licks his lips. He has not fully considered this most pertinent of enquiries. "No one else has to die," he stutters at last. "Your wife can live. She can live far away from here. Safe. They just want you."

Odysseus's brow flickers, though what surprise he may feel is gone in a flutter. "Really?" he muses. "What about my father? My son? Will they not be bound by all the sacred oaths of Olympus to take vengeance for my death? Surely they too must die."

The logic is, alas, flawless. These rebels know it. The one who grasps Penelope holds a little tighter. The one who holds Autonoe seems to barely know she is there, so hypnotised is he by the Ithacan king – or rather, by the idea of the king, the reality hardly relevant to his feelings.

Odysseus, hero of Troy, I whisper in his ear. *Fear him, fear him – oh but fear him . . .*

"Your wife," their leader stutters. "Your wife. She can . . . Everyone knows you love your wife."

Odysseus's eyes meet Penelope's.

There is no smile.

No frown.

No cry of anguish, nor tremulous lip, nor gasping in despair.

Instead, he looks to her as she looks to him, and there is something there that is almost a conversation. A question, as though to say: *Is that so?*

It is Penelope who lets out a sigh.

Half closes her eyes.

Draws in just a fraction of a breath, holds it an instant, and:

"Oh my husband my beloved my dearest one don't care for me don't risk your life for me oh my Odysseus!" She babbles it all in one big breath, hoping that the speed of delivery will at least somewhat compensate for how little enthusiasm she has for the sentiment. When that breath is finished, she draws in another, raises her voice to a near shriek, furrows her brow and presses her eyelids shut in an effort to squeeze out a tear, blubbers: *"Flee my love! Save yourself! Save our son!"*

And then, having somewhat unnerved the man who holds her, and with more than a little concern for the blade pressed to her neck, she swoons.

It is a careful swoon.

She has hooked one hand about the arm that holds the sword

across her throat, just in case the whole thing gets a little out of control, and the other slips round her back to the folds of her tussled gown as she descends. Her eyes flutter – but do not close – and as she falls, her head bends upwards with a dragging of hair and curling of neck.

The sword that is held to her neck slips along her skin, scratching as it goes. It nicks her chin, a little slither of blood starting to flow – but the man who holds her does not run it across her throat. Instead he draws the blade away, unsure what to do as the queen of Ithaca droops in his arms. He lets go of her hair to catch her beneath an armpit as she descends, rattles and bobs her into some sort of standing position. His motion twists her loose and dangling feet, so she seems to spin on the spot, revolving to face him in her semi-stuporous state of feminine despair.

When her eyes open to look up into his, they are fully awake and aware.

His blade is by his side now, no longer against her neck.

Her blade, hidden carefully in her gown, is sharp and thin. He doesn't immediately notice that it's passed into him, but feels a strangeness as it's withdrawn, as of an unexpected releasing of pressure in his chest. Then he feels light. Then he feels heavy. Then he feels a long way away, yet still somehow present in his body. Only then does he look down and see the crimson billowing on her gown where it presses against his body, feel the blood rushing freely down the outside of his leg.

Only then does he feel the pain, and understand that he is going to die.

Autonoe had also hidden her blade when the men came; now she drives it into the neck of the man who holds her before he can understand what is happening. She shrieks, she screams, she kneels upon him as he falls and stabs again and again and again, roaring, howling, his blood spraying into her mouth, her eyes, across her skin, and still she stabs until at last Laertes pulls her feebly away, kicking and shrieking like the wounded wolf.

The final man turns from Odysseus long enough to see his friends die, and when he turns back, the last thing he sees is the blade of the king of Ithaca driving home.

CHAPTER 35

>>>

In the morning light, a counting of the dead.

The bodies of twenty-three rebels are thrown from the walls of Laertes' farm into the ditch below. It is bad tactics to fill your own defensive ditch with bodies, but Odysseus hopes that decency will prevail and someone from the other side will call for a truce and perform the burial rites that he does not have the time or energy to do.

Eupheithes says: "Let the crows take them! Let them stink and curse the farm of Laertes!"

Polybus says: "Some of them knew my son."

Gaios barks: "We will bury them!" and that, remarkably, is that.

A messenger is sent to request recovery of the bodies.

Odysseus makes a show of thinking about it, before agreeing – because he is an honourable man. The stench of their flesh was already swelling with the rising sun, and he is hoping to nap while the dead are dragged away.

Inside the farm, eight men are dead, another three wounded. The dead are buried. The wounded are led inside to groan and toss out of sight of the living. Laertes wrinkles his nose as the holes are dug. He is not a pious man, does not believe in things sacred or profane. Yet he feels his farm should be a place for snuffling pigs and rich drink, for the smell of fresh cooking in the evening and the caress of the first light of spring. Not a burial ground for the unsung dead.

Odysseus's fighting force is now twelve men, in various states of injury.

His fingers brush the feathers of the iron-tipped arrows and find he has eleven left.

Telemachus leads what few of his boys remain to gather up the ladders that are standing against the walls and break them down for kindling.

Odysseus stands upon the wall above the gates and looks towards the camp of Eupheithes and Polybus. He thinks there are perhaps sixty men within it. He wonders how long it will take for them to fetch reinforcements.

He does not think it will be long.

Laertes says: "Well, that's the last of the wine."

Eumaeus stutters: "I'm sure we will find more loyal men if we can just make it to the harbour . . . "

Telemachus says nothing at all.

In the yard, Autonoe fetches water from the well. She has washed some of the blood from her face, some from her hands. There is still crimson under her nails, across her gown. She shows no inclination to change her garb, seems hardly to notice it, though it is starting to itch something dreadful.

Odysseus looks for Penelope, and finds her standing by the door of the farmhouse, arms folded, the knife that usually she keeps hidden now tucked into a cord about her waist. She is watching the work of the yard, the burial of the dead, the flies crawling over unwashed blood. The cut to her chin has started to scab. She too does not seem much interested in washing the blood from her gown, and no one seems inclined to ask her to.

Odysseus watches his wife.

She watches him.

He lays down his bow.

His arrows.

His blade.

Descends from the wall; walks over, stands before her.

Looks her up and down again, sees the blood, the ice, the coldness of her eyes.

Tries to find the words.

The needful words.

The words he has never thought to say.

Looks to his father, finds no inspiration there.

Does not look to his son, is immediately certain he'll get nothing useful there.

Looks about the yard, blood and mud and death, sees Autonoe. She has found the hand of one of the rebels that Laertes severed. She carries it over to a freshly dug pit, throws it in, goes back to her business. Looks at no one and nothing, as if this world holds no interest to her at this time.

Turns back to his wife.

Says: "I . . . "

The words that should follow stick in his throat.

I put my hand on his shoulder.

This is it, I whisper. *This is it.*

He tries again. "You are hurt."

"What?"

"Your . . . " He indicates his chin. It seems somehow intrusive to indicate hers.

"Oh. It's fine."

"Your lady should tend to you."

"What use would that be?"

None, he must concede. Absolutely none at all.

A little while he stands by her, watching the nothing that she watches too. When he finally speaks, the words are almost too small to hear, snatched away by the breeze.

"I'm . . . sorry."

Penelope's face does not move, does not twitch, but her whole body seems suddenly to clench.

Odysseus forces his lips around the words, finds them both easier and harder on the second go. "I'm sorry. I have . . . I have failed you."

"Because I have a cut on my chin?"

"Because you are here. In this place where we are very likely to die."

She shrugs. "After you murdered the suitors, there were only so many likely outcomes. If I was to be hunted and killed, this seemed as good a place as any."

"Nevertheless. I am . . . sorry. For all of it."

"Sorry for all of it?" muses Penelope. "Which part of it? Be specific."

This is absolutely not the answer Odysseus was expecting, but then again, the blood, the flies, the weariness, the broken men all about.

Eleven arrows, he thinks. A dozen men. He smiled and simpered and didn't once punch Agamemnon. He can do this; he is, after all, extraordinary.

"For . . . not being honest with you, when I came to Ithaca," he says at last, thinking it through, each word a step on a thorny, winding road. "For acting in haste. Without judgement. You are right. I was testing you. I wanted to see if you . . . I was angry, so angry, but that isn't it at all. I wanted to be the master of my house. The master of anything. Anything at all. To have mastery. A man should be master of his wife, and I . . . I see that . . . that it is likely that you have kept a kind of peace here. You have kept a peace. I should have . . . It was not wise to break that without . . . I should have found another way. I was

280

so ... All I saw was betrayal, there have been ... These years have been ... "

He stops.

Looks again to his wife.

Sees contempt in her face. What are his years to her? What is his story now?

Tries again.

"I brought this upon us. Upon our land. Upon my father, our son. Upon you. In this place ... you could have died and I was ... and I am sorry. For that. Profoundly. As ... as your husband. As your husband."

"My husband." Penelope tries the words, tasting them with the same unfamiliarity as an apology might sit upon Odysseus's lips. "Which husband is that? The one who sailed to Troy never apologised for anything. The things he did were necessary. I understood that, so did he. He had no choice about sailing. And yet I was still left. The one who returned? Broke my peace. Sullied my palace. Slaughtered unarmed men and innocent maids. Brought destruction to my family. And now he says he is sorry. Well then. I suppose that's all right, isn't it?"

A flash of other women briefly before Odysseus's eyes: Circe, back straight, eyes on some distant place as he sails away. Calypso, brimming with fury at the command of the gods. He thought their sentiments at his departure somehow petty; sulking, lonely women who couldn't live without him. And yet here it is again, this tilting of bloody chin, this turning away of her gaze. Penelope has cleaned the blood from the knife at her side because it is a tool, and tools must be looked after. That has been her only real concession to the slaughter now splattered across her skin.

"The women," he says, and is surprised to hear his own voice speak it. "Your maids. For what we did ... for what I did. At Troy, all we spoke of was Helen – traitor queen,

281

opened her legs to a Trojan prince and so the world must burn. And Clytemnestra, killed my sworn brother, lay with another man, everyone said ... it was ... And you're right, of course. I barely know these isles. You do. It would weaken my position to kill the woman who has run them for twenty years, damage my state even further than it already is, but I was so angry, I was so ... and at the time I thought ... but I was wrong. It was ... wrong. Your maids. The women. It was ... unforgivable."

Does she shiver with the cold of the wind without, or the cracking ice of a soul within? He cannot tell.

No one will ever speak words of apology, tenderness or compassion to me, and I will never ask.

"When this is done, if we live – if we live – I will ask nothing from you. Nothing. No questions, no ... explanations of anything that may have gone before. Not your forgiveness. Not your love. I understand that now. If you wish to take your women and live apart, wife in name, queen in ... in whatever way will serve to keep the lands ... I will understand. I will not make you pretend to love me. I was wrong. I am sorry."

Odysseus does not know if he is lying.

He is not quite sure when he became incapable of telling the difference in his heart, but knows it has been that way for a very, very long time.

Penelope hates this man.

She knows it inside her, with every pulse of her heart.

She hates him.

She also wants to cry.

She wants him to hold her tight.

She wants to weep into his chest.

She cannot understand how she can feel so many things, all at the same time. Thought perhaps she had mastered the art of feeling none of them at all. Is a little disappointed to find that it is not so, that the feeling of an empty heart was perhaps just a disguise for the truth of a heart too full to comprehend.

I cannot look at her, in that moment. It hurts too much – too much, even for me. I cannot. It will break me.

Penelope gazes across the yard.

Laertes is looking at her, waiting.

Telemachus stands with his back to her on the wall.

Autonoe buries the dead.

She watches Autonoe the longest while, before finally, with every strength of fibre she has left in her, turning to look her husband in the eye.

"Walk with me," she says.

CHAPTER 36

>>

T he barricade is peeled back just enough from the gate of
the farm that two people can squeeze through the tight,
scarred gap.

They hug the walls.

Eyes watch them from the walls above, as eyes watch them
from the camp across the burned-out land. This is technically
a time of truce, a time to bury the dead, sing the funeral songs.
Despite this, if Gaios's men were not wounded, diminished in
number, licking their wounds, they would attack. Of course
they would. They would race across this bloody, ashen field and
try to hack down Odysseus and his wife right now. But they are
unprepared, and even if they were ready, their camp is deliberately positioned out of archers' range. In the time it would take
to gather men to hack at these two wanderers circling their little
fort, the attack would be seen, the alarm given, the wanderers
rushed back inside.

This will not prevent Eupheithes and Polybus fuming,
demanding more sentries about the farm, more men always on
watch. What if Odysseus actually tried to escape? they demand.
What if they tried to make a run for it?

Where would they go? Gaios replies, eyes weary and face

stone as he gazes upon his employers. You command the harbours, the roads, the sea. Where exactly do you think the king of Ithaca can go?

Well then; in this time of truce and funeral song, of not quite ready to not quite fight again, Penelope and Odysseus walk about the edge of the farm.

Outside the walls it smells less of blood, less of death. The wind carries the faintest whiff of the sea. The birds sing in the forest; the sky is sapphire streaked with thin white clouds. It is, Penelope thinks, a beautiful day to paddle barefoot in cold water with your singing maids, telling stories of things gone by, of dreams that you would never normally dare whisper could be true.

Penelope pauses as they walk to look across the land. She bends down to feel the soil, dry and scarred with ash, and then a little deeper – the life just below. She feels suddenly the blood that coats her dress, her neck. Inside the walls of Laertes' farm it was merely uniform. Out here, with the sky above and the isle bending away before her, it is filthy, obscene.

She sighs, straightens and walks on, Odysseus by her side.

He does not interrupt her contemplations.

She waits until they are away from the gate, away from Telemachus, and near the eastern edge of the forest, before she stops, hands on her hips, to gaze towards the line of trees.

Odysseus stands a polite distance away – close enough to hear, not so close as to intrude upon Penelope's contemplations.

Her eyes watch the darkness of the wood, though her voice, when she speaks, is turned towards him. "There were pirates. A few years ago. Did Telemachus explain? No – probably not. A suitor by the name of Andraemon grew impatient with waiting. He was a veteran of Troy, had friends, soldiers, who had not received what they considered their fair share from the plundering of that city and who therefore had turned, as these men always will, to raiding. The fear of Odysseus's name kept them at bay for a while – what if my husband returned, found that fellow Greeks had been ravaging his land? But as the years rolled by, his name diminished and the raiders grew more bold. Andraemon and his spies told them where to strike. He hoped by taking my people, burning my land, he could force me into a marriage. Peisenor tried to raise a militia to defend the island – Telemachus joined, of course, ridiculous child. But it was manned only by untrained boys, and led by captains who couldn't agree on whether it was night or day. When the raiders attacked, Peisenor's militia died. As they were always going to. So I raised my own."

Odysseus stands taut as his bow. This is it, he thinks. This is it. So obvious. Why didn't I think of it?

"Naturally there weren't enough men to go around, and folly to buy mercenaries, so I turned to more irregular options. A warrior from the east – a woman called Priene – entered my service and trained some of the women who felt inclined, as I was, to defend their own. They gathered at the temple of Artemis, learned to set traps, shoot bows, fight by darkness, to strike and run. The first battle they fought was against Andraemon's raiders. They fought Menelaus's Spartans too, when that time came. When people asked, 'How come all these pirates seem to be dying?' the priestess of Artemis announced it was a sign of divine intervention, and for the most part that seemed to do. The idea that the widows and daughters of Ithaca had taken up arms was, thankfully, inconceivable. It needed to be inconceivable. Your brother kings would have laughed at the idea. Ithaca defended by women? By weaklings and whores? Clearly it is ripe for the picking! Imagine the battles we would have had to fight then, fending off wave after wave of mercenary men who could not envisage how they might die by the hands of women. Better by far that no one could imagine. That no one ever lived to tell the tale. Better that we controlled the story."

She sighs, shakes her head. These things she describes – they seemed so mighty at the time, so huge and difficult. Now, she looks back upon them and they are small, distant, memories of a simpler world.

"Then you returned. I considered, and my captain advised, simply killing the suitors for you. But that would not solve our problem. If the name of Odysseus kept raiders from the western isles before, then the name of Odysseus must continue to do so again. Odysseus backed by an army of women? Absurd. It would destroy the prestige of that name to even hint at it being supported by anything other than warrior men bound by some ... manly thing ... " A loose wave of a hand; she cannot conceive of what use this honour might be now. "And if the name of Odysseus is destroyed then we're back exactly where we started. Islands defended by women. Easy prey. No. When the poets speak of Odysseus's return, they must say how he masterfully seized control of his domain by valiant force of arms, of how terrifying and relentless he is, so that no raider or petty pirate even thinks twice about threatening the western isles again. If Telemachus can be involved too – all the better. Odysseus will be dead one day, after all, and it is valuable to the story of the isles that his son is suitably bloodied before he goes. And there you were. After all this time, there you were – a shipwrecked sailor of Crete, my backside. You can't even do the accent right."

Odysseus is having to digest a little too much right now to take time to bristle, but as his wife has paused for breath, he murmurs: "If you knew me, why didn't you say something?"

"Because it was so blitheringly obvious that you were considering murdering me." She speaks these words as light as summer air, bloody fingers outstretched at her side as if she would capture the wind. He opens his mouth to splutter a denial, but she cuts him off without a thought. "If you had come to me as my husband, trusted me, then of course we could have worked together. But you came to my palace as a beggar, lied to my face. You were utterly oblivious to the realities of the situation, so obsessed with skulking around probing my sexual piety that you clearly weren't in a mood to stop and consider the possibility that I might have been *forced* to chastity, commanded to twenty years of an empty bed for the very simple reason that it was how I stayed alive. As if I would lay down my life, the security of my kingdom and my station, for such things as good company, companionship, tenderness, pleasure, intimacy, desire, yearning, a wanting to be seen, a longing to be known, faith in another, days of laughter and nights without fear – let alone with some idiot boy young enough to be my son."

I stand by Penelope as her words shimmer through the air, my knuckles white where they grasp my spear, the drumbeat of her heart echoing in my own.

Stay alive, stay alive, stay alive.

Be as ice, and stay alive.

"And if you had concluded that I had lain with another man," she continued, "obviously you would have slaughtered me as surely as Orestes killed Clytemnestra, regardless of the idiocy of such an act. I suppose you would have justified your brutality to yourself in some terms of honour, masking jealousy and petty pride. Chaste Penelope, doting Penelope – so much safer than clever Penelope, powerful Penelope, no? So no, clearly I couldn't tell you the truth of my situation. Of the power I have amassed, the warriors, the intelligence, the alliances I have made and broken in the name of peace – and in Odysseus's name, of course. Everything always in Odysseus's name. I have worked very hard to keep that name strong, you see. Not Penelope, queen of Ithaca, lady of the western isles. Just Penelope, wife of Odysseus. You see how it goes."

There is a smile upon her lips. It does not find anything funny.

Odysseus takes his time, thinks this through, feels his heart rushing in his chest. Says at last: "In the garden . . . I heard you pray." Another thought, puffed out in sudden understanding. "You knew I was there."

"You heard what you needed to hear."

"And the man you spoke with?"

"Kenamon. An Egyptian. When Andraemon's pirates first attacked Ithaca, he saved Telemachus's life, at great risk to his own. And then when Menelaus occupied the island, he fought against the Spartans to protect me, Elektra and Orestes. He could never be king, of course, and he knew it. But he felt a great deal of affection for your son, and was of much service. He might have been able to kill you, at the feast. Of all the men in the hall – I would say he stood the greatest chance. And I couldn't let that happen. Not he kill you, nor you kill him. So I sent him away. At least I was able to save one life."

"Did you love him?" Odysseus is surprised that he can say these words without screaming, without foaming at the mouth, without falling to his knees.

Penelope doesn't immediately answer, and again, Odysseus does not rage, does not sway, does not fall weeping to the earth. Instead, in her silence, he closes his eyes and thinks he sees . . .

Circe, singing in her house away from the sea.

Calypso, picking fruit from the stem, juice upon her fingers, upon her lips.

"Perhaps," Penelope muses. "I have spent so long, these last twenty years, burying any fragment of my soul that might even dream of desire that I hardly know any more. As a girl, I told myself that I loved you, because that is what girls are meant to do, but there was no time to really find out what that might mean before you were gone, and so this thing – this thing the poets speak of as so fundamental, so vital to being alive – I never had a chance to really explore its limits, determine its meaning. It seems to me that to love, one must most likely be open to the possibility of it, to consider that it is feasible at all. I have not considered it feasible. Love makes you vulnerable. I cannot afford a moment of weakness – it would destroy me, and everything I have built. Does it then strike despite my shuttered, shrivelled heart? I am not sure I would know it if it did."

I should take Penelope by the hand.

Artemis would pat her gently on the shoulder, as bold a display of affection as ever the huntress shows.

Aphrodite would twine her in her arms, nuzzle her lips into the queen's bloodied neck.

Even Hera, old, broken Hera, would tangle her fingers with Penelope's own, whisper in her ear: *I am with you, my lovely. I am with you, my dear.*

I do not.

I, who should exult in this woman, who should clasp her to me and cry out, sister, sister, my beloved, my dearest sister – I stand dumb as stone by her side, and do not. I want to, with every fibre of my being I want to, and think the wanting will break me in two, and do not move.

And Odysseus?

Odysseus closes his eyes again, sees Circe, sees Calypso, again, sees the fires of Troy, sees the seas opening beneath him as he clings on, clings on, clings onto the olive branch above the whirlpool, tries to banish it all, cannot. Has tried so hard, for so long. Thinks he will never be free of it.

Lets out a breath. Tries to think. Replays her words, struggling to make sense of them. "You drugged the suitors," he murmurs, revelation dawning so brightly he cannot keep it from tumbling from his mouth.

"Yes. Even with the best of your preparations, twenty men

against a hundred? The insanity of it. I was infuriated that you'd even try."

"They were unarmed, unprepared . . ."

"It was absolute folly and you know it. You were driven by pride and rage – nothing more. Even if you are not ashamed of yourself for your slaughter upon our sacred palace stones, you should be ashamed of yourself as a soldier and a tactician. Odysseus the clever. The sea addled your wits. I could afford to let you die, perhaps, and if lucky in the process you would eliminate a fair number of the men who threatened my security – but you had also dragged our son into it. Telemachus . . . for all his . . . I needed to be certain that he lived. He must live."

Perhaps she's right, he thinks. Perhaps he has too much salt sloshing around his skull. And yet, here it comes . . .

"The *maids* drugged the suitors."

"Of course. You didn't think I could do it?"

"They poured the drink, then they left the room. Sealed the doors."

"My maids," barks Penelope, "have been gathering information on the men of this isle since the moment you set to sea. It is astonishing the things people will reveal to someone they hardly see. Remarkable the confessions made to a nice smile after a cup of wine. I am, I think we can agree, a competent queen, but even with the best will in the world do you really think I could stay ahead of one hundred ambitious men without having claws in every one? The women you slaughtered were the guardians of your house. They were its walls, its spears, its bows. They were the soldiers who kept your kingdom safe. And Eos . . ." The name is a stone in her throat. She has to try and suck air past it, her lungs stuck on the sound. " . . . Eos was the best of them. She was the best. She held my hand when our son was born. She protected me. Shared my secrets. Caught me when I stumbled. Was the executor of every plan. And you hanged her from the columns of the house like ... like salted meat ... on the say-so of a bitter old maid and a boy. You have no idea the woman you killed. You have no idea the power she had, or what a blow you struck against yourself that day. You slaughtered the protectors of your own kingdom, and didn't even feel yourself bleeding as you killed them."

She is weeping now.

Her voice doesn't waver, and she does not look at him, and does not try to brush the tears from her cheeks.

I should hold her.

I try to move my hand towards her, and cannot.

There is no tenderness left in me. No compassion. I burned it all away, in war and wisdom; it is gone, and none shall ever know how deeply I grieve it.

Odysseus feels sick. He has this overwhelming urge to sit down, cross-legged, *plonk*, on the muddy ground until his malady passes. But Penelope is standing and so he must too. That is the way of things.

"What should we do now?" he asks, and no sooner are the words out of his mouth than he stops, corrects himself, shakes his head. "What do you need me to do?"

Penelope turns slowly, wipes her tears, and for it seems the very first time looks at her husband. "Are you asking my advice?"

"You are the queen of the western isles," he replies. "I only ruled a few years before I left. I did not imagine Troy, despite prophecies and warnings. And when I was there, I could not imagine Ithaca. You have ruled for twenty years. You have raised our son. This island ... these lands ... you are their queen. And I am ... sorry. I am ... truly sorry ... for everything I have done."

These are, Odysseus thinks, the most extraordinary words he has ever said.

He wants to hold his wife.

He wants to hold his wife, and to be held.

Instead, they stand a few steps apart, not touching, breath fast, as the sun climbs high through the glistening day, faces stained with salt and blood.

Penelope smiles.

It is not forgiveness, but at the sight of it Odysseus drags down a gasp, hauls back a shudder that ripples through his body. Does not know what this feeling is; wonders if it is hope.

Penelope, queen of Ithaca, lady of the western isles, turns from her husband to the forest, and raises her hand.

And from the shroud of trees, a woman steps.

She carries a bow in one hand, a knife at her hip. There is mud on her face, in her clothes; she moves as if she was born of the earth itself.

Then another joins her, a woodcutter's axe in hand, a javelin across her back.

Another, who carries twin blades on her hips; another with a sickle and a scythe. Here, a pair who might be sisters, carrying hunters' bows. There, a group with carpenters' tools who as children learned to set snares for rabbits, and now set traps for something bigger. There are maids of the palace, those who survived, knives gripped in white-knuckled fingers; widows with no sons left to help them gut the fish they catch upon the blackened shore; daughters who will never make a match.

From the forest, the women of Ithaca come. Anaitis, priestess of Artemis, emerges with her arrows and bow, her hair bound up in tight winding braids. Old Semele, hands like the wood she chops, and her daughter, Mirene, with shoulders like the proud old tree, axe on her back, bear-killing bow in hand. Priene comes last, Teodora at her side, the women parting to let their captain through.

"Well," muses Penelope, as they begin to flow from the forest towards their waiting queen. "Let us see what we can do."

CHAPTER 37

>>>>>>>>>>>>>>>>>>>>>>>>>>>>>>>>>>>>>>

Telemachus, at the approach of nearly sixty women armed with bow and blade, doesn't know what to do.

He calls out to seal the gates – seal the gates! – but his father and oh yes, his mother too, they are still outside the walls, and if these foul and muddy creatures of the blackened forest haven't killed them already he really must do his best to get them back inside. So he orders the gates pressed shut and sprints around the walls to try and spot his parents, to find them talking to a woman with knives on her belt, her thighs, her arms, her back.

"Father!" he calls out. "What is this?"

The woman with knives for fashion glances up, sees Telemachus, and her lower lip curls in displeasure. Then his mother – of all things, *his mother* – puts a hand upon the woman's arm as if somehow familiar, murmurs a few unheard words, and though her scowl barely lessens, the woman looks away.

"Let them in," Odysseus says. "Let them inside."

In the camp of Eupheithes and Polybus, Gaios calls an immediate muster, a rush of men.

He should have done so the moment two people slipped from the gates to stroll around the farm – but he saw no threat, no sign that they were fleeing, knew they had nowhere to go, so let it be. He is now regretting that decision.

There is no way the men of Eupheithes and Polybus can arm themselves and sprint across the charred distance between the camp and Laertes' farm in time to stop this unexpected gaggle of muddy figures who are now slipping from the forest into the safety of Laertes' walls. And what even are these creatures that have come from the wood? Gaios is no fool; he set watchers on the roads, on the hills about, and the only thing they reported seeing were the women of the isle about their daily business, whatever that may be.

"Who are they, *what are they*?" demands Eupheithes, quivering with a rage that seems to threaten to rip him open from the inside out, shaking from top to toe like the breaking earth.

Gaios has a terrible feeling he knows what they are, but cannot quite bring himself to believe it, to name it out loud.

"We will need more men," he says. Eupheithes bristles; Polybus looks almost ashamed.

Odysseus and Penelope are the last to return inside the walls of the farm.

The gates are shut behind them.

The women are already making themselves at home. They have brought food, drink, freshly killed rabbits and still-glistening fish. The men of the farm slather to see it, but do not approach, do not know what to say to such a sudden mass of women with quite so many arrows upon their hips as they bustle about the place.

Priene looks around with displeasure. Whenever she went with her queen – her first queen, Penthesilia, lady of the chariot and the roaming plain – inside Troy's walls, she found them stultifying, oppressive. She marvelled that anyone in their right minds would live this way, away from mother earth and father sky. Though her people were sworn to the kings of that city, throughout the war they raided the edge of the Greek camps, vanishing into the grasslands or yellow hills that swagged the region only to return with the sun at their backs the next morning to strike and vanish again. People of the horse, they had been. People of the wind.

Laertes' farm, she concludes, is if anything even worse than the cloying walls of Troy.

The old king whose little home is now a teeming fortress sees Priene, and she sees him.

He nods, once, and she is surprised to see what might almost be respect in the old man's eyes, an acknowledgement of her as – what? As a soldier? As a captain?

She nods in reply, then looks away, because she is not sure how one is meant to look upon a king who wears rags, who needs help, who perhaps – just perhaps – in his hour of greatest need says thank you.

Telemachus half runs down from the narrow wall, hand upon his sword, cheeks blazing red. He pushes straight past his mother to land squarely at his father's side, and, knuckles white where he still grips the blade, blurts: "Father?"

He just about keeps himself from blurting everything else he'd like to holler, to shriek. Such as: *What the flaming hells? What is this madness? Are these creatures friends? Enemies? Where did you find them? What are we meant to do with them? We cannot protect ourselves let alone so many women! Why are they here? Why do they carry weapons? Are they slaves come to bring us supplies? What is your brilliant stratagem, Father, and how clever must it be to involve, somehow, unbelievably, women?!*

Odysseus looks into his son's eye, and perhaps sees all of these questions – and more – burning within.

"You should ask your mother," he murmurs, a hand on Telemachus's shoulder to turn him to face Penelope.

Incomprehension momentarily flickers upon Telemachus's brow, followed by a growing fury. He faces the queen with blood upon the fringes of her gown, and blurts: "What have you done?"

Penelope is too tired for indignation, too weary for snapping voice, fiery retribution. Instead, with a sigh, she breathes: "I have raised an army of women to defend this island, my kingdom and you. This is Priene, their captain. Priene, this is my son, Telemachus."

Priene tilts her chin towards the young prince, but says nothing.

For a moment, Telemachus's jaw works like the mouthing of a suffocating fish. "What do you mean . . . an army?" he demands at last. "What do you mean . . . women?"

"As I say. An army. Of women. You may recall Andraemon's raiders, a few moons back? The ones who nearly slew you? They died in the end. They all died, didn't they?"

Telemachus looks from his mother to Priene, from Priene to Odysseus, and seeing nothing he can comprehend in their stony gazes, looks back to Penelope. "I . . . Women can't fight. Women can't fight. This is madness. Father, tell her, this is—"

"For pity's sake, boy!" It is Laertes who speaks, stamping a foot on the verge of almost childish petulance. "You think Andraemon's pirates were seen off by wishing very hard? You think Menelaus's Spartans turned round because they'd had enough of the fish? Grow up, idiot child! Or are you still just a wriggling infant your mother has to protect?"

Telemachus has been struck square in the breastplate with stone and spear, felt his footing go, smelled death just a moment away. It did not hit harder than his grandfather's words.

Priene says: "I'm going to arrange the watch."

This is, everyone can agree, a very good idea.

Odysseus is watching Laertes, and there is a look in the

corner of his eye, a smile almost upon his lips. *Old man — you knew. You knew.*

Laertes straightens up a little, jerks his chin once, a thing that might be agreement. He knew, all right. But no one ever asks Laertes ever, just a silly old fart, they say, don't treat him with the respect he deserves, think he's lost his edge. But he knew. Of course he did.

Telemachus sees perhaps a hint of this in his grandfather's eye, turns away in desperation. He has spent most of his formative near-adult years in the act of turning away, from one thing or another. "Father," he tries again. "Whatever this . . . this is. You cannot think that *women* . . . You cannot think we can . . . They will faint at the first sight of blood, they will run, they will break! Use them as a . . . a distraction, perhaps, by all means, we can still sneak out and get to Kephalonia, raise an army of men — an army of *men* — but surely you cannot intend to just . . . to just . . . " A limp gesture at all of this. All this impossible madness.

"They beat Menelaus's Spartans," muses Odysseus, his eyes focused on some place gently above and to the left of his wife's steady eyes. "Drove off raiders. They have bows, arrows, well kept. Stayed hidden when commanded, came into this place without fear, have not baulked at the sight of blood. And their captain . . . I saw women like that once. They had a queen, and whenever I heard her war horn sound I would tell my men that it was better to withdraw with what supplies we had than skirmish with her riders. Achilles killed her, in the end. No one said it, of course, but everyone generally agreed that he was the one to do it. The rest of us . . . kept finding reasons to keep our distance."

Priene helped carry the body of Penthesilia to the funeral fire. Even though she'd seen her queen fall, in death she could not quite imagine that it wasn't some cruel trick, some

298

illusion – perhaps this body she bore was merely a hollow disguise made of wax and straw, and her queen would return, leap from the bushes with blade drawn and gold about her arms and throat, glinting in the sun, cry – ah-ha, my ladies! I tricked you, so I did! It was all a test! This war, this life, this everything – only ever a test, performed for the merriment of the cruel and laughing gods.

Though she has turned away, Priene can still hear Odysseus. He has modulated his voice, speaks perhaps a little for her. It would be false to say more of Penthesilia than he has. It would be unhelpful, he thinks, to say anything less.

Telemachus's mouth opens and closes once more, before at last, with hands outstretched in desperation, his eyes anywhere but his mother's face, he makes a last appeal. "But Father . . . if people knew. If people knew! If Menelaus, if Orestes, if they knew . . . You are Odysseus!"

Odysseus does not fight with women and girls.

He barely even fights with his own men; they get in the way most of the time. This is what the poets will sing. Kings are wiser, greater than the meagre, petty men who die for them. This is the poison the poets drip into listeners' ears.

"Poems are sung by those and for those who stayed alive," Odysseus replies. "When the poets sing of the dead, it is because the living told them to. The first thing we must do is stay alive."

That is the end of it.

Laertes spits into the earth – an agreement of sorts, a sharp glob of moisture and phlegm to complement the moment. Waddles back towards the house, muttering: "Excuse me, excuse me – can't even get into my own house – excuse me!" as he weaves between the massed women.

Telemachus does not look at his mother.

Cannot look at her.

And she?

She pictures herself taking his hand.

Holding his hand.

Saying: Telemachus, I . . .

(What then?)

I did it for you.

All of this for you.

I thought my husband was dead, and the kingdom?

This kingdom?

I was never allowed to be its queen, not truly. No one bowed to my authority, no one respected my name. I was not Queen Penelope, I was merely Penelope, wife of Odysseus.

What is Ithaca then to me?

Nothing. All of this, nothing. Except that there was always you. My son. All this I did for you, your kingdom, your home. All this I did for the love of you. I wanted to keep you safe. I thought if I kept you safe, you'd understand how much I love you. I tried so hard, but there never seemed the right way to say it. The right way to show it. Too soon – too soon – you were the little man of the house. The little prince, the little king. Your father was gone and there were no men left to show you how it was to receive affection, to show you how to be loved, only bronze men who knew that the love of a woman was a weakness, a curse. I did not know how to teach you to be loved. I did not know how to be loved, to teach it. I'm so sorry, Telemachus. I should have told you. I should have told you everything. I just left it too late. All of it – all of this – too late.

These are the words she should say.

She does not.

Eos's feet swing before her eyes, and her hair is itchy, tangled, flecked with blood.

Besides, Telemachus is already strutting away.

Already gone.

CHAPTER 38

>>>

Once, on that fateful night the Trojans recklessly burned the ships of the Greeks who besieged their city, I was standing upon a hill gazing down to the smouldering ruins of the shore when my brother Ares approached. His armour glistened with reflected firelight and the crimson dawn; his hands, his bracers, his arms up nearly to his shoulders were smeared with gore, and where he walked the earth shrivelled and grew bitter. No grain can grow in his footsteps, only bright scarlet flowers with a heart of deepest black, which will in time wither to dry brown stalks that crack in the winter wind and blow away at last like dusty bone. Only then will the land begin to heal, a harvest that tastes of blood.

I did not move as he neared, though I held my spear and my shield tight. Though we had sometimes crossed blades in the fray, neither of us would unleash our full fury upon each other before these walls; even Ares knew better than to risk cracking the earth with our matched potency.

So together a while we stood and watched the crows and gulls swoop down to pluck at the soft flesh and open eyes of the nameless dead, until at last Ares shrugged and said: "It will be better now." I raised an eyebrow and waited, with as much patience as I can muster for my kin, for him to clarify his sluggish thoughts. He considered, gestured loosely towards the smoke rising from the edge of the sea. "They could have gone home. Now it will be hard. Now they must win. Or they must die. Even your favourite, little Odysseus – even he will have to fight hard now, having nowhere else to go."

"It was folly," I replied, with a shake of my head. "For precisely the reasons you say."

Ares' great brow furrowed, but he never asks me to explain or expand upon my thoughts. He is not one for nuance or curiosity.

I have no such inhibitions. Wisdom must war against ignorance; in that at least, my twin natures align. "I have often wondered, brother," I mused, "why, after so much vacillating, you chose to fight for Troy in this affair. They make no great sacrifices to you, as they do for Apollo, and have always been a people inclined to conquer through alliance and threat rather than actual war. I would have thought Agamemnon would hold your favour."

Ares shrugged, and did not answer.

"Perhaps Aphrodite?" I suggested, half watching him from the corner of my eye. "I know she has some fondness for the idiot boy Paris, as well as that half-blood princeling of hers, Aeneas. Perhaps she has . . . persuaded you?"

It is a source of endless frustration to me how persuasive one such as Aphrodite can be.

Still, nothing.

"Maybe you are tempted by the heroes of Greece who have come to this fight? Maybe you wish to balance things, lend your strength to the Trojans and thus prolong the battle? But no – that would imply that the petty action of mere mortals has any influence upon your decision."

A slight curl of his lips; something in this narrative displeases him.

302

"I did think it possible that you chose Troy because I chose the Greeks," I added with a sigh. "Balance — it is good that there is balance, and war is not war if it is merely a massacre of one great power rolling over the lesser. But you and I both know the consequences were we to fight as the gods we are, rather than temper our blows to this mortal field, and so . . . " I let my voice trail off. Let the silence sit between us. Waited for my brother to speak.

At long last, a grunting, a rumbling from deep within his chest. Slow, like the tide washing in, words upon his lips. "Doesn't matter."

I waited still, knowing better than to interrupt the god of war about his musings.

"Doesn't matter," he repeated, a little firmer, warming to his theme. "Greeks, Trojans. Win, lose. What they fight for — it doesn't matter. What matters is they fight. Battle doesn't care why you came. Death doesn't care why you died. War doesn't care why you bled. Blood is true. Fire is true. Everything else is just . . . " he shaped his mouth round the word, spat it out in contempt, "story. The spear doesn't care for it. The blade doesn't stop to ask why you came here, before slicing your throat. All these . . . stories . . . gods and men tell . . . to explain themselves. War does not care. Just words. All of it. Just words. Doesn't matter to me. You'll see. When your loved ones are dying. When these 'heroes' you care for so much are screaming in the dirt. They won't care what the story was that brought them here. They won't care what they thought they were, who they thought they were, as they lie dying. They'll be dead just the same. That's war. War is honest. Honest is wise. You should be grateful that there is something in this world — anything at all — that is true."

I nodded without looking at him, without signalling my agreement. I could feel his eyes upon the back of my head, feel his fingers about the haft of his blade. I knew how much he longed to match weapons with me. I had bested him before with tricks and guile, but even Ares can learn, was learning, would not fall for such things again. He didn't know which of us was stronger, and it thrilled him. And I also did not know which of us would prevail, if we fought to the actual, bloody end. That truth terrified and appalled me. It appals me still.

"One day," I heard myself speak the words, and was surprised, "I will make a new world. I will build a city of ideas, and the people who fight for these ideas will go to war knowing that they are not just killing and dying for some mad tyrant, soaked in blood. Not just for the strongest man who they themselves fear, not for some crude construction of honour, or prestige, or the need to prove themselves more violent than their neighbour. No. They will go to war and bleed and weep for a story – a story of a better world, of a world worth dying for. And this idea – it will spread by their stories, it will travel far and wide, and when they kill and when they bleed it will just be more fuel to the story, not blood for blood's sake but blood to wet the mouths of the poets as they sing of greater things. And one day these songs will have travelled so far, so far indeed, that there is no more need for blood, no more need for the blade – the land will have been watered with the lives of those who died to feed it, the song will be sung and the fires lit in a new temple, in temples of learning and wisdom. Not war for the sake of war, but war for the *story*, for the dream of a world made anew. It will take centuries. Maybe thousands of years. But I will do it. If Olympus herself must fall to see it done – so be it."

Ares listened.

Ares nodded.

Ares seemed – so strange – to understand!

And Ares said: "You'll fail. Your wise men. Your clever men. Your ... people ... with their ideas, their words, their stories.

A man with a sword will come and kill them all, not because he cares what they have to say, not because he is interested in some . . . story. Some . . . *philosophy*. But because he can. Because he can. When battle sounds and shield breaks, no one cares for stories. It's just the blood, and the death, and the blade. All your poets, all your ideas, all your philosopher-kings. They'll die pissing themselves in the end, begging for a warrior to save them. And when the warrior comes, he'll be big and they'll be small, and they'll thank him for it. They'll thank him for his boot on their necks. That's the natural order of things. Always has been. Always will. And you know it."

So saying, he departed, leaving me shivering upon the edge of the blood-flecked sea.

CHAPTER 39

>>>

In the farm of Laertes, Odysseus invites Priene to talk strategy with him.

She replies: "I answer to the queen."

He bows his head, polite. "Of course."

This surprises Priene. She thinks it's perhaps a trick – Odysseus, famously tricksy, will smile and scrape and say "yes how nice" while eyeing up just where to stick a dagger in your back – but no. He goes and fetches his wife, and does not object when Priene insists on the rest of Penelope's council – the priestess Anaitis, the maid Autonoe, the lieutenant Teodora, even old mother Semele – also being there. Instead he nods to each one with respect, one at a time, his gaze lingering longest, most thoughtful on Autonoe's face, before at last he gives her a little bow, a thing that might almost be ... Priene is not sure ... perhaps some sort of apology? It is meaningless, of course. An apology to Autonoe would be a lifetime in giving, it would be a labour of Hercules, and she is pretty sure that Odysseus is only fighting this fight with the purpose of never labouring again. But still.

But still.

Autonoe's fingers twitch around the hilt of the knife on her hip, and she looks away.

Even though these women have fought battles together, run a kingdom together, with Odysseus now standing amongst them they are silent, shuffling feet, waiting for him to speak. He clears his throat, looks to Penelope. "My queen?"

Penelope appears for a moment as surprised as anyone to hear the deference in his voice, the polite turn of his hands, yielding space, breath to her. But she hesitates only a moment, then turns her head a little so he is barely in the corner of her vision, to look upon the women of her council.

"All right," she says. "Polybus and Eupeithes. What are we going to do?"

Priene looks away from Odysseus. Easier, she thinks, to speak without him there, but so be it. Penthesilia put up with blinking foolish Trojan men at her council, yabbering on about pitched battles and heroic deeds; Priene can do the same. "We can hold these walls," she declares. "Against our bows they do not have enough men to get through. But that won't help for long. They can just choose not to attack, wait for reinforcements. Their numbers will grow."

"Can we sally out?" asks Odysseus. "Take the fight to them?"

Priene is primed to hear mockery, condescension in his voice – but no. He sounds curious, a soldier learning about the nature of the troop with which he is serving, a craftsman with a valuable tool. "We don't fight direct battles," she replies, not quite believing in the patience in her tone as she answers him. "We lure men into traps. We shoot them from afar. Overwhelm them with superior numbers. If we could coax them into the forest, we could take them, but that would mean abandoning this farm. We are better trying to bring them into range of our bows than meeting them in open field."

"Midnight raids?" he asks, as if discussing digging a new well. "Burn their camp, see how many we can kill in their sleep?"

"Perhaps. But they have had watches set every night, and now that they have seen us enter the farm, they will have doubled that. I would love it, king, if your enemies were foolish and stupid. Unfortunately they are not."

"In my experience, men tend not to fear women. Perhaps they will attack anyway?" suggests Anaitis.

"We can only hope that they are foolish enough to throw themselves against us," Priene replies. "I have ordered the archers to wait below the wall, to mask our numbers and strength. Perhaps they will think we are just ... fleeing women?" She struggles with this concept. Who would look upon a woman who has nothing left to lose, who cares nothing now for her own safety, and *not* see her as dangerous? And yet when Troy fell, Priene also saw how mothers, daughters, widows lay down to die upon the edge of the shore, for in losing everything, they had also had ripped from them that part of the soul that screams get up, get up, fight! *Get up and fight!* It occurs to her that this is the single cruellest thing that warlike men steal from the women they prey upon.

I brush my fingers down her cheek, and for a moment she seems to almost feel my presence, to curl towards it like a cat.

"Captain." Odysseus is nodding to Priene, bowing almost, a hand raised, palm-up, towards her. "These are your soldiers. What would you have us do?"

Priene is so surprised for a moment she doesn't answer. Then: "We can wait one night. Tend to your injured, see if perhaps we can bait your enemy into an attack. And if they do not come to us ... then we shall have to see about going to them."

Odysseus bows his head. Priene looks to Penelope, and sees her queen almost shrug. She is as uncertain of what to do with the deference of this king as anyone else in the room. Priene shakes her head. This is not a problem for her. Husbands and kings – they are mysteries for some other kind of woman.

CHAPTER 40

>>>>>>>>>>>>>>>>>>>>>>>>>>>>>>>>>>>>>>>

The afternoon fades to dusk, the dusk to night.

The women sit around fires in the centre of Laertes' yard, and eat, and sing.

They are slow to sing at first. There are men – not just men, but royal men, men of power and judgement – upon the walls, standing in doors. They are not used to hearing women's voices raised in anything other than the songs of mourning, in wails for the dead. Priene does not understand this. In her home, the women and the men both sang together – there is much harmony, she would explain, in such music. Baffling you Greeks don't try it more.

Priene likes it when her women sing. She hopes that the sound will confuse the Greeks camped across the burned-out field. She hopes it will make them wonder just what manner of creature has set foot inside these walls, make them underestimate perhaps the quality of maid that shelters now within the farm. She would like her women to sing, and when they stop, she will order the fires doused and bid the women stay hushed and silent, in the hope that their quiet lures her enemy into something rash.

But more than that.

Secretly — more than that.

Priene likes the women's music. Sometimes even, very occasionally, likes to join her voice with theirs. She sings these songs — these foreign songs — badly. Thinks she sounds like a strangled lizard. But no one seems to care, and it is ... pleasing ... to do something with others that is not merely fight, kill, bleed, fall.

I envy her that. It is not fit that a goddess should envy a mortal, and yet I am wise enough to be honest about the bitter reaches of my raging soul.

It is Anaitis, priestess of Artemis, who sings first. She has lived so long away from the stares of men that she is almost now entirely oblivious to them. Besides, she believes that her goddess would enjoy a melody in her name, and that is more important than any slack-jawed gaping of some would-be king and his battered soldiers. So she raises her voice in a song of the forest, in praise of the boar and the arrow that slays it, and the women of Priene's band have spent enough time hiding around the temple of Artemis that they all know the tune, and slowly join in.

I look around, and there she is. Artemis dislikes walls and farms that have turned her wild lands into fields for grain. But for this song, sung this night, she has come, and sits on her haunches now on the roof of the farm, long arms about her bare knees, silver bow at her side, listening to the melody rise in her honour. I settle myself down near her — not too close to interrupt her reverie, but near enough that I need not raise my voice to be heard.

Telemachus stands on the wall with his back to the yard, face out towards the enemy. Others who stand watch are turning to look, beginning even to smile at the strange sound of music, but not he. He will not flinch from his duty to hear some feminine tittering. He will not deign to glance upon these girls and old haggard maids who are supposed to be his saviours. The reality of their presence is incompatible with the story he has told himself about who, and what, he himself must become.

Anaitis's song has opened the door to another. Teodora sings, a more merry tune, the song the fisherwomen sing when repairing their nets, a thing of little verse and endless echoed chorus that grows louder and more absurd the more it is repeated. Artemis sways along to it, with a glee that seems almost calculated to spite her brother Apollo's more refined tastes. The god of music has always understood that stories are weapons, as potent in cutting people down as welcoming them in.

I do not sing, nor sway, nor show signs of pleasure or displeasure or anything in between. I am the mountain; I am the midnight sky. I think that I am damned, whatever that can mean to one who is already entirely alone.

Laertes snores on a pile of straw. Now that the women are here, he sleeps like a fat, well-petted dog, utterly without care.

Autonoe sits near the fire, shoulder pressed close to the body of another, a maid's arm across her back. She says very little, laughs not at all, but smiles once, grimly, at a joke only she can hear, and does not sing.

Teodora takes Priene's hand in hers, whispers in her ear.

Priene smiles, murmurs back. For many years after Troy, every smile upon her lips was a strange thing, experienced with the shock of one who remembers that they are breathing, and having remembered, finds it almost impossible to experience anything else but slow, conscious breath. That has changed, these recent years. Now sometimes Priene finds herself smiling and doesn't even notice it.

As the moon turns towards the horizon, Penelope goes to bed.

She doesn't have a bed to go to any more, but like her father-in-law will sleep curled up on the floor, some straw laid down for pillow beneath her head, a rough cloak of undyed wool thrown across her shoulders. She has made some slight effort to wash the blood from her gown, but there is only so much water to be drawn from the well, and it must be shared amongst the women for drinking, not washing, and so resigned she lays herself down with a hem of crimson. Others will sleep here tonight – Teodora has already arranged the patterns of watch, of who will wait with bows ready beneath the farm walls, and who will rest, nooked into the back of some other maid. But not yet. For now the room is empty, save the queen, as she lays her head down.

Nearly.

Odysseus stands in the door.

She does not notice him at first, busy as she is with trying to arrange those few thin twigs of comfort she has into something resembling a kind of pillow. Then he opens his mouth to say something, and doesn't know what, but even that little indrawing of breath catches her attention, and she bolts up, hand reaching for a blade.

For a little while, that is all there is.

He in the door, she upon her makeshift bed in the darkness of the shallow room.

She does not speak, does not move.

The last time she lay down here to sleep, her rest was disturbed by violent men; she thought perhaps she might die, in this very place. She was surprised at how familiar this thought seemed, how little it mattered.

Then Odysseus says: "You should have a guard at the door."

"Thank you," she replies. "But I think there are enough guards about the farm tonight."

"But at the door," he declares. "After what happened. So you can feel safe. You should know. That there is a guard. At your door."

"Safe?" She tries the unfamiliar word, rolls it round her mouth, but Odysseus is already busy folding up a cloak – stolen

312

from a dead man, but no one need know that – into a rest for his head, fussing about where it should lie, what the least annoying position might be for a man to sleep in the corridor outside his wife's door – near enough that of course he can leap into action and defend her at the slightest sign of danger, but not so dominant that other women, tiptoeing their way to bed, risk walking on him where he lies.

He finds a position he judges adequate, nods once in self-congratulation at the choice, turns again to his wife.

"Well then," he says at last. "I will bid you goodnight."

"I don't need ... " she tries, but he is already closing the door that divides them, and settling down to rest in the corridor in front of it.

CHAPTER 41

>>>

The men of Polybus and Eupheithes do not attack that night.
Nor the next morning.

Nor by the early afternoon.

Instead, they prowl in little knots just beyond arrow's range, circling the farm, sending out small bundles of unarmoured servants and slaves to forage, watching the gate, guarding the road. They were caught by surprise when a column of women marched boldly in; they will not be surprised again.

A messenger comes for the rebel fathers, then is sent away.

A few hours later, another comes, and stays a little longer, before departing back down the road to the palace, far below.

Priene, Penelope and Odysseus stand upon the walls, watching their enemy's camp, watching messages come and go.

"They are waiting," says Priene.

"For what?" asks Penelope.

Priene's lips thin, but she does not answer.

"Reinforcements," Odysseus says, and the warrior-captain by his side seems almost displeased to find herself agreeing with him. "They are waiting for more men."

Word has spread: the suitors are dead.

On Kephalonia, a mother falls to the ground, clutching the pain in her chest.

On Zacynthos, a father does not understand. Does not understand. Someone else's son, you mean? Someone else's child?

In Elis, a brother swears vengeance.

In Calydon, a sister says: "But he only left a month ago. I gave him his cloak."

What is less clear – what the messengers are unsure about – is why they died. Some say Odysseus has returned. Surely, they say, that makes it all right? A king doing the thing that kings do. People whisper, well well, if it was Odysseus . . .

. . . but that does not change the way the fathers hear it.

Priene watches the camp of Polybus and Eupheithes, and sighs. "So much for a quick battle."

"What happens if they are reinforced?" asks Penelope.

"Depends how many men. Right now our numbers are roughly even. But should they double their contingent . . . we would have the worst of it."

"So what do we do?"

"We have to go to them." Priene does not like these words, hates what they imply. But times are what they are – you do not always get to choose your battlefield. "Before they raise enough men to overwhelm us."

"By night?" asks Odysseus, but Priene is already shaking her head.

"Archers need to see what they're hitting," she replies. "And we are running out of time."

In a shadowed corner, a whisper near the pigsties between a queen and her captain:

" . . . word from Ourania?"

"None yet."

" . . . her messenger, Mycenae . . . "

"Nothing came to the temple before we marched here. Will Elektra come?"

"Yes. I don't know. Maybe."

"Does Odysseus know?"

"Know what? That Mycenae may or may not send reinforcements? That Ourania's messenger may or may not have made it to Elektra's side? No. He does not know. I have told him nearly everything, but that? What use is it to say that this thing may or may not happen? It is too uncertain to be real."

Priene tuts, clicks her tongue in the roof of her mouth, but does not disagree. There was a time when she swore an oath – *Death to the Greeks!* – and she is not sure how she feels now about her safety being possibly dependent on the daughter of the greatest of all her foes. And yet . . .

. . . and yet . . .

. . . she looks about at her little army of women, and knows with a certainty as strong as any soldier's heart beating before the killing blow that she would have them live.

"Well then," she mutters. "Let's assume we're on our own."

The women muster in the yard.

They do not form neat ranks, like Telemachus thinks they should.

They stand in little huddles, bows in hand, talking.

Their talk is not heroic, not brave.

They tell silly jokes.

Laugh at stories they've heard a hundred times before.

Gossip.

Telemachus shakes his head. Achilles' Myrmidons never *gossiped*. They stood in ordered rows, silent before the fight, contemplating only the job that had to be done, the valour with which they would face death. Further proof, as if he needed it, that this whole business is folly.

316

Odysseus knows better. He knows that the Myrmidons were amongst some of the snarkiest, gossiping little tattle-tales of all the armies of Agamemnon. Whenever he sat around their fire, it was all who had slept with whom, who kept avoiding latrine duty, who tricked whom in some stupid game. Fart jokes and discussions of heroic sexual deeds – none real, all wild, boasting fantasies – defined most of the conversation he'd overheard or participated in beneath the walls of Troy. Topics that were not discussed included: who to tell should a man die. Who was loved and might now be left behind. Who was mourned. Who was missed. What it might feel like to be wounded, to lie there bleeding out slow. Whether a man favoured a quick end, not even seeing the blade that slew him, or whether he'd rather know what was coming, have a little more time – just a little more – to say goodbye.

He did not think he would hear this same tenor of conversation from the women in the yard, but listen – just listen. There it is. Stories of that time someone broke their leg chasing their own goats up the mountainside. Tales of fisherwomen who couldn't even catch fish, of that young man – what was his name? – with the funny accent who told those dreadful jokes. He's gone now, of course. All the young men left and never came back, but ah well. Ah well. You get on, don't you?

Odysseus becomes aware of a presence by his side. Penelope. She doesn't have a bow or spear in her hand, and for a moment this briefly surprises him. He half expected her to appear fully clad in armour, ready to fight. But she has no skills, no training – she would just be a liability that the others would be forced to defend, and no one needs that. Instead she stands next to him, arms folded, watching the women as they check, for the fifth or sixth time, their arrows, their bow strings, the sharpened tips of their spears.

He has been avoiding her, since sleeping outside her door. It is hard to avoid each other in a place as small and crowded as this, but he's been doing his best. He thought it was, in its own kind of way, a courtesy. He is therefore surprised to find that she has sought him out.

"Familiar?" she asks at last.

"In a way. I am used to seeing this from the other side of the wall, of course."

"Did you do much fighting on your way back? You must have been doing something in those ten years, I mean."

"I was . . . There was . . . I spent a lot of time stranded."

"Stranded . . . somewhere safe?"

"Yes. Some of the time."

She nods, once, briskly, not meeting his eye. "Good. I mean, not good that you were stranded. But at least you weren't having to fight to survive every night. And your men, were they . . . ?"

"They died. In the storm."

"But you survived."

"Yes."

"Perhaps some of them did too?"

"No. They didn't."

"You seem very sure of that."

"I am."

The bowels of the sea open, again − again Eurylochus is drowning, clawing for the air, Polites howls as the mast of the ship cracks in two. Odysseus remembers the smell of meat, of beef, the way the eyes of the cattle of the sun rolled in their heads, still living though their bones were broken, staring back at him from the flames. "I am," he repeats. "I am certain. They died. I lived."

Penelope thinks this sounds like conspiracy, murder even. Wonders how the poets will phrase it, should their ballads ever be sung. "Were you . . . alone then, when you were lost at sea?"

"For some of the time. Not for all."

"And did you go mad?" She asks the question as if she were asking after a minor malady; a nail that has grown strangely into skin, or a cut almost too thin to see.

Odysseus considers the question with the affable quiet of one for whom it is not an entirely new thought. "I'm not sure," he says at last. "At every stage of my journey, it seems like I look back on the man I was before as if he was a stranger. What man was it who sailed to Troy? I can't remember. I see his actions, remember them as if they were me, myself. And yet they are somehow distant, a performance in my mind, a thing rehearsed again and again, not real. When I was found by the daughter of King Alcinous, it was as if I became yet another person, the man who I needed to be to get through this next encounter. And when I came home and killed the suitors, it was another man again, just repeating, again, whatever it was that I thought was needful to survive. Perhaps that is all that is left now. When the sea has taken everything else away, the only thing that remains is a man who wills himself to live. No soul of note. No character worth any mention. Just flesh, hanging on."

This is the most truth Odysseus has ever spoken in his life. He is amazed how easy it comes to him. He suspects it is something of the disposition of all these women, rubbing off.

There was a time too, thinks Penelope, when she was a girl who laughed; a wife, curious about her husband. A mother, delighting in the gurgling of her child. These things too have passed. They were washed away by necessity.

"It would be unhelpful if you die," she says at last. "After all this. It would make settling matters on the island . . . even more problematic. You can be mortally wounded, if you absolutely must, but it is necessary that you linger on long enough for the poets to say that peace was restored to the land of Ithaca, Telemachus fought bravely and took his throne and then Odysseus died happy, at last, surrounded by the family who loved him. But if you die today, on this field – that would be most inconvenient."

Odysseus uses what strength he has not to look at her, not to turn his face away from his contemplation of Priene's army as they gather by the gate.

"And if I don't die, and am not mortally wounded? If I live say . . . another six moons, or ten, or maybe even a few years beyond that?"

"That would also be politically adequate," she replies, proper as the sacrificial priest, brisk as the blade across the white bull's neck. "The power of your name cannot defend Ithaca for ever, of course. But if it buys us a few years of peace, that will secure us the time to rebuild an acceptable-seeming army of actual men dressed in bronze, renew our fleet, increase our connections with allies and friends who pitied me but will treat fairly with you, and so on and so forth. In short if you cannot die valiantly in a poetic manner, I would ask that you live long enough for us to guarantee actual stability from which to defend the island when you die of more natural causes in some distant future."

And does this mean you love me? roars the heart of Odysseus.

And softer, beneath: *Does this mean you can forgive me?*

"I would ask for your blessing," he muses. "But you may not wish to give it."

"I just did," she answers. "I think you will find I did."

At last, the husband turns to his wife. She meets his eye, nods once. This is how she looked, he thinks, when he sailed to Troy, all those years ago. There were no tears, no sobbing upon the harbour walls. She is a princess of Sparta – she understands that there are certain things that need to be done.

"My lady," he says.

"Odysseus," she replies.

How strange it is to hear his name said this way, he thinks. Not as some curse – the man who killed a city. Not as some cry of desperation – the captain who watched his men drown. Not in hollow despair as he sails away from a witch's island, nor in the mouths of startled kings astonished to find him washed up in rags upon their shores. *Odysseus!* cries the ghost of Agamemnon. *Beware all wives!*

Odysseus, laments the spirit of Achilles. *I would rather live a humble life than walk upon these hollow shores of death.*

And yet now, in Penelope's mouth, it is simply a name.

How strange, he thinks, it is to simply have a name.

He picks up his bow, nods farewell to his wife and takes his place amongst the women preparing to fight.

CHAPTER 42

>>

The gates are opened a little before sunset.

The women sally out.

Some twenty stay hidden behind the walls, at the bottom of the stairs, ready to run up and fire upon a command.

Another thirty – Odysseus amongst them – step out into the blackened field that looks towards Gaios's army. Priene and Teodora are at their head. Anaitis and Penelope stand upon the walls, Telemachus by their side.

I should be with you, Father, he exclaims.

No, son, Odysseus replies. *Whatever happens, Ithaca will need a king.*

And then, a moment of thoughtfulness, a thing that he feels shouldn't need to be said and yet somehow is essential: *Listen to your mother. She knows how to rule this land.*

Telemachus splutters, but cannot argue with his father on the brink of battle, if at all, so returns to his place upon the wall, to watch and obey.

Eupheithes and Polybus are summoned from their tents the moment the gates are drawn back, and even before the women are fully out in the field, Gaios has his men arranging themselves in a line. They put those with shields at the front, an

322

acknowledgement of the power of the bows in the women's hands, but do not advance, even though the gate to the farm stands open at Priene's back.

"Well?" snarls Eupheithes, as the men wait patiently for their captain's command. "They're just . . . just women! The gate is open! What are you waiting for?"

Gaios clicks his tongue in the roof of his mouth. He has worked for many different employers across the seas of Greece, and generally speaking prefers either military men who understand things without needing to be told, or civilians who are appreciative enough of their own ignorance to leave him alone to get on with it. Polybus and Eupheithes are neither of these, but he is willing to treat them with a little more sympathy than usual, given the manner in which their sons have just died.

"They want us to advance to within range of their walls," he replies, arms folded across his bronze chest. "They have more archers waiting below, and plan to run behind the safety of their gates once we are close enough."

"But . . . but they're women!" Eupheithes is struggling to get this point across, to get his thick-skulled captain to understand.

Gaios never saw Penthesilia fight, but that was because his captain, much like Odysseus, felt it was judicious to stay away from the warrior-queen and her roaming tribe. He was always very appreciative of that particular bit of strategic wisdom, when he was a mere soldier at Troy. "Spread out," he orders his men. "Loose formation. Make it harder for them to focus their fire. Do not let them clump you together – and do not be tempted to charge. They will run out of arrows sooner or later. Hold your place."

His men obey, stringing themselves out into a long line across the edge of the field, shields up, chins down. Tall men try to make themselves a little bit smaller; larger men are suddenly aware of their bare calves and unprotected necks, wondering

323

just how accurate Odysseus and this strange army of huntresses can be with their bows.

Across the field, Priene watches this all and sighs. "Not stupid. Not like normal Greeks."

"We should still test them, perhaps," muses Odysseus. "If we can take out even a few, it may provoke the others to charge."

Priene is a little annoyed to find herself in agreement with the Ithacan king. But she has fought with annoying people before, even from her own tribe – she knows how to manage her sentiments later. "Find your range," she calls to the women. "Move when they move. If they charge, or even seem like they might, retreat. Do not stand and fight."

The women murmur their agreement – Odysseus has never heard consent to a command given in quite that way before – and slowly begin to move forward. They spread into a lazy curve out from the gate, stopping here or there to notch an arrow to a bow, raise it, fire. The first few arrows fall well short of the feet of the waiting men, so again they advance, raise, fire.

Semele's daughter, Mirene, is the first to find her range. The arrow does not hit a man, but slips past his ear to land, *thunk*, in the dead earth behind him. The men are at the absolute limit of where the arrows can pierce, wound, kill. The women cannot see the whites of their eyes, nor hear their breath, nor see the way their shoulders rise and fall in rapid exhalation with each shot that is let fly. That is good, in its way. It makes those they are trying to kill seem somehow distant, abstract – mere straw-stuffed targets rather than creatures of flesh and blood.

Odysseus stands between Semele and Priene; nocks an arrow to his bow, takes aim. He has eleven arrows left. He chooses a man whose shield is small and round, almost in the Illyrian style, a thing meant for close-quarters stabbing and driving with its hard, thin edge. His first shot is true, but the man has been watching Odysseus as Odysseus watches the man, and the instant the shaft leaves the string he is scuttling crab-like out of the way. The looseness of the formation gives him plenty of room to scurry to the side. Odysseus clicks his tongue in the roof of his mouth, slots another arrow to his string, looks for another, less alert target.

Behind the shield-carrying men, more men are assembling. They have pouches of stones and leather slings. They stand behind their armoured companions as if they were rabbits skulking behind trees, stepping out only when they are ready to throw – winding up the shot to quickly release.

The stones fall short of the women's feet, but Priene's scowl deepens, though she does not flinch.

Odysseus spies a man who is not looking at him, whose attention is fixed on an archer who seems to have singled him out as her personal splitting-tree. He raises his bow, lets fly. Though lured by the sight of a woman with death in her eyes, the man seems to sense the arrow of the Ithacan king flying towards him, for at the very last moment he turns his head and raises his shield.

The tip of the arrow tears straight through the wood, stopping palm-deep on the other side, the head quivering before the soldier's eye.

Odysseus has nine arrows left.

The wind drifts through the trees, and no one gives a great battle cry, and no one howls, and no one roars insults, and no one charges, and no one flees. On the shores of Ithaca, the waves beat in peaceful contentment. The rebel slingers dart forwards now and then to release their stones, but to run into the range of the bows is more than they are really willing to do, and their shots still fall short. The archers send their shafts towards the lines of bronze men, and some hit a shield, and others strike a plate of bronze, but most fly a little wide or are easily evaded by the waiting soldiers.

This also is a true part of battle – the part that is rarely sung by the poets. Skirmishers stinging at each other like the buzzing bee. Usually they are merely a cover for a larger army to form, buying time for stronger, heavier troops to line up at their backs ready to charge. But with the farm at Odysseus's back, and the spear-armed men of Gaios beside the scurrying slingers, there will be no charge on either side. No rush into destruction, no flailing of blade or crying out of death. Instead the arrows fly and the stones land flat on the ground, and when finally a man does fall, is struck with an arrow through the leg, it is so surprising that he himself can hardly believe it.

I feel irritation nip at the edge of my breast – exasperation even that the rebel men are merely standing there, merely facing their foe, not charging into the fight. It is of course wise – so very wise – that they are not letting themselves be lured beneath the farm's walls, and I would usually respect that, applaud it even. But today their stubbornness stands in opposition to my goals, and as I grip my spear and toy with taking a little more direct action, I turn my head – and see him.

Just for a moment, there he is.

Whispering into Gaios's ear.

His helmet is pulled across his brow, his shoulder turned so that his whole body is drawn away from me, but I would know his presence anywhere. He whispers of the things that Gaios and his men will do to these women when they are beaten. He whispers of power and blood, of beating down with fists, of faces smashed in, of how, when they catch Odysseus, they'll make him watch what they do to his wife, what they do to his son, his father, and when all of his family have had their tongues cut out, their noses split, their bodies ravaged – but still alive, oh yes, still alive – they'll string up the Ithacan king and cut him up one piece at a time and feed him to his kin.

Gaios listens, and does not blink, barely seems to see the

arrows that fly towards him. Perhaps that is Ares' great trick – not strategy, not cunning, not the wily wisdom of the clever plan. Perhaps all he does is blind his loved ones to the possibility of their own deaths, showing them visions merely of what it is they will do when they are the only ones left alive.

I grip my spear, feel the lightning power ripple through my veins, the divinity spin about me. Athena and Ares should never war, should never rip the world in two, but in that moment I taste blood in my mouth and feel the fury beat in my chest. I am ashamed of it. Ashamed to grasp my blade in wrath, to think of fighting for sentiment, for passion, for love. And yet it burns within me, and for a moment Ares raises his eyes to me, and sees.

He sees, and lifts his mouth from where he has been whispering in Gaios's ear, and grins.

Weak, he whispers. *Broken.*

I open my mouth to retort, to scream fury, vengeance, denial – but can make no sound. No witty quip, no pithy put-down, just hot pulsing in my neck and dumb, ignorant stupidity on my tongue.

Ares sees it, and laughs. I raise my spear to challenge him, but he is gone, spinning away in a blight of crows, and the men of Polybus and Eupheithes do not flinch, and they do not charge.

"Enough," says Priene, as another slinger sends an ineffectual stone towards her head. "They are not going to take the bait and we are wasting our shots."

Slowly, the women cease firing, lower their bows.

The slingers on the other side, rather than seize the opportunity, also stop hurling their stones, as if waiting to see what new threat this development might bring.

"If we cannot bring them into direct battle, they will starve us out," Odysseus muses, as Priene orders her women back behind the walls. "They will fetch reinforcements, and we will starve."

"Perhaps," Priene grunts. Then, with the pain of one pulling a splinter from her own torn flesh: "You are meant to be good at strategies. Do you have one now?"

Odysseus shakes his head. Not exactly *no*; perhaps merely *not yet*.

Priene tuts. They are out of time for *not yet*.

CHAPTER 43

>>

In the night: Odysseus wakes with a start, but it is too late.
Autonoe is already above him, knife in her hand, blade resting at his throat. The farm is quiet, the women sleep or are on watch elsewhere. He is the only one who lies in the corridor, guarding the door to the room where his wife lies dreaming.

He is not sure if Penelope will even pretend to investigate when in the morning they find him lying there with his throat cut. He is not entirely sure he can blame her.

For a while, the two watch each other, king and maid, in the shadowed dark.

They do not speak.

Autonoe does not feel there are any words necessary for this moment.

And Odysseus – for almost the first time in his life – cannot think what he might possibly say. This is almost a relief, he nearly gasps with wonder. Is this how it feels – is this what it is like when the struggle ceases? Is this really the death he feared all along?

Yet Autonoe, her knife ready at a king's throat, does not strike.

Watches Odysseus a while.

Then slowly – extraordinarily – sheathes her blade.

Watches a little while longer, just to make sure they understand each other.

It would appear that they do.

She rises.

Turns away.

Drifts back into the dark.

The next morning, Polybus and Eupheithes' reinforcements arrive.

They are nearly eighty men, including plumed soldiers of Nisos, father of Amphinomous, with an entourage of slaves and women leading mules laden with weapons and supplies at their back. No sooner do they reach the rebels' camp than they begin to expand it, digging new ditches and pitching tents that seem to quickly grow to encircle the whole farm in a thin, ragged line of spears and cloth.

Odysseus stands upon the farm walls with Penelope and watches as the rebel women lay their cooking fires and fetch water from the stream. "I don't suppose," he murmurs, "that any of those women are allies of yours?"

"Perhaps," Penelope replies. "But I can hardly send my maids out to enquire, can I?"

The women of the farm no longer bother with pretence. They set regular watches upon the wall, make no effort to hide their numbers, and when night falls, one of the bravest slips down a rope from the side of the wall to crawl on hands and knees through the dark towards the forest, to get a message out, seek help. She is the smallest, fastest of this troop – Priene doubts very much if more than one can get through, even in the dark, without being discovered.

"Go to Ourania," Penelope tells her, before she departs. "Find Ourania and ask her whether her cousin ever made it to

Mycenae, or if Pylos will answer our call. Tell her of our condition. Tell her ... tell her in the name of Odysseus."

The messenger nods, rubs mud into her cheeks, her hands, her hair. She is a wild thing of sticks and dirt, and Anaitis gives her the goddess's blessing, but she hardly needs it, for Artemis is already there by her side, running with her through the woods.

Through the day, the sounds of building, sawing. Trees fall in the forest, leaves billowing up as timber splinters down. Telemachus asks what it means. Priene replies, and he is briefly surprised that it is her standing by his side, and not his father.

"They are building another ram. More ladders. They will attack with everything they have."

Telemachus again looks for his father, but Odysseus is not here – inside, perhaps; sleeping, maybe, waiting for the assault. So, having no one better to talk to, he wonders: "Can we hold them off?"

Priene does not reply.

By nightfall, the battering ram is visible from the walls of the farm. This time they are building a roof for it, a protective covering to keep at bay the stones and arrows of the defenders. This will take time; Odysseus thinks they will not be ready until morning. Priene agrees. "You Greeks always did like to build big things slow."

The only exception to that rule she can think of is a horse, made from the timbers of the great ships. Its crudeness gave it a kind of beauty. Perhaps that's why the Trojans thought it was a gift.

"You were my enemy at Troy," muses Odysseus, a hint of regret tingeing the edges of his voice. "If we survive this, will that have changed?"

"No," Priene replies, light as the silver moon. "Even if you were not a Greek, I would kill you for what you did to the maids. But Penelope is right – the isles need to have a king. You are the least awful choice. The one with the greatest story. If you die now, it will be harder to keep them safe." A jerk of her chin towards the women, milling about the yard. "They are my soldiers. I am their captain. I have a duty of care."

Autonoe is watching the two of them from the corner where she is piling stones; Odysseus studiously does not watch her back.

The women do not sing that night.

Laertes asks if Anaitis is going to do some divining, have a look at some entrails or something of that sort. Anaitis replies that she's pretty sure divination would, at this stage, tell them what they already know. There will be a battle. It will be hard. They could all die in the morning.

"What is the point of priests," demands the old king, "if they won't even tell you what you want to hear?!"

Penelope sits by Odysseus, in the shadows away from the fire as it slowly burns down through the night. Their son is sleeping, curled up in a ball, though if you woke him he'd deny he'd even closed his eyes. Laertes put a cloak over him when no one was looking. Priene snoozes, her head in Teodora's lap. Teodora sits with her back against the wall, eyes half closed, fingers sometimes brushing along the edge of Priene's short, tufty hair.

Odysseus says: " ... We shouldn't even have had to stop there, but my men were already angry that they hadn't received their fair share from Troy. I asked them what fair share – the city had been besieged for ten years, everything of value had already been bartered away by her kings for weapons and grain – there wasn't anything left to take, and what there was Agamemnon and his brother took mostly for themselves. Ithaca isn't powerful enough to command the Mycenaeans to give us

332

plunder, what do you expect me to do? But they had imagined that there would be wonders inside those walls, and we'd let them. Ten years – you have to give people something to hope for, something to make it all worthwhile. When they didn't get what they wanted I thought they were going to mutiny, coming home empty-handed . . . so we raided the Cicones on the way home. They'd been allies of Priam and I thought . . . poorly defended, most of their men dead at Troy, it would be . . . We were wrong. I was wrong. The men did things and I . . . If they couldn't find gold then they wanted women, they wanted . . . Would you like to hear that I made them stop? Would you believe me?"

Penelope shakes her head.

Odysseus speaks to his hands, to his grubby feet, to the ravaged earth. "No. If they couldn't have gold they could at least have flesh. That is what I decided. That is what a commander does. But a force of Ciconians had got out before Troy fell, left before the celebrations, the horse. They arrived while my men were . . . We were lucky as many escaped as we did. Poseidon didn't hate us then."

"Did you . . . do things too?" Penelope asks. Odysseus tries to hear the judgement in her voice, the rage. If it is there, it is beyond his power to discern.

"I . . . There was an island ruled by a woman – a witch, you might say – and another where there was a nymph and she was . . . They had power, you see. It was so very strange. The land was theirs. The skies, the earth. Medea had power, of course, but she gave it up for Jason, did terrible things in his name, and in the end he betrayed her – Father always said she was considered a curse on the *Argo*, that she made everyone uncomfortable, but Father has never been comfortable with . . . a great many things. These women, though. One look and you just knew, the things you would normally do, the way you would normally ... show your strength ... it was meaningless. All of it."

Circe: *We should lie together, seal our pact.*

Calypso: *Darling, you couldn't hurt me if you tried. But do try, if you want. Oh but do.*

Odysseus has done terrible things.

He didn't think they were terrible, at the time.

He thought they were what men did.

The things that needed to be done.

He is beginning now to understand.

He fears understanding. Shies away from it. He is, of course, a curious man. An extraordinary man. The sirens, the sirens, they are still singing to him! He will never be free of their nightmare cry, and he is proud of that torment. But still ... curiosity like this, the kind of curiosity that might reveal him to be something he does not want to find himself to be. The kind of curiosity that might dare to contemplate someone else's point of view, the woman screaming no, no, please, no ... it nauseates him. It terrifies him. And he cannot help but wonder: if the mere whiff of this imagining threatens to break him in two, then just how cruel is the mark his life has left on those who crossed his path?

He cannot dream.

Dare not imagine.

Will die without ever quite mustering the courage to look, like so many heroes.

Penelope is also refusing to consider certain questions.

Questions such as: can she be near a man who has taken the flesh of women as substitute for chests of gold?

Can she permit a man to touch her who once wrapped his fingers round Calypso's throat as they tossed in lovemaking, tears in his eyes, horror in his throat, and wondered why the nymph laughed when mortals should have died?

Does she believe in redemption?

Does he understand that he needs to be redeemed?

Does she believe a word he says?

Penelope does not consider any of these questions. Deliberately and thoughtfully she ignores them, because to consider them is unhelpful to her now. The reality is that if they survive, she will have to do what she has to do.

For a moment she half closes her eyes, and thinks she understands the tiniest part of her cousin Helen's predicament. Helen made no sound that first night after Menelaus took her from Troy, as he held her down upon the rough deck of his departing ship, blood still smeared across her naked skin. When he said, *Show me what you did with Paris, show me what he liked*; when he snarled, *Tell me you're grateful to be fucked by a real Greek, say thank you, say thank you!* she said thank you, thank you, thank you as he pushed her until she bled. And upon returning to Sparta?

Upon returning to Sparta, she sat by his throne in the great hall and smiled and said oh how nice it is to be home, how wonderful, goodness it's so lovely to be back. Did you pick these flowers yourself? Oh they're gorgeous – simply divine!

And did not think. And did not stop to wonder, or muse upon the lives of others, or hope for the future, or dream of the past.

Because what else was she to do?

Sometimes, Penelope decides, there comes a point where you have done just about as much work as you can possibly do to be as adaptive as you can possibly be. Sometimes you need someone else to change – someone else to meet you halfway – for the next thing to arise. To make something new.

Odysseus is saying: "We had fair winds from the isle of Aeolus, and he gave us treasure too – better by far, I think he decided, to give us some reasonable gifts and send us on the way with a big belly than to not give us anything at all and risk a raid later. He judged it perfectly – enough gold to satisfy me and my men, not so much to make it seem he was too rich. We were so close, I could see the southern tip of Zacynthos, I thought . . . this is it. This is it. I was already planning what I'd get the poets to say. Enough praise to keep trouble away, not so much that Agamemnon or Menelaus could take offence, think I was diminishing their labours. You have to get it just right, sound strong enough, but not too strong. Never say you could compare with Achilles, but say instead . . . you gave him advice. Adjacent to brilliance, neither behind nor in front of it, merely . . . complementary.

"That was what I was thinking when the storm came up. It blew us straight back to Aeolus, but this time he'd had a chance to raise his own men, knew that the warriors of Greece were likely to be passing through, secured his palace gates and felt safe enough to say hello again, sorry you're in trouble again, but no – no. You absolutely cannot wait in my ports. After that . . . my crew . . . A dead wind can be as bad as the gale, the hunger, the thirst . . . I had heard stories of what happens when men drink salt water, but never seen it. They shrivel up from the inside out, like old fruit in the sun. You would have thought that madness would be a blessing by the end, but even mad they know what's coming for them. They knew what was going to happen. We raided what isles we found, stole food and cattle, killed . . . where we must. Saw things I would have accounted impossible. When the storm finally smashed the last of our ships, I was almost relieved. At least, I thought, it would be quick. But the will to survive, you just . . . you just want to survive. I should tell you that I thought of you. Of our son. Would you believe that?"

"No," she replies. "I don't think I would."

"No," he agrees, with a little shake of his head. "Although later I thought I really should have been thinking of you both. Ten years of Troy, the years at sea . . . these things grow distant.

Fog-lost. Coming back to Ithaca, murdering those men ... If we survive, the poets will have to say I did it all for you."

"Of course." Penelope's voice is light, easy. "That makes perfect sense."

They sit together, side by side, as the night curls towards the dawn.

CHAPTER 44

> >>>>>>>>>>>>>>>>>>>>>>>>>>>>>>>>>>>>>>

The attack comes at first light.

I will not report it as the poets shall.

Not heroes and valiant conflicts, not great and tragic cries greeting the rosy light of day. These leave no place for the nameless ones, the forgotten ones, the ones who fought side by side until they had no more breath to give, no more blood to bleed upon the greedy earth.

Gaios's men construct a battering ram, this time with a crude wooden roof to shield its carriers from falling stones and arrows. It is ostensibly on wheels, but the wheels have been stripped from an uneven cart barely able to carry its own weight, and it is poorly made to cover rough ground. As a result, its approach to the gate is excruciatingly slow, a constant tide of men flowing in and out of it to relieve one man who is as much carrying the thing as he is pushing it towards its destination.

To shelter from the archers on the walls, the men of Polybus and Eupheithes have hewn together rough wooden pallets, which may be carried forward by three men at a time in little bursts of movement, and which at any time six or seven huddle behind, armpit-tight in the crude shelter it affords. Behind these now advance more knots of men in their little groups, heads

down and arms tucked in against the flying shots of their enemies, and behind them slingers and even a few archers who are
there to even the odds. Neither of these have much chance of
hitting the women raising and lowering their heads upon the
walls of Laertes' farm, but that is not their purpose. The threat is
enough to make it harder for the women as they rise from their
positions on the walls to take their time about aiming, to really
level their bows, before an arrow or a stone flung from below
flies too close to their skulls and *whoosh* – their shot is taken too
fast, too soon, goes wide.

Thus, on all sides, do the rebels advance.

Behind their advancing men, Polybus is shrunken like the
withered crow, but Eupheithes stands stiff and straight. I feel the
touch of Ares upon him, see the blood in his eyes, the sword at
his side. He wants to be the one to kill Telemachus. He doesn't
care if Telemachus has been subdued, captured, bound, stripped
naked and brought bleeding before him. He still wants to strike
the final blow, while Odysseus watches. He wants to see if
anyone else living can understand the pain that he himself is in.
He wants to know that he isn't mad; that what he feels someone
else can also feel; that he is not alone.

From the wall, the women rain down first arrows then, as
the ram draws nearer, stones.

Priene prowls along their lines calling out encouragement,
telling each archer to remember what she has learned, to find
her target, to relax as she releases the arrow from the bow. As the
battering ram nears the gates, the women hurl burning torches
down upon it, trying to catch the timber beneath which their
attackers shelter.

Gaios has predicted this, and wet hides have been stretched
across the top, smothering the flames. Still the women keep
throwing, urged on by Priene, while to the sides the better
archers line up their shots at the men huddling beneath the

smoking roof of the ram as they start to swing it back and forth against the gate.

The first man to die is a mercenary from Patrae. He only came to join this fight because Eupheithes promised good gold, and it seemed like an easy win. He is slain by an arrow fired from Semele's bow, and his body is at once shoved aside by a man who not three hours ago he drank water and wine with, and who he swore was as good a fellow as any he had known, who now takes up his place upon the ram. The next man to die is a slinger, who knew Eurymachus a bit and thought he was all right, by the fairly low standards of the isles, and has come to this battle more because his colleagues seemed to care, and he didn't feel he could let them down. He falls before he can release his first stone, and takes a little while to die, bleeding out crimson from his ruptured belly.

Other injuries begin to mount, from splinters of wood to scratches of stone. The first of the women to die is Eunike, whose father was one of those very same who died by a Ciconian sword after he refused to let go of the woman he was dragging half-naked by the hair towards the fleeing Ithacan ships. Eunike never knew her father, and Odysseus cannot remember his name either. She is hit by an arrow fired by a man who loved Amphinomous, who knew Amphinomous as a good man, a man who would have been a worthy king, and who thinks he would have been mortified to be fighting women and girls – what strange times these are.

The women on the wall do not stop firing when Eunike falls.

They do not look at her body, do not say her name.

To do so would break them, and this is no time for breaking, so they do not.

Instead, Autonoe and Anaitis rush to the girl's side and, seeing the angle of her head, the arrow through her chest, pull the shaft free, close her eyes, carry her body inside, whisper a prayer, and then return to the yard to hand more flaming torches to the women on the walls.

The roof of the battering ram begins to smoulder, the wet hides finally curling and giving way to blackened char as some of the flame tossed upon it begins to catch. Not enough, though – not enough. The ram smacks again, again, again into the gate, bouncing back cracking timbers. Laertes calls for help, and Telemachus and three of his men press their shoulders into the barricade of furniture and wreckage that has been piled against the inside of the gate. It is strange, Telemachus thinks, that he is down here trying to hold the gate, instead of on the walls throwing stones. He resolves that should he live, he too will learn how to use a bow.

On the walls, Odysseus picks a shot, takes it.

Another slinger falls, and another. A third arrow strikes a shield raised to block it; a fourth rips into the edge of a moving pallet, skipping past the exposed shoulder he'd hoped to spear. He has five arrows left. He looks to the women around him. Some still have a dozen shafts in their quivers; others are down to three or four and now are trying to focus instead on throwing rocks and flaming brands as the enemy draws near. To his left, Teodora hurls another torch, then ducks as an enemy stone whisks by her ear. Below, Odysseus sees his wife rushing to the cracking barricade, pushing her shoulder into it by Laertes' side, and he knows that this time, the gate will not hold.

Priene knows it too, for she is already in the yard below, gathering up those women who do not have a bow or who have already shot their arrows, arranging them phalanx-like before the splintering timber. She manages to make two rows of women, seven in each row, with hunting spears bristling between them. "If a man grabs the shaft of your spear, your sister will stab that man!" she barks. "Do not let them grab! Do not let them close!"

It is not the most inspiring speech Odysseus has ever heard, but it is to the point.

The gate shudders and something rends inside it, sending a tumble of broken furniture back as the whole thing begins to buckle. Smoke and flame are now licking from the battering ram – too late. Odysseus slithers round the back of Teodora as she levels her bow, hears the gasping of a woman struck by a stone who now sits, legs dangling, on the edge of the wall, blood upon her lips. Descends to join the line of women arranging themselves by the gate, stands by their side, arrow notched, barks: "Penelope! The gate is going to go!"

It occurs to him that this is the first time he has said his wife's name, and she has responded as if that were in some way ... natural. She scurries away from the barricade as another slam of the now-blazing ram sends it tumbling backwards, Laertes by her side. Telemachus skip-hops backwards, nearly crushed by cracking wood as the gate slams open, splintered timber and broken hinges, revealing smoke-blackened faces and gleaming spears on the other side.

The barricade, though it has not held the gate shut, at least slows down the incoming men as they try to scramble inside. Odysseus can take his time with his shots, picking out the lead warrior to send an arrow straight through his breastplate and into bone. His corpse is another obstacle that must be removed, another thing to be kicked aside before the attackers can get into the yard. Odysseus kills the man who takes his place, and the next, and the next, but for all he is adding bodies to the obstruction, the gap created by the broken gate is being widened, so that now more than one man, two, three, can start to push through the tumbled mass of broken wood that stand between them and the courtyard.

Odysseus feels for the quiver at his hip, and knows he has no more arrows. Instead, as the women move forward to fill the mouth of the gate, spears poking and thrusting to form a new wall to obstruct the attackers, he takes his place on the left side of their position, sword drawn, to cut at any hands, fingers or knees that venture too near. Priene is on the other side, a blade in each hand. The lines of women are just wide enough to fill the gate, and for a moment this is all the battle is – waving spears from the attackers bumping against the wobbling weapons of the assembled women as each tries to take a few precious paces away from each other.

The blazing battering ram is now becoming a problem for the attackers, an obstacle that limits how many of them can get into the gap it has made. Men try to pull it back, create a slightly wider opening that soldiers can tumble through, but the acrid smoke tingles eyes and chokes lungs, filling the gateway with an itching, suffocating weight that makes it harder to see, to fight.

Another woman falls, and another man.

Neither has ever killed before.

They came here because they didn't see another choice. They looked and they looked, but they were not wise enough – the world they lived in was not wise enough – and so here they are, dying in battle.

I catch them as they fall, breathe into their hearts: *You fought well. Your death had meaning.*

This is all my frozen heart can give them.

Artemis steadies the aim of Mirene as she levels her bow towards an archer in the field below, whispers: *The crows will take him*, releases the shot, and another man dies. I glance towards the blazing battering ram, now fully alight, and see for a moment Ares standing beside it, his face turned upwards, bathed in fire, tongue out as if he would drink the falling shards and blistering sparks. He has not come for Ithaca, not for the western isles, not for Odysseus, nor for the future of any realm. He doesn't care that women fight, or men fight, or who lives, or who dies. He is here merely because there is burning, and he loves the flame.

I catch the arm of a woman with a spear who is about to waver, push her feet wider, drop her weight a little more into her hips, snarl: *Stand!* But when I look again, Ares is gone, his cup full of the screams of the dying and the stench of flame.

The rebels do indeed try to grab the spears of the women who face them. The women are not used to fighting like this – not to holding a line in a tight space, to standing their ground instead of firing and running. It takes them a moment to remember the lessons Priene has imparted to them, to watch each other's weapons, to slice at any man who'd touch a sister's shaft. Teodora is down from the wall too, her bow drawn, pressed in between the shoulders of the women as she looks for a shot in this tight, choking space.

"Hold together!" roars Priene. "Hold together!"

Penelope is kneeling on the wall now beside a woman bleeding from a tear in her skull where a stone flew by. Autonoe and Anaitis drag another into the shelter of the house; Mirene looks about her for more rocks to drop on the attackers below. Semele reaches for the arrows at her side and finds she has shot all but one, seems for a moment more paralysed by that than if she'd had none at all. I roar to Artemis, surprised to hear myself calling to her over the crunch of battle and the snarl of flame: "Kill their captain!"

She glances down at me from where she stands upon the wall, then nods and looks across the field. Her sharp eyes find Gaios immediately, and she whispers in Semele's ear. The old woman turns, seeks out the distant figure, raises her last arrow, notches it to the string, takes aim.

It is not by the will of Ares nor the whims of any god that the stone from below finds Semele. Nor does it hit her particularly hard – but she is old, and beneath the years of fetching water and carrying wood, there are parts of her that have grown gaunt and thin. I hear the crack of bone beneath her sun-shrivelled skin, and the little gasp from her lips. Artemis catches her before she can tumble all the way from the wall, eases her down, shielding her head from another shot. Mirene begins to look up from her place, but I turn her gaze away before she can see her mother gasping on the wall, and instead catch Autonoe by the wrist, yank her towards the fallen widow.

"Anaitis!" cries the maid, and the two rush towards Semele.

Artemis, however, is already shaking her head. She does not like to let animals suffer. She closes Semele's eyes, kisses her on the forehead, presses her bow into her chest, the arrow still notched against the string.

Below, the gateway itself is now near enveloped in flame. I feel my lips curl – an unbecoming rage, nothing I would ever dare let my brother see – and reach for my champion.

Priene.

Odysseus has served me well, so many times, in so many ways, but I need him to live.

I *want* him to live.

Forgive me.

Instead, I step to the right of the line of spears, lower my helmet across my brow and raise my shield.

"Tabiti, Tabiti, lady of the flame!" I cry in the tongue of Priene's people. "*Hvarnah, vahagn* – glory and war!"

The line of spears buckles. Shoulders tire, arms waver, and it begins to break.

And for the first and last time, Priene sees me.

She sees *me.*

"Blood and victory!" I roar, and as I do, Priene raises her voice as well, snarling like the lion. I push her up and onto the broken barricade, sweep her past the swaying line of her women's spears, clear a path for her with a huff of my swirling breath, and as she leaps into battle, I hear Teodora cry for her captain, her women cry for their leader, but I sweep it all aside.

"For the eternal fire!" I cry, putting my shoulder next to Priene's as she smacks aside the first spear of her enemy. "For the mother of the earth!" I exclaim as she slips past a rebel's guard to ram her blade up into his jaw. "For our sisters!" She ducks a wild swipe of a small shield and slices across the back of the arm that would have dared to beat upon her. "*For the queen!*"

Priene's battle cry is the roar of the wolf across the endless midnight plain.

It is the cry of the eagle as it falls from the sky.

It is the cracking of Troy as the great towers tumble to the ground.

I feel her gods stir about her – even here, even so far from home, I feel their hearts beat a little faster at their daughter's call, their flame tingling upon the edge of my dominion. I brush a spear aside without looking, step back a pace and let them in.

From the east they come, the lady of the burning river and the father of the racing horse, the mother of the sacred earth and the father of the cattle herd – they spin around Priene now as once they raised their voices for another warrior of their kind, for Penthesilia when she crossed blades with Achilles. They turn the edge of her sword to deflect a strike that would have split her skull; they steady her feet when she is about to fall; they catch her breath before she can lose it all in a gasp; they make stumble a man who thrusts with his spear for her gasping belly. I fight with them, join my blade to theirs, cry to the women behind: "Push! Push now!"

"Push!" roars Odysseus. "Push forward!"

The women take a step forward with their spears, and another, Priene now dancing out before them, almost through the gate and into the flames of the battering ram, laying a path of blood as she goes. She does not hear Teodora call for her to come back. She does not hear Anaitis cry that the men are broken, that they are fleeing before her, that it is enough, enough, please, enough! Her gods are hungry for the blood she spills, and for a moment so am I.

She is not here to kill. She kills so that her women might live. Ares has no power; he is diminished, he is tiny before her might. I raise my sword in salute to her as another man falls before her, join my voice in her battle cry as the rebels begin to buckle, to break, to stagger back from this whirlwind from the east. "Sisters, my sisters!" I call, and *sisters, my sisters* whispers the wind as Priene blazes, as men fall, as men turn, as men begin to run.

She feels the stray blade that catches her across the ribs, but thinks it is only a scratch.

Only a scratch.

Rages on a moment more, a minute almost, until she reaches to slice the tendons of a man who flees from her, lashing out for the backs of his knees — and stumbles.

Feels light.

Feels sore.

Tastes something liquid and strange rising upon her lips.

Her gods catch her before she can fall, and a moment later Teodora is there too, holding Priene under the arms as around her the rebels flee. Already women are pouring from the ruined gate, coughing and spluttering through the flames, rushing to recover the arrows they shot. Priene has trained them well, scavengers amongst the dead; I see Artemis with them, pointing to those arrows that did not immediately break, to any weapons that might be salvageable, ordering those who can hear to gather up stones that they might be able to throw again.

Laertes is standing inside the ruins of his smoking gate, coughing and spluttering and shaking his head. Odysseus watches the retreating foe. Teodora holds Priene tight, and will not cry. Those women who are not on the field are now standing in a silent knot around their captain, half blind and panting, their minds not yet still enough to understand, to see. Penelope kneels by her side, takes her bloody hand. Priene did not remember choosing to lie upon the earth, yet here she is.

Mother earth, she whispers. *Father sky.*

The gods of the east are already withdrawing, but they leave behind a golden trail in the sky, a thread spinning through the clouds. My kin, if they spot it, will try to blast it away, outraged that a deity of some other land dare mark our celestial tapestry. I will stop them. In this, they will not cross me.

"Priene?" whispers Teodora, squeezing her hand tight. All about are the bodies of the dead; Teodora has to half-kneel on the arm of one, not sure whether she should try to move it out of the way to make more room to be by her captain. "Priene?"

The warrior smiles upon her lieutenant, and then upon her queen, standing behind. Thinks of something important to say. Looks at the men slaughtered all around. Knows that she did this. Is satisfied.

Feels at last a word, strange and welcome, slip into her breath. *Home.*

They burn her body in the flames of the ruined battering ram, which is still ablaze.

CHAPTER 45

>>

They cannot repair the gate.

They fill the mouth of it with as much debris as they can, hammered together into some crude and ragged form. It will hold against the shoulders of men. It will not stand for more than a moment against another battering ram.

Then they count their dead.

Nine women are buried, another eleven too injured to fight.

They count the dead men who laid siege to them, and it is more – far more – but not nearly enough.

In the camp of Eupheithes and Polybus, the former roars: "They are broken! Their gates are down! We go again!"

And Gaios snaps: "We tend to our wounded and rest! They will die easier tomorrow than today!"

He is, tactically speaking, entirely correct. Eupheithes understands then that Gaios does not know how it feels to have lost a son.

Odysseus stands by the remnants of the gate. His father comes to his side. "All right," says Laertes. "Now's the time. Your wife, your son. They need to go down the back wall while it's dark and slip away. Eupheithes and Polybus have too many scouts to get everyone out – they'd be spotted and hunted down – but if you put on a good distraction, a big old song, draw the eye away – they should make it. Your Penelope's got this woman – Ourania – who can get them to Kephalonia. Leave just enough of us behind to make a good showing. At least our deaths will give them a bit of time, a fighting chance."

"You aren't going to run?" asks Odysseus.

Laertes snorts, a rich, liquid sound. "At my age? No thank you. I'll cut my wrists if I think they're going to make my death slow."

"If you're sure."

"Course I am! You think I'm stupid? Now, this distraction. Did you ever do any of that one-on-one duelling nonsense when you was at Troy? Good at making a big show in front of all the other *her-oes*?"

Laertes takes his time over saying "heroes". He's met plenty – sailed on the *Argo* with a whole bunch of them. Didn't think much of them then. Thinks even less of them now.

"I duelled for Achilles' armour after he was gone," Odysseus recalls. "But that largely involved a battle of wits. Against Ajax."

"Isn't he the fella who went mad, killed a load of sheep then topped himself?"

"That's the one."

"Not sure that's the standard of tactical brilliance we're dealing with right now."

Odysseus sighs. "I'll go speak to my wife."

Odysseus speaks to his wife.

Penelope says: "Yes, I think I agree with your father's assessment. Myself, Anaitis, Telemachus—"

Telemachus blurts: "I'm not leaving."

Penelope tries: "Telemachus, it's—"

Her voice – it hardly matters what she says – only makes

things worse. "I am staying here! I am not running away like some . . . some cowering dog."

"You need to live to avenge me and your grandfather." Odysseus is pronouncing on truths as solid as the mountain, as needful as breath. "You cannot do that if you are dead. There are three or four women who know the forest well. You will slip out with them before sunrise and—"

"I am not leaving you and Grandfather to die!"

"You are no use to us if you are dead!" Odysseus doesn't shout, except when tempted by the sweet song of the sirens. He is renowned for his measured manner and strict patience. But tonight he is as close to death as he has ever come, and once again – *again* – he is having to put up with pig-headed stubborn fools who threaten even the minimal plans he has. He has learned to expect this from your average Ithacan soldier, and indeed your standard Grecian king. It is utterly insufferable to have to put up with it from family.

"I'll go anyway." Penelope is blunt and to the point. "If you die, I'll need to make sure it's Orestes who sits in judgement over these isles. He's a young king and not especially remarkable, but he won't choose anyone too barbaric to rule on his behalf." Not too barbaric feels about all anyone can really angle for, given everything. "I'm taking Autonoe," she adds. "They might not violate a priestess of Artemis, but they'll definitely rape my maid, as well as any other woman they take alive. I know you cannot hold the gate for long, but please do keep that in mind when fighting."

Penelope has led her women to their deaths. She knows that now. She cannot think on it. To think on it is too painful, and she will never forgive herself.

Eos, Melitta, Melantho, Semele, Priene . . .

She wonders what it was all for, and has no really solid answer.

"It won't come to that – Father, tell them it won't come to that," blurts Telemachus.

351

"You should take Autonoe," Odysseus agrees. "And in the morning I will walk out into the field and surrender to Polybus and Eupheithes on condition that the women go free."

"What? Father, you can't, that would be—"

"Do you think you can persuade them?" Penelope asks.

"Perhaps. Those who survive should get off Ithaca for a while, seek shelter elsewhere, and I wouldn't entirely trust to a fear of Artemis to protect her temple either, once Polybus and Eupheithes have had time to think about things. Naturally they'll kill my father and son . . . "

"Naturally," drawls Laertes.

" . . . but if Telemachus is already gone, we may be able to deceive them. Put one of his friends in his armour, perhaps, leave him and my father standing by the gate. They might not look too closely, assume that I'm also surrendering them when I surrender myself."

"I am not leaving!" Telemachus nearly wails the words. "I am not leaving you!"

The room turns to stare at him, blinking in bewilderment.

No one is entirely sure how Telemachus got this way. Is the boy really so dense?

"You cannot make me," he pants, lower now, every breath a shudder. "If you try to make me leave, I will shout. I will bring the whole forest down. And I will be killed in the dark along with Mother as surely as if I had stayed."

Laertes rolls his eyes.

Odysseus wonders if this really is the boy he left behind.

Penelope stands, hands clasped in front of her. She rarely speaks when in this pose, but now she raises her head, looks her son in the eye. "Is this what Priene died for?" she asks. "Are *you* really why so many are dead?"

Telemachus sways, tries to out-glare his mother, and looks away.

352

She looks a moment longer – a last moment longer – then turns from her son. "I will seek refuge with Mycenae. So long as Orestes and Elektra can get their men on Ithaca before anyone else, the western isles should be safe. The people will not suffer too greatly. Father . . ." A nod to Laertes, followed by a moment to consider some suitable farewell. Laertes picks at a little graze upon his wrist as she does, peels off the scab, chews it, grins, waits. Penelope sighs. "All things considered, you could have been a lot worse."

Laertes claps her on the shoulder. "You can't hold a party for piss, but you did all right as a queen, girl."

She turns to Odysseus. "When you negotiate for the safe passage of the women, do not worry about whether they can keep their weapons. Priene taught them to use every blade in a kitchen, every knife you might want to gut a fish with. They will scatter, become invisible, and maybe one day – if needed – they will re-emerge."

"I will keep that in mind."

She thinks about it a moment more, then adds: "It would have been interesting to get to know you again, husband."

He bows a little, wants to take her hand, and does not. "Likewise, my lady. I feel . . . that had things been different . . . I would have been honoured to hear your story."

At last, and almost with a wrench, Penelope turns to Telemachus. He does not look at her, fingers drumming on the hilt of his blade, lips rolling in and out of his mouth as if he might try to chew off his own face. "Telemachus. I have failed you. I lied to you. I let you down. Hate me if you want. But you are the son of the king and queen of Ithaca. You have a duty – not to me, but to these islands – a duty to live."

She wants to hold him.

To clutch him unto her and scream and beg, to fall upon her knees and implore him, live my child, live. Live. Live.

For a moment she considers it, but then what would be the point? Perhaps in her old age she might feel a little bit better for having done all she could to save her son – but that is no reason, given that it is doomed to fail. That's just a little show, put on for her own comfort, her own self-worth. Nothing true in it at all.

So Penelope draws a muddy cloak about her shoulders, nods farewell once more to her family, calls Autonoe and a few women of the wood to her side, and in the darkest hour of night climbs up onto the wall of the farm.

By the gate facing the camp, Odysseus gathers the remaining women. They dislodge enough debris to make a small passage to the outside world, where the burning ram still sparkles with heat, where the ashes of Priene still smoulder upon the blistered earth. They carry torches, to draw the eye. It is Anaitis who leads the songs. The priestess of Artemis did not learn any of the funeral songs of the isles in her service to divinity – Artemis does not consider death a remarkable or notable thing – but she is still a woman of Ithaca. The women of Ithaca have a long history of grief.

They raise their voices, and sing.

They sing of broken promises, of lost lives.

Of widows, mourning.

Of wives, betrayed.

Of daughters, left to die of a broken heart.

Odysseus and Telemachus are silent. They do not know these songs. The poets of kings are all men, and sing the songs the men command. It is not considered fit that women and slaves should make music. It might suggest that they are as full of soul, and sorrow, and story as any prince seated upon a golden throne.

In the camp of Polybus and Eupheithes, the soldiers listen.

They too have never heard these songs.

How strange, they think, that the women have these secrets in their voices.

Artemis stands beside me on the wall. There is ash and blood drawn across her face, her knuckles white where she holds her bow. I glance to the forests behind her, and see the rising fog, the thick, growing mist, and know it is hers.

"Thank you," I say at last, eyes turned to the singing women below.

"I'm not here for him," she snaps, eyes flashing to silent Odysseus. "When this is done, I will leave these islands."

"I understand."

"Was it worth it?" she demands. "Is *he* worth it?"

I think a long time before answering, and when I do, I turn to finally look upon my sister. "No," I say. "He is not. But he is the least bad option I could see, until this world changes. Until everything in this world is made anew. His story — it is all I have."

Her scowl deepens, but she doesn't pull away, and the fog continues to thicken, wrapping itself around the flames, the walls, the fleeting shadows of Autonoe and Penelope as they scramble into the dark.

Artemis is warm by my side, her breath silent and slow. "I have fought ... so long," I murmur, as obscurity washes upon us. "I have done everything in my power to be ... *relevant*. To make the world about me wise, to make wisdom greater than war. I have failed. Men fight and die, and for what? Glory and power and spite and pride — nothing more. Gods and kings spin their stories, and in their stories it is good to die for one man's pride and to give thanks for the chains that are put about the necks of every child born less than a king. And I thought ... if I could not wield power through wisdom, or mercy, or justice, then perhaps I could take power in this other way. Perhaps if I became like these men of blood and cruelty, that would be enough. So I banished from my heart all hopes of tenderness, compassion, longing or kindness. I turned away friends for fear of being wounded, laid aside love as a danger, punished women for the things men do, denied my loneliness and refuted my fears.

"Poison. All of it. Poison. And still not enough. I am too cruel for women to love me, too tender for men to deign to grace me with respect. Where does this leave me? Why – I have fallen so far that to have men honour my name, my divinity, I must make myself an adjunct to *his* story." I level my spear at Odysseus, with neither malice nor praise, a simple truth, a silent man amongst women, singing. "My power should have broken the world, should have cracked the palaces and remade them anew. Not as goddess-who-appears-like-a-man, but as a *woman*, as strength-of-woman, as arm-of-woman, as wisdom-of-woman. But I could not make it so. Instead I must *contrive*. I must bend myself into some other shape, make some other story in which the poets praise *him*. A mere man. A petty mortal. They will call him wise. They will sing *his* song down the ages. The story of Odysseus is the last, greatest power Athena has left. They will speak his name, and after, mine. That is all the power I have."

Artemis listens.

Considers.

Shakes her head. "If your story is more important than them," a jerk of her chin towards the women singing below, "then your story isn't worth shit."

So saying, the lady of the forest departs, stepping into the night, which at once twines her in its embrace, as the fog rises off the sullen land.

In the gate of the farm: women sing, torches raised.

In the camp of Eupheithes and Polybus: the men listen, silent, to a sound they have never heard before.

The scouts they have arrayed about the farm are

listening too, their minds turned from their duties, the fog cold against the skin.

I do not need to bother to lay my divinity upon them, for Artemis has already worked hers, and as the fog thickens to a blanket in the night, Penelope, Autonoe and three ladies of the forest scramble down a rope from Laertes' farm, and in secret blackness, slip away.

CHAPTER 46

>>>

When dawn breaks, Gaios's men are already assembled.
The gates of Laertes' farm are broken, barely hanging
together. The earth is scarred with blood and broken arrows.
The smoke of the funeral pyre still twists, bitter in the grey
morning air. Women line the walls, quivers on their hips, faces
smeared in ash.

This battle will be bloody – but not long.

Polybus and Eupheithes stand behind the ragged ranks
of men, arms folded, heads held high. Gaios does not think
Polybus has eaten for at least three days, is not sure he has
seen him drink either. Eupheithes might well be the same –
but then he is fuelled by something more than mere food
and water.

"A last fight," Gaios tells his soldiers. "A final—"

He is interrupted by a man on watch, who calls a warning.

He turns to see the source of distraction, the cause of this
calling-out.

Through the ruins of the farmhouse gate, a man comes.

He is recognisable instantly. Not that Gaios knows his face,
or the squat shape of his hairy form, but he simply walks in a
manner that is at once knowable, even across this bloody field.

358

He walks like a soldier, weary before the break of day; but even so, there is a pride there he cannot shake.

Odysseus, sword at his side, no helmet upon his head, shambles to the limit of a good archer's range from the farm, and stands alone. At his back, in the gate, his father and son stand watching, both armed, out of sound of any conference.

"That's Odysseus," hisses Eupheithes. "That's him! Kill him!"

"What's he doing?" asks Polybus. "Why is he just standing there?"

"He wants to negotiate," Gaios murmurs, almost too astonished to believe it. "He wants to surrender."

"No surrender," snarls Eupheithes. "No mercy!"

Gaios looks at the two fathers, then to his own assembled troops. It occurs to him that most of the men he killed when he fought at Troy were those who'd already lain down their arms, were already kneeling in the dirt. He asked his captain, what do we do with these? And the captain had replied, women and children as slaves. We can't take the rest.

That was not how Gaios had thought he would be a hero, but after all this, who was he to let his comrades down?

"Kill him!" Eupheithes chants. *"Kill him now!"*

"You and you," Gaios barks, pointing at two of his best. "Come with me. The rest – wait my command."

"You can't," snarls Eupheithes. "We bought you, we bought you, he is ... *No mercy!"*

But Gaios is already walking across the black plain, towards Odysseus.

He waves for his escort to stop some fifteen paces away. He wonders if he can match blades with Odysseus for the time it will take his men to reach him and save his life, should this all go wrong. The soldier within him is not so foolish that he wishes to try, but there is another part of Gaios's soul, the part that has been infested with poetry, that has heard the songs raised by clever-tongued men, that wonders. That yearns to know. What would it be like to be the man who kills Odysseus?

In person, without the fury of battle upon him, Gaios is surprised by how small and old the Ithacan king looks. His hair is laced with grey, his shoulders curled, his skin scarred by salt and sand. He stands a little crooked, arms loose and slightly too long by his sides, as if he has grown all out of proportion. He has not washed the smoke or blood from his clothes or skin. There is no gold about his head or wrists. Even his sword looks second-hand, pillaged from a poor man's chest.

Gaios slows, out of the reach of a blade but within easy conversation distance.

"What's your name?" asks Odysseus.

As a warrior at Troy, Gaios often wondered how it would be to have a great king ask after him, want to know him, pay him attention. It never happened, of course.

"Gaios."

"Gaios," Odysseus repeats, turning the name about his mouth, a habit of a man who is prone to forgetting his own soldiers' names and knows that is not a good trait for a noble king. "And did I kill your brother, Gaios? Your friend?"

It takes Gaios a moment to understand, then he shakes his head. "No. I didn't know any of the suitors personally."

"But you serve their fathers."

"I have sworn to do so, yes."

"And you take that oath seriously."

"If you are wondering whether I am some pirate who can be bought . . . yes, I take it seriously. And even if I was another kind of man, I do not think you have the gold to buy me, king of Ithaca."

"I might do, if I was king," Odysseus replies with a smile. "Honestly, in all the fuss, I didn't have an opportunity to check the treasury."

"I did," Gaios blurts, a little flare of pride, a burst of something that for so long was kept silent on the beaches of Troy. "I went through your palace, once you were gone, examined every nook and corner. There was nothing there but dust and blood."

"My wife is hardly going to hide her wealth somewhere it could be so easily found – but I do take your point. This is not exactly the homecoming I was planning," concedes the king. "Nor did I envisage having to defend my family with an army of Artemis's chosen from the unexpectedly fortified walls of my father's farm. Yet here we are."

"Here we are," Gaios agrees. "You have something else to say?"

Odysseus cranes his neck a little, peers past Gaios towards the distant Eupheithes, Polybus. "Should I be talking to you – or to your masters?" he enquires.

"All they want is to kill you," Gaios replies with a shrug. "That is all I am required to do. I do not see why, if I can kill you without losing more of my men and time, I should not do so and consider my work fulfilled."

"And your men will obey you, should we reach some accord on that matter? You have that authority?"

"Do you? Did your men always obey you? Do the women?" Gaios asks, head tilting a little to the side, hands on hips, surprised to find himself curious about this strange, bloody king.

Odysseus considers the question, then laughs. It is a bigger sound than Gaios feels it should be, entirely lacking in humour. "For a while I relied upon the authority of being a captain and a king – but when war drags on, such things lose their meaning. Then instead I told my men that they could obey me and live, or oppose me and die, and given everything, I hoped that would induce a degree of obedience. But I have been surprised more often than I'd like to admit. What about you? How many of your men will survive if you come at my father's walls again?"

"Enough," Gaios replies. "Enough to count."

"Very well. Let us say, Gaios, that you attack again. The gates to my father's farm are destroyed, as you see, but the women on the walls will kill more than half of you before you take the farm, and I will personally see to it that in the fight, I seek out you, and you alone, and with my dying breath drive a sword through your spine. I think you understand how attentive I can be to these things. Or we can reach an agreement."

"I'm listening."

"The women march out of here, and I lay down my sword."

Gaios looks again towards the farm, towards the waiting huntresses upon the walls, then back to Odysseus. "And your family?"

"My father has already offered to slit his own wrists rather than put up with the indignity of whatever your masters have planned for him. It is a pity – they were friends once."

"And your son?"

"My son ... I think he will be inclined to fight. I cannot prevent him. I have done my best to persuade him to flee, to save his own life and raise a rebellion in my name, but he seems entirely opposed to the idea. He has been brought up, I think, on a certain kind of story. A certain kind of notion as to what it is to be a man – you understand, yes?"

Gaios thinks perhaps he does.

"However," Odysseus continues, "what I would ask is that when you have backed Telemachus into a corner and are about to seize him despite his most valiant efforts, you kill him quickly. No doubt your employers will want some grisly business for me – I understand they probably have feelings on this – but my son. My son has not ... does not deserve, I think, to be part of my folly. It was I who decided to kill the suitors, after all. I take full blame. I cannot compel you to do

362

this, but I would ask as a term of my surrender that when you do have the opportunity to kill my son quickly, as a warrior, you take it."

"I think I understand. You are asking a lot, for a man who has lost."

"A man who will make your men pay, when I lose, and pay considerably."

"I am willing to consider your terms."

"I would require an oath."

"The women – if I let them leave – their weapons . . . "

"They will leave them behind. You will give them a little time to disperse and never hear of them again. They will go back to what they are – widows and unmarried maids, weaving cloth, tending their herds, pressing clay and fetching water from the stream. You will never look for them, nor know their names, and they will not trouble you."

"And your wife?"

"She will retire to a temple, and never set foot on Ithaca again. When I am dead, her name will be meaningless – I think we both understand that."

"There are always those who want vengeance."

"You are going to kill a king," Odysseus replies simply. "And his father, and his son. Is that not enough blood to suffice?"

Ares whispers no.

Ares whispers no, no, not enough, not enough, never enough! Take and take and roar and rage because you want it all to mean something, it must mean something, it must have been for something and since it cannot be for anything good, let it be for power, let it be for fury, let it be for dominion by the strong upon the weak, power, *power, POWER!!*

I see it in Gaios's eyes. The words of my brother are buried deep – so deep. I cannot merely twitch my fingers and pluck them out. But there is something else too – something that has buried itself deeper even than the power of the gods. I nearly laugh to see it, to hear its whisper upon Gaios's soul.

There is a *story*.

Gaios is not sure where he heard it, what poet it was who sang of something more than the tyrant's blade and the endless curling tides of blood. But somewhere it slipped into his conscience and has been digging its way through ever since. Another kind of hero. Another way of being a man.

"Very well," Gaios says. "The women lay down their arms and may retreat. And the men?"

"There are barely any left standing," Odysseus replies. "I would ask that those you capture you treat kindly."

"I cannot promise it. But I think you know that."

Odysseus smiles. "Who did you serve under, Gaios? At Troy? Who was your captain?"

"Diomedes."

"Ah. Of course."

"You and he were sometime friends, no?"

"Sometime rivals too. With Diomedes, a little bit of both was often the most productive brew. Were you well rewarded from your time at Troy?"

"No."

"No. I imagine not. If my wife was here, she'd ask if you took your rage out on the women. She doesn't understand . . . some things. However well we tell the stories, I doubt we will ever really convey the truth to their hearers. You know what I mean, yes? My son does not."

"Have you told your men that we will kill them if you surrender?" asks Gaios, eyes dancing to the open gates of the farm.

"No. Do you think I should?"

"Yes."

"If you don't mind waiting, I can head back there now . . ."

Gaios raises a hand, an almost-apology, stopping the Ithacan where he stands. "I find myself wondering," he muses, "if this isn't some trick. Everyone says that Odysseus is the great trickster. I've seen proof of it myself."

"I would be delighted," sighs Odysseus, "if this were a ruse. Truly I would. But as you can see – this is all that is left at the end of my journey. What a disappointment it turns out to be."

Again Gaios looks to the farm, then back to the king. It does seem so very simple. He is not sure what to make of that. "Very well," he says at last. "Give me your sword, and the women go free."

"And my son? I would appreciate that oath in the name of sacred Athena that if you see the opportunity to slay him quickly, you will take it. I will not have him lingering in shame and suffering while Polybus and Eupheithes exact their revenge."

"I swear it." Gaios's voice is firm, honest, true. "In the name of Athena and all the gods of Olympus."

"Thank you." Odysseus sighs, a note of relief upon his breath. He draws his blade – with his left hand, a little awkwardly, the point towards the ground. Holds it a moment, seems surprised almost by its weight, isn't sure which dead man he stole this weapon from. Then turns the hilt towards Gaios.

The rebel captain hesitates a moment, takes a step, hesitates again. Waits for the attack, the betrayal. Doesn't see it. But still the story – the story! The story of Odysseus, it is there too, that other worm twisting through his mind. He looks at the king's weary eyes, his patient, empty smile, and still signals his two lieutenants to come up to stand by his side before he takes another step, and at last clasps the hilt that is offered to him.

There is a howl from the farm of Laertes.

It is faint enough, where Gaios and Odysseus stand, that they could perhaps pretend they had imagined it. Certainly they do their very best to ignore it. Gaios pays Odysseus the respect of not staring too particularly over the king's shoulder to where his son now falls to his knees, Laertes' hand upon his shoulder, holding back the young prince in his horror and despair. The women are already coming off the walls, forming up, ready to march out.

"Well," murmurs Odysseus, as the cries of his wretched son fade into sobs at his back. "I think our business is done."

"Indeed," Gaios concurs. "If you wish, we can wait here until the women are fled."

"I would appreciate that. If you would be kind enough to signal your men not to advance while they retreat into the forest?"

Gaios nods to one of his lieutenants, who scurries back towards his line. Odysseus in turn raises an empty hand towards the farm. Teodora raises her palm in reply. She still holds her bow, has one of Priene's knives hidden beneath her tunic, another on her hip. No one – not even a king – will take these blades from her.

The women do not march out in any particular order. Rather they pick their way out in little groups, some running straight for the forest, other walking steady and slow, heads raised and shoulders back, towards the rising sun. Mirene, her mother's body buried in the soil she leaves behind. Anaitis, eyes fixed upon the watching men, as if she cannot quite believe it. Otonia, a feeble gift of silver wrapped between her arms, a parting farewell from her master. By the time these leave the shattered gate of the farm, half the women are already melted into the forest, like the fox before the hunting dog. Teodora stands by the gate until the last of them have gone, then she sets aside her bow and walks into the trees, and does not look back.

Only Telemachus, Laertes and their men remain, awaiting the end. Telemachus kneels gasping upon the ground, sword in hand. Laertes pats him nicely on the shoulder one more time, raises his head, nods towards his son, turns to say goodbye to his house, his pigs, given how fond he is of the snuffling creatures.

Odysseus lets out a slow, shuddering breath and turns his back upon that place.

"Captain," he murmurs. "I believe your work is done."

Gaios nods, steps aside, gestures towards the waiting line of bronze men, the fathers of the slaughtered sons. Leads Odysseus away.

CHAPTER 47

>>

Polybus blurts: "You haven't bound him?!"
Odysseus looks somewhat pleased at this, satisfied that his legend is so great that even when surrounded by more than fifty heavily armed men, he still merits binding. Gaios sighs, orders rope brought, checks the knots himself as they tie Odysseus's hands before him, pushes him kneeling into the dirt at the fathers' feet.

Eupheithes looks from the king to the farm, where still Telemachus kneels on the bloody ground; says: "And the boy?"

"We will go fetch him," sighs Gaios. "And his grandfather too."

"Good. Bring them here."

Odysseus looks to Gaios, and Gaios nods once; he will remember his oath.

My lovely one, I whisper in his ear. *Ares wants you, but you are mine.*

Gaios has already picked thirty men for the task of taking the farm. He needs no more – not against so few, not when they are already broken. He will lead them personally. He will do his best to see that Telemachus does not survive.

As this little group of conquerors begins to assemble, Eupheithes stares down at Odysseus.

368

He is not entirely sure what to do, now this moment is come.

He has never personally tortured a man to death – at least, not in any meaningful physical way. He had rather hoped and assumed that others would do it for him. He had hoped it would make him feel better. He closes his eyes, tries to picture the face of Antinous, tries to hear the voice of his child.

A moment – Antinous, curling up on the floor before his father's fist, sobbing even though he was a grown man.

This is not the picture Eupheithes wants. His frown deepens, he tries again. *Antinous*, he prays. *Antinous. I have found your killer. I have brought him to his knees. Surely now you will be with me in some way that is not shameful? That is not guilt?*

"Eupheithes, Polybus," says Odysseus, and though he is captive, bound, diminished, there is still the voice of a king in his level tone. "I remember you. You were friends of my father, once."

Were they? Eupheithes wonders.

Certainly he remembers a young man – the man he used to be – laughing with some ghost who was Laertes. But they all died, all of them. Slowly, through years of poison and pain, the youth they had shrivelled, the hopes they held and the dreams they soared with, until all that was left of their lives was this. Just this, for ever and eternal, pinned in a moment of endless regret.

Another thought. If Eupheithes thinks about pain, he remembers one face in particular that was the cause of many years of its slow build, one name that otherwise he might forget . . .

"Where is Penelope?" he demands. "Where is this man's wife?"

"She left with the women," Gaios answers, level and clear. "She is gone."

"She will raise a rebellion! She will raise more . . . more of her women! She is clever, she is—"

369

"You are about to kill her husband, her father, her son," replies Gaios stiffly. "Do you think she will be clever after that?"

Eupheithes opens his mouth to shriek yes, yes, you don't know her! But the words die in the face of Gaios's gaze. There is something there, he thinks, he cannot understand. Does not want to know. So he looks away.

To everyone's surprise, it is Polybus who tries to strangle the Ithacan king.

He has stood silent all this while as soldiers gather and men talk, shaking, mouth like leather, fingers like feathers. Now, as if the quiet patience of Odysseus is too much to bear, he hurls himself upon the Ithacan, tries to beat him, to squeeze the life from him. His attack has the benefit of desperation, of the broken-hearted and soul-shattered man; but he is old, weak. A few of Gaios's men pull him off Odysseus before he can really get a good grip around the man's throat, though they themselves are not sure why they bother.

"Eurymachus!" howls Polybus. "Eurymachus! His name was Eurymachus!"

There are these words, these strange words that Odysseus has not yet fully mastered – "I'm sorry" – that he could perhaps utter. But no. They are still so fresh and new that to sully them now, to waste them upon men who are his enemy, upon those he does not consider worthy of their weight – he will not do it. Instead he draws down shuddering breath, rolls his shoulders, his neck, shifts a little upon his knees, searching through aches old and new to see if Polybus has added anything to the mix, and stares at nothing at all.

It is strange, he thinks, to be quiet at last. To let his voice rest, free his mind from stratagems. But not unpleasant.

He wonders why he didn't try it a bit more when he had the opportunity.

"Bring us the boy," barks Eupheithes. "Bring us Telemachus."

Gaios nods, calls to his men. "Behind me, to the gate, tight order, no drums."

No drums is the order given, and yet no sooner is it made than the sound of wood upon skin beats across the field.

Gaios's face flashes in irritation, looking to the source of the sound.

Again – *boom!*

And this time it occurs to him that the sound is not from his camp, nor even from the farm. Rather it is drifting from a little further away, carried by the wind that is turned by dawn's easy light.

Boom!

It is a marching drum, beating out a royal rhythm. It does not hammer for battle nor command a retreat. It is both more and less than that – a declaration of presence. A pronouncement that demands attention of all far and wide.

Boom!

Gaios looks to Odysseus, who, though bound, almost shrugs. He is as bewildered by the sound as any.

"What is this?" demands Eupheithes. "More tricks?"

"Draw up, facing the road," Gaios replies, and when no one moves in any haste, an added: "Now!"

His men wheel about, as Odysseus tries to shuffle in the dirt to peer between the legs of the assembling soldiers.

The drum beats, the drum draws nearer. In the farm of Laertes, Telemachus is now on his feet, sword drawn. Even Laertes has emerged again from his house, curiosity overwhelming his more sedentary instincts.

Boom, boom, boom!

The sound of the drum echoes across the curve of the rough, ravaged land, and there are other sounds too, as of feet on dry earth, as of metal clanking, the snorting of horses, voices, the solitary blast of a horn.

They see the dust before they see any people, dry and grey, rising from the disturbance that now beats upon the earth, shudders the sky. A pair of soldiers set to watch the road come running, faces flushed crimson, whisper in Gaios's ears. The veteran shudders, but does not flinch, gives an order of: "Hold steady! Do not draw your blades!"

When the standard appears over the brim of the hill down which the lazy road winds, it is briefly dazzling. A golden circle, decked with dyed horsehair. On it is a face with a thoughtful smile and two long, oval eyes, large ears protruding from the side of the disc into which it has been beaten. It bears no resemblance to the man whose presence it is supposed to proclaim, but he is dead, and so now that distinction hardly matters. Gaios recognises it first, followed at once by those of his company who fought at Troy.

It is the face of Agamemnon, etched in gold, borne aloft by a soldier in a plumed helmet, his gleaming armour barely smeared by the dust of the road. Next comes a column of men marching three abreast, the horn of bone and the ox-skin drum, leading amongst their glittering mass six figures upon proud horses.

Four of these six ride behind the other two, and we can name them: old Medon, crabbed Aegyptius, proud Peisenor, clever Ourania. They are dressed in their finest garb, which is a choice their maids will regret when it comes to cleaning it from all this tramping across the hills of Ithaca.

In front of them ride two figures whose garb is finer still. Penelope's gown is borrowed from one of Ourania's chests, and sits a little loose about the collar, a little short about the leg – but it will do for now. Next to her, the woman who rides a horse of midnight black offsets this quality with the gold and silver that glistens brightly about her fingers, her wrists, her neck, her head. Her diadem is not excessive, but on Ithaca, not excessive is more than the ornamentation of the finest of crowds. The drum beats, the horn sounds, and she is Elektra, daughter of Agamemnon, daughter of Clytemnestra, sister of Orestes, and at her back march two hundred men, and by her side rides the queen of Ithaca.

Mycenae has come.

Hair as black as her mother's, skin like the waning moon, Elektra is small, with tiny, delicate fingers and wrists you think might break if gripped too particularly. They will not. She does not carry a blade, though sometimes she has been tempted to wear one at her side, just to see what it is like. She has her brother for such things, and does not need to dress herself in the ornaments of men to know how power feels.

The riders pull up their horses some fifty paces from the line of Gaios's men.

The drum ceases.

The sharp tip of the standard that bears Agamemnon's face is driven into the ground, so his visage may still stand upright, watching all.

Elektra waits upon her horse, Penelope at her side, the wisest men of Ithaca at her back. She is in no rush. She lets her men fan out behind her, two lines deep, forming a long arc that at once threatens to curve around and crush Gaios's men. Only when this is done, with a little nod to her companions, does she dismount. She hands the reins of her horse to a warrior adorned with a crimson cloak, checks briefly to ensure that the gold upon her brow has not wobbled with her movement, smoothes down the front of her garb, holds out her hand to Penelope as the Ithacan queen dismounts.

Penelope takes the fingers that are offered.

It is a sisterly picture as pleasing as any one might wish to paint upon a vase. Two fair and uncorrupted ladies, who might now be about the gathering of fruit or the serving of sweet wine, walking together in perfect companionship.

As they walk, two hundred armed men move behind them, matching their pace, a line of spear and shield a glistening cliff at their back.

They make no demands, give no warnings or battle cries, nor flinch at the sight of the ragged men arrayed before them. Rather they drift towards Gaios's line as if it were not there, and truly, it is as if it is not.

Gaios gives the order for his men to stand aside a breath before they were about to crack and run of their own volition. Better, he decides, to be seen to command a surrender than to be forced into it by his own troops throwing down their spears.

"Honour guard!" he even manages to bark, in a moment of some slight composure.

His voice drifts across the field, and on the face of Elektra there is the tiniest flicker of a smile. His men scurry to form two new lines behind Polybus and Eupheithes, fixing their faces in something resembling respect, swords categorically sheathed at their hips. The only flaw in this otherwise excellent motion is that it reveals that which their bodies had momentarily before obscured – the king of Ithaca, bound and kneeling upon the ground.

Elektra stops the moment she sees this. Grips her cousin's fingers tight, half turns to Penelope, murmurs: "Is that him?"

"Yes," the queen replies, a twinge of regal displeasure curling the corner of her mouth. "That is Odysseus."

Elektra's hand flies from Penelope's, a finger uncurling in a furious line towards the king, his captors. "Release him! Now!"

No one rushes to obey. If they rush to obey, it might imply that they were in some way complicit in bringing Odysseus to this sorry state in the first place. Elektra does not have much height to rise to, but she tries nonetheless, swelling in her fury. "Of all the traitor dogs!" she barks. "If my blessed father were here, he would have you strung out as food for crows! You had better pray that my good cousin Penelope and dear friend Odysseus are only half as merciful as he!"

This speech is enough to tip the scales for a few more intelligent rebels, who now conclude that inaction is potentially more costly than even the slightly awkward act of freeing Odysseus from his bonds. Three rush forward at once, nearly tangle in each other's feet, cut the ropes, shove and scurry against each other in their enthusiasm to help him to his feet.

The Ithacan king does not know Elektra by sight, but he knows royalty, recognises the standard of Agamemnon, makes an educated guess. "My queen," he murmurs, half bowing to Penelope. "My lady," a deeper bow to the princess of Mycenae.

"My lord Odysseus," Elektra barks in reply, her eyes barely touching his face as they sweep across the field. "I received word from my dear cousin, your wife, of your return, but had not dared to imagine it would be in circumstances as shameful as this."

The messenger sent by Penelope through Ourania had in fact been very explicit and detailed about just how shameful these circumstances might be. When it comes to major military interventions on a very short schedule, Penelope always feels it is best to be clear and precise.

"And where is my dear cousin Telemachus – ah, over there, I see. How nice."

"My good cousin Elektra," adds Penelope with a smile that is all teeth and no lip, "is here on behalf of her noble brother Orestes, son of Agamemnon, lord of Mycenae, king of kings, greatest of all the Greeks, to show the immediate friendship and affection that there is between her father's exalted house and the house of beloved Odysseus. Her brother was alas held back by vital business, but will be here we have no doubt in . . . three days?"

"Four at the most," agrees Elektra. "He could hardly restrain his enthusiasm at the chance to finally meet noble Odysseus, so beloved of our father. He has sent word as well to Sparta and Pylos, to Corinth and Elis, calling for celebration and sacrifice in honour of this momentous event. You are lucky therefore that it is I, not he, who has stumbled upon this vile and treacherous assembly. I had no idea the people of Ithaca could greet their king so despicably. Who are your leaders?"

At least one man amongst Gaios's troop nearly raises his arm to point straight at Eupheithes and Polybus, but his wrist is grabbed before he can be too explicit. Odysseus, however, turns to the two old men. "These," he murmurs. "These are the men who would have seen me slain rather than take back my throne."

"I see." Elektra advances a little closer, looks the two of them up and down, sees nothing in either that leaves her impressed. "I would suggest chaining them to a rock for birds to peck out their innards, as Prometheus was; failing that, I suppose we could burn them alive."

"My lady," Polybus blurts. "My lady, we—"

"Did you dare think you could speak?!" Her voice is the lash, her eyes thunder. Her mother would be proud if she could see Elektra now. No one – not Gaios, not his men – twitches a finger in their master's defence.

"In fairness," Odysseus muses, "they had some cause. I killed their sons, you see."

"So?" Elektra demands. "My brother killed his mother, and it was noble and correct and sanctioned by all the gods. Warriors kill sons all the time – I hardly see the issue."

"I killed them in perhaps a less than . . . than entirely honour-able manner. I cut them down at the feast, the day they thought they were going to win my wife. Slaughtered them in their cups, left their bodies in an ignoble state for some little time. I was not thinking, you see, like a king. Merely a husband."

Elektra's eyes gleam as for the first time she looks Odysseus in the eye, takes him in – not as a political problem to be solved or a story to be told, but a man of flesh, standing before her. "Of course," she murmurs. "A husband. Of course. Such . . . noble passions . . . can inspire a man to dreadful fury. Why, my dear uncle Menelaus himself suspected that sailing to Troy would bring about a war that would ravage these lands for generations yet to come, but who could really fault him? He was also a husband, you see. Such things can be cruel – but understandable. You did not fight these men's sons honourably, because they had not acted with honour towards your wife. That is what the poets will say."

"I believe you are as wise as your father," Odysseus breathes. "Perhaps . . . a little more."

Elektra nods once, then jerks her head again to the old men before her. "And what of these? They have clearly sullied and dishonoured you past all bounds of mercy, and yet they too had cause. The burning alive may be a little excessive, given all you've said. Would you like my brother's men to cut them down, or to wield the sword yourself?"

A little cough from behind, a slight clearing of throat. "If I may." Penelope steps forward. "Perhaps it is just my weak and womanly spirit, but might not mercy in this one case be found? Exile, perhaps. There are temples, islands where they could go. What father would not seek to avenge his child? And what message, I wonder, does it send to these lands if the king of Ithaca follows blood with blood? What manner of man, the people might ask, has returned to them from so much war?"

There is a sound like a child tripping on a stone. It is the sound of noise sticking in Polybus's throat. The old man sways; he totters. Gaios catches him before he can fall. Polybus does not know what he feels – thinks perhaps he feels every feeling there is to know all at once. Perhaps this will burn him out, he thinks. Perhaps the fire of this will blaze so brightly that when it is done blistering upon his soul, he will never be able to feel again.

"Mercy?" Elektra's lip curl around the word. *"Really?"*

Penelope bows towards Odysseus. "My king? It is your kingdom. Your justice."

Odysseus looks upon the two old men who were once friends of his father.

I do not take his hand.

Do not slip my presence into his skull, nor whisper wise words in his ears.

I do not need to. My work is already done.

Master of my house, thinks Odysseus.

Strange how quickly these words change their meaning.

The feeling . . . is not as wretched as perhaps he imagined it would be. There are notions here – ideas of safety, of support, of being something more. He has never felt such things before. He will have to think on them further, once he has slept.

Odysseus feels more tired than he has ever known.

Perhaps, he thinks, that means he is finally home.

"Polybus, father of Eurymachus. Eupheithes, father of Antinous. You will leave my kingdom and never return. Your lands, your slaves, your goods are all forfeit. Your names will be sung as a curse, your sons forgotten, you will—"

Eupheithes draws his sword and hurls himself towards Odysseus.

He is old, a trader in grain.

He never even taught his son how to fight.

Odysseus steps aside, lets the old man's momentum carry him by, grabs his arm as he goes, turns it with an easy cracking of bone, drives the sword home.

Eupheithes gasps as the blade tears through him.

Staggers.

Falls.

His eyes stare wide as he looks around the field.

He is looking for Antinous.

He does not see him.

Then he dies.

Polybus thanks the Ithacan king for his mercy, and does not look upon his fellow fallen father as he is led away. The men of Gaios begin to disperse. They will not receive any reward for what they have done these last few days – but neither will they be slaughtered where they stand. That, given everything, is worth more than nothing.

Gaios remains. He too could flee, but he will not – not until all of those he brought to this place are gone. This he feels is some sort of duty; and besides, he has no interest in being a hunted rat for the rest of his days, however long or short they may be.

Telemachus and Laertes stagger across the short distance from the farm, since it is apparent that Elektra has no interest in going to them. "Oh," blurts Laertes, as he sees the princess crowned in gold. "You turned up then?"

"My dear and noble uncle," she replies carefully. "How glad I am to see you well."

Laertes snorts his sentiment, but his hands are shaking and he holds a knife between pale fingers, until Penelope eases it from his grasp.

Telemachus sees the body of Eupheithes, and the place where Polybus's corpse is not. "Is Polybus fled? Is he—"

"No. We have made peace."

"Peace? With traitors? With—"

"Son," snaps Odysseus. "Enough. All of it . . . it is enough."

Elektra clears her throat in the silence. "Well," she muses. "I can't imagine your dear father's farm is much accommodation at this moment. Perhaps if we withdraw to the palace? Penelope, sister, you must allow my maids to help yours restore a little . . . cleanliness to the place."

She hooks one crow-arm across Penelope's shoulders, and Penelope smiles upon the Mycenaean queen. "What a lovely idea," she murmurs. "We could talk about weaving and other ... *womanly* things."

The men part in a sea of bronze as the women turn away.

"You." Odysseus's finger lashes out to point straight to Gaios as the captain stands patiently by, awaiting his fate. "Where will you go?"

"To sea, I expect," Gaios grunts. "To whatever land will have me. If you let me."

"You fought well. Did not lead your men to their deaths for some ... ridiculous notion. I may have work for you, Gaios, soldier of Diomedes. If you'll have it. I am in need, you see, of men."

Gaios considers a moment. Then: "Didn't you once try to stab my captain in the back?"

"A misunderstanding. Diomedes and I were truly the closest of friends."

"All who followed you to Troy are dead, king of Ithaca." Gaios is too practical a man to infuse this sentiment with more than some trifling regret. "I am not sure if I would want to serve another hero such as you."

"That is ... understandable. Consider it for a few days. If you refuse, you may leave in safety, and know that I ... I was about to say that I will kill you should you ever return. But of course, that's absurd."

"Is it?"

"Of course. I won't kill you, Gaios, if you come back. But my wife will."

Odysseus pats the veteran on the back, then turns to follow his wife along the dusty road, leaving the bloody field behind him.

CHAPTER 48

>>>

At night – a feast!

This is where we began, is it not?

Feasting in the palace of Odysseus.

Except now there Odysseus himself sits, upon his long-empty throne. And his father has come down from the farm to sit in equal place next to him, and Elektra has her chair raised up to the same level, since she is there to represent her brother, king of kings, so overall the highest end of the hall is getting quite crowded. Finding lesser people to attend the feast proves a little tricky at first – so many who might come are slain – but Elektra packs the hall with her chosen Mycenaeans, and Peisenor and Medon and Aegyptius summon what few of their friends can make it in time and aren't too terrified of these current events. There are a number of Ourania's cousins, and nearly all of Ourania's maids, since Penelope's maids – those who are still alive – are still a little reticent about moving through the hall in too large a number, lest Odysseus notice them and remember that they exist at all, even slightly.

Anaitis comes down from the temple, along with a few of the women of the forest dressed in the least filthy clothes they can find. Teodora does not; she has mourning rites to sing for

381

her captain, for Semele, for the ones who are lost, and upon the hills of Ithaca incense now rises with the funeral dirge sung to the shadows of the dead.

Euracleia attends, fussing over Telemachus, who sits just a little below his father. Telemachus will always sit here – just a little below – and Euracleia does not realise that tonight is her last feast, that tomorrow Odysseus will say the exact same words Penelope always wanted to say: "Dearest nursemaid, the time has come for you to retire to a little farm far away, in honour of your service ... "

Eumaeus the swineherd has come, and just this once finds himself sitting with finer folk than he, who are too merry on the strongest wine Ourania can find to really complain about the old man's stench.

Autonoe watches from the kitchen door, her usual place of refuge, the portal she always guarded. Tomorrow she will ask for her freedom, and Penelope will grant it, and ask Autonoe how she feels about being a woman of trade, with many useful contacts in many far-off ports, and Autonoe will say that she will consider it – not now – but when the time is right, she will indeed consider it. She wears a knife upon her hip. She will wear it until she dies.

The maids of Elektra have added their labours to those already performed in removing the worst of the stench of blood from the halls, and painting is under way to cover up the more persistent marks with streaks of ochre and noble black, depicting perhaps some new facet of Odysseus's story – some particularly heroic stroke of genius that could only be performed by the kind of man who is absolutely, categorically capable of defending his kingdom from one and all.

The old stories wash away, in lines of crimson and yellow.

The bards are already trying out a few new songs, having gleaned some of the more pertinent details of Odysseus's return home from his councillors. These will be amended and tweaked over time, a verse added, a heroic deed substituted here or there. I will guide their mouths through this journey, so that in time the stories they sing shall be the spells I weave, the power I seek. I will be pertinent to the narrative, of course. Not as great as the great goddess should be, but great enough. Sometimes that is all one can be, when the last dice fall.

Speaking of the gods, there are a few come to tonight's feast. Hera has escaped Zeus's watchful eye for just one night, and sits proudly by the fire dressed in absurd lapis lazuli and gleaming gold. She says she is disguised as a mortal merchant, and yet it is so ridiculous that even her obscuring magics can barely keep people from gaping, staring at her alien presence. She will be punished for having dared to enjoy herself, dared to show her face for even a single night of merriment – but that will be later, and for now, at least, the palace welcomes her, queen of queens, lady of secrets, protector of wives.

Aphrodite peeks her head in for just a moment, then wrinkles her nose and says: "Can't they ever serve anything but fish?" and vanishes away in a flutter of fragrant perfume. But even that is enough that several burly men near the door begin to swoon, to stare into each other's eyes and whisper, *You know, we've shared experiences, you and I . . . experiences no one else will understand . . .*

I roll my eyes at her departure and its consequences, and cast around for the others. The one I feared is nowhere to be seen. Oh, Ares will come knocking at these palace doors again, blood upon his grinning lips and blade in hand – but his attention is as short as his nasty stabbing blade, and he has no interest in songs of wisdom and the deeds of women. In this regard, and perhaps in this alone, I will always be stronger than he.

Artemis stands awkwardly at the back, arms wrapped across her bare chest, quiver at her hip, a habitual adornment she has forgotten to remove, bow nowhere in sight. I slip close to her,

her nakedness, so natural in the forest now, a somewhat disconcerting sight in this place of civilisation; murmur: "Will you stay a while?"

She shakes her head. "The men's songs are no good, and the women here . . . do things differently now."

"There is still power to be found, if you look for it. Even the men could learn to sing your name."

She blinks at me, bewildered as my own precious owl. "What would be the point of that?"

I sigh, catch a passing cup as it travels by in the hands of a maid, turn it golden in my grasp, fill it with sweetest ambrosia. "One drink," I say. "Even the huntress must sometimes take her rest."

She sniffs it, wrinkles her nose, takes a sip. "Actually," she declares after a moment's pause. "It's not that bad."

Penelope, of course, sits below them all.

Below Odysseus, below Elektra, despite the latter's protest. Below Laertes, below even her son. His status has risen now his father is returned. No longer the whelp of a missing man, but a prince, son of a reigning king, the next in line to a safe and secured throne. He sits above his mother; he has no need of her now.

The queen of Ithaca surveys the feast, and for a moment sees only the dead and the departed.

Antinous and Eurymachus, leering at the maids, teeth stained with meat.

Amphinomous and his loyal lackeys, waiting their turn.

Kenamon, sitting apart, a stranger in this land, lost and far from home.

Penelope longs briefly for her loom, to be weaving again. She is aware that technically, she never actually finished making Laertes' funeral shroud. The whole business got away from her, as so many things did. There's the shroud to make, the sheep to bring in, timber to purchase, repairs to make to Laertes' farm; the autumn harvest is on its way, the storehouses need inventorying, the granaries too will need seeing to now that Eupheithes is no longer running things, and actually she'll also need to send word to some of Polybus's retainers about the old man's punishment, make sure the shipping lanes don't . . .

She opens her mouth to turn to Eos, to tell her maid all of this, remind her of the great many things that need to be done, in case her memory fails.

Eos is not there.

Slowly she turns back into her seat, fingers plucking at the air where a loom might otherwise have been.

Tomorrow, she thinks.

Tomorrow she will sit down with Ourania and they will discuss how to manage all these affairs. It might be that they need to buy some new women. Solid women, women who can be trusted to keep a secret, women who know how these games are played.

Not that Penelope is sure any more she understands how to play, now her husband is home.

Tomorrow.

Tomorrow the work will begin.

And I?

When the last song is sung and the shutters drawn back across the hall, how does great and mighty Athena celebrate this, the ending of these labours, the final verse of the story I have so carefully woven, the song I have sung?

I stand upon the highest point of Ithaca, my helmet from my face, my spear and shield at my feet. The gods are not watching now; they think this story finished, this journey ended. They do not understand, ignorant as they are, how it is merely the beginning.

I let down my golden hair.

Open my fingers, just a little, so they may feel the breeze.

Let it play upon my skin.

Let it tug upon my gown, shimmer across my lips.

Close my eyes and for a moment – just a moment – allow myself to revel in the glory of living, in the beauty of the endless sky, the fading sound of music, the touch of the earth beneath my feet, the embrace of starlight about my body. I think perhaps I could laugh. I think perhaps I might cry. I wait a little, to see if either of these things will emerge from within me, wonder how they will feel. I understand that I am desperate for their touch, and yet somehow yearning is never quite enough.

Then it passes.

Then it too is gone.

I return my helmet to my head, that no one might see me smile, or know when I despair.

Strap my shield to my arm, heft my spear, that no creature, mortal or divine, may ever touch me, ever draw near.

And like the last note of a song sung, I too am gone.

CHAPTER 49

>>>

A bed made from an olive tree. An oil lamp glows low by the open window.

Odysseus says: "Obviously Father is in Father's room, and Elektra is in Mother's, and I am not going to throw Telemachus out of his, after all he's been through – and if Orestes is coming, he will need ... but there are rooms further down the hall, now the suitors aren't ... now they are gone. I can have that maid ... I can have Autonoe. Ask Autonoe. Or another of the house. To bring some things in there. For tonight. For ... for as many nights as you ... as you wish. I have council tomorrow – Medon, Peisenor, Aegyptius, they are going to take me around Ithaca, apprise me of the situation. When Orestes has come and gone, I will sail around the isles too, take Telemachus with me, get to know my kingdom again. I think it will be ... very thorough. I understand it will only tell part of the story."

Penelope stands by the window, looking down to the sea.

How strange the ocean looks, she thinks, when one is not waiting for someone to sail upon it.

"Well then," Odysseus breathes. "Well. I will wish you goodnight."

He moves to leave, one hand upon the door.

387

"Wait," Penelope says.

He waits, hardly daring to breathe, one side of his face in darkness, the other in light.

"Wait," she repeats, turning her back now to the sea. "I ... It is not suitable that a king sleep in any room but his own. People will ... I do not know what we will be. I do not know you. You do not know me. But it is ... important. For Ithaca. For our son. That things seem to be ... what the poets must say they are. So you can sleep at the end of the bed, for now. Gracious, do you still snore the way you used to? I imagine it's only got worse – we'll deal with that. We'll deal with it. It is good for you to spend time with Telemachus. A great many things have changed since you were gone. Watch out for the cattle traders on Kephalonia, you cannot believe a word they say, and they would rather kill their own beasts than barter with you in a reasonable manner. And don't judge the situation on Leucas by what Aegyptius says. Their industry is not pretty, but it is highly profitable. They have become skilled in the working of tin, which they trade at extraordinary advantage with the barbarians from the north. Go. See for yourself. And when you come back ... when you come back, I will show you what this place has become. And we will talk some more."

"I would like that," he murmurs. "That sounds ... like an excellent plan."

For a little while longer they consider each other, looking for suitable words.

At last, a nod, a simple word from her lips, an acknowledgement of all the other words still unsaid.

"Odysseus."

"Penelope."

ABOUT THE AUTHOR

≫≫≫≫≫≫≫≫≫≫≫≫≫≫≫≫≫≫≫≫≫≫≫≫≫≫≫≫≫≫≫≫

Claire North is a pseudonym for Catherine Webb, who wrote several novels in various genres before publishing her first major work as Claire North, *The First Fifteen Lives of Harry August*. It was a critically acclaimed success, receiving rave reviews and becoming a word-of-mouth bestseller. She has since published several hugely popular and critically acclaimed novels, won the World Fantasy Award and the John W. Campbell Memorial Award, and been shortlisted for the Sunday Times/PFD Young Writer of the Year Award, the Arthur C. Clarke Award and the Philip K. Dick Award. She lives in London.

Find out more about Claire North and other Orbit authors by registering for the free monthly newsletter at orbitbooks.net.

Help us make the next generation of readers

We – both author and publisher – hope you enjoyed this book.
We believe that you can become a reader at any time in your life,
but we'd love your help to give the next generation a head start.

Did you know that 9% of children don't have a book of their
own in their home, rising to 12% in disadvantaged families*?
We'd like to try to change that by asking you to consider the role
you could play in helping to build readers of the future.

We'd love you to think of sharing, borrowing, reading, buying or talking
about a book with a child in your life and spreading the love of reading.
We want to make sure the next generation continue to have access
to books, wherever they come from.

And if you would like to consider donating to charities that help
fund literacy projects, find out more at www.literacytrust.org.uk
and www.booktrust.org.uk.

Thank you.

hachette
CHILDREN'S GROUP

little, brown
BOOK GROUP

*As reported by the National Literacy Trust